THE EVACUEE'S SECRET

DEBORAH KLÉE

Print book ISBN: 978-1-8380804-9-5 First Printed 2025

Published by Sherman House

BOOKS BY THIS AUTHOR:

Secrets of a Sunken Village Series:

The Evacuee's Secret - Book one

The Canary Girl's secret - Book two

Other books:

The Borrowed Boy

Just Bea

The Forever Cruise

The Last Act

Dedicated to *my* best friend and soulmate, Sherman.

PROLOGUE

May 1945

Louise stood outside the farmhouse door, a cardboard suitcase at her feet. Her lower lip trembled, the lump in her throat painful. She couldn't stop shivering; her bones felt cold as ice. Did they already know what she had done? Joan told her last night that she was being sent back to London. Louise assumed that meant she was going back home to Mum, but what if she was being sent to prison?

Louise turned to go back into the farmhouse to ask Joan, just to make sure, but the Red Cross lady came out. 'Okay. Jump in the car.'

No goodbyes. Becks Farm had been her home, Ma and Pa, her family, since she was evacuated from London, two years and seven months ago.

One of the new farmhands whistled as he clanked a couple of milk pails across the yard. Louise didn't recognise any of the lads and Land Army girls helping out. Milking the cows and feeding the chickens had been her job. Now, she had no place on the farm. Ma was staying with a friend in Harrogate. Louise hadn't seen her since the day of the accident. Pa had died in hospital. The most important people in her life-- gone. And it was all her fault.

There would be a post-mortem, and a police enquiry, Dicky had explained to her yesterday afternoon. The cause of the accident. The person to blame for Pa's death. And, as Dicky pointed out, if Louise was found guilty, she could be convicted of manslaughter or murder.

'But I didn't mean to. I loved Pa.' Louise had sobbed uncontrollably until Dicky took her into his arms. He was crying too. They clung to each other, as if their lives depended on it. He was her best friend. She loved him with all of her heart. A heart that was now breaking.

The Red Cross lady came out of the farmhouse. 'You ready?'

Louise nodded. 'Does Joan know I'm leaving now?' Surely Joan would come out to say goodbye.

'Yes. She's signed the papers.'

'Why am I being sent away? I'm needed on the farm.'

'I understand there's been a family tragedy. I'm sorry it's so sudden for you, but I'm sure your own mum will be glad to have you home. Jump in. We've a train to catch.'

So, this was it. Dicky said she had been seen with Joan before the accident. Did Ma know she was responsible? Joan had driven Ma to the hospital, following the ambulance. What had she told her? Louise took a deep shuddering breath but could not control the sob that escaped. Of course, Ma hated her.

'Louise.' Dicky came hurtling through the gate. Louise's heart leapt with joy at seeing him.

He was having difficulty breathing and bent over to get his breath. 'I've summat important to tell you. I didn't know yesterday you'd be leaving today or I would have told you then.'

'Neither did I. Oh, Dicky. I don't want to go. I'm going to miss you so much. I love you, Dicky.' A week ago, she would never have said this. Dicky was her best friend, not her boyfriend, but she realised with a physical pain, as she anticipated his loss, that she loved him deeply. Never to see Dicky again was unbearable. He was part of her. He made her whole.

'I love you too, Louise. I'm sorry. I was angry. I didn't mean to ...'

The car horn sounded, and they jumped like startled deer.

'It's okay, Dicky. I said lots of stupid things I didn't mean. We're always fighting, but I mean nothing by it. Oh, Dicky. I can't bear it.'

The Red Cross lady wound down her window. 'Get in the car or you'll miss your train.'

'But I've got to tell you...' Dicky's words were lost over the sound of the engine.

'We'll write,' Louise called out of the window as the car pulled away.

They drove out of the gate and Dicky ran behind them, waving. His pale face and round-rimmed spectacles, disappearing. Becks Farm. Her once perfect life getting smaller and smaller as the car bumped along the lane. She had left a piece of her heart behind and nothing would ever be the same again.

1

JULY 1963

'Lou. You'd better get down here, sharpish. A fancy limo's pulled up outside. Would you look at her from over the road? Out in her curlers having a good old gander.'

Louise had been halfway down the stairs, but on hearing her landlady's exclamation she did an about turn. A limousine? This was their first date. Where was he going to take her? He'd said, 'Out for a bite.' Obviously not in the cafe where she worked, but a limo? It was going to be somewhere grand. Her trousers were already halfway off as she stumbled back into her room, mentally scanning through other options. The navy and fuchsia crimplene dress. It was second-hand but looked Mary Quant-ish.

'He's coming up the garden path. I'm not answering the door to him in my overalls.'

'Okay. I'm ready.' Louise ran down the stairs, struggling with her zip.

'He's a looker. Nice suit. You've landed on your feet gal. I'll have to put up your rent now you're going all swanky on me.'

'Do me up, Doris. I don't know when I'll get back, but I'll try not to wake you.'

'Ooh, I'll be waiting up to hear all about it. But don't bring him in, mind.'

Louise rolled her eyes. She didn't even want to go out on this date. Edward Boyd, Eddie, had frequented the cafe where she worked since early March. The first time he popped in for directions because he was lost, but after meeting Louise, he returned daily. At least that's what the other staff said. Louise argued, it was because he liked Luigi's coffee. But he would only be served by her. They talked about books. He was reading Wuthering Heights on one of his early visits and lent it to her. Louise loved anything written by the Brontë sisters. The books reminded her of the Yorkshire moors where she had rambled with Dicky, her childhood friend. Jumping tumbling brooks. Running up hills to collapse breathless on heather, the world with all its possibilities stretched out before them. Dicky. The missing part of her soul. When she read Cathy's words to Heathcliff, *I am Heathcliff! He's always, always in my mind: not as a pleasure, any more than I am always a pleasure to myself, but as my own being,* she knew exactly what Cathy meant. Eighteen years had passed with no word from him. She had written soon after returning to London but didn't receive a reply. It made no sense the way he haunted her dreams. She had been little more than a child, and yet Louise knew she loved him.

The doorbell rang, and Louise mouthed goodbye before opening the door.

'Stunning.' Eddie's eyes appraised her. 'Ready?'

He had a chauffeur! 'Where are we going?' Louise said, as the car purred along the shabby street of terraced houses.

'Have you heard of Annabel's? My friend Mark and his wife, Annabel, opened last month. They do a good steak.'

Louise's jaw dropped. 'Annabel's on Berkeley Square? The one Peter O' Toole couldn't get into? I read about it in the paper. Don't you have to be high society or something?'

Eddie laughed. 'Let's just say I have connections. And only the best for you. It's taken me long enough to persuade you to join me for dinner. I've had to visit Kentish Town every day and drink weak, bitter coffee. But it was worth it. You're incredible, Louise Pearson. Clever. Beautiful. Kind. Tonight, I want to show you a better life. One where you don't have to scrimp around for every penny. Believe me, I've been poor. I know what it's like to have *and* to have not. And I can tell you, I prefer having money! So, let me spoil you?'

'You didn't say… I just thought…'

Eddie laughed. 'Exactly. You came out with me this evening because you wanted to be with me, not because of who I was or what I had.'

Thank goodness she had changed her outfit, but her dress and hair were woefully inadequate for London--may be the world's--most fashionable and luxurious club. 'But I could have had my hair styled, or something.'

Eddie faced her, taking her hands in his. 'I wouldn't want you to change a thing. I love your thick hair, the colour of conkers. You are natural. Unaffected. Your radiance will put all the debutantes and models in the shade.'

Debutantes. Models. There would be film stars. Rock stars. Louise's stomach fluttered with nerves and excitement. 'Are we really going in? Downstairs to actual Annabel's?'

'Bells. That's what they call it.' Eddie laughed, obviously enjoying her disbelief and awe. 'Here we are.' The limo had pulled up outside the gates of a grand Georgian house.

Louise took a deep breath. She was Cinderella arriving at the Ball. If only a fairy godmother would appear with a magic wand to transform her. Eddie led the way down some stairs into the basement. Perhaps they were heading for a staff entrance. That was it, he worked there and was sneaking her in through the kitchen. Louise let out her breath and tried to adjust her expectations.

The door opened into what Louise would later describe as an Aladdin's den. Her eyes darted around the room taking in the opulence, the golden glow of table lamps reflected in mirrors and bouncing off brass picture frames and fittings, deep red walls, paintings of nudes, some prints that looked Russian, a serene buddha sitting on the shelf of an alcove. Elegant. Warm. And soothing.

'Sit down. I'll let Annabel know we're here,' Eddie said.

Louise's jaw dropped as Eddie to steered her into the embrace of a plump velvet sofa. She sank into the cushions, feeling as though she had been transported to heaven.

Eddie grinned. 'Pretty special, huh?'

Louise could only nod. They were alone in this sumptuous, decadent cavern of a room. Soft music, the clinking of a glass, and a murmur of voices came from beyond the door. She watched as Eddie slipped out of the golden glow and, for a moment, she was alone. Alone with her thoughts. Lifted out of her exhausting, relentless routine of work, sleep, work and worry, she imagined for the first time in a couple of decades another life. One where she might be happy.

'Here she is. Louise Pearson.' Eddie presented Louise to an incredibly glamourous and beautiful woman. He was grinning as though she, Louise Pearson, was the prize--the celebrity everyone wanted to meet.

'Louise. Lady Annabel Vane-Tempest-Stewart.'

Louise jumped up. She did a half-curtsey. 'I'm pleased to meet you, Lady Annabel Vane-Tempest--'

'--Annabel. Please. Eddie hasn't stopped talking about you.' She gave a demure smile and then turned her attention to Eddie. 'Thank you, darling, for your generous contribution to the hospital fund. It has made a huge difference. Barts can now open a new wing. Dinner is on the house tonight. Mark and I are so grateful for your support.'

Louise followed them into the club where guests dined and danced. It was beautiful. Every corner was decorated and furnished with impeccable taste. The soft golden glow of lamplight, paintings, objet d'art, damask tablecloths, crystal glassware, gold-rimmed porcelain plates and vases overflowing with fresh flowers. Despite the glamour, the club generated a sense of deep relaxation and comfort. Beautiful people glided like swans. Apparitions in this dreamlike splendour.

'I couldn't eat another morsel. That was out of this world,' Louise said, with a contented sigh.

'We haven't looked at the dessert trolly.'

Louise grimaced. Lobster and steak sat heavy in her stomach. They had finished off a bottle of Chateau Neuf du Pape. All she wanted to do was curl up on that heavenly sofa and go to sleep. 'Maybe later?'

'Okay, Princess. Your wish is my command. If you could excuse me for a few minutes, I need to attend to some business upstairs. I'll ask Frederic to serve coffee.'

'What's upstairs?'

'The Clement Club. One of the original gentlemen's clubs. I won't be long. Are you sure you don't mind?'

Louise shook her head. 'I'm fine. More than fine. I'll enjoy people-watching and let my food go down so I can tuck in to more when you get back.'

'Good girl. Five minutes.'

Who would have thought Edward Boyd was so well

connected? He'd kept that hidden from her during his countless visits to the cafe. She didn't like to think that information would have influenced her. Louise had never been materialistic or impressed by status, but it was a pleasant surprise. She slipped her feet out of her shoes and wiggled her toes. The club's ambience, the warm feeling of a full belly, soft music and golden light; Louise felt as though she were bathing in tranquillity, washing away her troubles.

Women and men who looked as though they had stepped off the cover of Vogue. Louise studied one person at a time, taking in the cut and design of a dress, the shape of a stylish haircut. It reminded her of being thirteen, meeting Joan, the Land Army girl. Joan had seemed so glamorous, everything Louise aspired to be. What had possessed her to be so reckless, to put those she loved in danger? If only she could turn back the clock.

Eddie slid back into his chair, opposite Louise. 'No coffee? Hold on. Frederic?' He ordered two Irish coffees. When Frederic left them, Eddie took a long look at her. 'Something's troubling you.'

Louise sighed. 'Being here with you it's so … healing. I feel as though I could cast off all my worries and start anew.' She laughed at her foolishness.

'Then why don't you?' he whispered, gazing deep into her eyes.

'Some things are not easily forgotten. Or forgiven.'

'Whose forgiveness do you need?'

Louise shrugged. 'It's nothing. I'm getting maudlin. Too much wine.'

'Whatever it is, you can tell me.' Eddie reached across the table for her hands.

It was tempting to off-load. To share the secret that had weighed her down for so many years, and Louise could feel her resolve softening. 'I don't want to spoil a perfect evening.'

'You couldn't. I'm just happy to be sharing it with you. Who can't you forgive, Louise?' His thumb brushed the back of her hand as if coaxing out her secret.

Would it matter if she told him? Eighteen years had passed. Nobody had come looking for her. Louise extracted her hand from his grasp to finish her Irish coffee, but her glass was empty. Eddie must have signalled to Frederic, as within a couple of minutes, a shot of brandy was placed before her. Mentally reliving the day of Pa's accident, Louise barely noticed herself finishing the night cap. 'Too many people to name,' she said, setting her glass on the coaster. 'But most of all, I can't forgive myself.'

'Maybe if you tell someone, it will become easier. When we keep things to ourself they can grow out of proportion. I bet it's not as bad as you think.'

Louise took a deep breath. 'I did something stupid when I was a kid. A man who I loved like a father died as a result.' It felt as though she had set free the crazed beast trapped in her soul.

'So, it was an accident?' Eddie said.

'One that I caused. Intentionally. But I didn't mean Pa to die.'

A bottle of brandy had appeared. Eddie poured her another glass. 'Go on.'

Having started, there seemed no reason to hold back, so Louise told Eddie everything.

'Was the cause of the accident investigated?' Eddie said.

'I don't know. Probably. Nobody told me the outcome. Maybe they protected me because I was a child.'

'Does anyone else know you were responsible? That it was premeditated?'

Louise shivered. *Premeditated.* 'Dicky. My friend. He said other people witnessed my actions. I expected the police to question me, but they didn't.'

'And you say this happened eighteen years ago?'

Louise nodded.

'Then it's likely forgotten. A closed case. Forget about it, princess. I think it's time to dance. Shall we?' He grinned at Louise and when she nodded, led her onto the dance floor.

They danced until the small hours. When Louise left Annabel's that night, she felt as though the angst of the past eighteen years had been shed. She was as light as a lamb, relieved of its winter fleece.

'I'll look after you, princess,' Eddie said. 'Trust me. I'll keep you safe. You'll not want for anything money can buy. Promise.'

2

TWO YEARS AND TWO MONTHS LATER

Saturday 2nd October 1965

The plaintive notes of Patsy Cline's *Crazy* drifted down from the stage, as Louise did another tour of the bar area, collecting empty glasses. Patsy Hill, the daughter of a notorious bank robber, was entertaining a cluster of regulars. Louise didn't judge her; it wasn't Patsy's fault her father was a criminal, any more than it was Louise's being the wife of a gangster. 'You're one of us now,' Big Jim told her at their wedding reception. They had married seven months after that first date at Annabel's. Louise had no idea Eddie was a criminal, a key player in London's underworld. Maybe she should have guessed. Was deceiving herself because she wanted to believe he had inherited money, and it was his generosity as a philanthropist that made him popular with celebrities. By the time she found out Big Jim owned their flat and as good as owned them, it was too late.

'Leave them glasses, Lou. You get back to your man, or I'll have Eddie the Rick after me. He's already accusing me of working his princess too hard.'

'Thanks, Gloria. You didn't tell him I was earning a bit extra cleaning? I want to buy him something special.'

'Your secret's safe with me, babe. I'll pay you now as it'll be busy tonight.'

'The Kinks. Sold out I hear.' Louise had listened to many top bands here at the Tin Pan Alley Club on London's Denmark Street. Big Jim was part owner of the club and so his work associates had free entry. Eddie had rubbed shoulders with Mick Jagger, Paul McCartney, and Sandie Shaw. This had impressed Louise in the early days of their relationship. Now, she dreaded the inevitable late night at a club and the drinking and drugs that were part of the ritual. She always kept sober, afraid of letting her guard down. It was work, Eddie said. He needed to be seen. To network.

Gloria handed her a roll of notes. Her wages were paid into their joint account, but the cleaning work was extra.

'Thanks, Gloria. I'll be back at seven tonight.'

Louise enjoyed the walk to and from the club. Denmark Street was a musician's paradise, with shops selling guitars, keyboards and drums. There were recording studios and coffee bars where musicians hung out. Hippies loitered, browsing sheet music or record stores, hoping to see someone famous. It was a place where dreams were made and everyone wanted to be part of the magic. To catch a little dream dust. The music scene had not impressed Louise. It was Eddie with his suave sophistication and the promise of a better life. Gloria thought Eddie cherished Louise. Maybe he did, as a prized possession, but Louise lived in a gilded cage and Big Jim held the key. Eddie was a puppet. His every move dictated by the boss. If Big Jim told Eddie to do away with her, Louise was afraid he might. Thankfully, he had never been tested, but she knew where his loyalty lay--it would always be Big Jim first.

Walking gave her the space to think. She couldn't carry on living with Eddie. If it wasn't for Big Jim's hold over him, Eddie might have been a decent bloke, but he was in too deep by the time Louise married him. As far as she knew, Eddie's crimes were racketeering: illegal gambling, working as a 'rick' in Big Jim's casinos. He would sit in on a game cheating with marked cards. Big money was involved, but Louise was almost certain Eddie didn't use violence. She had threatened to leave him, if he did. It was then she realised he would never allow that. Eddie may not use violence, but he knew a man who did--several--and they would, if given the word. So, Louise had stashed away a bit of cash. Her escape fund. One day, when Eddie was on one of his business trips, she would take off.

She had put a pin on a map of the British Isles. Strathnaver Valley. It was at the top of Scotland, as far away from Eddie and the Mob as she could travel by train. Sixteen hours from Euston, changing at Inverness, then a mini-cab or hitching a ride from Kinbrace. If she took the night train, it would be cheaper. Some spare savings money would pay for a few nights in a boarding house until she found casual work: a pub, shop, cleaner. She would change her identity--a new name, cut and dye her hair. The idea of living in a valley again appealed to her. She'd even found a little village on the road map that Eddie kept in the glove compartment of his Jaguar. Bettyhill. It conjured images of a quaint village made up of stone-built cottages, a little stream running through its centre. And a bridge. Like the packhorse bridge in Thorncrest where she and Dicky had played. Maybe she could rent a room in a farmhouse cottage with an open fire. Get a dog. Go for walks. This dream kept her going. In a few months, she would have enough money to start a new life.

Louise glanced up at the bay windows of Big Jim and

Alice's ground floor flat before walking down the uneven steps to her basement flat. Although she rarely saw Jim or Alice at the house, she always felt as though she was being watched. When they first moved in, she had tried to befriend Alice but gave up after frequent snubs. Louise soon learned she wasn't famous, wealthy, or sufficiently glamorous to be included in Alice's golden circle. Gloria, the bar manager, was the closest she had to a friend. How could she forge a friendship without giving away anything about her life with Eddie? But Louise was good at keeping secrets. Maybe that's what Eddie saw in her.

The flat was silent, as always. When she started her new life, there would be an eager dog to greet her at the door. Maybe a couple of cats, too. Louise smiled to herself as she unzipped her boots. She left them in the hallway and padded through to the kitchen, where she filled a kettle and put it on the gas to boil. She took the roll of notes from her handbag. There had been other casual jobs over the past couple of years, each adding a little to her escape fund. While the water boiled, Louise went into their bedroom. Eddie favoured polished floorboards and luxurious rugs rather than modern wall to wall carpeting. Louise was glad. Ma Beck who had introduced her to the beauty of loose floorboards. A perfect hiding place in every home. Louise crawled under the bed a little way and eased up a loose board. She added the notes to the others saved in the jamjar. Here too was her diary. The one she had started writing when she was first evacuated. At that time, her entries had been regular. Since returning to London, it had only been used to record significant events, those times when she needed to confide in a friend. Her secrets were laid bare within its pages.

The kettle sung and Louise bumped her head. 'Ouch.' She wriggled out on her belly.

'What are you doing under there?'

Eddie was standing at the bedroom door, dressed in one of his dapper suits.

'I didn't hear you come in. My shoe. I lost one of my kitten-heeled shoes and I wanted to wear them tonight.'

Eddie gave her a long look. 'Did you find it?'

'No. But it's okay. I'll wear a different pair. You're home early.'

'Pleased to see me, princess?' He shrugged off his jacket and threw it onto the bed.

'Always.' Louise *was* pleased to see him. She didn't enjoy the life they lived, but Eddie was okay and, if she was honest, she always felt a little afraid when home alone.

'Want a cuppa? Kettle's just boiled.'

'I need something stronger. I was being watched at the Clement Club this afternoon. Plain clothes cops or something. I had to lose a lot of dosh.'

'How much?' Louise followed Eddie out of the bedroom.

'You don't want to know.' He went through to the front room to pour a drink and Louise darted into the kitchen to turn off the gas ring.

When Louise joined him, he held up a decanter of whiskey. Louise shook her head. 'Are you going to tell Big Jim?'

Eddie took a long slug. His face was pale. 'No. I won't tell Big Jim until I've won it back tonight. It makes me sick just thinking about it.'

'So, you're not going to see the Kinks at Tin Pan?'

'I'll try to drop in later. We're entertaining them after the show. A strip joint, probably. Hopefully, by then, I'll have sorted the trouble. Not a word to anyone.'

'You know I won't.' Louise reached for the decanter. 'Maybe I will join you.'

. . .

The Tin Pan Alley Club was heaving with sweaty bodies as fans crammed as close as they could to the stage. Louise's eyes smarted from cigarette smoke, her hands sticky with spilt beer. The lead guitarist blasted a final note, the sound reverberating against the speaker, and Ray Davies shouted, 'Goodnight.'

They had already played two encores. In another hour, the club would close. Big Jim had arrived in the second half and sat in a corner of the bar with a pretty young woman. Alice rarely joined him at music venues.

'Take a couple of magnums through to the boys,' he told Louise, as she passed by his table collecting empties.

'Of course. Is there anything else you would like?' Louise was always on best behaviour with Jim.

'Your fella. Where's Eddie, my man? He should be here entertaining our guests.'

Louise's stomach lurched. She prayed he would turn up any minute, his problem sorted. If not, there would be trouble for them both. 'He should be here soon. I'll get the champers.'

The boys were ready to leave and still no sign of Eddie. 'A word, Lou, in the back.' Big Jim nodded to indicate an office, which was upstairs hidden behind a two-way mirror. She followed him, praying that he wouldn't ask her questions about Eddie's whereabouts.

'I know I can trust you, Lou. I wanted to give this to Eddie tonight, but it seems he's not joining us.'

'He might still turn up,' Louise said. 'I know he was looking forward to entertaining The Kinks.'

'Maybe. But I can't risk missing him tonight, so I'm trusting you to deliver my message.'

Louise flinched, afraid Big Jim was going to punch her, or worse. If he knew Eddie had lost a lot of money, he might take it out on her. But Big Jim was reaching into his jacket pocket.

'Tell your old man there's a monkey in here. It says Randall Wolf is going to lose to Chad Tennessee on Monday the fourth. Wolf's manager knows the score.'

Louise took the brown envelope.

'That's a good girl. I've ordered a car to take you straight home. Can't have you walking the street with that kind of money.'

It was the first time Big Jim had trusted her with an important job. This was what she had feared. He was pulling her into the underworld. Until now, she could have pretended not to know what went on, but as time passed, it was getting harder. Already she was implicated and knew far too many secrets. She had to get away as soon as possible.

The lights were on in the basement when Louise's car pulled up outside. Eddie was never at home this early on a Saturday night. It didn't bode well.

'Hello, darling,' she called, glad to be safely home. There was no reply. Had Eddie come in and gone out again? She hoped he had caught up with Big Jim and their VIP guests.

Eddie was sitting in the front room, his jacket still on. She could tell from the tightness of his jaw and icy stare that something was seriously wrong. 'Sit down,' he said.

She waited. Bile filled her throat. The message and envelope from Big Jim forgotten.

'Fifty-two pounds,' he said.

Louise waited. But no more came. She was meant to know his reference. And then it dawned on her—the escape fund.

'I was saving up to buy you something special,' she said.

He conjured her diary from behind a cushion, and a wave of nausea swept through her. 'According to this entry, you're planning to bugger off. Don't take me for a fool, darling.'

'No. No. You've got it wrong. Maybe I did feel like that when I wrote it. You know how it is sometimes. I was probably in a strop about something.' Louise used her most persuasive voice, hoping to chivvy him out of his dark mood.

'You're not going anywhere. A word in the right ear and I'll see you banged up.'

Louise frowned. He wasn't making any sense.

'This.' He shook the diary under her nose. 'Your confession. Premeditated murder.'

Louise lunged for the diary, but he held it out of reach. 'That's private. There's nothing in there to incriminate me.'

'I'm sure your friend Joan will be interested to hear what you planned. And if the Fuzz aren't interested in closing a case, the newspapers will love your story.'

Louise felt sick. It was something she had always feared. The truth surfacing. 'Nobody will pay any attention to the ramblings of a fourteen-year-old.'

'Try leaving me and we'll test out that theory.'

'What about your secrets? You have more to hide than me.'

'I'll let Big Jim know, shall I? That you're threatening to squeal?'

'No. Of course not.'

'That's better. No need to fall out over a misunderstanding.' Eddie smiled. His hand darted back behind the cushion to reveal a jam jar. An empty jam jar. 'So, no need for you to save up for a rainy day, is there? I've told you. Anything you want. You just have to ask.'

He went to bed, switching off the light as he left the room. Louise sat in the dark, feeling as though her life had ended. She couldn't stay with him. But if she left … The diary entries were not enough to convict her of a crime. But the evidence she had hidden on Becks Farm in Thorncrest would be of interest to news reporters if Eddie carried out his threat to expose her. There *could* still be an investigation if new evidence came to light. Louse took deep breaths. She couldn't stay with Eddie. With Big Jim involving her this evening, things were only going to get worse.

Car headlights drew a curve across the ceiling. Louise closed the curtains. Tomorrow, Eddie would be sweet as pie, but he would be watching her. And she had to get away. It had been a mistake marrying him. She should have trusted her instincts.

I've got to go back. The thought came as clear as a directive. She had been running away for twenty years. It was time to go back and face up to what she had done. *I can't confess.* If she was found guilty of murder, she could face the death penalty. It was unlikely, but possible. *No*. Louise shivered and wrapped her arms around herself. She could find Ma and beg her forgiveness. Would that make things worse? If only she could talk to Dicky. But Dicky would have left Thorncrest years ago. He was probably married. An architect designing modern houses for fashionable new towns. *Go back. Destroy the hidden evidence.* And maybe. Just maybe. Find Ma. Her beloved Ma. Could Dicky still be in Thorncrest? Louise's heart fluttered at the thought of seeing him again. That decided her.

As gentle snores came from their bedroom, Louise took fifty-two pounds from the wad of notes Big Jim had given her and wrote a note to Eddie. *I've taken back what's mine—fifty-two pounds. Big Jim says there's a monkey in this envelope to see that Randall Wolf loses to Chad Tennessee, on Monday the fourth of October. I hope you resolved your problem at The Clement. I wish we could have had a different life together. I'm sorry, but I can't live like this. Please don't try to find me. Goodbye my love. Louise.*

Just before dawn she slipped out the front door, carrying the bare minimum—a change of clothes, her diary, and a copy of Jane Eyre. Inside was an inscription from Dicky; that book was her most treasured possession. Eddie could keep the jewellery and fancy clothes he had bought her. He would be angry rather than heartbroken. Angry and humiliated. But hopefully, the Eddie she had cared enough about to marry, the kind, considerate version, would respect her wishes and let her go. It was true, he could cause trouble by sharing her diary entries—maybe attract some media interest, but if he did, she would rather be in Thorncrest, where she could try to limit the damage by explaining herself to the people who mattered. Ma. Joan and Dicky, if they were still there.

3

MONDAY 4TH OCTOBER 1965

Louise crept out of their flat at five in the morning. A net curtain in Big Jim's window fluttered. She froze, watching the movement of a shadow. It could have been a hand or a cat walking across their window sill. All was quiet, so she ventured on.

A car crawled along the street behind her, then stopped. She kept her head down, relieved when she heard the engine die. Someone else returning home. Not Big Jim. A milk crate rattled by. Otherwise, all was quiet. But she could not shift the feeling that someone was following her. Every few steps, she spun around, but she was alone. *Me and my shadow,* Louise thought. *I'm afraid of my own shadow.*

At Euston Station, she bought a ticket for the 05:36 to Leeds. There were more people than she would have expected so early in the morning, some coming home from night shifts or parties, others, like her, heading out. She focused on the lone men: a youngish man further down the platform. A scruffy man who looked like he'd been sleeping rough. A business man reading a newspaper. Louise yawned. She would just have to check if any of them got out at Leeds.

If she'd found anyone to cut and dye her hair on a Sunday, even a shop to buy hair dye, she could have saved the cost of an overnight stay. But it had given her time to think. One moment she was excited to be returning to Thorncrest, the next terrified. Tired from a night of almost no sleep, cold and miserable, she had almost got back on the train to London but sense prevailed and she had checked in to a bed-and-breakfast before doing something stupid. And now she was here, standing in a layby, hitching a lift.

A Cortina slowed down and pulled over. 'Where're you headed, babe?'

'Thorncrest.' Louise slung her holdall over one shoulder.

'Hop in.'

'Thank you.' Louise jumped into the front seat. She was pulling the door closed when she felt resistance. A young man had grabbed hold of the handle. She held on tight. What if he was one who'd joined the train at Euston? She'd forgotten to check who got off in Leeds. He wasn't going to let go. Louise relaxed her hold, and he opened her door, leaning across to speak to the driver.

'Room for one more?'

'Why not? So long as you're headed in the same direction. Thorncrest for the young lady.'

'Perfect. Name's Pete.'

Louise was uneasy. Where had Pete sprung from? She hadn't noticed another hitchhiker. She huddled down in her seat, intending to say as little as possible. It had been a mistake sharing her destination with the men.

'Thorncrest.' The driver said, pulling away and into the stream of traffic. 'The valley that's about to be flooded to create a reservoir? We've seen lots of tourists and volunteers visiting. Everyone wants a last look at the village before it disappears.'

So, the day had finally come. Thorncrest was about to be submerged. A death sentence held over the valley since an Act of Parliament before the First World War. Everyone knew that one day it would be flooded to create a reservoir, but to the people of Thorncrest it was always in the distant future. It felt as though fate was drawing her back to the valley.

'What's your business in Thorncrest?' The driver looked in his rear-view mirror, addressing Pete.

'Work.'

'On the dam?' The driver asked.

'That's right.'

'What are you? An engineer?'

'In training. But yes. That's what I'll do doing in Thorncrest. Working on the dam,' Pete said.

'Then you'll be wanting High House?'

'Perfect. Thanks,' Pete said.

'What are you doing in Thorncrest?' Pete asked Louise. 'You didn't introduce yourself.'

She would draw more attention to herself by being secretive. The driver gave her a sideways glance. They were waiting. 'Um. Another volunteer. Like you said, there's lots of us. I heard they needed help. So here I am. Jane Cox.' It was the first time she had used her alias. It felt as though she were playing a part in a film.

Pete and Louise were dropped off outside what looked like a listed building, with red shutters at the windows and ivy growing up one side.

'Maybe I should go on into the village. See what needs doing down there. It's different for you being an engineer. You've something useful to offer. I'm just an extra pair of hands.' Louise needed to put some space between herself and this Pete fellow. He acted warm and friendly, but she didn't trust him.

'An engineer in training. I'm hoping to get some work experience. Come on. Nothing ventured, nothing gained.'

Louise followed Pete to a porticoed entrance at the side of the house. He did not turn back as he mounted three steps and pushed open a glass door. She caught the door as it swung back and, seeing a reception desk in the foyer, crept in behind him.

There was nobody manning the desk so Pete pressed the bell. Once. Twice. Nothing. He pressed again, keeping his finger in place this time, so an incessant buzz filled the high-ceilinged room.

'Okay. I'm coming,' a voice barked from above. Then, a man with tousled strawberry blond hair, wearing braces, his shirt sleeves rolled up to above the elbows, stomped down the sweeping staircase.

Louise tried to make herself small behind Pete's broad back.

'We're not taking any more volunteers. More trouble than they're worth. If you want to do good, go bother the Salvation Army.'

'I'm Pete Murray, trainee civil engineer. I sent my CV...'

The man rubbed his forehead. 'Did you? Can't say I remember, but it's a bit chaotic here. Our receptionist left with no notice and with that bloody bell going off every two minutes, I can't get any work done. But now you're here, you can help me.'

'At reception?'

'No. In my office. I need more civil engineers. Come on.'

The man had taken no notice of Louise. It was as though she wasn't there. He had ushered Pete up the first flight of stairs when she rang the bell again.

'What the heck...'

'I would be happy to man the reception for you, sir. Just temporarily until you have time to recruit a replacement.'

'You would?'

Louise scooted behind the desk, trying to look as though she knew what she was doing. 'Absolutely. I've done this kind of thing before.'

'I don't know what we can pay you. You would have to find your way around the switchboard and bookings. There's a manual under the desk.'

'I'll be fine. Why don't you get back to work and I'll take care of things down here?'

For a fleeting moment, the man looked uncertain, then he bounded up the stairs, calling over his shoulder, 'Thanks. I'm Sean Fitzpatrick. If anyone calls, take a message. Don't disturb me unless it's urgent.'

Pete grinned and gave her a wink before following their new employer.

There was a handwritten manual explaining: the fire procedure, how Mr Fitzpatrick liked his tea—white, four sugars--the booking-in procedure for workers staying at the hostel, and telephone numbers for the cleaner, plumber, and grocery store. Louise wondered whether it was still Braithwaite's.

The phone rang. Louise picked it up and searched for a name, anything that would tell her the name of the place where she was now working. An envelope addressed to... 'High House. How can I help you?'

'Your crew are ransacking properties that are still occupied. If you don't call them off immediately, there's going to be trouble.' The woman sounded distressed rather than angry.

'Hold on. I'll put you through to Mr Fitzpatrick.' It sounded urgent, and if there was anyone else on duty, Louise didn't know who they were or how to contact them. She wasn't even sure how to transfer the call to Fitzpatrick. However, she had watched her mum working a switchboard many years ago. You connected the caller and receiver by matching the plugs in sockets. *There was Fitzpatrick. Here goes. No light.*

'Are you still there, caller?'

'Yes, but you have to get someone down here now. I'm serious. There's going to be a fight, or worse. I'd get the police, but they won't get here fast enough. *I am. I'm on the phone now. Not Fitzpatrick. A woman.* I have to go. Please come quick. They need to be told to get off private land.'

Louise stared at the phone receiver—now a long, low tone. Fitzpatrick wouldn't welcome an interruption to his meeting, but this was urgent. She was curious to see what was upstairs. A musty, papery smell pervaded the dimly lit landing. A name in a brass bracket on each heavy wooden door. Fitzpatrick was the third door along.

He looked up over thick-rimmed glasses when she knocked and entered. At first, he seemed to have trouble remembering who she was and what she was doing there. Pete, who was standing at a table studying a plan, the corners held in place with paperweights, said, 'Hi Jane. How are things at reception?'

'Yes. Jane. It must be time for coffee,' Fitzpatrick said.

'No, Mr Fitzpatrick. There's an emergency in the valley. Some of your men are upsetting the locals, trespassing, they say, on property that's still occupied. They want us to call them off before there's a fight. It sounds as though some local lads are facing up to them. They've tried the police, but they won't get there in time. What do you want me to do?'

'We're a bit thin on the ground. Now the dam's finished, most of our men have moved on. I told you these bloody volunteers are more trouble than they're worth. Would you mind popping down there? Tell them you're following my orders and they're to return here? I'll deal with them later. Take a bike from the back of the house.' He looked over Pete's shoulder to point something out on the plan.

'But what about reception?'

'Lock the door behind you. Boarders will have a key and anyone else can wait.'

There were a few bikes in a bike shed and not knowing who any of them belonged to, she took one that looked the right size. It would be her first sight of the valley since she left twenty years ago.

It was all happening too fast. Less than an hour ago she had been standing on the side of the road, alone, uncertain whether she was doing the right thing in returning to Thorncrest. Now she was acting on behalf of the chief engineer resolving a dispute over an abandoned property. It was as though she had been catapulted into another life. In a way she had—Jane Cox's life.

Racing along the high road with the wind in her hair, Louise felt as free as a child. The moors cradled her in their autumn glory. Bronze, shades of green, and russet. Later she would explore. Find the school. Would the playground seem as big and scary as it had then? There was the lane that she had walked a thousand times with Dicky. Down into the valley. Her heart ached with longing for her friend. Where was he living now? The valley had seemed too small for him, even then, when the valley was their kingdom. He would have moved on, planted new roots, and expanded to become the amazing man he was destined to be. Unlike her. Louise's growth had been stunted like the trees of Thorncrest growing within the walls of dilapidated cottages. Trapped in 1945.

Becks Farm on a road to the right. She felt as though her

heart was being squeezed. Every fibre of her longed to be back in the farmhouse kitchen, Ma bashing out the dough for bread, or making a steaming mug of hot chocolate. As soon as Louise finished in the valley, she would cycle over and take a look. The thought of Ma being close by made her stomach flutter. Louise glanced once more over her shoulder and then freewheeled down the lane.

Not knowing where she was needed, she headed straight for Braithwaite's grocery shop and post office. The shop and church had always been community hubs. Whoever ran the shop now would know exactly what, where and when.

A woman was standing outside the shop, her arms crossed high over a checked overall. She was looking anxiously up the lane when Louise skidded to a halt.

'Shop's closed.'

'I'm representing Sean Fitzpatrick. I took a call reporting some trouble in the valley.'

The woman looked her up and down. 'I asked for Fitzpatrick. Fat lot of good you'll be.'

'I have his orders to send the troublemakers back to High House, where he will deal with them.' Louise worried she had given the impression that the volunteers were in the wrong before they had the facts, but she couldn't help her loyalties being with the people of Thorncrest.

'Best get down there, then. Ma Widdle's place. Its--'

'--I know,' Louise said as she took off.

A cluster of people had gathered outside Ma Widdle's. She could hear jeering and abusive language. Louise rang the bell on her bike several times. It had little to no effect. A couple of girls acknowledged her by pursing their lips and then muttering to one another.

'I'm here for Sean Fitzpatrick,' she shouted, pushing her way through the gathering.

A man with thick, curly black hair was nursing a bloody lip. A pretty woman with blonde hair tried to dab away the blood with a handkerchief, but he brushed her aside and held up his fists.

A young long-haired man said, 'Peace, man. We're just doing our job.'

The bloodied man grabbed him by the lapels of his fringed jacket. 'Get the hell out of here or I'll pummel you like I did your mate.'

A balding guy in a parka threw himself on the man and fists flew. The crowd chanted. 'Fight. Fight.'

Water. She needed water. Ma Widdle had the use of a well. She and Dicky had collected water for her in exchange for a couple of mint humbugs. Louise abandoned her bike and ran to the well. There was a tin bucket, possibly the same one they used all those years ago. Louise filled it, hoping she wasn't too late. A serious injury would be bad publicity for the project and would not please Mr Fitzpatrick. If she wanted paid work and somewhere to stay for a few days, keeping Fitzpatrick happy was her priority.

She threw the water aiming for both heads which were now locked in combat like a couple of stags, but the balding guy had dodged a fist, so the man with a bloody lip got the full impact as water drenched him.

Louise took advantage of the shocked silence to announce Fitzpatrick's message. 'So, fight over.'

Parka jacket and hippy-head muttered and turned to go back into the cottage.

'Now. Please.'

'We've got stuff inside.'

'That will have to wait. Mr Fitzpatrick gave explicit instructions you were to leave the property immediately and return to High House. I'm sure we can sort this out. It's bound to be a misunderstanding.'

The man with a bloody lip faced her. Louise's heart skipped a beat, noticing his stormy grey eyes and long lashes.

'Tell your boss that a compulsory purchase order does not mean the Corporation owns a property. Not until contracts have been exchanged.'

'Does the owner still live here?' Louise asked. Ma Widdle seemed ancient when she was a girl. Surely, she wasn't still alive.

'No. But her family owns this property until it's sold. The same as all the properties where sales have not been completed or ownership confirmed.'

Wet hair plastered to his face changed his appearance. Without the curls, there was something familiar about him. The blonde woman sidled up and slid a hand between the buttons of his shirt. 'You're soaked, Richard. Best get this off and dry out before you catch a cold.'

Richard. 'Richard Braithwaite?' Louise whispered.

The blonde passed him his glasses. There was no mistaking him now. Dicky. As a boy, his mam kept his hair short. She loved his hair longer and curly; it softened his face. Well, it would, if he wasn't scowling at her.

'Yes. Remember my name because if you're working for Fitzpatrick, I'm going to make your life hell. Thorncrest will not be bulldozed as though it never existed. My people. My family and community. Generations have lived and loved in this valley. When the end comes, we will leave with dignity. We will not be bullied.' His breathing was short and sharp. Louise was afraid he might have an asthma attack.

'I won't forget,' she said.

How could she forget her best friend? Surely Dicky would recognise her. Louise longed to tell him it was her. Louise

Pearson. 'I never forgot,' she whispered. But he was already walking away, his arm around the pretty girl.

Louise's legs wobbled as she climbed back onto her bike. She had imagined a scenario where she might come face to face with Ma Beck, and had tried to prepare herself, but not Dicky. She'd become convinced he would no longer be living in Thorncrest. Her head and heart responded as though she were still fourteen. She wanted to run after him shouting, 'Dicky, it's me! I'm back.' They belonged together. Her life without him now seemed unimaginable.

Plans to visit Becks Farm were forgotten as she cycled back to High House. Dicky was still here. Richard Braithwaite.

4

OCTOBER 1942

Seeing Yorkshire for the first time was like travelling to another country. Everything was different; the buildings in the town they passed through dark and imposing, like the illustrations in her Brothers Grimm book of fairy tales; and the hills—they enclosed her, magnificent and protective—leaning in, obscuring her view so that every turn of the road revealed a new vista. She was used to the countryside of East Anglia—flat with expansive views that rested her eyes. In comparison, Yorkshire was like a vibrant bazaar: the jewel-coloured moors—bolts of cloth being rolled out for her inspection—crowding her in.

Louise struggled to keep her eyes open, afraid to appear rude if she dozed off when the woman driving had kindly collected her from Harrogate Station. But she was exhausted: emotionally, mentally, and physically.

The last few weeks had been traumatic. Living with Aunt Emma—mum's sister—and her family wasn't ideal. Her cousins were all boys and so the three of them had to share a room giving one up for her and Mum's use. But Louise thought they had rubbed along well enough. Then—she couldn't pin-point exactly when—Mum had a falling out with Emma. Louise overheard the tail-end of a heated discussion because her name was mentioned.

'This *is* for Louise, not me,' her mum had said.

Embarrassed to be caught eavesdropping, Louise interrupted. 'What's for me?'

Aunty wiped her eyes on the back of a hand and left the room, saying she had to catch the last post. Mum never explained, but three days later they moved out of the terraced North London house into a bedsit in the East End. Maybe that was why Mum insisted she take up this offer of an evacuation to Yorkshire, even though they had agreed when her last evacuation was a disaster that she wouldn't go away again.

Then came a sleepless night worrying about where she would be going and how she would be treated. The last time she was evacuated, the couple who took her in were heavy drinkers. When the authorities discovered this, Mum said she was to go home rather than risk another unhappy placement.

There were tears at the station that morning when Mum saw her off.

'Now remember, ask a guard at York Station to show you where to board the train to Harrogate. Don't talk to anyone else unless you have to. Travel in the ladies' carriage and if there isn't one, make sure there's at least one other woman in your carriage, a respectable one mind, not a floozy. I've packed a sandwich in your suitcase, but don't eat it too early.'

'What if I don't like the people? Will you come and collect me?' Louise tried hard not to cry. She was thirteen next February, almost a grown up. Too old to be evacuated, she had tried to argue with Mum.

'You'll like them. They live on a farm, so you'll have more to eat than me. Maybe I should ask if I can come too.'

'Will you!'

'No luv. I was joking. Now get off with you before we both start blubbering. Write to me with your news.'

And so, the long journey had begun. Now here she was, clasping a cardboard suitcase on her lap as they drove through the Yorkshire countryside.

'German prisoners should be kept in their camps where guards can keep an eye on them,' the woman said and Louise jolted awake as the car slowed down to overtake a line of men in drab army uniforms.

Louise wondered if she had been dreaming. The men couldn't be Jerries, their enemy. She wanted to ask, but was afraid of sounding stupid. 'Where are they going?' she asked instead.

'Working on local farms. The Government in their wisdom, decided they might as well be put to use helping us keep people fed. Nothing good will come of it. People talk and we know *loose talk costs lives*. They'll report back to the Nazis. Tell them where to drop their bombs to cause most damage.'

For the first time since leaving home, Louise was terrified. Everything here was alien to her, even the dialect they spoke. How was Yorkshire safer than London if German soldiers were living amongst civilians? Why had Mum bundled her off like an unwanted package? Well, if she hated it, she would insist on returning home. But London was a very long way away and Louise felt helpless—dependent upon strangers in a strange land.

They turned off the main road into a narrow lane. Louise bit her lips together and tightened her hold on the suitcase. Could she ask the woman to drive her straight back to the station? She didn't have the money for a return fare.

'Here we are, Becks Farm. And look, you have a welcoming party.'

Louise peeked out from behind her case to see a slim woman with her hair styled in a Victory Roll. On seeing the car, the woman clasped her hands to her chest and then threw them up as if excited to see her. It was not the reception Louise had expected.

The woman called over her shoulder and a man appeared, accompanied by an old English sheepdog.

'Oh, let me look at you. Are you really twelve? You look so grown-up.' The woman held both of Louise's hands as she stood opposite.

'I'll take this up to your room if that's okay, Louise? Let her get in the door, Ma,' the man said.

'Of course. We're just so happy to have you stay with us and we want you to feel welcome. Thank you for collecting her, Mrs Ramsbottom. Pa will give you something for your collection box. Will you stay for some refreshment?'

'No. I'll be getting on. Mr Beck can make a donation through the church if he wishes. Goodbye Miss Pearson, Mrs Beck.'

The sheep dog nudged Louise, and she bent down to stroke behind its ears.

'That's Kara. She's taken to you already. Come on in. You must be tired from travelling. I'll make you a cocoa, unless you would prefer cold milk. We've cows and chickens, so milk and eggs are in good supply.' Mrs Beck winked.

Louise felt immediately at home when they stepped into the warm and cosy farmhouse kitchen. Mr Beck, Pa, showed her to her room. It was the first time Louise had a room to herself; she had been sharing with her mum as long as she could remember. It was a pretty room with a patchwork quilt over the bed and a milk jug filled with deep red hydrangeas.

'Ma asked me to pick some flowers this morning to

welcome you. Not much out at this time of the year, but that hydrangea is a beauty. I hope you like the outdoors.'

Louise nodded enthusiastically. 'I do. We had a garden in the last house where we stayed. Not a big one, but I planted some marigolds. If we hadn't moved, I would have planted some vegetables.'

'Grand. You'll do alright here. I'll show you where you can freshen up. I heard a rumour there's cake. I have you to thank for that. It's rare nowadays Ma will "waste" an egg on cake, but with a young'un around, maybe I'll get cake for tea more often.'

Louise couldn't have been happier living with Ma and Pa Beck on the farm. She loved helping Ma collect eggs from the chickens and working alongside Pa, digging up potatoes or riding alongside as he ploughed the fields. After a few days, Ma announced over breakfast that Louise was to register at the local school.

She had gone off happily enough, with Ma's reassurance that being new to the school, everyone would want to befriend her. The headmistress introduced Louise at assembly, explaining that she was an evacuee from London and they were all to make her feel welcome. Although well-intended, this announcement marked Louise as different. Heads turned to stare at her with looks of pity or wonder. If only one girl would befriend her, she would be okay, but Louise didn't know how to make the first move.

Being an only child, she hadn't much experience with childhood friends. Although she disliked her boy cousins, she knew how to talk to boys. Girls were, she discovered, more complicated. One to one she might have got on with some of the girls, but they seemed to band together on the playground with a hierarchy—Brenda Button being the leader, and it seemed Brenda Button took an instant dislike to Louise. It was a small school with children ranging from seven to twelve years of age. Until Louise joined the school, Brenda Button had been the eldest girl, so maybe she felt her leadership threatened. At playtime, when Louise asked if she could join in a game of hopscotch, Brenda said there would be too many. So, Louise stood by the white line dividing the boys' playground from the girls' and watched the boys playing at war.

When Ma asked about her day at school, Louise said it was good. She could put up with the rotten girls because life on the farm was like living a dream. London and the bombing seemed far away. She wished that Mum could be with them on the farm too, because it felt wrong to be so happy when her mum was living alone in just one room.

On Saturday, Louise went with Ma to Braithwaite's grocery shop and post office so she could post a letter home. It was the first one she had written since arriving in Yorkshire two weeks ago. There was so much to tell Mum, so it had taken a few days to complete. When Louise explained this to Ma Beck, Ma suggested she keep a diary, then when she returned home, she could share everything properly with her mum.

The shop bell rang as they pushed open the door to Braithwaite's. A boy a bit older than Louise sat on a high stool at the shop counter, swinging his legs and flicking the elastic on a catapult made from a Y-shaped twig. He glanced up when they walked in and Louise caught his eye before he looked away with an air of boredom and indifference.

'Good morning, Liz. Is this the evacuee you took on?'

Why did everyone have to label her "evacuee"? The boy dipped his head, but Louise was aware of him listening. She'd seen him on the boy's playground hanging around the bike shelter with the other older boys.

'Indeed. This is Louise Pearson. She's here to buy a diary and post her letter,' Ma said.

'You could use an exercise book or one of those hard-backed ones with lined pages. Nothing fancy, but something like that should do the job.'

Louise browsed the stationery shelf whilst Ma gave her grocery order. The catapult elastic twanged and the boy's feet thudded against the shop counter.

When Mrs Braithwaite said, 'Are you going to take on a German prisoner to help on the farm?' Louise gasped, and the boy toppled off his stool. They both stared at one another wide-eyed.

'I...I saw them,' Louise said, and then bit her lip. She hadn't meant to speak. Now all eyes were on her. 'They were marching down the road.'

'Aye. That would be right. The prisoner of war camp is on the road that you would have come in on. It's worth a thought, Liz. Now you've got her.' The woman, Dicky's mum, crossed her arms and nodded at Louise.

Ma put an arm around Louise. 'This one's a strong'un. And she has lovely manners. Pa and I are delighted to have a girl. But you may be right. I'll look into it, Else. See what it entails.'

Mrs Braithwaite rang up the total and Ma paid. Louise insisted on using her spending money to buy the hard-back book she had chosen for her diary. Mum had sent her off with a few shillings and so far, Ma had not let her pay for anything.

'Did you post your letter home?' she asked Louise as they left the shop.

'I did, thank you. Wouldn't you be worried if a German soldier worked on the farm?'

'They are only young men like our own, fighting in a war

because they have to. We would only take on a lad if we thought we could trust him. Times are hard and farmworkers scarce. I'll talk to Pa, see what he says.'

The following Monday, when Louise was walking home from school, the boy from the shop, Dicky, came running up behind her. 'Have you got a Jerry yet?'

'No. I asked Ma Beck about it after we left your shop. She said she would have to talk to Pa. I saw them marching along the road with the prison guards. What if they escape?'

Dicky let out his breath. 'I thought prisoners of war were meant to be locked up. If you get one working on the farm, will he have a guard with him?'

'I don't know. I hope so. A real German soldier, the enemy, on our farm.' The idea terrified and thrilled Louise in equal measure.

They walked along amiably, not feeling the need to talk. When they reached Becks farm, Dicky said, 'If you like, I'll show you the old mill.'

'I don't know. I usually help Ma Beck on the farm after school.'

'I'll come inside while you ask.'

Ma had been happy for Louise to traipse off with Dicky whilst she was busy in the dairy. She refused Louise's offers to help. 'I'll teach you how to skim off the cream and make butter once you've found your feet. For now, you're best letting off some steam. Go and have fun, but be back in time for tea. About five. And mind yourself when it gets dark. No climbing around derelict buildings and the like.'

'I'll look after her, Mrs Beck,' Dicky said, swinging his school satchel.

'Then leave your bag here. You can pick it up when you

return young Louise to the farm. Now, be off with you while there's still some light.'

As they tramped across a muddy field leaving the homely farmhouse behind, Louise became shy. Dicky's friendliness had been a balm to her wounded pride after being rejected by the girls, but now, as he swiped at the long grass with a stick, she didn't know what to say.

Dicky broke the silence. 'There are no proper roads in the valley. Just trees. They were planted when it was decided the village would be flooded.'

'What do you mean? Flooded?'

Dicky tossed his stick into the hedgerow and spun around to face Louise. 'Don't you know?'

She shook her head.

'Thousands of years ago. Maybe a million. The prime minister, or it might have been the King, agreed that Thorncrest would be flooded to make a reservoir so that the water could work the mills in Leeds. But then there was the Great War, and now this war. It's going to happen one day.' His eyes sparkled as he delivered this history in one breath.

Louise didn't know what a reservoir was or how water could work a mill, but she didn't want to seem ignorant and lose the one friend she had in her new home. 'If it's going to be flooded, what about the people and animals?'

'There's only our shop, Ma Widdle's place, and the polyphon man, Beaky. His cottage is stuffed full of polyphons. They're machines that play music. We can visit him another day. Mam says not to bother him, but he doesn't mind. And the church, of course.'

They tramped some more.

'Here we are!' Dicky spread his arms wide as they looked down on the valley.

Louise didn't know what to make of it. She felt as though

she had stepped into a magical land. The valley floor was covered in trees. They grew out of derelict buildings, their limbs stretching through windows, and missing roofs. Some of the stone buildings were unharmed and Louise wondered where Ma Widdle lived, and the polyphon man.

'Why did the other people move out?'

'Don't know. Do you want to see the mill?'

Louise nodded and followed Dicky over a little brick bridge. They stopped halfway across to lean over and drop twigs into the gentle current.

'What's it like living in London?'

'Nothing like this. But we have buildings with no roofs or walls because of the bombs. You can see the wallpaper and some of the peoples' things. Furniture and stuff. I once saw a house where the bed was unmade, as though the person had just got out of it, and a picture hanging lopsided on the wall, and I thought the house doesn't know that the people are dead and everyone can see in.'

'I hate the Jerries. My brother is fighting them. If I was old enough, I would too.' He pretended to hold a gun and made shooting noises as he blasted everything in sight.

'I hope we don't have a German soldier helping on the farm. Maybe if I work really hard, the Becks will decide they don't need one. They have a Land Army girl. Why don't they just get another one of them?'

'Because girls aren't as strong as boys.'

'Is that what you think?' Louise looked at his scrawny legs and skinny frame, then with a burst of bravado, she threw herself forwards and lifted him off his feet.

He giggled. 'Put me down. It's not fair. I wasn't ready for you.'

She could only hold him for a couple of seconds. As soon

as his feet hit the ground, he took off. 'Bet you can't run as fast as me!'

5

NOVEMBER 1942

Louise's first month on the farm had passed quickly. She didn't enjoy school but was quick to learn and had become a favourite with the teachers, if not the other kids. But the best time of day was after school, when she and Dicky walked home together. They would stop at the farmhouse for a glass of milk before running wild, exploring the valley until it was time for Louise to return to help on the farm.

'Does it make you sad to think that all the people who once lived here have left their homes empty?' she said, as they sat on the wall of an overgrown garden, a late-flowering Michaelmas daisy cushioning their backs.

'It used to frighten me. I thought the houses were haunted. But Mam said if they were, they wouldn't hurt me because they were probably my ancestors. Dead relatives.'

'I think a family lived here. A girl about my age and her two sisters—Beth and May. They played together in this garden and picked flowers to sell.'

'Why did they sell the flowers?'

'Because their mother was sick and needed the money to buy her medicine.'

'Where was their father?'

'He had to do some important work in a faraway land, but he got lost and so he didn't know that his wife was ill.'

'I like your stories. Where's your dad, Louise? You only talk about your mam and cousins.'

Louise sighed. She preferred to make up stories than talk about her life. 'I don't know. He disappeared when I was too young to remember. He could be fighting in the war, in prison, or dead for all I know.'

Dicky put an arm around her. 'You have Pa Beck and me. We'll look after you.'

Louise wanted to retort that she didn't need a boy to look after her, but she liked the warmth of Dicky's arm heavy on her shoulder, so she said, 'And I'll look after you.'

They followed the river to the mill, watching out for sticklebacks and frogs. A brown and gold fish darted in and out of the dappled shade. On the stone bridge, they stopped to lean over and watch the current.

'All the people in these houses worked at the mill,' Dicky said.

Louise sat on the bridge wall. 'One of the girls who worked there was in love with the mill owner's son, but they had to keep it a secret.'

'You should write your stories. One day someone will buy your books and you will be famous.'

Louise laughed. She liked that idea. 'What about you? What will you do when you grow up?'

Dicky tossed a twig in to the stream and they watched it nudge against the weed before making its way downstream. 'I'm going to be a carpenter. I'll build boats and barns. I'll build timber houses and make brand new villages. Not just here. All over the world.'

'Do you think we'll still be friends, then?'

'Always.'

They left the bridge and meandered on to the mill. This was where they usually spent their time. There were walls to climb and, as the mill had no roof, and spacious rooms, it was light and airy—unlike some of the other derelict buildings. Ma knew they went there and didn't object, so long as they did nothing foolish.

Today, they hung around outside the mill. Talk of the future, and the golden glow of the late afternoon sun warming the honey-coloured cottages had created a spell. The mill felt too mundane for a day like that. Dicky wandered over to a grand-looking house that stood close to the mill. He tried the door as they had done many times before.

'Do you think the people who live here might come back one day?' Louise said.

'No. It belongs to the Corporation now. They bought off all the houses.'

'Then why leave them empty? It's a beautiful house. I'd love to see inside.'

The windows were high, and so Louise looked for a boulder. 'Help me roll this over to the window so I can get a good look inside.'

Louise balanced on the stone as it rocked with her weight and peered through the smeared window. There was a fireplace and shelves of books. 'We have to go inside, Dicky; all of those books are going to waste.'

'We can't. It would be trespassing and we could go to prison.'

'But what if someone—a kitten—was trapped inside? We would have to rescue it.'

'But there isn't.'

'Are you sure? I think I hear mewing.'

Dicky climbed up next to her. 'That would have been the mill owner's house. I don't think we should break in, Louise. What if we get caught?'

'Who's going to catch us?' Louise wiggled the sash window. It took little to loosen it. 'Give us some room.' She elbowed Dicky off the stone and, crouching, put her weight behind her palms and pushed. The window resisted, then flew up with a rattle.

Shrouds covered the furniture. Lace cobwebs adorned the room. Somewhere in the house, a timber creaked. Louise shivered. Where was Dicky? Maybe they shouldn't have broken in. What if there was a ghost? Or somebody still living there?

'Dicky,' she hissed.

'Help me up.'

When Louise had hauled Dicky through the window and he had landed safely, they stood in a beam of light from the ebbing sun and took in the room. Dust motes danced like fairies, and Louise's courage returned.

'Let's explore.' She headed straight for the bookshelves. Up close, the books looked unexciting, brown and black spines worn and dirty. She pulled one out and blew away the dust. It was hard to decipher the title, so she opened it to find close print and hardly any pictures. 'I think it's about weaving and stuff.'

'Through here.' Dicky opened a door.

A grandfather clock stood beneath the stairs; its heart had stopped at twelve thirty-five. Louise imagined that moment. Had anyone been in the house to witness its last tock? To mark the occasion of its final chime? Louise felt as though they were being watched by ghosts, angry at the intrusion. 'Let's go,' she said.

'Not yet. Come and look in here.' Dicky had disappeared into another room off the hall.

Louise followed his voice and found him sitting in a high-backed chair behind an impressive-looking desk. 'Ah, Miss Jones. A pot of tea, please.'

'How come you're the boss?'

'Because I got here first. You can be my deputy if you like.'

Louise knelt in front of a wooden filing cabinet. The bottom drawer was empty apart from a bottle of ink and a folded sheet of blotting paper. She tried the next one up. Lots of boring papers with scrawled handwritten notes.

Dicky was opening and closing the desk drawers. 'Argh,' he screamed. 'This looks like the skeleton of a dead mouse.'

'You're such a scaredy cat. The top drawer's locked. What if there's something really valuable in there?'

'Like what?'

'I don't know. The family jewels. Or something secret—a treasure map?' Louise tugged at the rusty brass handle.

'There's a key in the desk drawer. Try this.' Dicky slid out from behind the desk to join Louise at the cabinet.

'It fits.'

'What's inside?'

'A metal box.' She lifted it out. 'But this is locked too! There must be something *really* valuable inside.'

Dicky peered into the drawer. 'Here's the key.'

They carried the box to the middle of the room and sat crossed legged on the worn Indian rug. The box stood between them, full of possibility. It was like an unopened Christmas present. Louise didn't want to dispel the magic by revealing what was inside.

'If it's valuable, do you think we should report it to the police or something?'

'No. Then we would have to tell them we had broken in.

Besides, the house and everything in it belong to the Corporation now.'

Louise sighed. 'That doesn't seem fair. If the people who lived here left in a hurry and forgot to take a family heirloom, wouldn't they want it back? We might get a reward if we return it to them.'

'Let's make a deal. Whatever's in the box will be our secret.'

'Forever?' Louise asked.

'Forever.' Dicky reached out his hand and they linked pinkie fingers.

'Okay. I'm going to open it.' Louise turned the key. She exchanged a nervous, excited look with Dicky and then lifted the lid.

'Lots of boring papers.' It was the musty, brown book all over again. 'Maybe there's a secret message in code.' Louise riffled through the yellowed pages of scrawl. They crackled and splintered like dry leaves.

Dicky took them gently from her hands. 'It looks like the accounts. Who's been paid with dates and amounts.'

Louise clutched the tin box trying to recreate the magic she had felt on discovering it, but it was like the Christmas she opened her mum's present to find a compendium of board games instead of the Flossy Flirt doll with eyes that could roll and said, *Ma. Ma.* Snakes and ladders, ludo, and draughts.

'I know,' Dicky said, as if sensing her dismay. 'This can be your secret box to collect things that will remind you of Thorncrest when you go back to London.'

'I don't want to go back. Not ever.'

The sun had gone, and the room felt cold.

'I don't want you to, either. I know, I'll give you something to remember me by.'

'I'll never forget you, Dicky.'

Louise's heart ached. She didn't know why. Her moods

seemed to do that a lot recently, extreme feelings of emotion that could change in an instant.

Dicky held out his fist and opened it to reveal a large multi-coloured marble. 'You can have this. I wish I could give you something better, like a ring or a necklace.'

Louise took the marble from his hand. Her fingers tingled as they brushed his palm. 'This is special. It's your lucky marble. I can't take this Dicky. You carry it everywhere. I know how much it means to you.'

Dicky swallowed hard and Louise noticed his Adam's apple. 'Not as much as you.'

Louise could hear the hum of tears in her temple. She shook her head to make them go away and her hair fell loose from its ribbon. Behind this screen of hair, she composed herself. When she looked up, Dicky was trailing the silky ribbon through his fingers. Louise's throat constricted; tears pricked her eyes. A tidal wave of love threatened to tip her off balance. It was a feeling unfamiliar to her. Scary.

'You can keep my ribbon. To remember me,' she said.

Dusk was falling as they walked home, hand in hand. 'Will you marry me one day?' Dicky said as they approached the farm.

Louise gave this some thought. She couldn't imagine loving anyone more than Dicky. Until that day, she had not experienced anything like the tenderness and devotion she felt towards this scruffy, earnest boy at her side. 'Yes,' she said. 'And we will live here, in Thorncrest.'

'But not in my parent's shop,' Dicky said. 'You've got a visitor.'

A big black car was parked next to the farm truck. Louise was nervous. 'What if they've come to take me back? I don't recognise the car, but it looks official.'

'We could run away. Hide in the big house. I'll sneak out after dark to get food from our shop.'

It was a romantic thought, but Becks farm looked cosy with the lights on. The fire would be lit. 'It's a bit cold. Let's see who it is first.'

The kitchen was empty, but voices were coming from the living room. Dicky shrugged his shoulders. His school satchel was on a chair in the kitchen. He picked it up and slung it over his shoulder. 'Do you want me to wait until you've found out who it is?'

'It's okay. I'll tell you tomorrow.'

Before Dicky had a chance to leave, the door opened and Ma Beck stepped in to the kitchen, followed by a woman in a black skirt and jacket, and a young man wearing the German prisoner of war uniform. Dicky gasped.

'Louise. Just in time to meet our new farmhand, Kurt.'

He didn't look like a German soldier. He was too young and kind of innocent looking. A clear, smooth face, and very blue eyes. Kurt shook her hand as though she were a grown-up.

'Kurt is starting work tomorrow,' Ma said.

Kurt, the woman, and Ma went outside to the car. Dicky must have left too, because the metal box he had been carrying was on the table.

6

MONDAY 4TH OCTOBER 1965

'I've had to let the volunteers go,' Fitzpatrick said to Louise, who was manning reception.

Louise wasn't surprised. She had gone in to Ma Widdle's when the volunteers left. The debris of butts from dismantled cigarettes, Rizla papers, and a plastic bag of tar-like resin explained why they had been anxious to remove their stuff. It had saddened her to see the old cottage, once cosy, now damp and neglected. Her rocking chair beside the range had a tapestry cushion worn to thin threads from years of use. A scratching and a scrambling had alerted Louise to a visitor. Ma Widdle's tabby would have seen off the water rat that bared its teeth at Louise, the intruder.

'All of them?' Louise said. She had not yet discovered how many workers lodged at High House or what they did.

'We only had two. Useless. The Corporation should send paid staff. I'm project manager and chief civil engineer. I can't be expected to nursemaid dope heads too.'

Louise smiled at his description. 'Will you be recruiting a receptionist?'

Fitzpatrick gave an exaggerated sigh, as if she had heaped more problems on to his overloaded shoulders. 'Can't you do it?'

'Maybe, but we haven't discussed pay or accommodation.'

'How about you work as my PA and stay in the hostel?'

Louise's heart leapt in gratitude. It would give her time to find the hidden evidence and, after meeting adult Richard and breathing in the beauty of the moors in their autumn glory, she was in no hurry to leave.

'Would you want references? An interview?'

'You just passed with flying colours. There's no job description—just whatever needs doing. I'll keep you busy.'

'I would have to be paid cash—casual labour. My situation is a bit complicated.'

Fitzpatrick waved his hand. 'Suits me. Less paperwork. So long as you sort out your National Insurance. It's up to you.'

Louise reached out her hand and after some hesitation, Fitzpatrick realised her meaning and took it in a firm handshake.

'I will need a proper briefing about the project if I'm to act on my initiative. I'm guessing you don't want to be involved in minor disputes, like today.'

'Good point. But I'm kind of busy.' He was checking his watch and backing away from her.

'Ten o'clock tomorrow morning when I bring you your coffee and biscuits?'

He frowned.

'Chocolate digestives.'

'That would be an improvement on Garibaldi. Done. See you then.'

. . .

That evening, she'd agreed to meet Pete for a drink at the hostel's bar. It was a comfortable room, a cross between a hotel lounge and student hangout in a hall of residence. The alternative was to sit alone in the dorm. As the only female resident, Louise had the women's dorm to herself, so she had chosen a bottom bunk close to the window.

'I didn't notice you when I was trying to hitch a ride,' Louise said, when Pete returned from the bar carrying a gin and bitter lemon for her and a pint of stout for himself.

'A clever ploy.' He grinned and took a sip of beer, leaving an edge of foam on his upper lip.

Louise frowned.

'You were bound to get a lift quicker than me.' Pete shrugged. 'You didn't mind?'

'No. Of course not. I doubt I would have landed this job and a room if it wasn't for you. Did you really send Fitzpatrick a CV?'

Pete grimaced. 'Really? Not exactly. I had one in case he asked. He needed an engineer, and I needed the experience. Fate brought us together.'

'And it seems fate nabbed you one of the best bedrooms in the west wing. How come you don't have to sleep in the men's dorm?'

'The construction workers in the men's dorm work unsocial hours. I guess I got engineer status. My bedroom's along the corridor from Fitzpatrick's. *Very* comfy.'

Louise was just grateful to have a bed for the night where she felt safe. She'd barely slept the last two nights and her body was depleted from one adrenalin surge after another. Sitting with Pete in the quiet lounge, being fussed over by Peggy, who was bartender, cook, and cleaner, felt natural. Normal. Life hadn't felt normal in a long while. Eddie would have realised by now she wasn't going back to him.

'Penny for them?' Pete said.

'Oh, I was just thinking how pleasant it is in here. What do you think the house was used for before the Corporation moved in?'

'It must have been a grand home at one time. She has beautiful bone structure. Have you visited this area before?'

Louise twirled the ice in the bottom of her empty glass. 'No. Just heard about it on the news and wanted to help out. See for myself. Fitzpatrick is briefing me tomorrow, but it would be helpful if you can tell me all you know about the properties in the valley. Which ones have been sold, and the ones waiting for contracts to be exchanged. I don't even know how high the reservoir will go.' The thought of Ma and Pa's home being under water horrified her.

'You'll have to look at the plan. Most of the properties have been vacated and contracts signed. The grocery shop—Braithwaite's, is causing a problem. Well, the owner is. Until he agrees a price and signs, we can't make any definite plans.'

Louise was surprised Richard was dragging his feet. She thought he would have been glad to give up the shop and live the life he spoke of as a teen—building timber houses, creating communities. Maybe having grown up in a condemned village, he wanted to create something new. 'Is he being offered a fair price?'

'Sounds like it. I don't know what his problem is. He's using his position as a lever to bargain on behalf of other residents who are being displaced. There's an old guy who recently went into a nursing home. He owns a load of jukeboxes.'

'Polyphons,' Louise said, without thinking.

Pete looked at her, bemused.

'I think they're called polyphons. I must have read about it.'

'Right. Well, they're valuable, apparently. And he wants

them to be taken to a local museum for the residents of Thorncrest to enjoy. Problem is the only museum that can take them is in York and you can imagine how that has gone down.'

'It must be hard for them, letting go. It's like when a person dies. People say they were ill for a long time and so it was inevitable, but it doesn't make their passing any less painful.'

Pete squinted, as if trying to make sense of her analogy. A shrug suggested he had no idea what she meant. 'Well, they need to get over it. We've limited time and a budget. The trial flooding is behind schedule because of the time it's taking to exchange contracts. Then there's the Church Committee making unreasonable demands about the replacement church. There are the graves to move as well.'

'The graveyard. I hadn't considered that.' *The graveyard.* If Ma had died, she would be buried there.

'You'd think these things would have been settled years ago. It seems building the dam was the easy part of the project. Although Fitzpatrick probably isn't the best person to be consulting with the community. Doesn't exactly have people skills.'

Maybe she was just tired, but Louise felt an overwhelming sadness. Pete spoke of fate. It felt as though she was meant to return now, to help the people of Thorncrest at a time of incredible loss. Ma would need her. It would break Ma's heart if she had to watch the farm disappear underwater. Outsiders didn't understand. Knowing the valley would be flooded one day did nothing to ease the pain.

'Do you want another drink?' Louise said, standing up. Pete handed her his empty glass.

Peggy was at the bar. 'Did you have enough to eat? If I'd known to expect you, I would have made summat special.'

'Pie and chips were perfect. Thank you, Peggy. You're a good cook.'

'My Bert says I am. Want to have a look at the evening paper? I can get you a daily delivered from the village, if you'd like me to.'

Louise took the newspaper from her. 'That's kind of you, but I'll buy my own newspapers. Give me an excuse to pop in and out of Braithwaite's—keep in touch with locals.'

'Aye. It will that. Here you are love. One and six.'

Louise carried their drinks back to the table, the newspaper tucked under one arm. Pete had started a conversation with a couple of men at another table, so Louise placed his beer where he had been sitting. She opened the newspaper. A story about the Post Office Tower opening in London on 8th October. On the next page, Parliament was still out on making a decision regarding the death penalty. Louise shivered. Then, remembering the date, she flicked to the sports pages. She was just looking for confirmation. If Peggy hadn't handed her the paper, she wouldn't have bothered to look. But as she had. Boxing results were in small print. Louise ran a finger down the entries. *Randall Wolf*. There it was. Except. No, that had to be wrong. *Randall Wolf defeated Chad Tennessee*. She shut her eyes, trying to recall exactly what she had written on the note to Eddie. Wolf was meant to lose. What had gone wrong?

Louise's head was in her hands when Pete slipped back into the seat opposite her. 'Bad news?'

He had no idea. It was catastrophic news because if Randall Wolf won, it meant Eddie had not handed Wolf's manager five hundred pounds for him to lose. Big Jim would think she hadn't passed on his message. And, if that wasn't bad enough, he would think she had stolen the money. Big Jim would be after her. Her legs wobbled as she stood up. 'I. Sorry I …' She rushed to the bathroom.

When it felt as though there was nothing left in her stomach, Louise stumbled over to the sink to rinse her face. Her skin was cold and clammy. She didn't want to believe Eddie had stitched her up, but maybe the temptation was too great. He had to win back the money he lost in the Clement Club or answer to Big Jim.

There was a knock on the door. 'Are you okay, Jane?'

Louise took a deep breath and tried to make herself look presentable before opening the door.

'Sorry. Must have eaten something that disagreed with me. Maybe earlier today when I was on the road.'

Pete was holding the newspaper. 'I wondered if it was something you read?' His eyes met hers. *He knew*. Who was Pete Murray? Had he followed her to Leeds from London?

Louise was about to ask when Pete laughed. 'Not a Swansea supporter, are you? Seven nil.' He handed her the paper. 'Seriously, are you okay?'

As Louise lay awake into the small hours, she replayed that scene, searching for clues. For a couple of seconds, she was certain he knew. And he knew she knew. Then, snap, it was as if he was a different person. Had she imagined it? Why would anyone follow her from London unless Big Jim was protecting his money? And if Randall Wolf won the fight that afternoon, it would confirm Big Jim's suspicion. Pete Murray could be exactly who he claimed to be, a trainee engineer who happened to be heading to Thorncrest at the same time as her, or he was connected to the Mob. One way or the other, Eddie had set her up and Big Jim would be on to her.

7

TUESDAY 5TH OCTOBER 1965

After tossing and turning most of the night, Louise came to a decision. Wherever she was in the world, the Mob would find her, eventually. Thorncrest was as good a place as any to hide out, and if Pete *had* followed her from London, she could at least keep an eye on him if she stayed put. Bloody, Eddie. He was using her to get out of his own mess. She definitely gave him the right information. Louise could guess exactly what had happened. Eddie would have pocketed the five hundred pounds to pay back lost winnings from the Claremont and told Big Jim she had done a runner with the money. She would just have to make Jane Cox's short life matter, do what she had come to do before they came looking for her.

So, the following morning, Louise skipped breakfast and took what she now considered to be her bike from the shed. Her meeting with Fitzpatrick was not until ten, so she had time to visit Becks farm. The air smelt of autumn, a fresh washed scent of peat and fermenting fruit. Dew drops adorned the hedgerow, transforming spider webs to glittering jewels and anointing plump purple sloes. Louise welcomed the kiss of breeze on her cheeks as she headed for the lane that would take her past the turnoff for Becks farm and down into the valley. Their farm had been higher than the shop and church. Louise prayed that it wouldn't be submerged; she couldn't bear the thought of their beautiful farmhouse destroyed. And if there was no threat to the farm, then the evidence hidden in the milkshed and workshop was unlikely to be disturbed by anyone other than Ma Beck, and Ma already knew her secret.

A Land Rover pulled out of the track that led to Becks farm. There was little else down that way, so the driver was either lost, visiting Ma, or the current occupant. Louise's heart raced a little. If no-one was home, she could be in and out, mission accomplished.

It was weird returning to her childhood home, as nothing had changed in the scenery surrounding the farm. If she half closed her eyes, she could imagine being a young girl again, with Dicky at her side, planning an adventure in the valley. Dicky always at her side.

When the farm came into view, Louise stopped cycling. What if Ma was still living there? Her beloved Ma. The ache in her heart was a physical pain. If only she could hammer on the door, plead forgiveness—but that was selfish and naïve. Ma mustn't see her.

The gates to the farm were padlocked and behind them, someone had erected a hardboard fence to stop anyone from looking in. Ma and Pa would never have agreed to that. It was ugly. Louise leant her bike against the gates and walked the length of the fence, trying to find a gap to peer through. The hawthorn bush offered a glimpse, but only of the far side of the house, away from the door and front yard. A wheel barrow had been filled with apples from the orchard. They looked fresh. Someone was living there. She would question Fitzpatrick on Monday. Retrieving the evidence would not be as simple as she had hoped.

In the valley, a newspaper boy was leaving Braithwaite's a sack slung over one shoulder. He reminded her of Dicky as a boy. She slipped into the shop, half hoping to bump in to him. The same woman was behind the counter as before. The one who had phoned High House asking for Fitzpatrick.

'Good morning.' The woman gave her a warm welcome and Louise let go of the anxiety knotting her stomach.

'Jane Cox. I didn't get a chance to introduce myself properly when we last met.' Would it be a step too far to extend a hand? Louise decided not to take the risk.

'Aye. What can I do for you?'

There was no reason for her to enter the shop, apart from a curiosity to see how much it had changed. It had not. The woman now facing her with her arms crossed over an ample bosom could have been Mrs Braithwaite herself, if time had stood still. 'A packet of chocolate digestives, please.'

'Did you want me to add them to the High House order? It's going out today. Or are you in a hurry for them?'

'I'll take them now, thank you.' Louise wanted her first meeting with Fitzpatrick to go smoothly and she suspected chocolate biscuits would help.

'Any news about our new church?'

Louise understood now why she had been greeted so warmly—the woman thought she had insider information. 'Not yet, but I'm sure Mr Fitzpatrick will work with the Corporation to ensure there is a place of worship that meets with the community's approval. It's a beautiful church. Irreplaceable.' A lump formed in her throat. The people of Thorncrest would mourn the loss of their church as a family would a beloved mother.

A door slammed in a room behind the shop. Louise knew it was the back door and the stairs where footsteps now padded led to the maisonette above. She imagined Richard—her Dicky—now a tousle-haired man with eyes that changed like the sea, discarding his denim jacket and putting a kettle on to boil.

'The village will miss this shop, too.'

'Aye. Been run by the same family for generations.'

'What's the owner planning to do when it closes?' Her voice sounded a little too anxious. She turned the display stand of postcards and added offhand, 'Are there plans to open another shop above the valley?'

The woman sighed. 'I wish I knew. Mr Braithwaite has been like a bear with a sore head. Furious at your lot. He's going to have to make plans soon. Anything else for you today?'

Why was Richard being so obstinate? The trial flood was weeks away. Surely, he must have a plan for the future. It wasn't fair to his staff, and she could understand Fitzpatrick's frustration if Richard's reluctance to sign a contract was going to delay the project. She left her bike outside the shop so she could walk over the little bridge to the church where she had accompanied Ma and Pa every Sunday. As villagers greeted them, other farmers, people they supplied with eggs and butter, Louise had felt proud; she belonged to them. Everyone loved and respected Ma and Pa, and Louise felt the glow of this affection by association. She crossed the bridge with reverence, stopping mid-way to remember them and give thanks for their unconditional love.

The sight of the little church, surrounded by shrubs and trees, the moors towering behind—as though nature was doing its best to protect her—brought tears to Louise's eyes. How could this treasure be lost forever? The graveyard wall was marked with the letters of the alphabet so that burials could be neatly filed. It would make Louise's quest easier, but she didn't want to know yet. First, she wanted to step inside the church and imagine that it was 1944 and her world was still magnificent—full of love, hope, and dreams.

The hanging Art Déco gas lamps were just as she remembered them. Prisms of light from the stained glass windows danced across the stone flagged floor as Louise made her way to the pew where they always sat. The same kneeler, embroidered with a lamb and the words, *Lamb of God.* Ma told her she had embroidered it herself when she was a young woman. Louise kissed the kneeler before settling herself on it to pray. She prayed for forgiveness, as she always did, but it never eased her guilt. It was time to face the truth.

Louise gave one last backward glance before stepping outside. The obvious move was to head for B, but Louise wanted to take her time—to put off discovering Ma's fate. So, she walked along each row starting at W-Z. Ma Widdle died in 1952, aged 82. There were other names she didn't recognise.

A-D Elizabeth Beck 1890 – 1951. Louise gasped and fell to her knees. 'I'm sorry, Ma. I'm sorry.' It was too late. There would be no joyful reunion. No forgiveness or understanding. Louise was fourteen years old again, standing outside the farmhouse forlorn and unloved. She hugged her arms tightly across her chest and closed her eyes, imaging Ma's embrace, but her hug could not reach the emptiness inside. Why had she waited so long?

Pa's grave was alongside Ma's. There were no flowers. If she placed some now, it would arouse suspicion. Louise stood up and brushed off her knees. She glanced around, relieved that no-one had witnessed her display of emotion.

It was time to go back to High House for her meeting with

Fitzpatrick. It was up to Jane Cox to try to make things right for the people of Thorncrest. She owed it to Ma and Pa.

Louise was surprised to see a young woman sitting behind the desk in reception when she arrived back at High House. 'Can I help you?' Maybe Fitzpatrick had got it wrong, and the receptionist had not left. In which case Louise's time here had been short-lived and she would need to look for another job. It had seemed too good to be true, and now Louise knew why.

'Hello, I'm Jane Cox.'

Fitzpatrick joined them. 'Good, you've met, Fliss. I need to talk to you now Jane—in my office.' He turned and bounded up the stairs.

'Is he always like that?' Fliss said.

'I don't know. I'm new too. But he seems to get distracted. He didn't tell me that another receptionist was starting today.'

'My friend Lizzie's mum, Peggy, asked if I could cover a few shifts. Is that okay?'

'More than okay. Did Mr Fitzpatrick get his coffee and biscuits at ten?'

Fliss put a hand to her mouth. 'No, sorry. Should I…?'

'I was meant to. But if you wouldn't mind making him a mug of coffee, I'd better go up and see what he wants. Here, I bought some chocolate digestives.' Louise gave Fliss a conspiratorial smile.

His door was ajar. 'Come in. Come in.'

Fitzpatrick was sitting behind his desk. The plan of the valley that Pete had been poring over was on a table in the centre of the room. Louise glanced as she passed by, hoping to get a glimpse of Becks farm.

'We're behind schedule. Way behind. These people have had nearly a century to get used to the idea. How much notice does a person need? I don't have time to be nice. To listen to the Church Committee and smooth ruffled feathers. You're good at that.'

'How do you make that out? You've only known me a couple of days.'

'You diffused the situation when a fight broke out between our men and the locals. Whatever you did worked. So, now I've lightened your load on reception, I thought you could handle PR.'

Louise frowned. Peggy had found Fliss because she knew they needed two people to cover all the shifts. Now, it seemed she was being given extra duties. It would make her unpopular with the locals, including Richard, but it would make it easier to protect their interests. To give something back to the community that had once welcomed and supported her.

'Okay. But what exactly do you want me to do?'

Fitzpatrick beamed. 'I've got a list. Hold on.' He rummaged through some papers in his in-tray. 'Ah. Here it is. Sort out the new church and graveyard. Rehouse valuable items.'

Louise held up a hand to stop him. 'Whoa. Sort out the church? That's huge. Break it down for me.'

Fitzpatrick sighed. 'Building work has started on a replacement church. The Church Committee has suggested what is required, and the architect has taken that in to account in the design.'

'Good.' Louise was relieved that despite his brusqueness, Fitzpatrick recognised the importance of involving parishioners in the church design.

'So, just keeping people updated. Communicating. And then there are the valuable items.'

'The stained glass windows, the gas lamps?'

Fitzpatrick shrugged. 'Who knows? It seems there's a lot of

attachment to stuff, like those old jukeboxes. We need to find homes for everything where there's no clear ownership.'

'If you can keep me informed, then I'll do my best to communicate with the community. Have you thought about holding regular meetings?'

'We had one or two early on, but they just throw up more problems.'

'Of course, I'll represent you in listening to and responding to individuals, but I really think you ought to have regular meetings. I can set them up. Suggest an agenda and see that they run smoothly.'

He nodded and returned to his list. 'You'll need to finish the job of clearing out properties. Our contractors will pick up heavy items.'

'Who owns the empty properties?'

'On paper, everything belongs to the Corporation once contracts have been signed, but try telling Braithwaite that.'

'Well, we were trespassing if the contract hadn't been signed on Ma Widdle's... I mean Brackbarn cottage. Who's representing the owner?'

Fitzpatrick shrugged. 'Some distant relative. I don't think they're raising any objection, just difficult to get hold of. The Corporation handles the legal side. I'll give you the details so you can communicate direct. Did you say something about chocolate digestives?'

On cue, Fliss arrived with two mugs of coffee and a plate of biscuits.

Louise took her mug over to the table to study the plan. She could trace her finger over the paths where she and Dicky had traipsed. Over the stream to the mill. Across the valley to another derelict mill. That one had been a pile of stones, even then. The wood where they had built a camp from logs and bracken, huddling together within its damp, peaty walls, listening to the patter of rain on leaves.

Fitzpatrick joined her at the table. 'The reservoir will probably come up to that blue line.'

Louise's eyes darted from the irregular oval of blue to Becks farm. It was just outside the line. 'Don't you know exactly how high up? What about this farm here?' She put a shaking finger on Becks farm. 'Who does it belong to?'

'The Corporation, in the absence of known ownership.'

Louise couldn't remember Ma and Pa having any family. It was sad to think the farm had been deserted all these years. She wondered when Kara, their dog, had died and if her remains were buried on the farm. 'I went by that farm this morning. It looked as though someone has been living there or using it.'

'Then they're trespassing. The dam has attracted visitors to the area—probably a load of hippies making themselves at home. Don't worry, we'll throw them out if we need to. Have you seen the dam yet?'

Louise shook her head, unsettled by an image of strangers making themselves at home like the weasels and stoats in the book *The Wind in the Willows*, at Toad Hall.

'It's a fine feat of engineering. A magnificent structure.' Fitzpatrick became animated as he explained the technicalities of creating a reservoir. 'This reservoir will provide fresh drinking water for thousands of people. The need is far greater than the loss. That's why I get so frustrated with the opposition. The only properties occupied are Horatio Beacon's house and the post-office. Mr Beacon recently moved into a nursing home. Braithwaite has appointed himself as Beacon's spokesperson. We'll have to get one of the legal team to visit Beacon. Braithwaite causes too many problems.'

'Why is he holding things up? Have we offered a fair price for the post office? I understand it's been a family business for generations.'

'If it was just about agreeing on a price, we might have moved on, but he wants a guarantee the reservoir will come to no higher than the estimated level. It's really none of his business. If he's planning to buy land immediately above the valley, then he's a fool. If you can persuade him to sign the contract and let us get on with planning the flood, then you'll be worth your weight in gold.'

Louise understood Richard's concern. If the reservoir came up any higher, it would flood Becks farm. She didn't want that either. It would break her heart. But what could they do? Ma and Pa were no longer there and if Fitzpatrick was right, there was nobody to inherit the land. It belonged to the Corporation by default.

'Why can't you give him the reassurance he wants? Is it likely to come up any higher?'

'No. We're ninety-nine percent certain of the reservoir dimensions, but they were estimated early on in the planning. Experts will be visiting to reassess. Take measurements. Check water volume. That kind of thing.'

'Ninety-nine percent?'

Fitzpatrick nodded.

'So, almost certain? You don't think we'll have to clear out this farm?' *Please say we won't. Please say Becks farm is safe.*

'If we do, I'll let you know. It shouldn't be a problem, as we don't have to get anyone's permission.'

'It's sad though. Seeing buildings that were once loved submerged. A bit of history lost.'

Fitzpatrick shrugged. 'You can leave the biscuits.'

Louise took this as her dismissal. Ma and Pa never mentioned the possibility that Becks farm might disappear beneath the reservoir. Plans must have changed over time. Maybe Richard was resisting out of a loyalty to them and maybe—just maybe—because he was holding on to precious memories of their childhood. She wanted to tell him she understood. If there was any way she could prevent Becks farm from being flooded, she would join him in his protest. But Fitzpatrick said it was ninety-nine percent certain that wouldn't happen. Louise desperately wanted to talk to Richard. He was bound to recognise her. How could he not when he was a part of her? The thought of their reunion was both exciting and terrifying. What if he hated her for what she had done? He hadn't replied to the letters she sent after leaving Thorncrest.

8

NOVEMBER 1942

'Why did you leave without saying goodbye?' Louise broke an unsaid rule by approaching Dicky in the school dining room. He was carrying a tray of food to his usual table.

'Dicky's got a girlfriend,' George, a stout boy who was following Dicky, chanted.

'Because of *him,*' Dicky hissed, widening his eyes.

'You mean Kurt?' Louise boldly sat at the boys' table opposite Dicky. She was fed up with the stupid girls and their whispering. Dicky was her friend. Why shouldn't she talk to him at school?

'Kurt. That's a Jerry name,' George said. 'Whose Kurt?'

'The Becks have got a Jerry working on the farm,' a boy with red hair and freckles said. 'Me mam told me they were getting one.'

'They should keep them locked up,' George said.

'I think he seems nice.'

Dicky rolled his eyes, and Louise wished she had said nothing.

'My Da is in Germany shooting the Jerries. They are the enemy.'

Dicky shot Louise a sympathetic look. 'Who wants my spam fritter?' It was enough of a diversion for Louise to slip away to the girls' table, taking her roly-poly jam pudding with her. At least the girls ignored her.

It wasn't until they were walking home together that Louise told Dicky Kurt would work on the farm six days a week. 'Ma says that Pa needs a younger, fitter man to do some of the heavy work.'

'Has he started yet?'

'He was meant to arrive after I left for school today.'

'It just doesn't seem right to me. My brother Frank is fighting for our country. His mates getting blown up and shot. The thought of a Jerry working on your farm—it's just wrong. Don't talk to him. Why do the Becks want him there, anyway?'

'Ma says the Government is trying to rebuild our country and as it's the Germans' fault, they can help repair it.'

'How does working on a farm do that?'

'You know, Dig for Victory. Farms feed the nation. I don't know, but with rationing, I guess it's important we produce as much food as possible. That's what Pa says, anyway.'

'There are Land Army girls to do that.'

Louise didn't want to argue with Dicky. Since the moment he gave her his lucky marble, she had imagined being in love with him. He'd asked her to marry him, so they were kind of engaged.

Louise shrugged, 'You're always saying boys are stronger than girls. Maybe that's why they need a male farmhand and with all the fit young men at war.' Louise shrugged.

'Maybe.' He sounded subdued, not even latching on to Louise's concession that boys might be stronger—it was something she always refuted with a passion, often demonstrating to Dicky her strength over his.

'Do you want to visit the polyphon man?' Louise said. She couldn't bear to leave Dicky like this—cross and moody.

'Is the Jerry there now?' Dicky said, scuffing his foot in the gravel.

'Probably.' The truth was, Louise wanted to meet Kurt. To establish her role within the farm before he got too comfortable.

'No. I'd best be getting back. See if we've had a letter from Frank. At least when we get one, we know he's still alive.'

It was the first time Louise had said goodbye to Dicky at the gate of the farm; they always spent time together after school. She watched as he descended into the valley. At the end of the lane, he turned and, seeing her still there, blew a kiss.

Ma wasn't in the kitchen when Louise stepped inside. She wouldn't be expecting Louise for another couple of hours. She filled a pail with chicken feed and fetched the egg basket from a shelf in the pantry. Kurt would see that she was just as important to the farm as any Land Army girl or prisoner of war.

'You're back early,' Ma said, coming out of the cowshed.

'I'll feed the chickens and then see to the new batch of butter,' Louise said.

The barn door creaked open and Kurt followed Ma out into the sun. He smiled shyly at Louise.

'Thank you, pet. I'll make a start in the dairy. Why don't you take Kurt with you? He hasn't met the chickens yet?' Ma smiled at them both as though Kurt was a friend of the family, not a prisoner of war.

Louise didn't want to be alone with him—not because she

was afraid—he just made her feel self-conscious and awkward.

'Can I carry your bag?' Kurt said, nodding at the pail of feed.

'It is a bucket, or a pail, not a bag.'

'Then, let me please to carry your bucket.'

Louise led the way to the hen-coop. 'Hello my chickadees,' she chirruped.

Kurt watched as she threw handfuls of feed. 'My family has a farm in Bavaria. This is good for me, to be back on a farm. Maybe I can be of help.'

'You can throw some of the feed, if you like.'

Kurt took the pail from her. 'I will take the *bucket*.' When the pail was empty, they checked for eggs.

Two small brown eggs from Dilly, nothing from Martha or Jemima. 'I collected a few before school,' Louise said.

Kurt sat on his haunches and trailed his hand through the straw. Then he fell onto his knees and sifted through it. Jemima flapped her wings and squawked.

'Beweis.' Kurt showed Louise his open palm.

'No. That's a broken egg shell. *Egg shell*.'

Kurt laughed. 'Okay. Egg shell. But it is beweis too. How you say? Evidence! Yes. This is evidence that the hens have been eating the eggs.'

Jemima pecked Kurt's hand, and he yelped. 'You have been caught, Miss Jemima.'

Louise was dismayed. The chickens were her sole responsibility. Ma was teaching her how to make butter and cheese, but looking after the chickens and providing eggs for the table and market was her job. 'Why would they eat their own eggs?'

'If an egg breaks and they have a little taste, then they get, how do you say gewohnheit?' Louise frowned, and he mimed putting food into his mouth rapidly.

'Hungry?'

'No.'

'Into a habit?'

'A habit. Yes.'

How many eggs had they lost? Just one egg was a person's daily ration gone. Why hadn't she noticed this herself?

'Maybe it was a rat?' Louise knew about ratting; the Land Army girls did a rat catch soon after she arrived at the farm.

'Maybe.' Kurt shrugged. He teased the straw some more, running his hands along the floor. Louise joined him and within a few seconds uncovered a recently broken shell.

'This hen I think is broody,' Kurt pointed to Dilly. 'Maybe her nest could be moved away from the other chickens?'

Louise nodded. Dilly had been producing the most eggs. She kept a record in her diary. 'Will that stop them from eating the eggs?'

As Louise was saying this, Jemima tried to peck at the yolk. 'Go away. Naughty girl.'

'I know how we can stop them eating the eggs,' Kurt said.

Louise thought Kurt would tell Ma and Pa about the lost eggs — she was prepared to forgo her ration for a week or more to make up the loss, but he didn't. Two days after discovering the broken egg, Louise returned from playing in the valley with Dicky to find Dilly happily settled in a new nesting box away from the other hens.

She went in search of Kurt and found him in the milking shed. His head was resting on a cow's flank as he sang quietly in German. Louise stood at the door, listening. His voice was calming and gentle. The cow shifted position and Kurt rubbed his hands over her hide.

'Du bist schön.'

'Do you always sing to the cows before you milk them?'

Kurt turned and smiled. 'Come and help me.'

'I can't. I don't know how to milk.'

'Then let's make a deal. You teach me English, and I will teach you how to milk the cows. Yes?'

'Okay.'

Kurt carried a milking stool across the barn. As he bent down to position it, the light glinted off a charm around his neck.

'What's that?'

His hand shot to his throat and a worried expression furrowed his brow. 'It is all I have of home. My mother. She gave it to me on my birthday. A Saint Christopher.' He fastened the top button of his shirt, hiding the chain. 'Are you ready to milk the cow?'

Louise nodded.

'First you sing.'

She giggled. 'What shall I sing?'

'What did your mother sing to you when you were a baby?'

'You mean a lullaby.' She thought hard but had no recollection of being sung to as a child.

'Copy me,' Kurt said. He sang a line in German and Louise repeated.

It was a simple verse. Unfamiliar words curled around her tongue and came out as a melodic whisper. Kurt leaned into his cow and Louise rested her head on her cow's belly just above the udders.

'Like this.' He stroked his cow as he hummed, and she did the same.

'When the cow has relaxed, the milk will come easily.' He pulled the cow's udders in a steady rhythm and milk filled his pail.

Louise had never tried milking a cow. The thought had

repulsed her, but now she wanted to impress Kurt. She felt the teat and recoiled.

'Wait. First, we must clean her.' Kurt wiped a damp cloth over the bulging pink udder.

'Did you make a new nesting box for Dilly?' she asked, her eyes fixed on the muscle tendons flexing in Kurt's forearm.

'It gave me something to do in the evening. Does she like her new home? Sit here.'

Louise pulled her stool closer to the cow's udder. 'Yes. Thank you. Do you think Jemima will stop eating the eggs now?'

'Maybe. But I have another plan.' He grinned. 'It is something I learnt on my farm at home. Now take hold of a teat in each hand.'

Louise tried to wrap her fingers around each teat and pull, but the cow complained, shuffling around and Louise made some distance to protect her toes.

'Like this.' Kurt made a ring with his index finger and thumb. 'Then, like you are playing the piano. One. Two. Three.' He curled each finger into his palm.

Louise tried again. This time, a little milk spurted out.

Kurt nodded. 'That's right. Keep going.'

They worked in silence. It felt peaceful—the occasional low from a cow, the swish of milk as it hit the pail. The scent of hay and cow dung was surprisingly comforting. Louise felt like a small animal, safe and protected in the barn's warmth. Kurt had filled four pails to Louise's, which was a quarter full. Her forearms ached.

'You are a fast learner,' Kurt said. 'Now you must teach me some English.'

'Your English is good. What can I teach you?'

'Then tell me every time I say something wrong so I can

get better. Tomorrow, when I come to work, can you have some mustard ready?'

'Mustard? Are you sure that's the word?'

'Yes. Mustard. If you can get it.'

'Did you tell Ma and Pa Beck about the hens eating our eggs?'

'No. You are the boss of the chicken coop. I told you. Is that okay?'

Louise nodded. 'I'll try to get some mustard, but it may be tricky.' She couldn't take mustard from the pantry without telling Ma. Until she solved the egg problem, Louise wanted to keep it to herself.

Pa had been delighted at her success in milking a cow. 'We will make a farmer of you, Louise.'

'I'm going to spend more time after school helping on the farm.'

'There's no need love. We have Kurt and the Land Army girls. You enjoy your childhood; it will pass soon enough.'

'I'm almost a teenager. So, not really a child.'

'That you are. Now, if you're ready for bed, I'll make your cocoa.'

Louise felt tired after milking the cows. She would need to build up the strength in her arms. 'Can I have my cocoa in bed?'

'What about the next instalment of our story?' Pa said.

Louise had been making up a story about the mill owner and his daughters. 'Okay. Just a short one. Now that I'm going to be doing more on the farm, I'll need a good night's sleep.'

9

NOVEMBER 1942

As she walked to school, Louise's thoughts were with Kurt and the challenge of finding a jar of mustard. A check of Ma's pantry had been fruitless—there had been a jar of home-pickled onions but unless Kurt was planning a feast of cold cuts, that would not do the job. Why on earth did he want mustard? Louise couldn't help thinking he had the wrong word, despite what he said.

'Is that what you wear in London?' It was Brenda Button.

Louise, startled out of her thoughts, checked to see what she had put on that day. Her usual brown school tunic and white shirt. 'It was the uniform at my old school.'

'But those shoes! I thought London was meant to be a fashionable place. They look like orthopaedic ones. Oh! Have you got a deformity? I'm sorry.'

Behind her, a couple of girls giggled. Louise glanced down at her feet, half expecting to see some hideous footwear in place of her brown and white lace-ups. What was wrong with her shoes? They were light and practical for the muddy tracks.

The other girls wore clogs. Brenda's were green, the other girls' brown or black.

'Why don't you wear a skirt instead of a tunic?'

'Because she's flat-chested. What a baby, wearing white socks.'

The three girls crowded around, penning her in. Louise tried to walk through them, but they closed the gap.

'Where's your boyfriend Dicky Braithwaite?' The girls giggled.

'Look at her pretty little plaits.' One of the girls tugged Louise's hair. 'Did your mummy plait your hair? Oh, I forgot —your mummy is in London getting bombed.'

'What does your mam think about you living with a Jerry?'

Louise used her elbows to nudge her way out.

'Oi. That hurt.' Brenda nursed her arm, feigning injury.

A foot tripped Louise from behind and she slid on the mud, landing face down. The girls shrieked with laughter and ran away as the school bell rang.

Her raincoat was splattered in mud, her white socks now a muddy brown. Louise undid her coat to inspect the front of her tunic. There was a dribble of mud on the skirt. She rubbed it with a handkerchief and it smudged into a dirty, wet splodge, spreading the width of two hands.

'We're late.' Dicky wheezed behind her. He stopped, hands on his knees, gasping for breath. 'You'd better go on.'

'What's wrong, Dicky?'

'Asthma. I've got asthma. It makes me breathe funny when I get out of breath.' He gasped some more and Louise felt a weight of responsibility. Should she run for help or stay with him?

His breath evened. 'I saw those girls bullying you and I wanted to stop them. So, I ran. But I'm not much good at running. I would've seen them off if I'd got here in time.'

The bell rang—its final warning. The children would be lining up on the playground, as the prefect swung the brass bell.

'Let's not go to school today,' Louise said. 'We're already late and I'll get in trouble because my uniform's dirty. Besides, you *are* sick.'

'I'm not sick. It's just asthma. We'll get in worse trouble if we play truant.'

'We can say that we were needed on the farm. Your friend Billy was off school to help stack peat. I'll say that Ma and Pa needed all hands on the farm because there was an emergency. The cows broke loose or something.'

'Then we'll get in trouble with the Becks and my parents.'

'If the school tells them.'

They took baby steps towards the school. The babble of children silenced. Louise imagined them all sitting down at their desks. 'If we go to school now, we'll get in trouble for being late and everyone will go on about us arriving together.'

'Brenda will tell on you.'

'I don't care.' Louise had made her decision and now a day without boundaries lay before her. It was exhilarating and unsettling. 'You'd better hurry if you're going to school.'

But Dicky made no sign of leaving. 'Let's go visit the polyphon man.'

Mr Beacon—Beaky--was in the turf shed when Louise and Dicky, on hearing his voice, ventured in to the backyard. They helped him by carrying peat into the house and setting it alongside the fire. Then, they fetched water from the well. These two jobs earned them uninterrupted time in the polyphon room, with no questions asked.

It was like a museum filled with upright polyphons resembling polished grandfather clocks and box ones, all lavishly decorated with beading and inlaid wood.

'These discs have tiny bumps and holes.' Dicky pointed to a golden disc in the window of an upright polyphon. 'When the cylinder here rotates over them, they make music.'

'It's beautiful.'

'Pick a tune.' Dicky pointed to two rows of white labels with song titles in italics.

Louise didn't know any of them. 'Find something jolly.'

'Okay.' Dicky took a penny from a pile alongside the machine, dropped it into the slot, then slid the bar to The Washington Post March.

'Da da. Da da. Da-da, da-da, da...' Louise recognised the tune as one played at funfairs and parades.

Dicky marched around the room, pretending to play a trumpet. Louise followed, buoyed up by the energy of the music. Dicky turned and, laughing, took hold of her hands. They twirled about the room, giggling and breathless.

Louise ran to another polyphon, a pretty maple box. There was only one disc to play — a waltz. She wound it up, then closed her eyes, imagining herself at a ball. A magnificent ball-gown, the golden glow of chandeliers. As she moved to the music lost in her dream, Dicky put an arm around her waist and then they were moving together, waltzing. She could feel his breath on the back of her neck; his warm hand in hers as if they belonged together. When the music stopped, they carried on dancing.

'You smell nice,' he said.

Her cheek brushed against his. She could feel his warm breath in her ear. Dicky brushed her hair back from her face. 'You're the prettiest girl I've met. But that's not why I want to marry you one day.'

Louise let go of his hands and laughed. 'Why then?'

'Because you tell great stories. Because you like doing the

same things as me, and you're not silly like some of the other girls.'

'Brenda Button?' Louise snarled.

'Not at all like Brenda Button. And you make me laugh.'

Louise laughed. 'Why would I want to marry you?'

'Because I'm handsome, strong and brave.'

'Hmm.' She posed as though considering. 'I wouldn't call you brave. You're a bit of a scaredy cat, if we're being honest.'

'True.'

'But you did run to my rescue this morning when Brenda Button pushed me over.'

'So, just handsome and strong. I'll take that.' Dicky bowed.

'Have you got anything to eat?' Louise said. 'I'm hungry.'

Mr. and Mrs. Braithwaite had gone to market, leaving a shop assistant in charge of the grocery store. Dicky told Louise to wait out of sight whilst he crept in through the back door.

'I'll get us a packet of biscuits or summat.'

'Do you sell mustard in your shop?'

'I think so. Why?'

Louise hesitated before telling Dicky about Kurt and Henrietta, the egg-eating hen. She knew how much he resented the prisoner of war.

'And he told you to get some mustard for him? That's not right. He's having you on.'

'Maybe. I don't know. But can you see if there's a jar of mustard in the store? I'll pay you when I get my egg money.'

Dicky returned ten minutes later with a packet of Rich Tea biscuits and a jar of Coleman's mustard. They ran across the bridge and found a place to sit by the river. It was getting cold, and damp from the river bank crept into Louise's bones. The biscuits were dry and stuck to the roof of her mouth.

'When do you think we can go home?'

'It's only two fifteen. Another hour? What have you collected for your box?'

'Apart from your marble?' Louise didn't tell Dicky that she had put the broken eggshell into the box to remind her of that day with Kurt. 'Nothing much.'

'I got this for you. To remind you of today.' Dicky handed her a shiny brown penny.

'Did you steal it from Mr Beacon?'

'Of course not. It's from my money box. I went up to my room when you were waiting for me. It will remind you of our first dance.'

Louise held the penny to her heart. 'I'll keep it always.'

'I'll walk back to the farm with you. I think it's going to rain.'

Dicky was quiet as they ambled as slowly as they could—it was still too early to arrive home from school. As they neared the farm, he said, 'Have you heard of mustard gas, Louise? They used it as a lethal weapon in the last war. What if your German prisoner is planning to gas you all? Maybe he needs the mustard to make a bomb.'

10

NOVEMBER 1942

Kurt was carrying a bale of hay on his shoulder. 'Did you find the mustard?' He looked as though he was trying not to grin, and Louise felt the warmth of their shared secret. She nodded and winked at him. 'Good. I will meet you in Miss Henrietta's parlour. First, hay for the cows.'

Louise helped Kurt distribute a couple of bales of hay between the cows.

'Tomorrow, we will bring them in for the winter. They will need lots of feed. No grass to graze on.'

Louise nodded solemnly. She was trying to learn everything there was to know about dairy farming. One day, she would work alongside Pa. If Land Army girls could farm, then she too would become a farmer.

'I don't want to go back to London. Never ever,' Louise said, stroking the hide of a cow's belly.

'I will be glad to return to my home when the war is over. There, I will work on the family farm.'

Louise's skin prickled to hear Kurt talking about the war. It reminded her of Dicky's objection to their friendship. When the war was over, one side would win. Kurt was the enemy.

At two in the morning, this realisation woke Louise with a jolt. Her brushed cotton sheets were damp with perspiration, but Louise shivered. There was a bomb in the hen-house. She had planted it there herself. Louise threw back the eiderdown and felt beneath the bed for her slippers. Dicky was right. Kurt was trying to blow up the farm.

A full moon lit the yard as Louise stumbled in her nightgown past the cowshed. Heavy breathing came from within, and then a gentle low. Louise wondered if cows had dreams.

She unlatched the hen house door and crept in. The scent of ammonia and warm hay was stronger at night, with no whisper of fresh air. She should have brought a candle; it was too dark to find the bomb.

That afternoon, Kurt had plucked one of Dilly's newly laid eggs from beneath her billowing breast. Then, as Louise gathered the remaining eggs to fill her basket, he had rolled it from palm to palm.

'Do you think Henrietta has stopped eating the eggs?' Louise said. There were certainly fewer eggs than she expected. Soon, Ma was going to ask questions, and Louise would have to admit her failure.

'Maybe not. But if you have the mustard, then we will put into operation my secret plan. But first, I will need a bowl, a pin, a sharp knitting needle, and a …' he mimed sucking through a straw.

'Ma doesn't knit. I'll fetch her darning needle and the other things.'

'And the mustard,' Kurt called.

When Louise returned carrying a basket, a tea-towel spread over its contents, Kurt led her to the barn where Pa stored broken bits of machinery. There was a workbench littered with curls of wood. Kurt brushed them to aside and took the bowl and needle from Louise's basket.

'First, we make a hole at the pointed end. He eased the darning needle into the egg. Now, the other side. We'll need a few holes, then...' He wiggled the needle to widen the hole. Kurt looked around the barn and discovered a length of wire. 'This will do.' He pushed the wire into the egg. 'I break up the yolk.'

Louise watched as Kurt inserted a straw in to the top of the egg, then he held the egg over the bowl and blew. A stream of egg white, then the yolk dribbled out of one end.

'Now the egg is empty. Feel.' He placed the fragile shell in Louise's palm. It was as light as air.

Kurt took the bowl of white and yolk outside and returned with it empty. Louise worried about wasting an egg, but unless they stopped Henrietta, there would be more waste. 'Pour the mustard in to the bowl.' Louise did as he said. 'Now suck it into the egg.'

When a shot of mustard found her mouth, Louise knew the egg shell was filled.

'We hide this egg in the coop. When Miss Henrietta takes a peck, she will decide that eggs do not taste so good. See?'

'And she will break her habit.' Louise added, remembering Kurt's explanation why hens ate their eggs.

'Exactly.'

It had seemed so innocent. It was only when Louise woke from a nightmare, her sheets sodden with sweat, that she realised. The egg must be a mustard gas bomb. Dicky had tried to warn her, and now she had put Ma, Pa, and the animals in danger.

Henrietta squawked and flapped her wings. That set off Dilly and the others. A confetti of feathers, grazing Louise's eyelids, settling on her hair and nightgown. 'Hush. Hush.'

She fell to her knees and raked through the straw, careful not to set off the bomb. What should she do when she found it?

Bang A shot rang out. *Bang. Bang.* The Germans had come for them. She scrambled to her feet. Her legs shaking. She felt as though she were a blancmange.

'Come out, you thieving scoundrel.' It was Pa's voice.

Louise crept out into the night. Pa was aiming his gun right at her. 'I'm sorry. Pa.'

'What the heck are you doing out here, lass? Shivering in your nightgown.' He put his hand on her forehead. 'You've a raging temperature. The cold air will bring it down some, but we need to get you back inside. Come on. Ma will put you right.'

'There's a bomb in the hen house. Mustard gas.'

'I'll see to it, pet. Let's get you in the warm.'

The next day, a doctor visited and diagnosed measles. 'It's been going around the school,' he said. 'Keep her at home until she's free of spots.'

Louise explained to Ma and Pa about the mustard egg. It was a crazy plan, but it worked, because the hens had stopped eating their eggs. 'It was Kurt's idea. I just thought the hens had stopped laying.'

'You're a good team,' Ma said.

Louise snuggled under her covers and dreamt of Kurt—how they would get married and manage the biggest farm in Yorkshire. Ma and Pa would visit for tea, and express amazement at what they had achieved together. Her own mum did not feature in this fantasy; London felt like a million miles away.

A week later, Louise was feeling better. She was curled up in Pa's big chair by the fire, with Kara at her feet. The scent of freshly baked bread wafted from the kitchen, mingling pleasantly with traces of Pa's pipe smoke and burning peat. Louise wiggled her stockinged feet into Kara's thick coat, trying to commit everything to memory. One day this farm—Ma and Pa, who she had come to love, would be in the past and her life would be in London. The war couldn't go on forever, although Louise was hoping it would. One side would eventually win and that would change her life and Kurt's. One of them would lose, but what would that mean? She wanted nothing bad to happen to Kurt or his family — despite them being German. Why couldn't Dicky accept Kurt was her friend?

'A visitor for you, Louise,' Ma called from the kitchen.

Dicky! She hadn't seen him since the day they played truant. And danced together.

'How are you, Louise? Me mam said it was measles. But I've had it, so no need to worry 'bout me.'

'Did you get into trouble for missing school?'

'I didn't need to say anything. Miss presumed we had measles—well, you did. Nobody said anything 'bout me missing a day. It's been boring without you. Here, I got you summat.' Dicky handed her a package wrapped in grocery paper.

It was a thick book with a glossy frontispiece. 'Jane Eyre.'

'I bought it at the church sale. Have you read it?'

'No.' Louise turned the heavy cream pages, breathing in the delicious scent of print and paper. 'What's it about?'

'A girl called Jane, who's poor and works as a governess for a man in Yorkshire. I read it while I was waiting for you to be well enough. But someone had read it before. It's not new.'

'It's the best gift, Dicky. I love it. I've read all of Pa's farming magazines and the newssheets, so this is tons better. What did you think of it?'

Dicky sat on Ma's chair opposite Louise. 'I read it every day after school. I couldn't be with you, but reading the book made me feel like I was. I know that sounds stupid. It's just that Jane, she was living away from home, like you. And she was clever, and wise, and not afraid of anything.' Dicky blushed.

'Like me?' Louise laughed. He had fallen far too serious.

She expected him to put her in her place, but he said, 'Summat. But much older. She wasn't as much fun as you, though. Oh, and there's a spooky part. I liked that bit best. Anyhow, when are you coming back to school?'

Louise hugged the book to her. She felt guilty, wishing Dicky would leave so that she could start it straight away. 'When all the spots have gone.' She pushed up the sleeve of her dress and inspected an arm.

'I can't see nought. You sure they've not gone already?'

'Maybe,' Louise whispered. 'But I'm not going back to school until I've read this book. Besides, there are a few blotches on my back that you can't see. I want to get back to the farm—milking the cows and looking after my hens. Oh, and going down the valley after school. It won't be long.' Louise yawned and stretched.

Dicky took the hint. 'Right you are. Well, I just wanted to say, get well soon. Oh, I nearly forgot.' He pulled a card out from beneath his school jumper. 'I made summat for you.'

When Dicky had gone, taking with him a loaf of bread for his mum and a few eggs, Louise inspected his handiwork. He'd done a good job. She smiled. A decorative border of pressed autumn leaves—the reds, gold, and bronze still vibrant, framed his handwritten message: *Get Well Louise. I miss you. xxx* Later, she would add his card to the marble, penny, and broken eggshell in her memory box.

11

THURSDAY 7TH OCTOBER 1965

The site of the new church had been marked on a map and so Louise cycled via the building site en route to her meeting with the vicar. It wasn't far from the original church—less than a mile, but above the valley.

Two days had passed since her meeting with Fitzpatrick and in that time she had seen or heard nothing of Richard Braithwaite. There was plenty to do in the office to keep her occupied, and she told herself this was why she had not returned to Becks farm to retrieve the evidence which would confirm that she, Louise Pearson, was responsible for the fatal accident. But Louise knew it was because she was afraid of what she might find. The farmhouse kitchen wrecked: paint daubed on walls, excrement, empty beer bottles, uneaten food rotting. She couldn't bear to see Ma and Pa's beloved home ruined, and the intruders might still be in the farmhouse, drunk or stoned.

Louise propped her bike against a tree and picked her way across the muddy building site, heading for a Portakabin where she hoped to find the site manager. A long, loud wolf whistle alerted the other workmen to her presence. Two hob carriers stopped work to leer.

'I'm looking for the site manager,' Louise said, trying to sound haughty.

'Round the back, luv.' The man nodded to indicate behind the Portakabin.

As she walked away, there was laughter, and Louise suspected she was being set up. There were some portable toilets behind the Portakabin and a white van with Bellamy Brothers emblazoned on one side. Louise's body responded as blood rushed to her head. It took a few seconds for her brain to catch up; she had seen that van before, or one like it. Where? Louise darted behind one of the portable toilets, unsure why she felt unsafe. Donuts. The scent of donuts frying. Where had she been? There were market stalls. The van. A man leaning against it eating—he'd offered her his bag of donuts. Eddie was with her. That's it, Haydock races. The Sunday market. The man—Billy the Weed—Bellamy. He had a market stall. On the way home, Eddie told her the Bellamy family worked in construction and property. That explained why a van with the Bellamy logo was on site. Nothing to spook her. Louise crept out from between the portable toilets, afraid of embarrassing one of the men who would not be expecting to see a woman. A man opened the passenger side of the van and jumped down. It was Pete Murray. Louise shrank back into the shadows. Something didn't feel right. Her heart quickened. If Pete was working for Big Jim, he would know Billy the Weed. They were watching her—she knew it. But what could she do? Where could she run? Here, in Thorncrest, working for the Corporation, she was safer than out there alone—on the run. Maybe this little scene was intended to spook her, to make her leave the safety of Thorncrest. A chicken running from the coop straight into the path of a waiting wolf.

Louise stayed hidden as she watched Pete march over to the Portakabin, whistling. The white van drove away and Louise followed Pete back to the Portakabin.

When the site manager opened the door and Louise stepped in to his office, Pete said, 'What are you doing here? I thought you had a meeting with the vicar this afternoon.'

'I did. I do. I wanted to get an update on the new church first, so I'll have something to tell him.'

'Good move.'

'Did you drive?' she asked Pete.

'Got a lift. Room on the back of your bike for me?'

Louise laughed. 'You're too heavy. It's hard enough cycling up and down the hills around here without your weight. How are you getting back?'

'I'm taking him,' Geoff, the site manager, said before giving Louise an update on the new church.

It was being built with York stone from a disused mill and was ahead of schedule. Louise tried to keep focused on these facts, repeating them to herself as she cycled on to Thorncrest Church for her meeting with the vicar. But she was afraid. It was too much of a coincidence, the Bellamy Brothers showing up here in Thorncrest.

When she pushed open the heavy door and stepped into the warm, incense scented nave, she found it empty. 'Hello,' she called, not wanting to raise her voice, as it felt irreverent. A clink of crockery. Louise strained to hear. There was movement at the back of the church. A chair scraped. 'Hello?'

The vicar came out of a door tucked to one side of the pulpit. Sunday School. Louise remembered sitting in a semicircle as they listened to a bible story—one about a prodigal son. She had thought it unfair that the boy who had wasted all of his money and behaved badly should be favoured over the dutiful son.

'Come on in. We've just had a pre-meeting.'

Louise's heart sank. This would not be the cosy, getting-to-know you chat she had expected. 'Okay.' She took a deep breath and followed him into the meeting room.

There were two other people sitting at the table, the woman from the shop, and the pretty girl who had been with Richard when they met outside Ma Widdle's cottage.

'I am, of course, Reverend Tobias Cummins. This is Kaye White, who I think you met at Braithwaite's grocery. And Fiona Simms.'

Fiona stood up and offered Louise her hand. Her fingers were cool, her handshake firm. Louise felt the girl's eyes sizing her up and withered a little inside. 'Nice to meet you.' That sounded pathetic. She wasn't at a tea party.

Louise coughed and stood a little taller. 'And you…' *was it, Mrs or Miss White?* '…Kaye.' Her first name hung between them awkwardly. '…White.'

Louise's palms were sweaty and her throat dry. Everyone's eyes were upon her. She wanted to turn and run.

'Sit down. Perhaps we could have a refill, Mrs White? A bit of a break before we get down to business?' Reverend Cummins said, before excusing himself from the room.

Mrs White disappeared into a kitchen off the vestry, leaving Louise and Fiona facing one another across the table. Today, Fiona's hair was pinned up in a French pleat. Although younger than Louise, maybe by ten years, Fiona seemed more self-assured in how she carried herself and in her direct gaze. 'So, you are the Corporation's latest device. What did the Reverend call you? Public relations officer? A bit late for that, don't you think?'

'I don't really have a title. But if that means to improve two-way communication, then yes, that's why I'm here today.'

The Reverend returned just as Mrs White pushed a trolly of tea things into the meeting room. 'Good. You're getting acquainted. Modesty may have prevented Fiona from explaining her family are *The* Simms.'

Louise waited for further explanation, as the name meant nothing to her. Fiona gave a coy smile and sipped her tea.

'So, let us begin.' Louise felt as though she should bow her head in prayer. 'Perhaps you could start, Miss Cox, with an update on our new church.'

Louise's thumb brushed the skin where her wedding ring once sat. 'Jane is fine. I met with the site manager before coming here today. The work's ahead of schedule. It's bigger than this church, and although it won't be as beautiful—how could anything compare to Thorncrest Church?—–it's being built with York stone from the old mill, so it will at least fit in to the environment. And, as you know, very close to the current location.'

'Above water.' Fiona smirked.

'Yes. On the edge of the valley.'

'The reservoir,' Fiona corrected, and Louise blushed.

'We've all seen that much,' Kaye White said. 'What we want to know is when will it be complete? There will need to be a period between the last service here and the first in the new church. Fixtures and fittings will need to be transferred.'

'Don't forget the graves,' Fiona said.

'We will have to consecrate the ground. Moving the graves of loved ones will be a delicate operation. I'll need to prepare and support my parishioners through the ordeal. It's not something that can be rushed.'

Louise listened to their concerns with growing anxiety, she wasn't equipped to take on such an important role. The project was poorly resourced with personnel. Someone with far more experience and expertise than her should be sitting at this table.

'As you know, I'm new to this role and so I can't answer all of your questions right now. But I'll communicate your concerns to Mr Fitzpatrick. We're planning to hold regular public meetings.'

'We should have had them from the outset.' Fiona was a bit fierce and scary.

'Better late than never.' The vicar pursed his lips. 'We've invited Sean Fitzpatrick to numerous Church Committees, but he has refused to attend.'

'I didn't know I was meeting the committee today,' Louise said.

'This isn't the committee, just a couple of members who can report back with me. Not that we have anything new to share. It's all very disappointing.' He shook his head and shuffled his papers together.

Disappointing the vicar felt like a severe reprimand. 'I'm sorry. If I had known what was expected, then I would have come better prepared. How about I return in a couple of weeks with answers to all the questions you have raised?'

'A week would be more acceptable. We need to plan the last service here, and families are distressed about the moving of graves. I can't offer comfort to parishioners when I'm not kept informed. I'm sure you understand, Miss Cox.'

'Is that all?' Fiona looked at her watch. 'Richard is picking me up and I don't want to keep him waiting.'

Louise's heart leapt at his name. Richard. If only she could jump into his car and drive off into the sunset with him. As the tea things were collected up and the vicar chatted with Fiona, Louise daydreamed their reunion. He would look once and then a second time, not trusting his eyes. 'Is that you,

Louise Pearson?' He would step closer, his beautiful grey eyes taking her in. 'I can't believe it's you.' They would stare at one another, an energy between them. And then he would hold out his arms for a hug.

'There he is,' Fiona called over her shoulder before stepping out into the autumn sunshine.

Louise followed, shielding her eyes from the sudden glare of light. When she looked for Richard's car, they had already gone.

12

FRIDAY 8TH OCTOBER 1965

The community of Thorncrest spread wider than the valley; with dwellings separated by farmland, the population was sparse but covered a broad area surrounding the valley. Despite the geographical distance, the silent moors and interrupting hills, news travelled fast. In Ma's day it had been through exchanges at the market. *A pound of butter and did you hear the Jones's girl had twins?* Louise didn't know how news spread beyond the valley today. Braithwaite's had always been a source of local news, but she couldn't ask Kaye White about Richard and she wanted to know *everything*. What his life had been like after she left Thorncrest. Why he hadn't moved on to fulfil the dreams of his youth?

Louise wondered whether the accident had severed his life in the way it had hers. She had broken dear, sweet, loyal Dicky. Hurt him through her selfish actions and ruined his life. By staying away, it had made matters worse. When she got back to London, Louise had poured out her heart to Dicky. Asked...begged...for his forgiveness, but he hadn't replied to her letters. Her mum forbad her from writing to Ma Beck. She said Louise must let her grieve her loss, and a letter from her would cause too much distress. If only she had returned when Ma was still alive. But Dicky–Richard–was.

The need to be with him, to reconnect, was overwhelming. Everything else, fear of being convicted, or Big Jim finding her, receded just a little as this need propelled her carelessly towards him. Louise caught herself; she had to manage her emotions or she would end up dead. Big Jim was no fool. She *had* to keep her identity a secret from *everyone,* even Richard. One slip and he would find her.

'Sorry, I'm late, Jane.' Fitzpatrick's booming voice jolted Louise into the present. She had coaxed him into a routine where they had a daily update over morning coffee.

Fitzpatrick poured himself one. 'The contract's been signed on Brackbarn. There's already a skip down there. Take one of the construction lads with you and clear it. How are the other properties looking?'

'Mr Beacon is in a nursing home, but his cottage hasn't been emptied. He has a collection of polyphons. We agreed we would find a museum to take them.'

'Blast. Another of Richard Braithwaite's causes. Can't you do something about him?. Did you find Beacon's family? Can't we deal with them instead of Braithwaite? He doesn't have any legal power as Beacon's representative. See Beacon in the nursing home. Tell him we've got to move his stuff and then put it in storage.'

Fitzpatrick was going to put her in direct opposition to Richard unless she could find a way to make everyone happy. 'I'll phone the nursing home.'

'Maybe I should ask one of the villagers, someone from the Parish Council, or church, to be present when I empty Brackbarn. Mrs Widdle's family is still alive and we don't want any accusations made at a later date.'

'Good idea. So long as it doesn't hold things up.' Fitzpatrick's knee bobbed up and down, a sign that he was impatient to finish the meeting and return to what he considered more important tasks.

'We still have to discuss the church and your public meeting.'

Fitzpatrick sighed and looked at his watch. 'Can't that wait? I need to head over to the dam.'

'No.' Louise had learnt to be firm. 'I've answered none of the questions raised by the Church Committee. It's only the promise of a public meeting that's keeping them from anarchy.'

Fitzpatrick snorted. 'Anarchy? The vicar and his blue-rinse brigade?'

Louise had an image of Fiona Simms leading a revolt of angry villagers carrying pitchforks and torches. 'You haven't met Fiona Simms.'

Fitzpatrick frowned. 'Name sounds familiar.'

'One of *the* Simms, apparently.'

'Hell. The CEO of Simms Building Society?'

'I don't think Fiona is.'

'If it's *that* Simms, then her family is extremely influential. What has she got to do with the vicar?'

Now she had his attention. 'Fiona Simms was with the vicar when I met him. We need to give them some answers and show we're listening before things get out of hand.'

'Yes. I see what you mean. Okay. Set up the meeting. Is that all?'

In need of more coffee to prepare her for the day ahead, Louise made a fresh pot and carried a tray through to reception where Fliss now worked full time. They shared the women's dorm and had become good friends.

'My boyfriend's band is playing at the Coach and Horses this weekend. Come with me or I'll have to sit on my own when he's playing.'

'I'd love to. I can't remember when I last had a proper night out. This coffee and the promise of a wild night might just get me through the next few days. I have to clear out the last cottage without upsetting the village, negotiate clearing out Mr Beacon's property including moving the polyphons to York—which is definitely going to upset Richard Braithwaite, and arrange a public meeting that could well turn into a riot.'

Fliss laughed. 'Ouch. I don't envy you your job. I hope Fitzpatrick's paying you danger money.' She scrunched up her nose. 'Not sure a Saturday night at the Coach and Horses will be wild. They play rock 'n roll, so we can dance. And I'll buy you a gin and bitter.'

'Deal!' Louise downed her coffee. 'I'd better get going. But first, can I use the phone?'

'Sure, you can sit here. I need to pop to the ladies.'

Mrs White, who worked at Braithwaite's, was on the Church Committee and the Parish Council, so Louise rang the shop.

'Braithwaite's.' It was Richard.

Two seconds passed, and Louise felt like a teenage girl. Goosebumps prickled her arms.

'Is that Richard Braithwaite?' It gave her time to even her breath.

'Speaking. Who is this?'

'Jane Cox,' she whispered, her heart shouting, *it's me, Louise.*

Silence. She raised her voice, trying to sound business-like. This wasn't the time to reveal herself. 'Jane Cox from High House. The contract for Brackbarn has been signed. We're clearing it out this morning and so I was phoning for Kaye White, as she's on the parish council, to see if someone from the council would like to be present.'

'Kaye's busy looking after her grandchildren today but I can be there. What time?'

Louise's heart knocked hard against her sternum. 'I was planning to start work in about half an hour.'

'Okay. I'll get there as soon as I can.'

They were going to come face to face. He would know her. He had to. At last, they would be reunited. Two pieces of a jigsaw fitting together, filling the space in the centre of her soul. There was so much she needed to say. Would they even get round to clearing Ma Widdle's cottage? She didn't care. All that mattered was seeing him.

As Louise approached the cottage on her bike, she looked for Richard, imagining him to be waiting, perhaps perched on the garden wall. A catapult in his hand. She grinned to herself as Richard and twelve-year-old Dicky merged in her mind. But there was nobody outside, just an empty skip waiting to be filled. She let herself in.

The cottage was in a worse state than Louise remembered from her previous visit. The armchair by the fire gave the impression that things had remained almost untouched since Ma Widdle vacated Brackbarn. Louise did not know whether she had died there, or in another house, or hospital bed. She hoped it had been the former: that Ma Widdle had died in her armchair, her grey/blue tabby cat curled up in her lap. The boy who was coming to help lift things onto the skip had not yet arrived, and so Louise rolled up the sleeves of her blouse, pulled on a pair of rubber gloves, and grabbed a black rubbish sack.

Damp wallpaper had peeled away from the bedroom walls and fell in swathes of faded roses. There was a crack across the ceiling, and Louise worried that the roof was about to cave in. She tugged a striped mattress from the iron bed and flung it down the stairs. A mustard blanket, mildewed pillow, and chamber pot went into the black sack. That left a threadbare Indian rug, and a standard lamp. Louise kicked the mattress ahead of her down the stairs, following with the black sack.

As she worked, her senses were on high alert, waiting for Richard. Her heart jumped at every noise, the sighing of floorboards as the house creaked, a magpie's caw. When she stepped outside, there was still no sign of him or the lad who was to help her.

The ghosts of herself and Dicky came laughing down the lane. He was boasting of his superior strength and intelligence until she tackled him to the ground. It had been there, on the flattened grass near the well. Would he recognise her? They knew each other so well. And yet, there was no recognition in his eyes when she tipped a bucket of water over him. Louise smiled to herself. She was still getting the better of him. But she didn't want to fight him over the Beacon property. He was being a good friend to Horatio Beacon, a man who had been patient and kind to them when they were children.

A couple of hours later, Louise had dragged out everything for the skip. The buzz of a moped gradually became louder until it appeared, meandering towards her, dodging the tree roots.

'About time,' Louise said to the boy when he climbed off. 'I've finished in there, but this lot has to go in the skip.'

'Cool.' He leaned against the wall of the cottage and rolled a cigarette.

Richard wasn't coming. He said he wouldn't be long, and it was now midday. A ball of disappointment lodged in the pit of her stomach. There would be another opportunity. Richard couldn't avoid her forever. It was time to go, calls to make about the polyphons, arranging the public meeting, and—Louise hated to even think about it—making an appointment to visit Horatio Beacon in the nursing home. Richard would be furious if she didn't at least prepare him, explain that she needed to talk to Mr Beacon to get his permission to move his belongings.

'If Richard Braithwaite or someone from the Parish Council arrives to oversee the disposal of items, show them what's in the skip. I would have made an inventory, but there's nothing of value.'

Back at High House, Louise booked the school hall for a public meeting. It was the same school she had attended with Dicky, although closed to pupils for several years. It now served as a community centre. Louise was looking forward to seeing inside.

She had one week to prepare for the meeting: publicising it, and the more challenging task of organising Fitzpatrick so that he could give an informative report on progress and answer questions. Louise wasn't even sure Fitzpatrick had the answers. If he did, he wasn't sharing them with her.

Next on the list was calling the museum in York to organise the collection of polyphons. The phone on her desk, the one she shared with Pete, who was rarely in the office, rang.

Louise picked up, 'Peter Murray is away––'

'––I know. It's me, Fliss. I've got Richard Braithwaite on the line. He wants to talk to you and he sounds mad. Not crazy mad, just really, really cross mad.'

'I'll go crazy mad if you don't connect me now,' Richard interrupted.

'I'm sorry, Mr Braithwaite. I didn't think you could hear.'

This wasn't how she had imagined their reunion. Somehow, she needed to get him to trust her, to see her as a friend, not an enemy. 'Hello, Richard. Mr Braithwaite. I was hoping to see you earlier today at Ma … at Brackbarn cottage.'

'That was the plan. So why didn't you?' He was yelling at her as if it was her fault he hadn't turned up.

'I was there for over two hours. I can't hang around all day in the hope you'll show up. If you did, you would have seen a full skip, which you are free to inspect.' This wasn't going to plan.

'How do we know you haven't pocketed any items of value?'

'Really? What exactly do you think might lurk in the corners of that dilapidated cottage? Priceless jewels? A treasure map?'

He gave a soft chuckle. 'Okay, we will have to trust there wasn't anything of value.'

'There wasn't.'

'Okay. The reason I got delayed was Horatio Beacon. I got a call from the nursing home. They wanted me to visit to try and calm him down. He's worked up about his polyphon collection. Afraid it won't be preserved for the people of Thorncrest, he's refusing to eat and barely sleeping. You can't move it to York. It means so much to him. Beaky's a war hero. Doesn't he deserve your respect? A little patience while we find somewhere local for them?'

She could hear the desperation in Richard's voice and wanted to help. Beaky had been good to them as children. He deserved her love and care, but what Richard was asking may not be possible. 'I want to help. Truly I do. But you must understand the Corporation is working to a tight time schedule and budget. Maybe if I visited Mr Beacon with you in the nursing home, I could reassure him that his collection will be well cared for and appreciated by York Museum?'

'That would finish off the poor man. He's recovering from a stroke. It's bad enough he won't see his home again, after living there all his life and you want to tell him you're moving his precious collection to a museum twenty miles away? You're not visiting him with me and I'll warn the staff so they don't let you near him.'

Louise took a deep breath. Somehow, she had to arrange for the removal of Beaky's possessions in a way that wasn't going to alienate Richard and do it quickly. An impossible mission. 'Okay, what do you suggest? We need to empty Mr Beacon's cottage within the next week. We can keep all his things in storage, except the polyphons. We've found a home for them with York Museum, so unless you, or Mr Beacon, can identify another museum in a location that's acceptable, that is where they have to go. I'm sorry, but that's the best we can offer.'

'Okay. Give me a few days to come up with something.'

All morning she had anticipated a reunion with Richard, her heart skipping a beat every time a floorboard creaked or a cat cried. It felt wrong to be working in opposition. They both wanted the same thing, to preserve precious memories of their valley, to treat those who lived and worked there with care and respect. She prayed Richard could find a solution for Beaky. But she was more concerned about Richard's future. The valley would soon be flooded and, as far as she knew, he had made no plans to move the shop. This was his chance to create the life he had imagined as a boy. Something more than running his family's business. Maybe if she convinced him the reservoir plan was as good as agreed, he would finally let go and say goodbye to their valley. If her reckless behaviour as a teen had trapped him in the past, then she owed it to Richard to set him free. He could do so much more with his life. And Louise wanted to be part of that life.

'Before you go,' Louise said. She had to say something now before she changed her mind. Before it was too late. 'Mr Fitzpatrick wanted me to update you on the reservoir.'

A silence. Her heart thumped. The flood would almost certainly be contained within the boundaries on the plan. Fitzpatrick had as good as said so. Waiting for confirmation was just a formality. A teeny white lie. But it would give Richard the permission he needed to make plans for the future.

Louise took a deep breath and continued. 'You were concerned about the dimensions—how far up the water would come. We can confirm that the level will be as estimated in our plan. Mr Fitzpatrick would have shared that with you.'

Richard let out his breath. 'Thank you. That means a lot.'

In the silence that followed, thoughts chased through Louise's head. The first, joy that she had set him free. *The world is your oyster, Richard. You owe nothing to no one. Just yourself.* Then doubt. She had told a lie. A big—huge—lie. If Fitzpatrick knew, he would sack her on the spot. Richard would be angry too. But it was 99.9 percent certain. There was no way they would flood Becks farm. If there was the remotest chance, Fitzpatrick would have asked her to clear it out by now. She had just given Richard permission to live his life. That was all. There was no need for Richard to take responsibility for everyone who had once lived in the valley. As Jane Cox, she could take on that role—fight any battles on their behalf. Save Becks farm if necessary.

13

9TH OCTOBER 1965

The Coach and Horses on Saturday night was not as glamorous as Tin Pan Alley and the band were not The Kinks, but they were good. Louise hadn't expected to enjoy herself so much. Everyone seemed to know each other. It was like a party of friends.

'Two halves of bitter shandy,' Louise shouted to the barmaid.

'Get pints. Save you fighting your way to the bar,' said a man to her right.

Louise had seen him talking to Fliss's boyfriend Dion when they were doing soundchecks. 'Too late.'

'Make that another two halves,' he said to the barmaid. 'On me.'

Louise went to object, but she was learning that things were done differently in Yorkshire. It was a kind gesture. 'Thank you.'

'Go on. I'll carry them over.'

When their drinks had been distributed, Fliss got up to dance. 'Coming Jane?'

'No, I'll sit this one out.' She watched Fliss and her friend Mike boogie across the floor. The band was playing, *I'm a Believer*. It was the last song of the first set and Louise was pooped. She'd danced most of the evening and perspiration was cooling on her neck. She took a sip of shandy.

'Can I take this seat?'

Louise's hand shot out to secure Fliss's chair. 'No, sorry.'

'Jane Cox?'

It was Fiona Simms. Louise wished the village wasn't quite so small as it meant she could never really escape from work and being 'on duty.'

'Hello, Fiona. I didn't expect to see you here.'

'I wouldn't miss it. I love this band. Unless you go into York, there's not much that goes on around here. I expect you're missing London.'

Louise replied without thinking. 'What makes you think I lived in London?'

'A lucky guess going by your reaction.'

Damn, she had given too much away. 'Not London. The suburbs.' That could be anywhere: Kent, Surrey, Essex.

'Now we are going to take a short break. Thank you for being a great audience.'

Fliss and Mike were returning to their table.

'I wanted to talk to you. Shall we step outside for a moment?' Fiona said.

Louise didn't want to talk to Fiona about the project and she didn't want to hear her talking about Richard. But it was important to keep the Simms family happy, so she reluctantly followed Fiona's neat behind. It was chill outside the pub and Louise regretted not putting on her coat. She wrapped her arms around herself and shivered.

'Mind if I smoke?' Fiona extracted a cigarette from a fancy oriental-looking case. 'Want one?'

Louise shook her head. She hoped they wouldn't be out there too long. The sky was clear, hardly any cloud cover to dim the bright expanse of galaxies. It filled Louise with awe every time. It was hard to believe this was the same night sky as the one in London.

Fiona blew out a long plume of smoke. 'I wanted to thank you. For holding off on the jukebox things and persuading Richard to sign the Corporation's contract. He's been using it as an excuse to put off planning our future.'

Our future. Louise gritted her teeth. Fiona was Richard's girlfriend. She had to learn to like her. 'I didn't persuade him, just updated him on plans.'

'Well, I'm glad you did because together we have steered him in the right direction.'

'Has Richard made plans for after the flood?'

'He has.' Fiona took a long draw of her cigarette. Louise's gut told her this would not be good. 'Richard's finally accepted Daddy's offer. They're going into business together Braithwaite and Simms, a chain of department stores across England. The first one in Ripley. And you'll be pleased to hear we are making room to accommodate Mr Beacon's collection. To be honest, I think that was what decided it for Richard. He was so upset over those jukeboxes. The silly boy. Anyway. I wanted to thank you, darling.' Fiona stubbed out her cigarette with the toe of her kitten heel shoe, grinding it with a swivel of her hips.

'Well. Nothing has to be decided yet. I won't cancel arrangements with York Museum until I've had confirmation from Richard. It's a big decision.'

'Oh, don't worry about that. I'll get him to sign first thing. It's wonderful news. Maybe now we can think about getting married.'

'I'll find somewhere else for the polyphons. Richard

doesn't need to sign the contract to save them. Tomorrow. I'll come up with something tomorrow. I promise.' Louise was gabbling.

'Why ever would you do that? No. You and the Corporation are happy. I'm happy. Daddy is. And so is the dear old man in the nursing home.'

'And Richard? Is this what he wants?'

'Oh, Richard never knows what he wants. So long as he keeps everyone else happy. And as that is exactly what he's doing, he'll be elated.' Fiona laughed at her joke. 'No, seriously, a major investor in his business? Of course, he's happy.'

Fiona was like a runaway train flattening everything in its path. Louise had to stop Richard before he signed the contract, and somehow find a home for the polyphons. He couldn't really want this—a future in retail. The Dicky she knew would be appalled.

Louise was trying to think of a way to slow things down when a voice called, 'Jane.' She turned to see Pete wrapped up in a hat and scarf. 'I didn't know you'd be here.' He kissed her on the cheek.

'I'll leave you two lovebirds,' Fiona said.

'We're not. Never mind,' Louise said to Fiona's retreating back.

'What was that all about?' Pete asked when they were alone.

'Apparently, Richard Braithwaite is going to sign the contract.' Louise was thinking ahead. She would meet Richard, confess to him she had lied. Anything to stop him going into business with the Simms. Surely Richard hadn't changed that much.

'That will make Fitzpatrick's day. Are you going in? It's freezing out here.'

'I will. Just need a minute.'

Pete shrugged. 'Okay. I'll have a drink waiting for you. Gin and bitter?'

Louise nodded. 'Thank you.'

One last look at the stars—was one of them Ma watching over her? *I've messed up Ma. Again.* Was she being as selfish as Fiona in trying to influence Richard? Maybe he wanted what Fiona and her family offered. Financial security. His mum would be overjoyed to hear Braithwaite's might one day be a chain of department stores. Frank too. It was their dream. Not Dicky's—Richard's. But maybe it was now. What did she know? Richard and Fiona were happy together. There was no place for her in Richard's future. It was too late. Far too late. Ma and Pa dead, and their valley soon to be flooded.

If her coat hadn't been inside, she would have gone straight home. She no longer felt in the mood to party.

The band were playing, *I Can't Get No Satisfaction,* when Louise slipped back inside to fetch her coat and make a quick getaway. Fliss was on the dance floor. Two gin and bitters had been left for her, and Louise felt guilty. Everyone here made her feel welcome. Valued for being herself, not Eddie's wife—except she wasn't herself, she was Jane Cox. Coat on, Louise took a sip of her drink. She would thank Pete and ask him to let Fliss know she had gone home. Fliss, whose bright red hair was flying around as she twisted and turned, arms and legs pumping to the music. Louise smiled; she would hear all about it later when Fliss crept into their dorm trying not to wake her.

Pete was in the far corner, tucked into a shadowy alcove. Louise tried to attract his attention, but he looked away, then nodded at two men who were heading towards him. Their tailored suits looked out of place in a country pub. The sort of thing Eddie might wear. Big men, tall and broad, and they lumbered over to Pete like a couple of grizzly bears. So, nothing like Eddie, who was slim, elegant, and suave. Pete greeted the men with a hand on a shoulder, a shaking of hands. It was all too familiar. Louise had witnessed similar exchanges in the Tin Pan Alley and upstairs at Annabel's. The hairs on the back of her neck stood to attention. She watched and waited.

Mike, Fliss's friend, stopped to chat. 'Great set. Having a good time?' Whilst they talked, Louise kept her eyes on Pete and the men.

'I'm getting a round in. What are you drinking?' Mike said.

The two men strode past them and out of the pub. 'Let me buy this round,' Louise said. 'I've been supplied with drinks all evening.'

She shrugged off her flimsy anorak—the first thing she grabbed when leaving London, and went to the bar. 'You sit down. I'll get Pete to help me carry them back.'

On hearing his name, Pete turned. 'At your service.'

Louise reeled off the list of drinks, adding his pint of stout.

'Who were those men I saw you talking to?' she asked, as they moved glasses onto a small tray.

'George and Mickey?' he answered without hesitation. 'What did they look like in their suits? A couple of gorillas.' He laughed.

'They didn't stay long.' Louise tucked a bag of peanuts and two packets of crisps between the glasses.

'On their way out to dinner, a posh restaurant in Harrogate. Mickey's wife's birthday or something. They're brothers-in-law. Is that it? I'll carry the tray.'

'No. Those two pints, but I'll carry them. So, what were they doing here? And how do you know them?'

'Why the interest? I told you, Mickey's married. I thought you only had eyes for me.'

Louise gave a half laugh. 'Funny.'

'They're contractors working with us. Didn't you recognise them from High House? I told them about the band. They planned on coming along tonight to support Fliss, but then Mickey's wife sprung this on him. It's not her birthday until next week, but she got it into her head they would join the men in Harrogate for a weekend away.'

'I was going to leave but got waylaid,' Louise said, as they manoeuvred themselves away from the bar carrying the drinks.

'I'm not staying late, so I'll give you a lift back if you like.'

'On your motorbike?' Pete had acquired a rusty old Triumph since arriving in Thorncrest.

'If you're okay with that?'

Louise hesitated. She wanted to believe Pete, that the two men were innocent contractors, but she was spooked. If she got on Pete's bike, he could take her anywhere. Back to Big Jim.

'It's okay. I'll call a cab.'

'Don't be daft. It's not like calling a cab in London. You could be waiting hours.'

'Okay.' Louise sighed. 'Thank you.'

Outside the pub, surveying the motorbike, she had second thoughts. 'Don't you have motorbike helmets?'

'No. Sorry. Have you done this before?'

Louise shook her head as she climbed on behind him.

'Hold on tight so you move with me when the bike goes around a corner,' Pete shouted over the roar of the bike's engine. 'Ready?'

She clung to Pete's waist and tried to relax, to go with the flow, afraid she might tip the bike over if she resisted. After a couple of turns, the road was a straight run and Louise's muscles relaxed, her mind wandering. Was there anything she could do before Monday to stop Richard from signing the contract? Finding a new home for the polyphons would help, but she had already tried, as had Richard, and it was proving impossible.

They were back in minutes. Her cheeks felt raw from the wind, her hair standing on end like a toilet brush. Pete secured his bike and followed Louise to the front of the house.

'Night, Jane.'

'Before you go, Pete. Those men. George and Mickey. Do they work for Bellamy Brothers?'

'Ha! I knew you fancied one of them. Yes. Bellamy Boys.'

14

DECEMBER 1942

Travelling home to London for the Christmas holiday, that first year at Becks farm, Louise felt years older than when she'd left just ten weeks ago. Ma and Pa had driven her all the way to York, so that she didn't have to change trains.

'A day out for me,' Ma had said, and Louise, sorry not to be exploring the city with them, immediately felt guilty because going home to Mum should have been the best thing ever.

The train's momentum slowed. A woman opposite Louise packed away the matinee baby jacket she had been knitting and fastened her coat. Excitement bubbled in Louise's belly. So much had happened in the past few weeks; Louise wondered whether she would look different to her mum—older and more worldly. The train jolted and the woman opposite, who was now standing, clutched hold of the seat. Louise breathed in deeply and tried to compose herself. Mum would be standing on the platform searching for her little girl. To think that she had been frightened of leaving London.

'Can I help you with your luggage, Miss?' a train guard enquired, before lifting down Louise's suitcase. 'What have you got in here? A ton of potatoes?' He winked.

Louise grinned. Not quite, but she had butter, cheese, some carefully packed eggs, and a special treat from Ma — her Christmas present to Louise and her mum. They were going to have a wonderful Christmas. Not in the tiny bedsit. Mum had written to say they would spend Christmas Day at a friend's house. Louise was glad her mum was making new friends. Christmases with her aunt and uncle had been fun, but different was good. Living in Yorkshire had proved that.

Most of the train's passengers had disembarked: men and women in army uniform, a mother and her three children, an elderly woman with a walking stick. A couple of sweethearts were hugging and kissing, oblivious to anyone else. It was so romantic. Louise took her time savouring the moment. Wanting her reunion with Mum to be special—memorable.

Mum wasn't on the platform. Louise struggled with her case. It was the first time she had lifted it as Pa saw her onto the train. Maybe Mum had been held up in traffic. A sick feeling churned in her stomach—the memory of bombs and air raid sirens. Louise followed the flow of passengers through the ticket gate, presenting the ticket Pa had bought at York station. It seemed so far away now.

There was still no sign of her mum. Now Louise was seriously worried. She was planning to telephone her aunt when Mum's voice carried across the ticket hall.

'Louise. Over here.' Mum strode towards her, waving both arms. Louise sighed with relief and picked up her case.

'Sorry I was late, darling. I got a lift, but Joe stopped on the way to pick something up from a friend.'

Before Louise could ask, *Who is Joe?* the man in question

joined them. He wore a shabby suit and rakish hat, which he lifted on meeting her. 'So, this is our evacuee returned home?' He extended a hand. Louise took it and her inner-self shudder.

'This is the friend I told you about, Louise. Joe has invited us to spend Christmas with him in his flat.'

In all of her imaginings about the first Christmas home—and there were many—never had a Christmas with Mum and a sleazy-looking man featured. When Mum mentioned a friend, Louise had imagined a kind, joyful woman—maybe one with an interesting past like an actress or a RAF pilot—or with a daughter who would become Louise's best-friend. A younger girl who would be fascinated to hear about Louise's life on the farm and would look up to her. Christmas in a family home with laughter, games, and songs around the piano.

'You didn't tell me she was a strapping gal. Hope you're not going to eat us out of house and home,' Joe chortled.

'Oh, you are funny, Joe. Louise will be no bother. You'll barely know she's there. Isn't that right, sweetheart?'

Louise glared at her mum, but she didn't seem to notice. Joe had taken off, and they followed in his wake, her mum carrying Louise's case.

'Sorry luv. I wanted to meet you alone, but Joe insisted. He's been so kind to me. I'm not sure how I would have coped living on my own. We'll have a jolly Christmas together.'

'Ma Beck sent some eggs and cheese. Something else too, but it's a surprise.' Louise wanted to tell Mum everything about life on the farm. She'd brought her diary to help her remember.

'That was kind of Mrs Beck. I hope you thanked her.'

'Right. You girls wait here and I'll bring the old chevy

round.' Joe left them standing in front of the station and set off down the road to find his car.

As soon as he was out of earshot, her mum said, 'We're going straight to Joe's place. I've kept the bedsit on, but I barely live there now.'

Disappointment fuelled Louise's anger. 'Why didn't you tell me? If I'd known I was going to play gooseberry, I'd have stayed on at the farm where at least I'm wanted.'

As soon as her words were out, Louise regretted them. Her mum blanched and her eyes filled with anguish. 'Oh, sweetheart. Of course, you're wanted. I've been longing to see you. It's just with this war, and being single—it's hard. Joe looks after me.'

An old Sunbeam car drew up. It made a loud, spluttering sound, causing people to turn and look. Joe waved from an open window as if the attention focused on his car was a good thing. Louise wanted to hide. It was so embarrassing.

'Come on darling. We'll soon be home and you can tell me all your news.'

The car had two front seats, with a narrow bench behind them. Louise clambered into the back, cramming herself and her suitcase into the limited space. Joe revved his engine, and the car lurched forward.

The first night at Joe's flat, Louise slept undisturbed on the sofa. There was only one bedroom. Joe made a bit of an effort, asking about the farm, and unsuccessfully attempted a card trick. Louise almost felt sorry for him. But any sympathy eroded by Christmas Eve.

The day started off okay. Joe went out, saying that Louise and her mum needed time together. They made paper decorations from newspaper and Louise told her mum all about the farm—how she was in charge of the chickens and had learnt to make butter. They peeled swede and Brussel sprouts for Christmas dinner the next day.

'I managed to get a chicken but no Christmas cake or mince pies this year,' her mum said.

Louise couldn't wait until the next day. 'I've got something special from Ma Beck. Hold on. I'll fetch it from my bag.'

It was wrapped in a white cloth. The scent of cinnamon and currants took Louise back to the farmhouse kitchen. 'Ma made us a Christmas pudding. It's made with breadcrumbs instead of flour, but I'm sure it will taste just as good, if not better. Ma is an amazing cook.'

'She really ought not to have gone to any trouble. It's not as if we are family.' Mum sounded annoyed rather than pleased and Louise was cross on behalf of Ma, who had gladly taken the trouble because she was kind and wanted them to have a wonderful Christmas.

'It's Christmas. People do nice things for each other at Christmas—especially with there being a war on,' Louise said.

Her mum's face softened. 'Hark at you, sounding like a wise old woman. You're right. It *was* kind of her and I'm grateful. Joe will be too.'

Mum prepared a Christmas Eve tea: corned beef sandwiches and a can of fruit salad served with carnation milk. They waited for Joe, but when he still wasn't home by seven, they ate it without him.

'I'll save Joe's for him,' Mum said.

Joe arrived home an hour later, a bit merry from a drink with some mates down the pub. Louise was used to going to bed early as her days on the farm started soon after sunrise but it was Christmas Eve and so she made an effort to be jolly, laughing at Joe's jokes and sipping sherry—because it was Christmas—even though she hated the taste.

Mum was drinking too, and before long, it seemed as though Louise's presence was forgotten. Joe played a gramophone record. At first, they all danced, but when Bing Crosby started crooning *Somebody Loves Me,* Mum and Joe smooched around the room as if she wasn't there.

It was late. The journey from Yorkshire the day before had tired her. Louise's back and stomach hurt. She wanted to tell her mum, but it was impossible to have a quiet word with Joe in the room. When he left them for a few minutes, Louise took the opportunity.

'Mum, can I go to bed? I'm really tired and achy.'

'Not really love. There's only the one bedroom. We'll all go to bed soon.' She blew Louise a kiss as Joe returned.

It felt like hours before Joe slumped into an armchair and fell asleep, an empty glass in one hand and a cigarette in the other. Her mum removed the cigarette and stubbed it out in the ashtray.

'Get changed in the bathroom, Louise. I'll fetch some blankets for your bed.'

In the bathroom, Louise pulled down her knickers and was shocked to see blood. How had that happened? She hadn't hurt herself there. She tried wiping it away with a sheet of Izal toilet paper, but there was so much it coated her fingers. Louise didn't know what to do.

'Are you alright in there, darling?'

'Mum. I've hurt myself,' Louise whispered through a crack in the door. 'I'm bleeding.'

Her mum slid past Louise and locked the bathroom door. 'Don't worry, sweetheart. You're just having your period. I told you all about this.'

Louise remembered vaguely. 'That was ages ago. You didn't tell me it would happen now. Today. What am I going to do?' It was a catastrophe. She was in a strange man's flat the day before Christmas. Everywhere was closed for the holiday.

'I've got a couple of sanitary towels here at Joe's in case of an emergency. I'll fix you up for the night. Don't say anything in front of Joe, it would embarrass him. Please don't get any blood on the sofa.'

'I'm scared Mum. I want to go home to your place. I don't want to spend Christmas here. My tummy aches.' Louise couldn't stop her tears.

'Shh. You're just tired. I'll get Joe to bed, then I'll sort you out. Wait here.'

Louise sat on the toilet, her head in her hands. Why couldn't this have happened on the farm? Ma would have known what to do. If she had bled a few days ago, they could have cancelled her visit to London. *I want* to *go home to Ma,* Louise cried to herself.

Christmas Day was little improvement on the evening before. Joe had a hangover and so they had to creep around until the afternoon, when he finally emerged from the bedroom. They ate Christmas dinner at three in the afternoon. Louise gave her mum the needle case she had spent weeks sewing under Ma's direction. Joe ridiculed it, saying her mum had no use for such a thing as she didn't know the meaning of make do and mend. It was meant to be a joke, but Louise thought it unkind. Mum's present to Louise was an orange and some notepaper for writing letters home.

'Joe brought home the orange for you.' Mum beamed.

'There's more where that came from.' He winked and her mum giggled.

Louise wanted to save the orange for Ma but her mum insisted on Louise eating it almost straight away—in front of them both—which was embarrassing and spoilt any enjoyment she might have had from the delicious citric juice trickling down her throat.

It was the day after boxing day and time for Louise to return to Yorkshire. Mum got up early to make a sandwich for her to eat on the train. Joe wasn't up and so Louise crept into the kitchen to spend a few precious minutes with her mum before leaving.

'How are you feeling, sweetheart?'

'Better. I've stopped bleeding. Will it happen again?'

Mum put down the butter knife, and hugged Louise. She stroked her hair. 'Many, many times, but you'll get used to it, I promise. It means you're becoming a woman.'

'I don't want to be a woman.' Louise's lower lip quivered. 'I'm not ready.'

'Don't cry or you'll set me off. Have you packed your things?'

'Can we go to the station on our own, like the last time you saw me off?'

Mum laughed. 'You silly thing. Why would we do that when Joe can drop us off in the car? Besides, me and Joe are going on someplace.'

'Where? Doesn't Joe have a job? And why isn't he in the army?'

A shadow fell across the room and Louise looked around to see Joe standing behind her.

'I'm popping out to buy some fags. Want anything from the corner shop, doll?'

Louise slipped past him, wishing she were invisible. Their murmured voices carried, then her mum's tinkling laughter. Her mum was happy. Louise knew she should be glad for her, but it made her feel as though she no longer belonged.

'Joe didn't pass his medical,' Mum said when they were

alone again. 'He's sensitive about it—feels it makes him less of a man. He keeps busy doing this and that. Helping people out. Now you have some fancy notepaper; I expect lots of letters.' She hugged Louise tight. 'This war can't go on much longer. You'll soon be home. Just don't grow up too much in the meantime.'

15

JULY 1943

Louise and Dicky had been looking forward to haymaking week since Pa first mentioned it over breakfast one morning.

'Farmer Jeffreys will need our help in yonder field.'

'Aye. And the Fordson,' Ma said, buttering the toast.

'The tractor and some manpower. I won't ask Kurt. Folk are sensitive about prisoners of war working on farms and as it's not our farm. But Louise can help and that young lad, Braithwaite's boy.'

'Help with what?' Louise didn't know yet whether she was proud to be offered as a useful pair of hands to Farmer Jeffreys or indignant on Kurt's behalf.

'Hay making. Jeffreys' old mare can't pull a loaded hay wagon, so I'm lending the Fordson. We'll need lots of hands to turn and bale.'

Ma wiped her hands on her apron and joined them at the kitchen table. 'I'm not sure, Pa. It's hard work. And what about school?'

Now Louise was determined to help. 'Loads of kids get days off school to help with harvest. *Please* Ma.'

The second week in June, Dicky arrived early in the morning to start work.

'You young'uns wait here. Susan will pick you up in the hay wagon.' Pa puttered away in his tractor.

'Ma said Pa's really proud of that tractor. It's an old one from the war agricultural people, because of us having to plough fields for crops. They took away his horses for the war, but Farmer Jeffreys couldn't get one and he only has an old mare.' Louise felt like a proper farmhand in her breeches—Ma had cut down an old pair of Pa's.

'Will that Jerry be helping too?' Dicky said, as they sat side by side in the back of the hay wagon.

'I hate it when you call him that. No, but you've reminded me. Wait here. I've got to tell him something.'

Dicky sighed. 'Susan will be here any minute. You haven't got time.'

'Tell her I'm in the cowshed. I'll be two minutes.' Louise didn't wait for a reply.

She could hear Kurt humming and pushed open the door. The cows and their calves were grazing in the lower meadow, so the barn was empty. Kurt stopped sweeping, then discarded his broom and went into the farthest corner. He squatted down to investigate something.

Unseen, Louise delighted in watching him at work; his sleeves rolled up, exposing blond hairs on his forearms, the outline of his back muscles as they strained against his shirt. Kurt gave a low whistle.

'What is it, Kurt?'

He turned, surprised to see her. 'This stone is loose. A sharp edge. It is not good for the cows.'

'Let me see.' Louise knelt beside him. 'Gertrude doesn't stand that close to the wall. How loose is it?'

Kurt stood up and looked around. Louise guessed what he needed and fetched a shovel from outside the barn. She handed it to him. The flagstone lifted easily.

'We can cement it back in. I thought you were making the hay.'

Louise beamed. He remembered. He was going to miss her. 'I am, but I wanted to let you know I'll ask for a bale of hay so when you've finished scrubbing the floor, we can make it cosy for the cows.'

'Cosy?' Kurt laughed at her.

'There you are!' Susan, the Land Army girl, burst into the barn. 'Come on Lou. We've lots to do.'

Kurt was holding the flagstone. 'So, you think Miss Gertrude will not be disturbed by this loose stone? That she will be cosy?'

'I do. I wonder how it got loose. Maybe there's something hidden underneath.'

'Ah buried treasure.' Kurt winked. 'I think Susan is in a hurry. Have a good day making the hay, Louise.'

Dicky tutted and rolled his eyes when Louise climbed back onto the wagon. 'What was so important you had to make us late?'

'We're not late. Susan didn't mind, and it *was* important.'

Dicky leaned over the side, ignoring Louise as they bumped along the lane. She knew he was sulking. The wagon slowed down and turned onto a farm track.

'Get ready to open the gate,' Susan shouted from the front.

Dicky turned to face Louise and grinned. She knew he was planning to beat her to it. The wagon had barely come to a stop when Louise leapt off.

'Hey. I was going to do that.' Dicky laughed as Louise

dragged the gate open. The wagon passed through and she secured it shut behind them before jumping back in.

'You can do the next one.'

Three gates later—Louise let Dicky open and close two—they joined the men, boys and Land Army girls in a field covered with mounds of hay.

'Grab yourselves a hay rake,' a young man said.

Susan went all girly, giggling and making eyes at him. 'I've not done this before, so perhaps you could talk me through the process, Mister…?'

'Simon. Simon Jeffreys. It would be a pleasure…?'

'Susan.'

Dicky and Louise exchanged an exasperated look. Those two were obviously going to be flirting all day. Young men were in short supply and so Louise understood the attraction. The son of a farmer, Simon Jeffreys, had been exempted from conscription to the army.

Louise and Dicky were set to work a swathe each. The grass had been cut and spread out, but it was still green in places.

'Use both hands on the rake to turn the grass and spread it evenly across the swathe,' Simon said, demonstrating. 'See, the underside is green. That all needs to be pale yellow. A couple more days if the weather stays fine.'

'What if it rains?' Louise said.

'Don't even think it. Forecast is good. As they say, let's make hay while the sun shines. I'll leave you to it as I'm needed for bailing the hay that's dried.'

'I'll give you a hand,' Susan said. And they drove off in the hay wagon.

Louise played with her rake, feeling its weight. 'Ready?'

'Yep. This is easy. I bet I finish before you.'

And they were off. Forking and turning the grass while the sun crept higher in the sky.

By eleven o'clock, Louise's blouse was sticky with perspiration, her hands raw with blisters, her calves and thighs ached, and she had cramp in places she didn't know possible. Dicky was a long way ahead. *He can't be doing as good a job as me,* Louise thought. A bee buzzed around her face, and she swiped it away. Ma had prepared some lunch and wrapped it in a cloth, but Louise had left it in the hay wagon. As if aware that the rhythm of her work had been interrupted, Dicky turned towards her. Then he threw down his rake and walked back along the swathe, a bag slung over one shoulder.

'Want a drink?' He waved a flask at Louise and she realised she had drunk nothing since leaving the farm.

The other farm workers were scattered about the field, some ahead of them and others behind.

'When I get a farm, I'll buy hay for the cows,' Louise said.

'Is that what you're going to do? I thought you wanted to write story books.'

'I can do both. But if you want to grow grass and make hay for me, you can.'

'No. That's okay. It's harder work than I realised. And this is just the morning of the first day. Shall we stop for lunch? I know it's early, but we've been working for hours,' Dicky said.

Louise sighed. 'I left my sandwich on the wagon.'

Dicky reached into his bag and triumphantly held aloft a brown paper bag. 'You can share mine. Fish paste.'

'Thanks. We can share mine later.'

Dicky took off his shirt and lay it over the cut grass. 'The grass is scratchy. You can sit on my shirt.'

He was wearing a white vest beneath his shirt. There was muscle where there had once been soft flesh. Louise's mouth felt dry.

'So, are you going to sit?'

Louise realised she had been staring and blushed. 'Yes. Thanks.'

He handed her half of his sandwich and they ate in silence. It felt awkward. His proximity. The way he was Dicky, and yet he wasn't. When his bare arm brushed hers, Louise felt as though her skin had been scorched. There was a time that they had play fights, rolling around like a couple of bear cubs but now everything felt wrong. She brushed breadcrumbs from her breeches. When she glanced up, Dicky was watching her with a faraway look in his eyes.

Louise scrambled up and adjusted her clothing, tucking in her blouse and fastening a button. 'Put your shirt on or you'll burn in the sun.' She averted her eyes as he dressed. When he was fully clothed, Louise could look at him without feeling awkward.

'Why don't we work together? I'll turn the grass and you can spread it?' Dicky said.

Louise's hair fell forward as she worked, and the sun felt hot on her neck. She should have listened to Ma and brought a hat. Tomorrow she would come better prepared. The dry grass swished as Dicky worked ahead of her. Swish. Swish. Pa's tractor rumbled in a nearby field and the birds called to one another. It was hard to believe that on the other side of the English Channel, men were fighting for their freedom. That in London bombs were dropping—devastating lives. Hoot. Hoot.

'What was that?' Louise said, shielding her eyes from the sun to scan the sky.

Dicky leant on his rake. 'Over there.' He stepped closer to Louise and put a hand on her shoulder to guide her in the direction he wanted her to look. 'A barn owl.' His arm fell lightly across her back.

The owl flew straight at them, its talons stretched out like witch's fingers. Louise gasped and, without thinking, turned her head into Dicky's chest. He stroked her hair, pinning her to him, and she felt comfortable. Comforted.

'Look, he's caught something,' Dicky said, pointing with his free hand.

She turned to catch sight of the owl's pale yellow underbelly and the grey tail of its prey. 'Nature's cruel,' Louise said. The little field mouse had perhaps been enjoying a feast within a thatch of dried grass. The next second, he *was* the feast in the talons of a predator—terrified and helpless.

'Nature isn't cruel—it's the natural way of the world. It's man who's cruel. The Germans are executing people in cold blood—thousands of them, mostly Jews. Have you heard about the concentration camps?' His body tensed and he stepped away from her.

Louise knew a little; she listened to the radio with Ma and Pa on Sunday afternoons. She knew about the brutality of war, that Hitler was persecuting Jewish people. Pa had explained what that meant. Hitler was sending them away from their homes and work to concentration camps where they had to live together. That's why they were at war. But it felt so far away, here, in a field of hay with birdsong and sunshine.

'Yes, of course I have,' Louise replied. 'But "courage, cheerfulness and your resolution will bring us victory." "Dig for Victory!"' She thrust her rake above her head.

'Do you think I could look eighteen?' Dicky said, ignoring her attempt to lighten the mood.

'No. You don't even shave.' Louise threw handfuls of grass at him. 'I look older than you.'

Dicky glowered, then as Louise bent down to gather more

grass to throw, she felt his hands stuffing some down the back of her blouse.

'You swine!'

They tumbled around having a grass fight. Now, as comfortable with each other as they had always been—a couple of kids. Best friends.

But Louise was afraid Dicky might lie about his age to get into the army. Anyone could see he was still a boy—fourteen. Only he wasn't. He was becoming a man. Why did everything have to change? Why did they have to grow up?

16

MONDAY 11TH OCTOBER 1965

When she wasn't fretting over the Bellamy Boys, and their real purpose of being in Thorncrest, Louise had spent the weekend replaying her conversation with Fiona, trying to convince herself that nothing had yet been decided. Richard would never agree to her father investing vast sums of money to build an empire of department stores across the UK. The Richard she knew hated capitalism. His reluctance to sign a contract had nothing to do with the sum offered for his business. He was holding off so that he could protect the interests of people like Beaky, and through a false sense of loyalty to the Becks, who would know nothing about the flood. Louise was curious to know how much the Corporation had agreed to pay Richard. It would be enough to fund a new venture. He could do anything. Be anything. The Dicky she knew and loved would hate the idea of being a retail business tycoon.

On Monday morning, Louise waited for her ten o'clock meeting with Fitzpatrick. There was a lot to discuss, with the public meeting scheduled for Friday, but top of Louise's list was delaying the completion of Richard's contract. He wouldn't sign up to anything with the Simms until that was agreed.

'Well done, Jane.' Fitzpatrick stepped into the office, rubbing his hands together. 'I don't know how you did it, but you've put the project back on schedule. Braithwaite signed this morning.'

'He can't have. I only spoke to him on Friday.' Louise was dismayed.

'What did you say to make him change his mind?'

She couldn't tell Fitzpatrick. He would dismiss her on the spot. 'I just reasoned with him. Richard Braithwaite isn't greedy. He just wanted reassurance that the church relocation, Mr Beacon's cottage, and any other homes and businesses displaced would be treated with sensitivity and respect.' Louise shrugged.

'Good. Good. Well, you can tell them all that at the public meeting.'

'I'm not telling anyone anything. You're the chief engineer and project manager. I'll set everything up, but you'll need to give an update.'

'Okay. Just let me know what I need to say. Where is it being held?'

Louise had told him several times. 'The old school.'

'Got it. Is that all?' Fitzpatrick stood up. 'I'm meeting a health official today about the relocation of graves. So, lots to do.'

Louise muttered as she rode her bike uphill to the old school. It wasn't as if he had recruited her with any intent. If she hadn't hitched a ride and met Pete, Fitzpatrick would be on his own—headed for disaster. And that was exactly where she was headed if the reassurance she had given to Richard proved to be wrong. Fitzpatrick had said the reservoir boundary would almost certainly be as drawn on the plan. It was just a matter of ticking boxes. Belt and braces. Not that he had said that, exactly, but as good as. Richard had been a bit quick off the mark signing; Fiona must have been on to him all weekend. But that didn't mean he had to go along with her plans. Louise would talk to him. Remind him of the plans he had as a boy. He was bound to recognise her, anyway.

And then her kangaroo mind jumped to Pete Murray. How did he appear out of nowhere as soon as she hitched a ride? Did Pete say he was going to Thorncrest first, or had she already told the driver? Maybe it was time to run. But where would she go? If Pete had followed her here, he would alert Big Jim as soon as she tried to leave. Louise wobbled on the bike as she tried to look behind her, paranoid that she was being followed. With her mind preoccupied, she almost missed the school.

It looked much smaller. Had it really felt so imposing when she first attended as a child? If not for Dicky, her loyal friend and protector, she might not have survived those first few weeks.

Louise parked her bike in the bike-shelter. It looked exactly the same from the outside: weathered corrugated iron providing a makeshift roof. Used only by a male teacher and a couple of older boys it was cloaked in mystery and folklore—an unexploded bomb was rumoured to be buried there, a hand that would come out of the ground and grab your leg if you ventured in after dark. Today, it smelt of cat's pee and Louise made a hurried retreat.

She pressed the doorbell of the headmistress's house that adjoined the school building. Today, the caretaker lived there. He came from the side of the house carrying an armful of logs.

On seeing Louise, he put them down and brushed off his hands.

'Jane Cox? Sorry, I must have lost track of time. I'll get the keys and show you the hall. You should easily get a hundred in there, if not more.'

They walked past classrooms now used for adult education classes. 'You can still sign up for this term if anything interests you.'

'Not sure I would have time for any classes. Maybe creative writing. I used to write stories when I was younger.'

'Shame we give up doing the things that bring us joy. Now, here is the hall.' He switched on the lights as the only natural light came from small windows set high in the wall. There was nothing to distract pupils in assembly or windows to smash during PE.

'A kitchen through there. A couple of tea urns, a bit ancient, but they still work. Have to light the wood-burner to warm them. We're behind the times here. Should invest in something more modern but same old story—not enough funds. What do you think?'

Louise imagined Fitzpatrick standing where the head-mistress once had on the stage at one end of the long hall. It would be better if they set the chairs out in a semi-circle, maybe several rows and Fitzpatrick in the centre—on the same level.

'Would you help set up the chairs?'

'Aye. But they're child size ones, I'm afraid. Is that okay?'

There wasn't much alternative. Louise had no idea how many people would attend. She nodded. 'If we set up for fifty people, could you add rows of chairs if they are needed?'

One job ticked off the list, Louise thought as she cycled back.

Fitzpatrick would be busy with the health official and so she decided to track down the mobile library to discover how much interest there had been in the public meeting. The paths that she and Dicky once took cross-country were hidden to her. If they were still there, she didn't recognise them and so she kept to the road that circled the valley. As she pumped her pedals uphill, a delicious scent of burning peat triggered childhood memories of sitting by the fire with Kara, the sheepdog at her feet. There were a few cottages dotted around and most of them would have fires. Her eyes searched the horizon for Becks farm and that's when she noticed a spiral of smoke.

Louise braked, trying to glimpse the farm through the trees. But it was out of sight. And now she could no longer see the smoke. A rage engulfed her. If squatters were living in Becks farm, she would bloody well throw them out. They might fool others, but she knew exactly where the chimney smoke curled on the horizon; she had watched for it as a child when she hurried home from school, or back up the valley, knowing Ma would be waiting for her with a loving word and a mug of cocoa.

Breathless and sweaty, Louise skidded her bike to a halt. A faint smell of peat smoke hung in the air, but it had infused the valley, giving no clue to its source. She had lost sight of the chimney smoke when she turned into the lane. Now she had reached the farm, Louise felt foolish. It wasn't the farm as she knew it, not with the hardboard lining the perimeter. Becks farm had always been welcoming, the open gates like arms inviting all who passed to enter. Had she wished so badly for the farm to be inhabited—for Ma to be there waiting for her—that she had imagined the chimney smoke?

A magpie cawed. A faraway hum of traffic. The bleating of a lamb. All was still. Now she was here, Louise knew what she had to do. Retrieve the evidence. She examined the Hawthorn bush. It was deep, and the branches looked spiky, entwined around an elm tree, and there, around its roots, an animal had burrowed beneath the hedge, creating a dipped tunnel. Louise searched for a sturdy stick. It wasn't ideal. A spade and pruning shears would have the job done in minutes, but with a bit of effort... She scraped furiously at the soil and whacked the branches until the opening was big enough to crawl through. Twigs scratched her scalp, sharp stones scraped her knees, and her hands stung from a quarrelsome nettle, but she fought her way into the farmyard.

Lying on her back, gasping, Louise caught sight of the wheelbarrow. The scent of fermenting apples tickled her nose. She closed her eyes, cradled by the earth of the farm. They weren't fresh apples. She had imagined what she wanted to believe. Nobody lived on the farm. Inside wallpaper would be peeling off the walls, mice would have the run of the place nibbling the wood, making nests in the armchairs. The farmhouse was as dead as Ma and Pa. She didn't know what was worse, unwelcome intruders making themselves at home, or decay and squalor from years of neglect.

First, she ran to Pa's work barn. It was unlocked, as it had been when she lived here. The day of the accident, when strangers had invaded their home, someone had locked the barn door. Confirmation that Louise was not to be trusted. Inside, little had changed. A worn tractor tyre rested against one wall; in another corner, a rusty plough once pulled by horses – a relic from bygone days. The smell of paraffin and grease brought back memories of Pa, bent over a piece of machinery. His delight when everything fitted back together. 'All it needed was a bit of love and elbow grease,' he would say.

She knew exactly where she had hidden it. The empty oil drum was still there. Louise rolled it to one side, and a spider ran out. But there was nothing beneath the oil drum or the surrounding area. After a good search, she gave up and moved on to the cowshed.

Earth wedged the doors partly open. Unable to shift them, Louise squeezed in sideways. It took a while for her eyes to adjust to the dark. The shed smelt of damp stone and a faint odour from years of housing cattle. A milking pail and three-legged stool were the only evidence that this had once been a milking shed. Someone, Ma probably, had cleared out the barn and scrubbed the flagstones clean.

Louise had hidden the incriminating evidence in Gertrude's stall, beneath the straw where a flagstone was loose. Kurt had said the loose stone was far enough away from where Gertrude stood to cause any harm to her hooves. The day she removed the stone to hide her wicked secret, her hands had been trembling. She'd covered the newspaper-wrapped items with damp soil before replacing the stone. It had been a little raised until she used all of her weight to press it down. Nobody would pay any attention to the loose flagstone. Ma and Pa didn't even know it was loose.

With no cow stalls to define the space, and working in the dark, Louise wasn't sure exactly where to find her hiding place. She worked her way around the walls, feeling each stone as if wiggling teeth to find one loose. There it was. Just a little give. But Louise knew this was the one. If only she had planned this better, she might have brought a screwdriver or some other implement to ease out the stone. Over the years, it had become embedded, and she imagined it to have grown roots that now clung to the farm and shared its pain.

After several attempts, she finally levered the stone up, disturbing an army of woodlice. But there was no newspaper package. Out of desperation, Louise spent the next hour trying different stones, but none of them would give. The letter and Saint Christopher were no longer there.

. . .

Louise barely noticed the three-mile bike ride across the valley as her mind worked through the implications of what she had discovered. It could be innocent; the evidence found and removed by someone clearing the farm and then destroyed without a second thought. *Or* Eddie had got there first. Her stomach dipped; she felt nauseous. Did Eddie have a contact working for him in Thorncrest? Pete? Her legs felt like jelly and her feet slipped from the pedals as she careered down the hill. When a cluster of cottages and the mobile library came into view, Louise squeezed her brakes and willed her brain to focus.

Esther, the librarian, was assisting a couple of small children up the steps into the library when Louise arrived. She left her bike propped up against a dry stone wall and joined the children's grandmother, who was lifting a toddler out of his pushchair.

'There was nothing I loved more than choosing a book from the library when I was a child,' Louise said.

'Wish I could find time to read one myself,' the woman replied. There was something familiar about her.

'I don't read as much as I used to. It helped me escape when things weren't good at home, especially when we had to sit in the air raid shelter,' Louise said.

'From London, are you?'

Louise had spoken again without thinking. 'I spent some time there when I was a nipper.'

The woman peered at Louise. 'Don't I know you?'

'I've not been in the area long.'

Fortunately, they were interrupted by the little girl exclaiming. 'Granny. Granny. Look what I found. Pippi Longstocking.' She held the book aloft. It was indeed a prize. Louise had loved those books herself.

'It gets her learning to read, anyway,' the woman said. 'I'd better help Dylan choose. He's not such a big fan of books.'

When the family left, Louise shared a cuppa from Esther's flask. 'I envy you your job,' she said wistfully. 'Spending all day with books. Helping children discover them.'

'I wouldn't change it for the world.'

'That woman thought she knew me,' Louise said.

'Susan Jeffreys. They have a farm. I think she came from London too. A Land Army girl in the war. A romantic story—well, it is when she tells it. Fell in love with a local farmer's lad and came back to marry him after the war.'

Louise remembered her. The day they made hay. The day that she discovered the loose flagstone with Kurt. Susan had been there.

'Are you here to borrow a book?'

Louise had been staring into space with her mouth open. She gathered herself together. This was no time to fall apart. 'Oh no. Although I would love to. Have you managed to distribute leaflets about the public meeting?'

'I have. I ran out of them within the first week.'

'But you had enough to distribute at all of your stops around the valley?'

'I made sure of it. Don't worry, word of mouth is the way news travels around here. The new reservoir is the main topic of conversation, well, the relocation of the church and graves. It's so sad. I don't think any of us can really believe it, despite growing up knowing what was planned. It was always going to be too soon.'

Louise needed time to recover from the shock of seeing Susan Jeffreys. It was possible Susan had helped Ma Beck clear out the cowshed. They knew each other and if Susan was living on a neighbouring farm… The thought of Susan reading Louise's adolescent letter made her cringe. It would have been harmless if not for the tragic accident, because her words made clear her intention.

Louise's plummet into despair was interrupted by Esther passing her an open packet of ginger biscuits. 'Why not borrow a book, now you're here?'

Clinging on to this thread of normality, Louise scanned the titles; some covers on display, others packed closely together in alphabetical order. Jane Austen: Pride and Prejudice, Emma, Sense and Sensibility. Then, the Brontës.

'I'll need some ID. A birth certificate, or driving license whenever you can drop them in.'

Louise didn't have an identity. She didn't even have wage slips with a National Insurance number. Jane Cox was like the mist on the moors, insubstantial and transient. And yet she felt more like herself than she had in twenty years. If only she could stop time right there, before everyone discovered her true identity. Before Big Jim or one of his hitmen made an appearance.

'Have you chosen one?'

Louise knew without having to think. 'Have you got Little Women?

17

NOVEMBER 1943

Sundays were like a precipice: the void between one week starting and another finishing. They were to be endured. Louise loved the extra time she got to spend with Pa, suffered Sunday school, treasured reading time, and hated homework. But it was Kurt's and Dicky's absence that clouded the day. Outside was dark and dreary.

'Don't think that rain is going to let up,' Pa said, standing at the kitchen door.

'Then close the door and come inside. It won't hurt you to sit still for one minute,' Ma said.

Pa made a face at Louise and she giggled.

'Don't forget, I have eyes in the back of my head,' Ma added.

Pa kissed Ma on the cheek as she washed up. 'I'll take the paper then.'

'That's right. Take the paper and yourself into the living room. I'll make us a brew and a bit of bread pudding. Get that fire stoked up.'

Louise loved those rare moments when the three of them got cosy together around the fire. Pa would take her usual chair, but Louise was happy to sit in a more upright one away from the fire, just to be in his company. Kara was delighted to see Pa, too. She did a little dance, turning circles before Pa patted her head and she settled at his feet with a contented sigh.

'I'm going upstairs to fetch my book,' Louise said. Ma had found her a copy of *Rachel* in a jumble sale.

When Louise came downstairs and opened the door to the living room, Pa was reading something out loud from his newspaper.

'He didn't have much of a life after his wife died. Poor man,' Ma said.

'Poor man? He should have hung.'

'How can you say that, John? He was acquitted of murder.'

'Only because they couldn't find enough evidence.'

'And what if they had hung him and he was innocent?' Ma examined her darning and made another stitch. She noticed Louise. 'Good, you've got your book. Bring that chair closer to the fire, pet. I'll pour the tea.'

'Who are you talking about?'

'A local man accused of murdering his wife in the shop where she worked. They say he hit her with a wheel brace. It was found in the reservoir near where he worked. But he was acquitted and released. Then, this week he was out cycling and got knocked down by a car,' Pa said.

'Do you think someone killed him on purpose? Maybe his wife's angry lover. And … he killed his wife because he discovered her having an affair with … um.'

'You and your overactive imagination. You should write down your stories,' Ma said.

'The death penalty is an incentive not to kill,' Pa said. 'The day we abolish it, we'll have blood on our hands. The world will go crazy thinking it's okay to stick a knife in someone because you don't like the way they look at you.'

'What do you think, Louise?' Ma put down the sock she was mending and looked thoughtfully at her.

Louise blushed, flattered to be asked such an adult question and nervous that her response may seem uninformed. 'I think if someone does something really bad--something evil, like murder--then they should pay the price with their life. A life for a life.'

'And what if an innocent person is found guilty?' Ma said.

'If they are innocent, then they won't be found guilty.'

'If only it were that straightforward. Unfortunately, we sometimes get things wrong. Things are not always what they seem, however convinced we might be,' Ma said.

'Did you say summat about bread pudding?' Pa said.

'I'll get it.' Louise was glad to leave the room and Ma's scrutiny. She felt as though she had failed in some way.

The news story and debate were forgotten when Louise returned with a plate of bread pudding. Thick, raisin encrusted slabs, with a precious sprinkling of sugar. The conversation had turned to Land Army girls. Susan had a family crisis and was returning to London.

'I've asked the WLA for cover, but it would mean offering the girl a room. The hostel's full,' Ma said.

'When will Susan be back at work?' Pa pushed the tobacco down the bowl of his pipe.

'It's hard to say. Her mum is seriously ill. Poor Susan. What do you think? We still have one spare room.'

'Aye. It'll be hard to replace Susan. She's a good'un. A hard worker and no trouble, but we need all the help we can get.'

'I could do more,' Louise said.

'You do plenty, lass. You're going to get a good education and do us proud.' Pa winked at her and struck a match to light the bowl of his pipe.

'She already does that.' Ma smiled lovingly at Louise.

It was a memorable afternoon, the fire crackling, the taste of cinnamon and nutmeg, the smell of Pa's pipe smoke, and Kara's gentle snoring. Ma dropped off to sleep, her fingers still pinching the darning needle. That afternoon, Louise had felt as though she was stepping into adulthood. Leaping the precipice. Tomorrow was Monday—back to school with Dicky—and then helping Kurt on the farm.

Dicky seemed moody as they walked home from school the next day.

'Have you heard from Frank?' Louise said as they ambled up the lane.

'Yes. He doesn't sound like himself. I wish that he'd stayed here. That I was old enough to fight, instead of him.'

'Why would you want to go to war?' Louise remembered Dicky saying he would lie about his age to fight, and a shiver ran down her spine.

'I don't. It's just that Frank is the one with all the ideas about our shop. He belongs here. Ma and Pa miss him more than they would me. I'm not saying that they love him more. It's just that Frank would get Ma all excited about the future. How he would make Braithwaite's a name—a chain of shops all over the country. Like Woolworths, but better. Pa has no ambition—but Frank... I've not seen Ma's face light up since Frank's been gone.'

'I'm sure she loves you both the same. You'll make her proud when you're a renowned carpenter building a magnificent village of timber houses, never mind one crumby shop. In fact, you can build her shop and anything else she wants to see in that village. And you can build a castle for me.'

'I will. Can we hang out today like we used to when we were kids?'

'Okay. We haven't visited the Mill House for ages.'

They cut across the fields. Now Louise was older, Ma no longer insisted on her reporting home first, so long as she was home before dark.

'Ma and Pa were talking about the man who was accused of murdering his wife,' Louise said, as she followed Dicky along a footpath bordering a field.

'Aye. I saw it in the paper.'

'Do you think people should be hanged when they've murdered someone?'

'An eye for an eye. A tooth for a tooth. Isn't that what it says in the bible?' Dicky said.

'Yes. But what if a person is hanged and they're innocent?'

'What if they are guilty and set free, then they kill again?'

'Which one is worse?'

'Don't know and don't care. Hundreds of our men are being killed every day in Leros. These are men—not much older than me. They didn't sign up, thinking they would be blown apart. Arms and legs severed. Who cares if they hang a murderer?'

Louise felt the age difference between her and Dicky. He was only one year her senior, but there were times like today when it seemed more.

Dicky stopped walking and looked over his shoulder. 'Stay there. The water's risen so we can't jump the stream. I'll find a log or summat.'

The stream was usually just a trickle of water, often entirely dry in the summer. Today, the water gushed with force, heading down the valley into the river below. Dicky tested the weight of logs, searching for a suitable bridge.

'I know you want to do more to help the war effort, Dicky. I feel the same way. Just because we have a prisoner of war working on the farm, it doesn't mean I'm less patriotic than you.'

Dicky looked up and then lobbed a log across the stream.

'Ma and Pa were talking about taking on a new Land Army girl because Susan has to go home to look after her mum or something. Anyway, I said to Pa I wanted to do more, and he said I could have an allotment.'

She waited for Dicky's approval. He seemed to give her words some thought, then he smiled. 'Good for you.' He held out his arms and lifted Louise into them.

'What about the log?'

'It's okay. I've got you.'

And she felt safe in his arms. No longer the scrawny little boy she played rough and tumble with. Louise turned her face into his chest, his scent so familiar. She could feel the beat of his heart. As her lips grazed his shirt, she pursed them in a secret kiss. He held her for three heartbeats before setting her down on the other side of the stream.

'Your feet are wet,' she said.

He smiled. A sad wistful smile, as though he knew something that she didn't. 'Come on, Land Army girl.'

Louise followed him, placing her feet in the prints he left behind. Her heart ached for it to be like old times, but they had both changed.

'Do you remember the time we skipped school and danced to the polyphon music?' she said to his back.

He stopped walking, then continued. 'He was a war hero, Horatio Beacon. Did you know that?'

'Yes,' Louise sighed. That's all Dicky wanted to talk about, the war. This one and the one before. He probably didn't remember their dance, how they had almost kissed. Dicky was her best friend, but he had grown up, and the affection he'd declared as a boy now seemed forgotten. It was time she grew up too.

18

NOVEMBER 1943

The new Land Army girl, Joan, was in the spare room unpacking her things when Louise got home from school.

'Shall I go up and ask if Joan wants a brew?' Louise was tired of waiting for her to come downstairs and say hello.

'She had one before she went up, and that was a short time ago. Go on up and say hello. She won't mind being disturbed. I dare say she has brothers and sisters back home. I'll make a lamb stew with a scrag end I got in exchange for milk and eggs.'

Louise thundered up the stairs, then stopped on the landing. Joan was eighteen. Maybe she should have changed out of her school uniform. But everything that she had was practical —mostly handed down from her boy cousins and adapted to fit. Louise untied her plaits and then tried to run her fingers through her hair, but it was too thick and tangled. Instead, she turned her head upside down, intending to throw it back, creating a cascade of waves.

'Sorry, I didn't see you there.'

Louise unfolded to see a pair of shapely legs in nylons. How had Joan purloined nylons during the war? 'I felt faint, so I put my head between my legs.'

'Oh no. You'd better sit down.' Joan took her hand and led her into the spare room. 'Hold on, I'll make some space. I brought far too much, but it won't all be farm work. There are bound to be dances, and I didn't want to look like a country bumpkin. You're from London, so you'll know what I mean.'

Louise forgot she was meant to feel faint. Her mouth fell open as she took in the array of clothes and underwear spread across the bed. Pink camiknickers! Silk. With creamy lace trim. Joan snatched them up and then a suspender belt. 'Sorry about that. I'll tidy up a bit. Wasn't expecting a visitor.'

'I thought you had to wear a Land Army uniform.' Louise said, as Joan put away her clothes.

'We do. But not *all* the time. Please tell me there are dances. And there must be some men left behind. Farm boys don't have to go to war.' She was standing at the tallboy, where Ma had rested a mirror, raking through a cosmetics bag. 'I had an American boyfriend in London.' She winked at Louise in the mirror. 'He wasn't much to look at, but a catch, if you know what I mean?' Joan swivelled and presented a stick of lipstick. 'Want to try it?'

Louise wasn't sure how to position her lips for Joan to slick them with lipstick. Her attempts made Joan giggle.

'Like this,' Joan demonstrated. 'You have good skin and pretty eyes. Do you have a boyfriend?'

'Not really.' A few months ago, Louise secretly thought of Dicky as her boyfriend. He had promised to marry her one day but things were different now. He didn't think of her like that. She had to stop hoping he would notice she had grown up and turn her attention elsewhere. Joan was asking if there was someone special and Louise realised there was.

'There's someone I like.' Louise blushed. It was the first time she had admitted to having a crush on gorgeous Kurt.

'Then we have to get him to notice you. Let me do your hair.' Joan twisted Louise's hair into rags and pin curls. Then, she tied a headscarf over it. 'In the morning, brush it out and pin back the sides like this.' She demonstrated on her own hair.

A cow bell sounded from downstairs. 'That'll be Ma telling us tea is ready. We've got lamb stew.'

'That's the best thing about living on a farm. Good grub. Will Ma mind you wearing lipstick?'

'I don't know.' Even as she said it, Louise started rubbing it off with the back of her hand.

'Tell you what. You can have this little bit. If you're going to wow your boyfriend with those curls, it would be a shame not to make the most of your pretty face.' Joan handed Louise a lipstick that was almost flat in its silver case. *Hot Lips.*

The next morning at breakfast, Ma served Louise a boiled egg and then did a double-take. 'What's Miss Rita Hayworth doing in my kitchen? Where's my Louise?'

'Do I really look like Rita Hayworth?'

'Prettier. But I hope you're not going to go silly on me. Start behaving like those London farm girls. We all have a job to do, fighting for victory—whether that be on the battlefield or the farm. There's no time for frippery. Not while good men and boys are giving their lives for England. Now, eat that egg and get off to school. I dare say your friend Dicky will appreciate your efforts—at thirteen you're bound to get romantic notions—but keep your head, lass.'

Louise blushed at the mention of Dicky. She didn't want him, or Ma, thinking she had done this to attract his attention.

If Dicky thought she was so desperate for him to like her that she had put her hair in rags, she would die of embarrassment.

'Where is Joan working today?' Louise asked, hauling her satchel over one arm.

'Pa took her out to help plough the fields. If she can handle the tractor, it will cut down some of his work.'

Dicky was unbearable on the way home from school: Kicking stones. Mumbling into his scarf. Slouching. He didn't mention Louise's new hairstyle. As they neared the farm, Louise stopped to search her bag for the nub of lipstick.

'Why are you so cross today, Dicky?'

'I'm not. It's just everything stinks.'

Louise closed her fingers around the lipstick. She was desperate to find Joan and Kurt—to show off her new look, but Dicky was her best friend and when he was miserable, she suffered too. 'What's going on?'

'Me Mam was crying last night, 'cos Frank hasn't written for some while and she's scared summat has happened to him. You've gone all girly, and I spilt ink over my homework before I handed it in, so now I've got to do it again.'

'What do you mean, I've gone all girly?' Louise tossed her curls, although they had flattened somewhat in the damp air.

Dicky scowled. 'Is that the most important thing I just said? Girly! Fussing with your hair instead of listening to me.'

'I heard what you said. You spilt ink on your homework and your mum is worried about Frank.' She rolled the lipstick between her fingers. 'Do you like my hair?'

'No.'

'Fine. Well, if you want to be sulky, that's up to you. I'm guessing you don't want to hang out if you've got to redo your homework?' Louise widened her mouth and applied the lipstick as Joan had taught her. She pressed her lips together. 'See you at school tomorrow?'

'You look like a tart with that muck on yer face.'

'Dicky!' He had never spoken to her unkindly before. It felt like a slap across her face. 'That's a horrid thing to say.'

'I'm sorry.' He reached out to touch her hair, but she stepped away. 'You don't need makeup to look pretty.' He sighed. 'Everything is going wrong today. Let's hang out in the Mill house.'

'No, thanks. I don't have time. Sorry about your brother and everything, Dicky, but I've got work to do on the farm.'

Joan came out into the yard, wearing her Land Army gear —a knotted headscarf covering her hair. 'Are you going to introduce me to your *friend*, Louise?'

Dicky buried his hands in his pockets. 'I'd better be off. Nice to meet you.'

Joan watched him amble along the lane. 'Hope I didn't interrupt anything.'

'No. We had already said goodbye. How did you get on today?'

Joan linked her arm with Louise's and they walked to the farmhouse. 'I'll drop my school bag and then I've got to milk the cows and see to my chickens.'

'I'll take it. I'm finished for now. I'll see if Ma's got a brew on the stove and wash this filth off. I drove a tractor today. Who'd have thought? Women can do anything a man can. The war has proved it. Let's see what happens after the war. Do you think women will be allowed to carry on flying planes and the like?'

'Will the war ever be over? What happens if we don't win?'

'What kind of talk is that?' Joan shook her head.

'Did you meet Kurt?' Louise said, but Joan was out of earshot. The farmhouse door banged shut behind her.

Louise headed straight for the cowshed. Outside the door, she pressed her lips together to refresh the lipstick and teased her curls. Why couldn't she have bumped into Kurt this morning when she still looked like Rita Hayward?

If Dicky's response to her new look had been flat, Kurt's was the opposite. 'I love your hair like that. Very pretty.' He gazed at her and Louise's knees wobbled.

She tried to act nonchalant. 'Oh that. Joan set my hair in rags and pins last night. Have you met Joan?'

'The new Land Army girl?' Kurt moved over to make room for her on the milking stool next to him. 'We said hello.'

'What did you think?'

Kurt rubbed the flank of his cow and started to milk. 'She seemed nice.'

Not glamorous. Or gorgeous. Had he noticed how stunning Joan was?

'Do you think she's attractive?' Louise kept her eyes on the task of cleaning her cow's udder.

'I didn't notice. So long as she works hard on the farm and helps Mr Beck. He does too much for a man of his age. I do all that I can, but they need more farmhands. It is not good for his heart.'

Louise smiled. Kurt had not noticed Joan—but he had noticed *her* hair. *It's pretty,* he had said.

19

MONDAY OCTOBER 11TH 1965

'The health official's arrived. Dolly Lombard. We've put her in the West wing and her team in the dorms. Two of them women, so we'll have room mates. Fitzpatrick's been in a meeting with her all afternoon,' Fliss said, when Louise arrived back from visiting the community library.

Louise raised her eyebrows. 'Good for her. I couldn't get him to concentrate that long on anything that wasn't to do with engineering for.'

'I think he's a bit scared of her. She's a force to be reckoned with, that's for sure.'

The phone rang and Louise mouthed, 'See you later.'

'Hold on.' Fliss put one hand over the receiver. 'It's for you, Jane. Richard Braithwaite.'

It was as though she had summoned him with her thoughts. He had been on her mind all day. But now was not the time to discuss the Braithwaite Simms enterprise.

'Jane?' Fliss raised her eyebrows and nodded at the phone receiver on her desk.

Louise picked it up. 'Richard.' She tried to sound neutral. Professional.

'Jane Cox?'

No, it's me, Louise Pearson, she wanted to shout. One week had passed since the day she threw water over him and in that time, they hadn't met since. Louise cradled the phone as if she were hugging him. 'How can I help you, Richard—Mr Braithwaite?'

'We've found a home for the polyphons. I can arrange for them to be moved tomorrow if that's okay.'

'Fantastic!' He had found a solution. There was no need for him to go into partnership with the Simms.

'Yes. I visited Beaky this morning. He's overjoyed. His collection will be on display for everyone from Thorncrest and surrounding areas to enjoy. He's a legend in these parts. Now he can rest, knowing his wishes have been met. Those polyphons are like his children.'

'Where are they going?'

'The new premises for my shop. Well, department store. Braithwaite and Simms.'

'Oh.' Her voice was small. 'I'm surprised. Kaye suggested you might not continue with the shop.'

'I wasn't sure. But I am now. Anyway, you wanted them moved.'

'We can hold off if you want to find somewhere else.'

'No. It's okay. I can have them moved tomorrow.'

'Tomorrow?' There was nothing she could say to stop him. 'Are you sure? I mean, if you don't really want to open another shop. We wouldn't want you to feel pressurised into something you didn't want.'

'Do you want them moved or not?' he snapped, irritated now.

'Yes. Thank you.'

'Okay. I'll meet you at Beaky's cottage midday tomorrow.'

It took Louise ages to get comfortable on the lumpy mattress of her bunk bed that night. The nylon sleeping bag and thin pillow with sharp brown feathers piercing its surface had not bothered her before, but tonight she could not settle. Fiona's father must have secured the new premises, knowing Richard would eventually cave in and accept his proposal. Mr Simms was no different to Big Jim, a man who was used to getting his own way—a man who assumed everyone would fall in with his plans—and acted as though they already had, regardless. Richard was going to marry Fiona. Louise had only just found him and now she was going to lose him all over again.

Louise bashed her pillow, trying to make it more comfortable.

How was she going to face Richard tomorrow and keep up an act? If he recognised her, she would come clean. He would keep her secret. Maybe it wasn't too late to stop him from marrying Fiona. Thoughts went round and round in her head.

She must have dropped off to sleep because she dreamed that Ma and Pa were still living at Becks farm. She was talking to them about a dance for the people that had passed away, using the polyphons for music. Then, she realised they were both dead, and woke with a jolt. Two women were giggling and crashing clumsily around the dormitory. The light went on.

Louise sat up in bed. 'Hello?'

'Sorry. Forgot anyone else was sleeping here. Where's the bathroom?'

By morning, Louise felt as though she had barely slept. The two women were asleep, one of them snoring noisily. She was tempted to crash around as they had, but instead crept out of the dorm carrying her shoes.

The key to Horatio Beacon's property had been in Louise's pocket all morning. A Chub key. She traced its edges with her thumb and thought of their old friend, the polyphon man. Visits from children must have plagued him over the years. They had to do a few jobs in exchange for time in the museum, but he didn't hang around telling them not to touch or boring them with lectures. It was as if he understood the magic of being in that room, with the freedom to explore and play tunes as they pleased. Poor old Beaky. She would have loved to meet him in the nursing home, to say thank you.

'You're early,' Richard approached from the opposite direction than the one she expected and Louise, lost in the past, and with no time to prepare herself for their meeting, was tilted off-balance.

She felt his presence behind her, a warm and familiar energy, but could not turn until she had arranged her face. There was nothing she could do about the love and passion in her eyes—unless she kept them closed.

'Good morning, Mr Braithwaite.' Louise spoke briskly. She extended her hand and then withdrew it, afraid of physical contact. 'Here's the key. Would you like to open up?'

'I can't wait. Honestly, I've been like a kid on Christmas morning. I've not been in this place for what must be twenty years.'

Dicky had not gone back. The last time they visited had been together. Louise took a long, juddery breath.

'How are you going to move them?' she asked, as Richard put the key in the lock.

'One of my delivery men is coming by. I asked him to

arrive at one. I wanted a bit of time here by myself first.' The door eased open to a dank, dark hallway.

'Oh, did you want to be alone?' The disappointment was crushing.

'No. I'd like to show you what all the fuss is about. We'll have to manage without artificial light. Careful of the pigeon droppings.'

Louise followed Richard along the hallway. Cobwebs hung like curtain swags from the wall mounted parraffin lamps, and clung to the picture rail. 'Alright?' He looked over his shoulder at Louise and held out a hand.

A flutter of wings at the top of the stairs startled her, and she grabbed hold of his outstretched hand. He chuckled. 'Old Beaky, keeping an eye on us.'

'Its in here.' A round brass door handle. Richard squeezed her hand, sending a current of electricity up her arm, and then let go to push open the door.

Light from long sash windows flooded the room. Sheets covered the polyphons, which stood like stately ghosts. It was quiet and still in that room. No obvious decay. Dust swirled up from the flagstones as they crept reverently between the machines.

'Let's inspect them one at a time,' Richard said. To Louise, he sounded like Dicky when he was pretending to be a grown-up, *Ah Miss Jones, a cup of tea, please.*

Together, they lifted the first sheet to reveal one of the tall polyphons resembling a grandfather clock. The gloss of burnished wood had not tarnished. 'It may have been these beautiful machines that led to my love of wood.'

'Are you a carpenter?' Louise asked. Her voice was hoarse. How could he not know it was her?

Richard sighed. 'No. I just love the look and feel of wood.'

'Did you always want to work in retail? I mean, a department store sounds impressive, but is that what you dreamed of doing as a child?'

'I had other ideas then. But you grow up. Life has other things in store for you and it's easier to go with the flow than try to resist. I think you'd agree, given the grief I caused, refusing to sign a contract until I knew the reservoir plan had been confirmed.'

'And now you have,' Louise whispered.

'Aye. All signed. You can open the dam! Let's look at another one. I'll show you how they work when I find one that I can start.'

Louise followed Richard as he uncovered one polyphon after another, marvelling at the inlaid wood, laughing at the song titles. He showed her how the disk turned, the bumps and dents playing a tune. 'My Darling Clementine' was the song he used to demonstrate. Louise stood so close to Richard she imagined the raised hairs on her arm tickling his skin. He was so engrossed in rediscovering the polyphons, he did not look directly at her, and Louise avoided eye contact. It was as though the clock had been turned back. If only it had, she would tell him she loved him. Would never let him go.

A lorry pulled up outside. 'That'll be Dave.' He left her alone in the museum whilst he went out to greet him.

It was good to be alone with her thoughts—and disappointment. The shrouds had all been removed. Just Louise and her ghosts. The maple box she remembered from her last visit was exactly where it had been before. Outside the window, Richard was busy inside the lorry with Dave. And so, she wound it up and as the disc turned, she closed her eyes.

The waltz. Louise wrapped her arms around herself and swayed to the music. She imagined dancing with Richard. She could summon the feeling of his hand in hers as if he were there.

And then he was. She opened her eyes to find him staring at her across the room. It felt as though a lightning bolt shot through her. All the lies and deceit fell away. They faced one another soul to soul. Finally complete. She stepped towards him. Reached out her hands. The air around them was electric. Neither of them spoke, and yet so much passed between them.

'I'll take this one first.' Dave broke the spell.

Richard looked dazed as if woken from a deep sleep. 'Okay. Thank you.'

His eyes lingered a while on Louise. He smiled, kind of apologetically. Then, it was all action; the men heaving the polyphons across the room, wrapping them up in sheets and packing foam.

Louise felt superfluous. She couldn't be around Richard and act normal. Why did Dave have to interrupt them at that moment?

She went outside. Richard was in the back of the lorry.

'I'd better be getting back,' Louise called up to him.

He jumped down. 'Meet me tomorrow. I'll show you where we are displaying them in Ripley. You didn't get a proper look before we were interrupted. We could continue where we left off?'

His meaning was obvious. There was so much they needed to say to one another. Why hadn't he replied to her letters? Was he really going to marry Fiona? It wasn't too late for him to change his mind. They would find somewhere else for the polyphons. She could do a fundraiser. Get the community on board.

'What time tomorrow?'

'First thing. No, make it eleven thirty. There's something I have to do first.' His eyes held hers.

Louise smiled. 'I'll see you tomorrow.'

She couldn't stop smiling as she cycled back to High House. He recognised her. Reunited at last. There was so much she wanted to tell him. How she had never stopped loving him. That she was sorry for everything—how she had behaved as a child, hurting him. 'Oh, Dicky. My darling sweet friend,' she murmured to the wind.

The only thing that could destroy her joy was Eddie. She wanted to believe he had left her alone to start a new life, but a sickening feeling in her stomach told her otherwise. Reality seeped in, as if mocking her. *She didn't deserve to be happy.*

If Big Jim thought she had done a runner with five hundred pounds of his money, he would have found her by now. His silence was scary. It meant he had other plans. She could wait for Eddie and the Mob like a sitting target or she could get one step ahead.

Back in High House, Louise found an empty office upstairs and closed the door. Gloria would be working alone in Tin Pan Alley, maybe with a cleaner or two, but nobody who knew Big Jim or Eddie. Please let Gloria answer, she prayed as the phone rang. She picked up on the second trill.

'Hello, darling. How's your grandma? Shame, her being taken ill sudden like that. Eddie told us, so we could arrange cover. When are you planning to come back?'

'I'm not sure,' Louise said, thrown by Gloria's upbeat voice. 'Have you seen much of Eddie? He's never home when I try calling him.' A lie, but she needed to find out what was going on.

'I thought he'd gone up to Yorkshire to bring you back. Didn't he tell you?'

Louise went cold. She covered her mouth. 'Um. Yes. Of course, he did.' She tried to slow her breath. 'I just wasn't sure when he was planning to get here. My grandma's still with us. Everyone else, okay? Jim and Alice?'

'Yes. As far as I know. Did you want me to leave a message for Jim?'

'No. Please don't bother him. He's a busy man. So long as everything's okay there. I'll be back soon.'

When Louise put down the receiver, she felt light-headed. Eddie knew her whereabouts. He would come for her, that was certain. And if he didn't, the Mob would. There was nowhere she could run. High House offered some protection as she was rarely alone. But she couldn't meet Richard tomorrow. His association with her would make him a target for Eddie and the Mob. He had to be kept out of the Mob's business at all costs.

20

WEDNESDAY 13TH OCTOBER 1965

Fitzpatrick sent his apologies for their ten o'clock meeting. Dolly Lombard seemed to demand his full attention. He wouldn't be happy with that arrangement. Louise was getting worried; the public meeting was on Friday and she hadn't received an update from him in days. Pete was out somewhere, and if any of the other contractors or Dolly's team were in High House, Louise hadn't seen them. She found Fliss in reception.

'What's this Dolly Lombard like?' she said, making herself comfortable in a chair that was intended for visitors waiting to see one of the team.

'Smokes like a chimney and drinks like a navvy. I'm surprised you didn't hear her in the bar last night.'

'I went to bed early. A lot on my mind with the public meeting on Friday. I've not seen Fitzpatrick since Monday and I was hoping to get some reassurance that all the questions raised by the Church Committee had been answered.' Louise stretched out in the armchair, which was surprisingly comfortable. Two nights with little sleep meant she was exhausted and could happily take a nap if a kind person threw a blanket over her.

Fliss wrinkled her nose. 'Going by the messages left for you, I don't think so.'

Louise cast aside her fantasy of resting. 'Okay. Hit me with them.'

Fliss rifled through some papers on her desk. 'Ah. Here it is. Reverend Cummins phoned. Nobody has been in contact about moving the stained glass windows and he wants to know when the church has to be vacated so he can arrange the last service. I said I would ask you to get back to him before the public meeting. He doesn't want any surprises on Friday.'

'I know the feeling. Have *you* heard anything about the relocation of the graveyard, Fliss?'

'Only that it's taking up all of Fitzpatrick's time.'

'You mean Dolly Lombard has. I need to talk to him too! It's a nightmare.' Louise covered her face. 'I'll visit Reverend Cummins today and do my best to reassure him, but it will be tricky because he knows as much as I do. Are we expecting Pete back in the office today?'

Fliss ran her finger along the entries in a big diary. 'He was meeting with the site manager for the new church this morning, then doing safety checks for the dam.'

'What do we know about Pete Murray?' Louise frowned.

'What do you mean?'

'Did Fitzpatrick get references for him? Where's he training as an engineer? Has there been any communication with his college?'

'No idea. You would have to ask Fitzpatrick. Why? Has he done something wrong?'

Louise shook her head. 'No. It's just that his employment here was very casual for a man with so much responsibility. I'm probably being overcautious. I mean, I'm in the same position turning up here asking for casual work and next thing I'm a public relations manager! Nobody could be less qualified or experienced than me. Yet here I am.' Louise sighed.

Yesterday she felt elated, daring to dream. Today reality was driving her, quite possibly, over a cliff edge. Best kill dead any lingering hope of a happily ever after. 'Richard Braithwaite was going to pick me up at eleven this morning. He wanted to show me where the polyphon collection was being displayed. Would you mind phoning him to say I can't make it? There's too much to do before the public meeting.'

'Okay.' Fliss made a note.

'And if you see or hear from Fitzpatrick, *please* make sure he talks to me, asap.'

Louise set off with a heavy heart. Richard would be disappointed, but not as disappointed as her. It was no good thinking of what might have been; it was for the best. She sighed. There was work to do. She pedalled faster.

First, she would go to the new build in the hope of finding Pete. He would have some up-to-date information. It had been an indulgence to hide away in her dormitory last night. She should have met Dolly Lombard and talked to Fitzpatrick.

Then, she would go on to the church or vicarage in search of Reverend Cummins. Keep focused on work. Try to forget about Richard. The look of recognition in his eyes. The warmth that flooded her heart. If Dave had not interrupted them, would they have embraced? It felt as though they had and yet they hadn't touched. He would be disappointed to receive Fliss's call. He would think she didn't care. It was for the best. If Eddie thought she was romantically involved with Richard, or sharing information about him and the Mob, it would get back to Big Jim. And Big Jim would have no hesitation in arranging what he called, 'damage limitation.'

Louise slowed her bike as she approached the building site.

The church looked almost complete now the roof was on. There were no builders today and so Louise left her bike on its side and stepped carefully around puddles to take a closer look. It could have been anything: a hostel, a homeless shelter, a Quaker meeting house. It was going to be hard persuading Reverend Cummins that it was a suitable replacement for Thorncrest Church.

A car and a white van were parked alongside the Portakabin, no motorbike. Louise walked up the steps to the office door and knocked. When there was no reply, she opened the door. The site manager was alone and on the telephone. He motioned for Louise to sit down.

'It's my lucky day,' he said, when the call ended.

Louise ignored his suggestive leer. 'Good news?'

'No. Having a visit from an attractive young lady.' He clicked his tongue.

Louise stood up. 'Well, I won't keep you long. I'm here to get an update for Mr Fitzpatrick, ahead of the public meeting.'

'No need. The boss has asked me to talk at the meeting. Friday, right?'

Louise thought it a terrible idea. But if that's what Fitzpatrick wanted … soon she would be gone. With Eddie on her trail, she had little choice.

'There was something else,' she said. 'The contractors employed to work on this project. Bellamy Brothers. Did you contract with them or was it the Corporation? Only, I can't find the paperwork and needed to clear something up about paying them.'

'The Corporation. I work with whoever I'm told. They were only here for a couple of days. Decent blokes. Don't believe all the rumours.'

'What rumours?' Louise *knew* there was something dodgy

about the Bellamy Brothers. Why else would Eddie know them?

'Quality Street gang. Been a bit naughty—the brothers, not the men working here. Well, not as far as I know. Friends of the Krays. As I said, you can't believe everything you hear.'

'No. Of course not. Well, thank you, mister…'

'Geoff. You're welcome. A pretty girl to brighten my day. Can't complain. Maybe next time you'll let me take you out to lunch or for a drink?'

Louise barely heard. They were there for her. She had to get away before it was too late. But where? There was nowhere she could hide. 'Okay. See you at the meeting,' she mumbled as she walked out of the office in a daze.

21

FRIDAY 15TH OCTOBER 1965

Louise stood at the door, greeting everyone as they arrived for the public meeting. Fitzpatrick, Dolly Lombard, Geoff––the site manager, and Pete were already in the hall preparing for the meeting and, as Fitzpatrick hadn't asked Louise to join them, she concentrated on practical arrangements.

The leaflet drops and canvassing had paid off. It looked as though everyone from Thorncrest and the surrounding area had congregated in the school that evening.

She spotted Esther, and a little further back, Richard. Her palms became sweaty at the sight of him and her heart beat a little faster. Louise tried to focus all her attention on Reverend Cummins and Kaye White, who had arrived together, but Richard's presence was a force field attracting her energy.

'I have high expectations of this evening,' the Reverend said, clasping his hands together.

Louise hadn't visited him as planned. She had left Geoff's Portakabin to return to High House, where she spent the rest of that day and the next in a whirl, planning her next move.

The Outer Hebrides? A remote island in the Shetlands? Would she be more or less conspicuous living on an island with few inhabitants? Foula was Britain's most remote, inhabited island. It had taken several phone calls to find out how she would travel and how much it would cost. Too much. And so, two days had passed when she should have been preparing for the meeting.

The Reverend's face was rosy from the wind, and his eyes glistened. Louise smiled. 'I hope you're not disappointed. We're all learning as we go. Every reservoir project is different, each with its own challenges, as I'm sure Mr Fitzpatrick will explain. But hopefully, you'll get answers to all your questions.'

Next was Esther, the librarian, with her lovely husband, Bill. Louise thanked her for promoting the event. And then there was Richard. She watched his hands as they reached for the information sheets. His nails were as jagged as they had been when he was a kid, a deep scratch on his right index finger. She resisted the temptation to place her hand over his and instead met his eyes.

'I'm sorry I couldn't meet you. I wanted to, but there was too much to do preparing for this meeting.'

He smiled, looking up through long dark lashes. 'Fliss said. It's okay.'

People were squeezing past without an information sheet or a personal greeting. 'Catch you later?' she said.

He nodded and Louise watched him walk away, reluctant to turn her attention to the next guest. At least Fiona wasn't with him. Louise hoped she was too busy to join them. Three more rows of chairs were required, which Jim the caretaker provided with no need for direction. Louise hoped that the rest of the meeting would go as smoothly.

Everyone was seated. Fitzpatrick, Dolly Lombard, Geoff,

and Pete were facing the audience from behind a table. It wasn't what she had planned. The point of having chairs in a horseshoe rather than facing the stage was to create a feeling of informality and intimacy. It was too late now. Louise settled into a seat in the back row.

'Testing 1 2 3.' Fitzpatrick spoke into a microphone. A screech of feedback. She could hear snatches of private conversation between him and Dolly. Louise covered her face, wishing she were somewhere else.

'Jane Cox?' Fitzpatrick was scanning the room. Could she drop to her haunches and hide? 'Ah, there you are. We need you up here.' Everyone turned to see who Fitzpatrick was addressing. 'Quick. Quick.'

She sighed and made her way to the front of the room. Voices hushed as she neared the makeshift stage.

'If you could introduce us and manage questions and answers. That kind of thing.' Fitzpatrick smiled and passed the microphone to her.

Louise took a deep breath. The room fell silent. Heavy with anticipation. 'Welcome everyone. It's good to see so many of you here today.' Richard beamed at her from the front row, and she basked in the warmth of his smile. She went on to introduce the panel.

So far, all was going well. The audience seemed appreciative that the chief engineer, health official, and site manager were present to give an update and answer questions. Richard winked and for a moment, she lost concentration. 'Um, yes. So, first I'll ask Sean Fitzpatrick to give an overview of the project.'

Fitzpatrick stood up and cleared his throat. 'We're on track for a trial flooding of the reservoir this year. What this means is …' Fitzpatrick started by reading an explanation of why a trial flood was necessary, but then abandoned his notes to explain the mechanics. The audience started to fidget.

Reverend Cummins raised his hand and Louise interrupted Fitzpatrick's monologue. 'We have a question. Reverend Cummins?'

'I would like to know when the church needs to be vacated so we can schedule the last service,' the vicar said.

'We're on schedule, so Thorncrest Church will be closed to the public from the first of November.'

Louise took the microphone from Fitzpatrick. 'Thank you, Mr Fitzpatrick. Will that give you sufficient time, Reverend Cummins?'

'We'll manage. Does that mean the new church will be ready before Christmas?'

Louise smiled. She was almost enjoying herself. It was like being a TV presenter. 'As the site manager is here, I'll ask Geoff Brown to answer that question. Mr Brown?'

She stole a glance at Richard. His eyes were on Geoff, but as if sensing her attention, he shifted his gaze to meet hers and smiled. They had eaten school dinners in this hall. Dicky on the boys' table, Louise on the girls'. Then, as now, she wanted to be sitting with him. Geoff was speaking and so Louise tuned back in.

'She's pretty much finished. Should be ready for you by mid-November.'

'How's that possible? The fixtures and fittings haven't been transferred from the existing church. The stained glass windows need to be removed by specialists. We've been telling you this for weeks.'

Geoff shrugged and held up his hands. 'Nobody said anything about stained glass windows. If you want them fitted, we'll have to knock down the walls and start again.' He gave a half laugh. A couple of people joined in, thinking it was a joke until they sensed a change in mood.

'What about the gas lights?' Kaye said.

'Have you seen how high the ceiling is in the new build? You can hang them, but you'll need really long chains,' Geoff said.

Louise glared at Fitzpatrick, willing him to say something that would restore peace in the room. Murmurs of dissatisfaction were building like rolling thunder.

In the back row, Fiona Simms stood up. Louise hadn't noticed her earlier. 'So, you're telling us that despite our stipulations, which were shared with you before work started, the most precious artefacts from Thorncrest Church will not be transferred to the replacement church?'

Louise took the microphone. 'Thank you, Fiona Simms. I'm sure we can sort out this misunderstanding. Mr Fitzpatrick?'

Fitzpatrick went a deathly shade of pale. He loosened the collar of his shirt. 'Of course, Miss Simms. A misunderstanding. I'm certain the architect was given a brief which made that stipulation clear. Jane Cox will look into this and we'll get back to the church committee as soon as possible.'

Louise felt sick. She looked at Richard, hoping to draw some comfort from his friendship, but his eyes were dark and stormy. His jaw clenched.

Please God, let Fitzpatrick be right. They would have to make things right. She tried to appear in control by nodding enthusiastically. 'Yes. Of course. This seems like a good time to introduce Dolly Lombard, who is advising us on the relocation of the cemetery.' Her upbeat voice did nothing to ease the tension.

'Surely, it will be alongside the new church,' Fiona said.

Why didn't the wretched woman sit down? The audience

twisted in their seats to face Fiona and Louise felt the shift in power. Richard crossed his arms and nodded in agreement.

'No. Not possible.' Dolly Lombard barked. 'The new cemetery must be a sufficient distance from the reservoir to avoid the contamination of drinking water. The new church is far too close to the perimeter.'

The room erupted with angry voices. None of this was Louise's fault, and yet she felt responsible. She daren't look at Richard now; he would be furious. Reverend Cummins nodded at Louise, indicating he wanted to use the microphone. Fitzpatrick looked as though the wind had been knocked out of him. There was nothing the Reverend could say to make matters worse and so Louise handed it to him.

The Reverend stood up. 'This is an emotional time for us all, but I'm sure with God's good grace we will find a new spiritual home and a resting place for those we have laid to rest in the existing cemetery. There will be a last service in which we can give thanks for Thorncrest Church, which has served many generations of families from this valley. We will announce the date as soon as possible. Now, let us be calm and respectful by allowing Mr Fitzpatrick and his team to finish updating us.'

The Reverend sat down and the room fell silent.

Fitzpatrick took the microphone.'Thank you, Reverend Cummins. We will do our outmost to resolve all the issues raised here today. Sadly, the location of the cemetery is non-negotiable for health reasons.'

If she had concentrated on her job instead of wasting time researching remote islands, they would have been better prepared. Why hadn't she noticed the new build would not accommodate the existing fixtures and fittings?

A distance separated them but she could feel the heat of Richard's burning rage. *We'll put things right*, she wanted to say.

But in truth, it might be too late. Their beloved church and the resting place of loved ones would soon be underwater and in its place a characterless monstrosity posing as a modern church, and a cemetery miles from anywhere.

Louise was about to take the microphone from Fitzpatrick to thank everyone for coming when he said, 'To end on a positive note.'

Oh, thank God, there was something positive. Louise had no idea what that might be. She smiled up at Fitzpatrick, mentally blessing him.

'The dimensions of the reservoir will be confirmed by the end of October. I know some of you have been eagerly awaiting this news. A team of experts will calculate the contours and, through some complicated formulas, estimate the volume of water needed. So, expect to see markers go up around the valley, in the last week of October, marking the perimeter of the reservoir.'

Her stomach plummeted through the floor. She wished she could follow it. Richard would hate her. She had lied to him and there was no way she could put it in a good light. Louise's hand shook as she took the microphone to close the meeting. All she could say was, 'Thank you for coming.'

Louise kept her head down on the pretence of gathering the water glasses. She felt the fire of Richard's accusatory look and flushed. When she summoned the courage to look at him, his seat was empty.

'An absolute, bloody disaster,' Fitzpatrick said. 'This is why I avoid public meetings.'

Louise wanted to say it had been a disaster because of poor communication and project planning, but that wouldn't help anyone. 'You said the specifications requested by the Church Committee were agreed and communicated to Head Office?'

'They were. I remember signing the letter before the "old you"—the girl who left before you arrived—posted it.'

'Good.' She lowered her voice so Geoff wouldn't hear. 'If the contractors have messed up, they'll have to put it right at no extra cost.'

She had done her best to reassure Fitzpatrick, but what could she say to Richard? He was at the back of the room talking to Fiona and Kaye White. She ought to go to him, but her legs wouldn't move. Reverend Cummins left before Louise could thank him for keeping the meeting on track.

'Coach and Horses?' Pete said.

Louise shook her head. 'No thanks. But could you drop me off at High House?'

Everyone had left, including Richard, although Louise hadn't seen him go. The idea of fleeing to a remote island was more attractive than ever. She was no good to anyone—especially not Richard. All she seemed to do was cause misery and chaos in his life. And now he would hate her.

The bike pulled away and made a wide circle of the playground to turn around. Pete sounded his horn twice and waved as they passed a small group of people. Louise turned her head to see Richard staring at her, Fiona and Kaye at his side. He watched as she left the school clinging to Pete's back.

22

SATURDAY 16TH OCTOBER 1965

High House was quiet. Dolly had returned to Leeds after the disastrous meeting. Her assistants had gone home for the weekend, as Fitzpatrick always did, and Pete was unlikely to get up before midday. Louise had to find Richard to say sorry. It had been too dark to see his face properly last night, but she felt his contempt and disappointment in her. There was nothing she could say to make things right, but she had to try. First, a Telex to Head Office requesting a copy of the building specifications and plans. If the contractor had ignored the instruction to incorporate the stained glass windows, then it was Geoff's problem to sort.

The Telex whirred across the ether with her silent prayer. In the silence that followed, Louise tried to summon all her strength and courage. She spoke out loud in an attempt to channel Ma's positivity. 'You got yourself into this mess. Find Richard. Apologise. See what Head Office has to say about the fixtures and fittings. Maybe the new cemetery can be located somewhere peaceful with beautiful scenery, and a little chapel of peace. Then you can decide what's next. One step at a time.' The words of a warrior. But Louise's heart was quaking.

Big Jim. Eddie. The Mob. They were on to her. Why else would the Quality Street Gang be in Thorncrest? Louise actually longed for the day when her only fear was being convicted of intentionally causing a fatal accident. Big Jim would have no mercy if he thought she had crossed him. Heart palpitations. Cold sweat. Louise took deep breaths. Fear would paralyze her and she had to take action. One. Step. At. A. Time. But her feet remained rooted to the spot.

The sound of Peggy's hoover broke Louise's stupor, and she pushed open the office door. Peggy switched off the vacuum cleaner.

'Sorry, lass. Didn't know anyone was working today. I'll just nip around with this and then I'll leave you in peace. Got anything nice planned for the weekend?'

'It's okay, Peggy. I just had one job, but it's done. I thought I'd do a bit of exploring.'

'Be careful. It looks fine now, but the forecast says it's going to turn.'

The air was crisp, the sun bright, but Louise took little notice of the beauty surrounding her as she cycled down the valley to Braithwaite's.

I'm sorry, Richard. I didn't mean to mislead you ... No. That would be another lie. *I thought the plan had been agreed.* Liar. Liar. *I didn't want a dotting of I's and crossing of T's stopping you from making plans.* Wrong. Wrong. Wrong. It made her sound scheming. Manipulative. That's exactly what she had been, but for the right reasons. There was nothing she could say that would make things right. Just 'sorry'.

A teenage girl was serving behind the counter. The door to

the back was closed. 'Are you on your own today?' Louise asked, attempting a cheery tone, despite the butterflies in her stomach.

'Yeah. What do you want?'

Louise's stomach rumbled; she had not eaten since lunch time yesterday. 'A cheese and pickle roll, please.'

The girl buttered a roll in silence. It was ten in the morning and she looked as though she would rather be having a lie-in. 'Anything else?'

Louise shook her head and paid. Outside the shop, she looked around the side to the door of Richard's maisonette. She didn't know what she hoped to find. Milk, newspapers and post would come from the shop, so the absence of these was no indication of him being in or out. No Land Rover at the back, just a delivery van. Louise rang the doorbell and waited, holding her breath.

The delivery man pointed from the open window of his van. 'Reckon he's up on the moors. Set off right early with a rucksack and walking boots.'

'Nice day for it,' she said.

He gave her an appraising look before turning up his radio and pulling away.

Louise scanned the moors, wondering which path he had taken. They had wandered the moors as kids but never further than Hunters Hall, a shooting house that stood proudly on the horizon, on the opposite side of the valley. A sorceress lived there, she had told Dicky, a woman who could command the weather. This sorceress watched over the moors and valley; she knew everything that you did — good and bad.

'What would she do if we met her?' Dicky had said, his brow furrowing.

'She would...' Louise loved having Dicky enthralled. 'Gobble us up!' She had thrown back her head and laughed, intoxicated by the fresh air blasting her lungs and the power to hold him captive with her imagination.

'She wouldn't eat me because I'm good. You're the naughty one, always getting us into trouble.'

They had run until Dicky had trouble breathing and then they collapsed on the heather cushioned moorland, arms and legs flung carelessly over one another as though they inhabited one body.

Louise had cycled around the valley and reached a path that would take her up the hill. Richard would have gone much further, but maybe she would see him from up there, or catch him on his return. She hid her bike from sight of the road and set off. The path took her to open moorland, and a steady climb to reach the hunting lodge.

At first, Louise enjoyed threading her way between hillocks and heather; she would never tire of the splendour—the rolling hills, peaks and troughs, waterfalls and tarns of the Yorkshire Dales. Mother nature cradled and soothed her troubled soul. With each step, her heart lightened just a little, until she felt she could let go and just be. Soon enough she would have to face reality, but here on the moors, just for one moment, she could pretend life was okay.

The climb became steeper, and Louise regretted her choice of footwear—flimsy plimsoles were not hardy enough for this terrain. She didn't remember it being so steep. They must have had more energy as kids. Louise tramped on. Way off in the distance, she could see a figure. He had paused to look down the way he had come. Could it be Richard? Louise picked up her pace, keeping him in sight. The sun dipped behind the clouds, creating swathes of shadow and light across the multi-coloured moorland. So many colours woven together, a giant tapestry of purples, burnt umber, peaty brown, and splashes of vibrant green—tender new crops on scattered farmland.

As Louise climbed onward and upward, she kept her eyes on the figure in the distance; sometimes it looked as though he was walking towards her and sometimes away. The shooting lodge was still above, but now to her left; she had veered off course. But if it was Richard... She picked up pace.

There was no sun now. It was getting cold and damp. Sweat chilled on Louise's skin. She ought to rest and eat her roll, but was afraid of losing sight of him.

It was really steep now. Her socks were damp from the rising mist. She could no longer see the lodge. Even the figure she had been following seemed to go in and out of focus as mist swirled, blurring the horizon. Desperate to halve the distance between them, Louise tried to jog, but it was impossible uphill. Her thighs ached with the exertion. Then her right foot slipped on a slick of mud and she fell onto all fours. Within a few seconds of falling, mist seemed to cloak her. She could see no further than the length of her arm. It was time to turn around and make her way back.

Progress was slow as she limped and stumbled, her ankle painful from the fall. She should have been able to mark her route by a view of the valley below, but the sorceress had punished her with what was now a thick fog. She just had to keep walking or crawling downhill.

Louise ate her roll but had nothing to drink. Her feet felt as though they were encased in ice. Her flimsy anorak gave no protection against the elements. It was three o'clock. Soon it would be dusk. She had to keep moving, but it was so hard.

She had been struggling downhill for over two hours. By now she should have reached the valley, but it felt as though she was in a wilderness. Disorientated, freezing, and in pain, she curled up in a ball, squeezing warmth from her body. Her eyelids were heavy, and she gave in, closing them for a few minutes. *Just rest your eyes,* Ma said.

Someone was wrapping a blanket around her. Arms lifting her to an upright position. 'Ma?'

Had she spoken? Her lips were dry and chapped.

'Drink. Just a little sip.'

The neck of a glass bottle pressed against her mouth. She greedily took a gulp, then spluttered. Brandy. It warmed her throat and chest. Louise covered his hands with hers and took another gulp. And another. She was so thirsty.

'Steady.' He tugged the bottle from her grasp.

Louise lifted her head. It felt so heavy. 'Dicky?'

His hands relaxed, and Louise took the bottle from him. 'I was looking for you.' She drank deeply, welcoming the way it warmed her body and softened her edges.

'You've almost finished the bottle. I should have brought water or a flask of tea.'

'No. That was lovely.' Her voice slurred. There was something important she had to tell him. The words muddled in her head. 'Dicky. I didn't mean to lie to you. I'm so sorry. For everything. I just wanted you to build houses. I wanted you to be happy and now I've made everything worse.' She hiccupped. 'The sorceress cast a spell.'

'Okay. Let's get you back to my car. Can you stand?' He supported her as she struggled to her feet.

'Ouch. My ankle. I think I sprained it.'

'Okay. Put your arms around my neck. I'm going to carry you.'

Louise put her arms around his neck. 'I thought your eyes were grey but there are blue flecks, like the sun coming out after a storm,' she said.

'Okay. Hold on.' One of his arms lifted her legs, the other held her close to him. He smelt of soap and fresh air.

'I was following you to Hunter's Lodge, but then you went the wrong way and I lost you.' She closed her eyes.

'The car's not far. I drove across the moor. You shouldn't have come out in this. You're not even wearing walking boots.'

Louise nuzzled her face against the warmth of Richard's chest, protected from the wind by the opening in his coat. She wanted to stay like that forever.

'Okay. I'm going to put you down now.'

When Louise felt her feet touch down, she opened her eyes. Richard released his hold to open the car door.

'Ouch. My ankle.'

'Okay. Hold on to the car and I'll help you in.'

When they were both seated and the blanket tucked around her, Richard started the car. Louise tried again to explain. 'Yesterday, I didn't know what he was going to say. I should have done. But I was afraid because of the…' she whispered. 'Quality Streets. You know. The chocolate men. Oh, Dicky. I'm sorry.' Louise's head was fuddled, and she didn't know whether she was making any sense.

The Land Rover lurched forward. 'Shouldn't really drive up here, but you could have been anywhere. You've wandered miles from Hunter's Lodge. I don't know who you were following, but it wasn't me.'

They stopped when they reached the road and Richard turned off the engine.

'Oh. Thank you.' It surprised her he wasn't going to drive her home.

'Don't move.' Richard got out. A couple of minutes later, he opened the back door, letting in a gust of cold air. 'Your bike.'

Louise shivered, and Richard handed her the brandy. 'You might as well finish it.'

'How did you know where to find me?'

'A woman from High House phoned the shop asking if

anyone had seen you. The shop was closed, but I thought I'd better check with Kaye. She said Julie was working today, so I called her.'

'The girl in the shop didn't know.' Louise drained the bottle.

'Better?'

She nodded. 'Thank you.'

'Maybe you ought to go to A&E. Hythermia.'

'No. Just need to get warm and rest this foot. But how did you find me?'

'I phoned Julie. She mentioned seeing a bike dumped in the undergrowth when she stopped off on her way home from work for a crafty fag. Meant to have given up and didn't want anyone to see. I checked it out. Recognised it as yours. Here we are.'

When the car stopped, Louise took his hand. 'Thank you, Richard. And I'm really, really sorry for everything. But he mustn't see me with you. That's why I didn't meet you. I didn't want him to know about us. We can't be seen together.'

Richard pulled his hand away. 'Drink a strong coffee when you get in and have something to eat.' He was abrupt, his tone harsh.

Peggy was waiting anxiously at reception when Richard half carried Louise in.

'Thank the Lord you found her,' Peggy clucked.

'She'll need a cold compress on that ankle,' he said, transferring her weight to Peggy's arm.

'Don't leave. I said it all wrong,' Louise said, but nobody seemed to hear. Peggy followed Richard out, leaving her in an armchair with her leg raised.

She must have dozed off, as Peggy gently shook her. 'I've made up a bed for you in the west wing. You'll stay in bed all day tomorrow and if I'm worried about you, I'll be calling the doctor. You could have died out there on the moor.'

Louise slept soundly. Her bed bigger and softer than the bunk beds in the dorm.

'How are you feeling this morning, lass?' Peggy backed in to the bedroom without knocking. But she was carrying a tray of breakfast.

'My head aches.' That was an understatement. It felt as though a vice was tightening around her skull.

'A bit too much medicinal brandy. I don't know what Richard Braithwaite was thinking, giving you the bottle. Bacon and eggs will see you right. When I come to collect your tray, I'll bring some ice and we'll take a look at that ankle.'

'No. It's okay. I'll get up so you can have the room back.' Louise adjusted her pillows and Peggy organised the tray on her lap.

'You'll do no such thing. When his nibs gets back, he'll have you doing somersaults. Enjoy being spoilt. Besides, you can't put weight on that ankle. Rest it now and it'll heal quicker. I see you've got a couple of books to read.' Peggy nodded at the two books on her bedside cabinet.

'I need to return my library book. But I can happily reread them both. Thanks for everything, Peggy. I really appreciate it. And you're right, it's a very comfy bed.'

The hangover would clear, and the swelling of her ankle, but her heart was not so easily mended. Richard hated her. Those beautiful grey eyes had flashed with anger. Lightning bolts. But he had been kind. His voice gentle. What had she said to make him angry? The scent of his body, the touch of

his hands around hers, resting her head against his chest--
these things she could recall, and relived each moment, but
her words—what exactly she had said—were a blur.

23

MONDAY 18TH OCTOBER 1965

'Telex for you,' Fliss said, waving a paper under Louise's nose, when she limped in to reception on Monday morning. Her ankle was less swollen, but it hurt when she put her full weight on it.

It was time to leave Thorncrest. She had failed dismally at everything: helping the community prepare for the flood, freeing Richard to live the life he dreamed of, and—Louise cringed at the memory—apologising to Richard for all she had put him through then and now. It was time to leave. If only she hadn't sprained her bloody ankle.

'Well? Good news or bad?' Fliss said.

Louise remembered the paper in her hand and cast her eyes down to read. She sighed. 'It couldn't get much worse. I'd better find Fitzpatrick.'

'I'll bring you both a pot of coffee. But later, I want to hear all about your weekend. Lizzie told me that dishy Richard arrived here on Saturday night, carrying you in his arms.'

'Assisting me to hobble in. Yes please, to coffee. Thanks, Fliss.'

Fitzpatrick had dark shadows beneath his eyes. 'What's the plan? Can you placate Fiona Simms? We don't want this getting in the paper. The Corporation can't afford bad publicity at this stage. They'll blame me. It's a bloody awful mess. I should have kept a better eye on that builder, Geoff. They just throw these things up, paying no attention to the spec.'

Louise clutched the Telex. 'I'm afraid it gets worse. I heard back from Head Office; I don't think the Church Committee's specifications were communicated to them. They're posting a copy of the plans and contract so we can check, but this Telex says there's nothing about using fixtures and fittings from the existing church and no mention of stained glass windows.'

'That's not true. I sent them myself, by post.'

'Recorded delivery?'

'Um no. I didn't actually post them myself.'

Fliss came in with a tray of coffee and chocolate digestives.

'Please, could you have a look on and around the desk in reception, Fliss? Mr Fitzpatrick asked the girl who worked here before to send an important document to Head Office. Apparently, it didn't arrive.'

'Sure. Reception was a bit of a mess when I took over. I'll look in the filing cabinets too.'

Louise took a deep breath. 'I can't stay, Sean. I know I said I would work until the trial flood, but something's come up.'

Fitzpatrick spluttered biscuit across the room. 'You can't leave, Jane. If it's about money, I'll talk to Head Office. Get you on the payroll. Head of something or other… Just tell me what you need to make you stay.'

Richard. Forgiveness. A clean slate. Eddie and the Mob erased from my life. 'I'm out of my depth, Sean. Friday night was a disaster. If I'd been on the ball, I might have helped things go more smoothly. You need an experienced assistant. It's not too late to find someone better suited to the job.'

'Rubbish. We need *you*, Jane. Look how you've won over the trust of local people, Fiona Simms, the vicar. They'll listen to you. Don't worry about moving back to the women's dorm. You can keep your room in the West wing. Have a biscuit.' He proffered the plate, with a look of desperation and hope.

Louise shook her head. 'Thank you for the room. If my staying meant Thorncrest would have a church worthy of replacing the one they're losing and a cemetery close by, then I would, no hesitation. But you can't promise me.'

'No. I can't. But if you were to leave now, it would be another blow to the community.'

Louise bit into her biscuit. He had her, and she resented it, because he was right. Ma would want her to do everything possible for the people of Thorncrest—they were kin. Fitzpatrick was watching her face closely.

'Okay. I'll stay until we've come to an arrangement that's acceptable to Reverend Cummins and the Church Committee.'

'Good. Good. Talk to Fiona Simms. Make sure she's happy.'

Louise sighed. 'I can't do the impossible. I'll talk to Fiona and Reverend Cummins, but I don't have any authority. Pete Murray will have to come with me.'

'Agreed. He's with Dolly Lombard's team this morning searching for a new location for the cemetery.' Fitzpatrick walked over to the window. 'If you go now, you'll catch him before he leaves.'

Louise phoned down to Fliss and asked her to waylay Pete. Peggy was making Louise's bed when she stepped into the bedroom to grab her jacket.

'Do you want me to drop your books off at the mobile library this morning?' Peggy said.

'Yes, please.' Louise blew her a kiss and hurried as best she could to catch Pete.

He was in reception, extolling the virtues of being a redhead; Fliss had a mane of auburn hair tied back with a green bow. 'Did you know 5th November is National Redhead Day?' he said, leaning against the desk.

Fliss giggled. 'I don't believe you.'

'It's celebrated across the globe. You knew that, didn't you, Jane?'

Louise was exasperated by him. He seemed so charming and affable. But so had Eddie. 'No. And I don't believe you,' she snapped.

Pete winked at Fliss and stood up. 'You wanted to see me, Miss Cox?'

Louise felt stupid. 'Yes. Thanks for waiting. We need to talk.'

'Then you'll have to come with me because I'm already late.'

They couldn't talk on the motorbike. Or when they met with Dolly and her team on the other side of the valley. A new location had been found for the cemetery. The right sort of earth, and sufficient distance from the reservoir to eliminate any risk of contamination. It was too far away from the church, but nobody on the team apart from Louise seemed concerned by this.

'I think you're becoming a bit of a Rocker. You'll be trading your bicycle for a Norton.' Pete laughed as Louise dismounted back at High House.

'I'd be happier if you had helmets.' Louise smoothed down her hair.

'The wind's brought colour to those pale cheeks. Was that all you wanted? A ride on my bike?'

'No, it wasn't. But it was worth chasing across the moors on your excuse for a bike because now I have some information to share with the Church Committee. Not good news—but at least it's something.'

'My time is all yours. If you rustle up some coffee, I'll park this round the back and join you.'

Fliss greeted her by waving an envelope triumphantly. 'Filed between Highways and Housing. I worked my way through all of them, shaking for loose papers. It was at the bottom between the suspended files.'

'Don't look so pleased, it's bad news.' Louise took the envelope from her. 'This looks like the one. Damn.'

'Sorry,' Fliss shrugged. 'But I'm still proud of myself for finding it.'

'Yes. Thank you, and congratulations.'

'What are we celebrating?' Pete said, joining them in reception.

Louise sighed. 'Fliss's super efficiency. She found the letter Fitzpatrick dictated with the specifications for the new church. It wasn't sent to Head Office. So, nobody else we can blame for this complete balls-up. Fitzpatrick wants us to placate Fiona Simms. I don't know how. Unless we promise to delay the reservoir until a new church is built, complete with the old fixtures and fittings and a cemetery alongside. And that is not going to happen.'

'No.' Pete slumped his shoulders and rubbed the back of his neck. For once, he didn't have a witty retort.

'I'll make you both a coffee,' Fliss slipped out from behind her desk.

Upstairs, Louise and Pete rehearsed what they could offer the Church Committee to make up for the massive blunder.

'How about a chapel of peace within the cemetery? It doesn't have to be lavish or big—just somewhere loved ones can spend some time in thought or prayer,' Louise said.

'Good idea. I'll check costings. We could make a small donation to a community fund.'

Fliss came in with coffee and freshly baked rock cakes. 'This might help. Oh, I forgot to tell you, Louise, Peggy returned your library books.'

'Thanks,' Louise said, as Fliss settled the tray on Pete's desk. 'Please, could you phone Reverend Cummins to arrange a meeting with him and Fiona Simms? And anyone else from the Church Committee.'

'When were you thinking?' Fliss said.

'As soon as possible. We really need to thank him for his support at the meeting and show him we are prepared to do all we can to make amends,' Louise said.

'Within budget and timescales,' Pete added.

Louise frowned at him.

'Well, we do. But I'll check with Fitzpatrick how far we can stretch them both.'

A meeting with Reverend Cummins and Fiona Simms was arranged for four o'clock that afternoon.

At Louise's insistence, Pete took the lead, explaining where the cemetery would now be situated.

'Really? That's the best you can do?' Reverent Cummins's face was ashen. 'It's going to be a blow to our parishioners. Many of them visit their loved one's graves when attending church. To cast them so far away from a place of worship feels callous. I'll do my best. Hold a special service. But this news is going to devastate them.'

'It's unacceptable. You'll have to go back and tell the

Corporation *No*. We don't accept.' Fiona thumped the table with her fist.

'I'm really sorry, but that's not an option. This is the only site that meets with public health requirements. I wish it wasn't,' Pete said.

'Maybe one day a new church could be built closer to the cemetery. In the meantime, how about a small chapel of rest?' Louise said.

'A chapel of rest. An excellent idea.' Reverend Cummins rubbed his hands together. 'And the fixtures and fittings? Will the Corporation pay for their safe removal and storage? I'll talk to the archbishop about where that might be.'

'Yes. Yes, of course.' Louise was relieved that the Reverend was taking things so well.

'Good. Then I'll turn my thoughts to the last church service here. Lots to do. Maybe we could celebrate Christmas in a barn. A *real* nativity.'

Fiona narrowed her eyes. 'You can tell Fitzpatrick that we are not impressed. Not impressed at all.'

'We are truly sorry for what can only be described as a monumental balls-up,' Pete said. The sincerity of his tone impressed Louise. 'If there is anything we can do to compensate for the stress caused, we would be happy to consider. Maybe a donation to a community fund?'

'Hmm.' Fiona batted her eyelashes at Pete. Was that a pout? 'There might be something you could do.' The commanding, I'm the most important person in this room voice, was replaced by that of a petulant child trying to get her own way. Louise was learning, Fiona always had to have things go her way.

'Try me,' Pete said, returning her coquettishness with a little flirtation.

'I will do just that.' Fiona grinned. 'Dinner at The Grange.

Saturday 23rd October. You, me, Richard and Jane. Mummy and Daddy will be in London so we'll have the house to ourselves—apart from the staff, of course. We will discuss how the Corporation might make amends for, what did you call it? Their monumental balls-up.' She laughed.

'If we're discussing church business, perhaps Reverend Cummins could join us?' Louise couldn't spend an evening with just the four of them. Richard was barely talking to her.

'That's very kind of you, Jane, but I have other commitments that evening. I'm content with a chapel of peace within the cemetery and the safe removal and storage of our stained glass windows and other fittings. And now I have a date to vacate Thorncrest Church I will get on with arranging the last service. You will let me know when it will be convenient to consecrate the ground for the cemetery?'

'Of course, Reverend Cummins. Thank you so much for your understanding. We really appreciate your kindness and support, particularly the way you calmed everyone down at the public meeting. I know Sean Fitzpatrick was incredibly grateful. He would have come here himself to say so.'

Reverend Cummins waved away Louise's thanks. 'He is a busy man. As am I. I don't mean to be discourteous, but if that is all, I really need to get ready for my boxing class.'

Louise's jaw dropped. She would not in a million years have put the Reverend down as a boxer. 'You box?'

He laughed. 'As a lad, I was a champion boxer for my county. Now, I hold a class for disadvantaged boys in Harrogate once a week. If I don't get there before them to open up the hall, they're bound to cause mischief.'

They all made a hurried exit. Outside the church Fiona said, 'I nearly forgot. The librarian, Esther, asked me to give you this, Jane.' She rummaged in her bag and with a flourish, presented Louise's copy of Jane Eyre.

Louise gasped. 'How did you? What …?'

'I was out riding and met Esther. She'd been walking her dog. We live close to one another; you could say we're neighbours. I said I was meeting you, and she popped inside to get your book. Apparently, it was handed in to the library by mistake.' Fiona was still clutching Louise's book.

Inside the cover was Dicky's inscription to her. Louise wanted to snatch it from Fiona's claws. She tried to appear calm as Fiona scrutinised her face.

'Thank you for taking the trouble.' She extended her arm and Fiona, after turning the book back and forth, handed it over.

'What's that?' Pete said, when Fiona had driven off in her MG Midget sports car.

'Just a book.'

Pete pointed. 'Can I have a look?'

Louise didn't want anyone else touching her precious book, but it seemed churlish to refuse when he had put on his charm to win over Fiona. She handed it to him with a shrug. 'It's an old copy I've had for years.'

Pete turned to the inscription. 'To Louise from her best friend Dicky.' He raised his eyebrows. 'Cute.'

'It's just an old book. Peggy picked it up with my library book by mistake.'

'Okay. Well, job done. Shall we go back and tell Fitzpatrick the good news?'

'Not quite done. We've got to get through Saturday evening first.'

'With my charm, it'll be a walk in the park. I've got Miss Simms eating out of my hand.'

Louise climbed on the back of his bike. If there was any way she could get out of Saturday, she would. The thought of spending an evening watching Fiona and Richard together was unbearable. But she was beginning to trust Pete. Maybe it was wishful thinking, to believe he was on her side. Her days were numbered. Eddie knew where she was, even if Big Jim didn't. But she couldn't go anywhere until she had made things right with Richard.

24

SATURDAY 23RD OCTOBER 1965

Louise spread her pink gingham dress across the bed. It was too much. She shouldn't have bought something so obvious. A photo of the one in Biba, and an image of Brigitte Bardot wearing something similar, had persuaded Louise to splash out a week's wage in Busby's, but now, draped across her candlewick bedspread, it looked a bit too flashy. It was vain of her, and childish, to try competing with Fiona's glamour. Richard was in love with Fiona. And even if he wasn't, he wouldn't be interested in Louise. Richard had good cause to hate Jane Cox and everything she represented—the loss of his village, the heartless destruction of Thorncrest Church and the graves of loved ones. They were her loved ones, too.

Fliss knocked on the door and entered without waiting for a response. 'Haven't you put it on yet? It's gorgeous! I wish I was a couple of sizes smaller so I could borrow it. This is a groovy room.' She moved to the window. 'Hey, you've even got a view.'

'I'm having second thoughts about wearing this, Fliss.'

'Why?' Fliss swung around, her eyes wide. 'You went into Harrogate to shop because you wanted to look your best. Don't tell me you're going to leave this fab dress in the back of your wardrobe and turn up for dinner in what, jeans and jumper?'

'No. You're right. It's just that it might look as though I'm trying too hard. I told Pete to dress up. Do you know what he's wearing?'

'Don't worry about Pete. He loves a bit of dapper. He could charm the birds from the trees.'

'We just need to get Fiona Simms on side. The Reverend is fine, but Miss High-and-Mighty wants us to beg for it. I told Fitzpatrick she wasn't worth it, but he wants us both to go. So, here we are…'

'What about your hair?' Fliss said.

Louise raked a hand through her short cut. Her natural curls would not be tamed and so the style she had on leaving the salon had long gone. 'This is okay, isn't it?'

Fliss pulled a face. 'Let me wash and style it for you—make it look a bit slicker. Stay there and I'll fetch my bag of tricks.'

As she waited, Louise glared at her reflection. 'It's the bloody party all over again. Dressing up, hoping to make an impression. Don't you ever learn Louise Pearson? It was Joan then. Fiona now. And…' Louise threw up her hands and laughed, 'I'm wearing a gingham dress, just as before.'

'Who were you talking to?' Fliss said, returning to the room with a hairdryer and an armful of lotions and sprays.

'Nobody. Just going a bit crazy.'

Forty minutes later, Fliss held up a mirror so Louise could see the back. 'What do you think?'

Louise admired her work. She had to admit she looked pretty.

. . .

Fiona lived in a grand house with a sweeping in and out drive. Fitzpatrick paid for a minicab to take and collect them. A motorbike ride would have ruined Louise's hair. There were stables and paddocks behind the house, according to their driver.

'Ready?' Pete said. Louise took a deep breath and nodded. He rang the bell.

A woman in a neat black dress and white apron opened the door. They entered a wide hall, which, despite its grandeur, looked lived in, with coats spilling over the inadequate coat stand, a hairbrush on the hall table and discarded wellies and shoes scattered across the parquet floor. A couple of Labradors came out to greet them. Fiona called from a room at the end of the hall. 'We're in the study.'

They took off their coats and were shown into a room where a fire crackled in the hearth. Fiona and Richard both stood up when they entered. Richard avoided making eye contact; he seemed as discomforted as Louise felt. Fiona looked effortlessly elegant and Louise was glad that she had taken the trouble to buy a fashionable new dress.

'Cocktails and then supper. I think we're having grouse or partridge. You do like game?'

Pete made enthusiastic noises and kissed Fiona on both cheeks. Louise hung back, hoping Richard would thaw and at least smile, but he barely acknowledged her.

'Sit. Sit.'

Louise positioned herself alongside Richard on a comfy, deep chaise lounge that faced the fire. They could stare into the flames and avoid eye contact.

Fiona signalled for Pete to sit in a chair close to her. 'I'm going to make the most of having you here, Peter.' She giggled. 'Jane can't keep you all to herself.'

'We're not ...' Louise paused. What had she been going to say? We're not involved?

Why did it matter? Let Fiona play her games. If it made her more amenable to the church relocation project, then their job here would be done. Louise just had to endure an evening of Fiona flirtating with Pete and ignore the fact that the woman was Richard's partner, lover, and best friend, and she, Louise, was the baddie. The one who couldn't care less about the people of Thorncrest. Friend of The Corporation. Enemy of the people.

'I see you're still limping,' Richard said.

'Good job you found her.' Pete's voice was upbeat, unlike Richard's gruff observation.

'What's that?' Fiona froze at the cocktail trolley, holding a bottle of whiskey she had been about to pour. 'You didn't tell me about this, Richard.'

'It was nothing,' Louise said. 'I'm fine now. Well almost.'

'Jane went walking the moors last Saturday, wearing plimsols and an anorak,' Richard said.

'Wasn't it foggy that day?' Fiona handed Pete a whiskey sour.

'It was sunny when I set out. When the fog descended, I lost my bearings and then I twisted my ankle. But as I said, it's almost completely healed now.' Louise wanted to change the subject. The purpose of the evening was to win over Fiona, and this conversation was not helping. She looked as though she wanted to throw the gin martini over Louise's head rather than placing it on a coaster.

'Well, we can't expect Londoners to understand country life. How long are you intending to stay in Thorncrest, Jane?'

She sensed a change in Richard's body tension and glanced sideways to see his hand clench. 'I don't know.'

'Long enough to see our village wiped out. Generations of

life and history submerged.' Richard said. He stood up and busied himself throwing logs onto the fire.

Richard seemed relaxed and completely at home in the Simms' manor. One of the Labradors ambled into the room and butted up against Richard, causing him to rock on his haunches. He tickled behind the dog's ear.

'I was rather surprised to hear the reservoir perimeter had not been confirmed. So was Richard, weren't you darling?'

Louise's heart sank. Pete didn't know about her lie. She had hoped Fiona would keep quiet on the matter—after all, she got what she wanted.

'We'll know in the next few days,' Pete said, oblivious to the tension in the room.

'Let's hope Becks farm doesn't go under. Not that it matters, with the owners long gone.' Fiona raised her eyebrows at Richard.

'I'm sure that won't be the case,' Louise said. Her heart quickened.

Richard finally made eye contact with her, his eyes blazing with fury. 'I will hold you personally responsible if Becks farm is destroyed by the flood.'

'I don't want that farm destroyed any more than you do,' she cried.

The Labrador's head shot up. Richard stroked his ears. 'It's okay, boy.'

'I understood the Corporation had taken ownership of that farm,' Pete said.

'Only by default. If you read the paperwork, you'll see I've been contesting the assumption that there's no legal owner.'

What did Richard mean? Ma and Pa were both dead; she'd seen their graves. 'Do you know something we don't?' Louise asked. 'I wondered if someone was living there. I'm sure I saw chimney smoke.'

'Then they would be trespassing,' Pete said.

'Of course, nobody's been living on that ramshackle old farm—just a load of rats. It's a blight on the landscape. Good riddance.' Fiona's tone sounded venomous. What did she have against Ma and Pa?

'It was a beautiful, homely farm--' Louise said.

'It's part of our heritage. Our history--' Richard said.

Both of them talking at once,

'-- I heard,' Louise added, her voice trailing off.

'-- the village's history, I meant,' Richard, added.

In the silence that followed, Louise was afraid to look at Richard. She had given too much away.

'I think it's time to eat.' Fiona stood up. 'Let's go through to the dining room. I hired some help for this evening. You wouldn't want to eat anything I cook! Isn't that right, Richard? I have other talents.' She gave him a knowing smile, and Louise resisted the urge to smack her in the face.

Thankfully, Louise was seated alongside Richard and opposite Pete. It felt good having him so close; she could almost pretend that they were friends again. The young Dicky would have laughed at the image of them both at a grown-up dinner. She wasn't even sure he would have liked Fiona.

The first course was awaiting them in the dining room. Melon wedges sprinkled with brown sugar and a maraschino cherry on a cocktail stick. Richard poured them each a glass of wine. 'A Claret, as we are having game. But if you prefer white?'

'No, Claret is perfect. Good choice. You were saying, Richard, something about preserving local history. The Corporation could help fund an initiative to collect and display memorabilia from before the flood,' Pete said.

'What a marvellous idea! This is why I wanted you to bring your wonderful man, Jane. He's not just good looking.'

'A shame the Corporation wasn't interested in preserving history when it failed to take the Church Committee's specifications into consideration. Those stained glass windows are precious artefacts,' Richard said.

'It's not Peter's fault, Richard. Apparently, *someone* failed to pass the spec on to Head Office.' Fiona shot a look at Louise. 'But Peter will see that the windows and lamps are fitted in a new chapel of peace to be built alongside the cemetery, won't you, darling?' She didn't wait for Pete to reply.

'How are you getting on with establishing the new grocery shop?' Pete asked Richard.

'We have a site and a moving date.' Richard popped a cherry in his mouth.

'Can I ask when that might be?' Louise guessed Pete was thinking about the project plan and potential delays to the trial flooding exercise.

'We'll move by the first of November. Don't worry, it will be ready for you to decimate before the trial flood.' He speared a melon chunk as though he were taking out Pete's eye.

'Well, if there's anything the Corporation can do to make the move smoother, let me know.'

'Oh, that's wonderful, Peter. If you could get us a little funding to help with refitting, that would be marvellous. Wouldn't it Richard? I'll send you a proposal. My father is excited about Richard's plans to develop the Simms emporium. Did he tell you we're planning a whole chain of them?'

'I thought it was called Braithwaite and Simms,' Louise said.

Fiona waved her hand as if swatting away a fly. 'Oh, we haven't decided yet, but Simms sounds so much more elegant, don't you think? It's a bit of a mouthful, Braithwaite and Simms.'

Louise heard Richard let out a long breath. Was he as exasperated by Fiona as she was?

'Are *you* excited by this new venture, Richard?' Louise looked directly at him.

'It's what my family always dreamed of. A department store to rival Woolworths.'

'Yes, but is this what *you* want, Richard?'

He met her eyes, then looked away. 'It means we can display the polyphons. Beaky was over the moon.' He smiled.

'Until we find somewhere else more suited for them,' Fiona said. 'They occupy too much retail space. Richard renovated a pair of gorgeous walnut counters. They give the place an authentic feel. Family grocers established in 1900.'

'1910,' Louise and Richard said in unison.

What had possessed her to say that? She daren't catch Richard's eye.

'You seem to know a lot about our valley, for a Londoner new to the area,' Fiona said.

'I have made it my business to talk to local people. It's important we listen to the community.' Louise's voice sounded clipped.

Fortunately, the hired help came in at that moment to clear away the first course and serve the main meal. Pete shot Louise a look. He frowned. She wasn't doing a very good job of winning Fiona over.

Fortunately, Pete stepped in. 'Your emporium sounds like a grand venture, Fiona. Here's to your success.' He raised his glass.

Louise noticed that Richard, like her, only half-raised his glass.

'If the Corporation can do anything to help ease the burden as you move out of the valley, I'm sure Mr Fitzpatrick would be amenable. We really do want to support you in any way that we can.'

'I'm pleased to hear that, Peter. I will let Daddy know.'

Louise kept her head down, afraid of irritating Fiona further. She reached for the red cabbage serving spoon at the same time as Richard. His hand brushed hers. For a millisecond, it seemed to rest against her. She met his gaze. Then he sighed and looked away.

Louise struggled to eat her meal. The partridge was tender but stuck in her throat. Anger and resentment radiated off Richard. Pete, in an attempt to shake off Fiona's manipulation —she was taking advantage of his relaxed state to wheedle promises out of him–focused on Louise, acting as though they were a couple.

Crepe Suzette was delivered on a platter and they all gasped in feigned delight to see it flambéed at the table. Fiona had gone to some trouble and expense to put on a good show, but she was making the most of it in getting what she wanted. Louise begrudgingly admired her. She had never gone after what she wanted.

'Jane. We know nothing about you apart from the fact you came here from London. If this get-together is about getting to know one another better, then I think you should tell us more.' Fiona held a cigarette close to her mouth, a signal for Pete to light it, which he did with a flourish.

'There's nothing much to tell. I travelled here from London to volunteer for the reservoir project. Pete and I arrived on the same day. That was the day I met Richard.'

'And threw a bucket of water over him,' Fiona said. She took a long pull from her cigarette, then breathed out a plume of smoke.

'Yes. Sorry about that, Richard. Anyway, I started as a

volunteer and then I was employed to work with Sean Fitzpatrick.'

'We know all that.' Fiona waved her cigarette. 'What I want to know is why here? What or who did you leave behind in London?'

Louise's heart hammered. Richard looked directly at her. Heat flooded her face.

Pete clearly sensed her discomfort. 'Jane has been a godsend to the project. And Fiona and Richard, you have been gracious hosts, but I'm afraid it's time to be getting home. I've eaten and drunk far too much. It has made me sleepy.'

'Please stay for coffee and liqueurs.'

'Our car is due in,' Pete checked his watch, 'twenty minutes. So, a coffee would be lovely, thank you.'

As they ambled back to the room where they had started the evening, Louise found herself alone with Richard.

'You're wearing gingham,' he said. 'It suits you.'

Louise smiled. 'Your family would be proud of the new Braithwaite's.'

They looked into one another's eyes. 'I'm sorry about the reservoir, Richard,' she said.

Fiona and Pete came in at that moment. Pete was telling a story in a voice that was too loud. Louise swallowed hard but could not shift the lump in her throat. As she drank her coffee and waited for their cab, Richard seemed to withdraw from her — avoiding any eye contact or direct conversation. Why did she always seem to hurt him when he was the person she loved more than anyone else in the world?

25

NOVEMBER 1943

Dicky seemed reluctant to leave Louise when they reached the farm. 'Want to hang out in the Mill House?' he said.

'It's too cold to mess about in the valley. Even in the mill. Besides, it gets dark by four.'

Dicky sighed.

'Okay. Why don't you come back to the farm with me? I have a few jobs to do first, but then we could play a game of Monopoly,' Louise said.

'I'll help with the jobs.'

Louise wanted to spend time with Dicky, to see him smile; he had seemed down recently, but she hadn't seen Kurt for a couple of days. Now, Dicky wanted to follow her around the farm, when all she wanted to do was sit on a milking stool next to Kurt and listen while he sang a German lullaby to the cows.

Ma greeted Dicky as though she hadn't seen him in months, and Louise felt guilty because she had rarely invited him in since Kurt's arrival on the farm. 'I'll phone your mother and say you're to stop for tea. Where are you going Louise?'

Louise stopped at the door to the stairs. 'I was going to change before milking the cows.'

'There's no need for you to help today. Joan can do your milking. Go and sit by the fire with Dicky, and I'll bring in a tray of cocoa and some boiled fruit cake.'

If she didn't do her chores, she wouldn't see Kurt. 'I'm going to change anyway. Get out of my school uniform. I won't be a mo.'

From her bedroom window, she saw Joan swinging her hips as she sashayed across the yard. How could she look so glamorous wearing breeches and covered in cow muck? Louise pulled on her angora jumper. It clung to her body, but something was missing. She posed in front of the mirror, wiggling her hips and pouting.

'Hurry up, Louise. I've made the cocoa.'

There was nothing much filling her trainer bra. Louise rummaged through her underwear drawer, all winceyette and flannel. When she was older, she would wear matching silk underwear like Joan. She tossed a pair of socks onto the bed. They padded her bra perfectly. Louise admired her silhouette.

'Louise!'

She ran down the stairs. 'Sorry, Ma. I was looking for the Monopoly board.'

'It's in the chest in the living room. Go through. Dicky's waiting for you.'

'I'm just going to pop out to see Kurt. I want to give him my fruit cake because I don't think he's tried it before.'

Ma called after her, but Louise didn't hear. She imitated Joan's sexy walk, a plate balanced on one hand.

Kurt wasn't in the cowshed, just Joan sitting on his milking stool.

'Is that for me?'

'Oh. Where's Kurt?'

'In the far field. I said I would milk the cows. Thanks for the cake, squirt. I see you've brought your boyfriend home. I hope he appreciates the trouble you've gone to dressing up for him. Tell you what. Take my cake inside and I'll join you as soon as I've finished here.'

So, Louise returned to the farmhouse with a plate of pudding and a dish of disappointment. Joan should not have chased Kurt away. Who said she could milk *her* cow?

'What a good idea,' Ma said, when Louise dumped the plate on the kitchen counter. 'We can all play Monopoly before tea. I've put a casserole in the oven. Pa will be ready in a couple of hours.'

'I could ask Kurt too.'

'I'm not sure that's a good idea, pet. He's here to work. Besides, he'll be collected and taken back before tea.'

'Back to prison, where he belongs,' Dicky said from the doorway. 'He's a prisoner of war, not a tourist taking a farm holiday.'

'Kurt lives on a farm.' Louise said. 'He knows more about farming than most of the farmers around here.'

'And how would you know that? A year ago, you were living in London and didn't know the back end of a cow from a bus.'

'Don't argue, children. What's that in your jumper, Louise?'

A ball of sock had slipped out of her bra and was now creating a bump above her navel. Ma took a closer look and Louise felt her cheeks go pink.

'Come here, you look like a sack of coal.' Ma pulled Louise's jumper straight. 'What's that lump? Oh, there are two!' Louise tried to wriggle away, to preserve a shred of dignity, but Ma thrust her hand up her jumper and extracted a ball of sock.

'Thanks Louise. They should be warm and toasty now. My feet are wet and frozen after stepping into that puddle. If you give me the other one, I'll change my socks.' Dicky smiled at her.

She should have been grateful, but all she felt was a burning humiliation. She fled the room, then on the stairs, pulled out the other sock and threw it back into the kitchen.

I'm thirteen, not eight. A teenager. And Dicky's fourteen. Why does Ma have to call us children? It's so embarrassing. I hate Joan. I love Kurt. Now everyone's downstairs waiting for me so they can play Monopoly. I can't face them. Joan thinks I dressed up for Dicky. Dicky knows I stuffed socks in my bra to look like breasts. I'm so embarrassed I could die. Why can't they all leave me and Kurt alone? Now, I won't see him for another day. Three days without seeing him. I wish Dicky would stop calling him a Jerry. He doesn't know Kurt like I do or he would understand not all Germans are bad.

Louise scribbled in her diary, waiting to be summoned, but nobody called up the stairs. She half-expected Dicky to come up and knock on her bedroom door, but it had been twenty minutes and nobody seemed bothered that she had left the room.

She changed into a familiar old jumper and swapped the breeches for a plaid skirt. If anyone asked, she would say it was warmer. But when Louise opened the door from the stairs to the kitchen, nobody seemed interested in her arrival. Joan, Ma, and Dicky were sitting at the table sorting piles of Monopoly money.

'I hate capitalism,' Dicky said. 'It makes people greedy. If it wasn't for capitalism, we would live in a thriving village instead of one strangled by trees.'

'You can't stop progress. Would you really want to go back to before the Industrial Revolution?' Ma said.

'I suppose not. But why did the Corporation have to buy up all our cottages and then leave them empty? It's corporate greed. Nobody cares about the people. Our village. My family has lived here for generations.'

'Mrs Beck tells me your family runs the grocery shop,' Joan said, fluttering her eyes at Dicky.

'Braithwaite's. A family business since 1910.'

'Is that what you are going to do when you leave school, Richard? Manage the shop?' Joan was looking tenderly at Dicky as if he were her age and not a schoolboy. Why was she calling him Richard? His name was Dicky. Louise coughed once. Then, when nobody took any notice, twice.

'Come and sit down, Louise. We haven't started yet.' Ma shifted along the table, making room.

'I saved the wheelbarrow for you,' Dicky said. 'But you can have the top hat if you like.'

'No. You can have the hat.' Louise remembered Dicky dancing to the polyphon. A top hat and cane would have suited him.

She wished that Joan and Ma had not joined in their game. Joan keptsidling up to Dicky as though he were her best friend. Even Ma seemed more interested in him than Louise, asking adult questions about retail and the impact of the war. Louise felt like a stupid little sister—one who stuffed socks in her bra to try to look older.

Dicky won piles of money and Joan teased him about being a capitalist. The aroma of lamb stew wafted from the stove.

'Pa will be back any minute.' Ma got up from the table just as the outside door opened, bringing cold air into the cosy kitchen.

Kurt stood behind Pa, blowing warmth into his hands.

'Summat smells good. Where's the latest Farm Journal? I wanted to loan it to Kurt. Wait here, Kurt. I'll have a look in the bureau.'

'Good evening,' Kurt said. He sounded awkward and formal. He knew Ma, Pa, and Joan, so it must have been Dicky making him feel uncomfortable.

'We've been playing Monopoly, Kurt,' Louise said, jumping to her feet. She should have kept on the angora jumper.

'Is that Louise's hair ribbon?' Joan said.

Everyone looked at Dicky, who was trailing a silky ribbon between his fingers. He blushed and shoved it into his pocket. 'Yes. I didn't notice I did that.' He cast an apologetic look at Louise.

'Things that mean a lot to us can be comforting at times of stress,' Ma said.

Kurt's hand slid to a chain around his neck. The Saint Christopher, he always wore.

'That is so sweet, and romantic,' Joan cooed. Kurt smiled.

Was it romantic? Louise stole a glance at Dicky to see if their remarks embarrassed him. Dicky didn't think of her that way anymore. But it warmed Louise's heart to see he still had her hair ribbon. Dicky stuffed it back into his pocket.

'Just a habit, I guess.' He avoided Louise's questioning look. Did they all know it was her ribbon?

'Here it is.' Pa returned to the room brandishing a magazine. 'No hurry to return it. If it's of interest, I'll save them for you when I've finished.'

'That is very kind. Thank you.'

When Kurt had said goodbye and stepped outside, Louise went after him. She didn't care what anyone thought.

'I wanted to save some fruit cake for you, but Joan ate it. I would have milked the cows with you. Just because Dicky stayed for tea, I didn't have to neglect my farm duties.'

'There was no need. We managed fine. It is good that you spend time with your boyfriend.'

'He's not my boyfriend,' Louise yelled.

'He is a boy. He is your friend?'

'He's just a boy who goes to the same school as me,' Louise said.

'Mr Beck asked me to give you this,' Dicky spoke from behind her. 'It's got an article on the Fordson tractor.'

Kurt thanked him and walked out to the lane where a car was waiting for him.

'I'm sorry, Dicky. I didn't mean that. It's just embarrassing when everyone thinks we are courting. You know you're my best friend.'

'I hate Jerries,' Dicky said. 'And don't say, Kurt's different.' He mimicked Louise's voice. 'If he were on a battlefield facing Frank, he would kill him. So, don't tell me he's sweet and kind.'

'He is. And he doesn't sulk and grumble like you.'

'Fine. I'll talk to gorgeous Joan. She appreciates my wit and intellect. But then, she's a grown-up, not a kid pretending to be a woman.'

26

DECEMBER 1943

When Louise joined Ma at the breakfast table, there was a thick envelope propped up by a salt cellar—addressed to Mrs E Beck in her mum's handwriting.

'I waited for you before opening it.' Ma was standing at the kitchen counter a bread knife in one hand. She nodded at the post.

Louise couldn't take her eyes off the envelope as she sat down. If her mum was asking Ma to return her to London, she didn't think she could bear it. Maybe Mum was ill, like Susan's mother. Fear. Guilt. Dread.

'I don't want to go back,' Louise blurted out, unable to contain herself any longer. 'My parsnips and leeks aren't ready for harvesting, and what about the sprouts I'm growing for Christmas? I've got orders. And my chickens! Who'll look after them when I'm gone? Oh Ma. I don't want to go back to London. I love my mum. But please don't send me back.'

'Hey. Hey. Don't get yourself worked up until we know

what your mother has to say. I waited for you so that we would find out together. How many slices of toast?'

'One. Thank you. But please sit down and read the letter first. If it's bad news, I won't want to eat anything.'

Ma tutted. 'There would be a lot less drama in this house without you, that's for sure.' But Ma put down the loaf of bread and sat opposite Louise. She used a butter knife to slit the envelope open.

Louise sat hands clasped together, eyes closed as she willed the letter not to bring tidings of bad news.

'There's another one in here addressed to you.' Ma handed Louise her envelope.

They each read their own letter. Ma sighed and shook her head.

Louise bit her lip. 'I'm sorry Ma. I won't be a nuisance.'

'For goodness' sake, I'm not upset you'll be staying with us. Pa and I will be overjoyed to have you. It will make it a proper Christmas.'

'But Mum shouldn't have asked.' Louise sensed Ma's disappointment in her mother and felt the need to defend her. 'It's just that she's living with her friend Joe and I don't think he likes children—not that I'm a child, but you know what I mean. Besides, there's not really enough room.'

'Well, I'm grateful to your mum. Having you stay is the best Christmas present Pa and I could have. I can't wait to tell him. Does this mean you can eat a slice of toast and a boiled egg?'

'Two slices of toast, please.' It was a relief that she wouldn't have to spend another dreary Christmas sleeping on the sofa in Joe's flat. All the excitement Louise had suppressed now bubbled to the surface as her mind conjured the perfect Christmas. 'Does that mean Kurt will work on the farm on Christmas day?'

'I doubt that, pet. The guards will want to spend time with

their families so they won't have the staff to escort prisoners. Besides, they will have their own Christmas dinner and festivities.'

'In a prisoner of war camp?'

'Aye. We would want the Germans to take care of our boys at Christmas—and it is the season of goodwill.'

'What about Joan? Will she be going home for Christmas?'

'A couple of days before and then she's back at the start of New Year. So, it will just be you, me and Pa.'

'It will be my best Christmas ever — spending it with you and Pa.'

'So, that's settled then.'

'Have you had any news of your brother Frank?' Louise asked Dicky a few days later as they made their way down the valley, slipping and sliding on snow and ice.

'We got a telegram to say he was missing a couple of weeks ago.'

Louise lost her footing and slid onto her bottom, grabbing a tree trunk for support.

'You okay?' Dicky offered his hand to yank her up, but Louise stared up at him.

'Why didn't you tell me? That's awful, Dicky. I've been going on about my mum and Joe, as if I had problems.' She couldn't get up. It was too dreadful. Poor Dicky.

He slumped down next to her, the tree supporting his back. 'I guess I didn't want to talk about it. I keep hoping that we'll get another telegram to say he's been found. The other day we got a letter from him. My mam was so happy she cried. We all were. It was a normal sort of letter, how he had spam for tea, met another lad from North Yorkshire, asked after the shop. Mam read it out loud. We were imagining him sitting on his bunk writing, joking with his mates. Then she read out, *It's cold here for November*.'

'*What's the date of that letter?* Da said. November 10th 1944. Three weeks before we got the telegram. It was like … I don't know…'

Louise pulled off her mitten and squeezed his hand. 'I'm so sorry Dicky.'

'I can't believe he's dead.' He swiped his eyes with the back of his arm. 'For a minute, he was in the room with us. Then the date. It was worse than when we got the telegram.'

'He's not dead. He's missing. There's still hope Dicky.'

'That's what I tell Mam. It doesn't help because she imagines him as a prisoner of war.'

'Maybe that's not so bad. Ma said that our soldiers in prisoner of war camps might have Christmas celebrations because the German ones are. So, maybe they treat them okay.'

Dicky pulled his hand away from Louise's. 'Let's not talk about it anymore.'

They clambered up, their bottoms and the back of their legs wet. Louise wanted to hold Dicky's hand, to hug him—anything to show how much she cared. But today he was distant, as though protecting himself within a fragile bubble. All she could do was be there. So, they traipsed down into the valley, every now and again, one helping to steady the other, as they slid on ice covering snow.

'I'm staying here for Christmas,' Louise said, when they reached the little bridge.

'Mam told me.'

'Oh. So, that's good.'

Dicky tossed an acorn from the bridge. It skittered on the ice, then rested. A marzipan fruit on an iced cake. 'Do you think it would take our weight?'

Louise had expected Dicky to be excited that she wasn't

going away for the holiday, or at least concerned that her mum didn't want her, but he had a lot on his mind. She watched him negotiate his way down the river bank, reaching for the branch of a tree, then sliding onto his bottom. At any other time, she would have laughed.

He sat on the bank and tapped a heel against the ice. 'Feels firm.'

'Don't stand on the ice, Dicky. Please don't.'

But he did. Arms flailing, legs wide apart. Louise had to follow him down the slippery bank. If he fell through the ice, she would need to act quickly. Anxiety outweighed annoyance. A feeling of incredible sadness, as though the life they once knew was buried beneath the ice—unreachable to them.

They heard the ice cracking before it splintered. Dicky made it to the bank in one leap. Louise threw her arms around him and they stayed locked together, their breath hanging as white wisps. His body was firmer, stronger than when they had wrestled as kids. Louise felt a stirring. An overwhelming desire to kiss him. Dicky pulled away first, saving her from the embarrassment of rejection. She had to stop thinking of him in that way.

'I'm glad you're going to spend Christmas here,' he said.

27

DECEMBER 1944

Dicky had insisted on walking her home after school. The old pattern of hanging out in the valley before tea had changed in recent months, first due to Louise's farm jobs, then inhospitable weather, and, more recently, a reluctance from Dicky to spend time with her. His rejection had hurt Louise. She had taken for granted his constant friendship. Losing this was like waking up to find the eiderdown had slipped off her bed, leaving her skin exposed to cold air.

'No more school this year,' Dicky said, as they climbed the hill to Becks farm.

'It will be a difficult Christmas for your family.' Louise avoided talking about Frank. He was still missing — not yet "presumed dead," but it was a conversation that Dicky would quickly close down.

'It's difficult for everyone. Lots of people have been bombed out of their homes.'

Louise felt a stab of pain. Dicky was talking about London.

He had always reassured her that everything would be fine at home, that her loved ones were safe. 'I guess my mum and cousins have been lucky.'

'Hope so,' he said.

'Why did you want to walk back with me? I mean, it's good to have your company, but is there something you wanted to do?'

'Last day of school. Christmas.' His voice was flat.

'Okay. We could make paper chains if you like. Or something else, Christmassy.'

'They're having a surprise party for you and I was invited.'

'Oh.' Louise felt a stirring of excitement, but Dicky had spoiled it. Why did he have to be such a wet blanket?

Her thoughts raced ahead. Kurt would be there and Joan. If Louise had known, she would have dressed up, put on some lipstick and perfume. Joan would have helped to make her look beautiful.

'How do I look?' Louise pinched her cheeks and pressed her lips together.

'Your nose and cheeks are bright red from the cold wind.'

Louise fluffed up her hair. 'But I look okay otherwise?'

Dicky's face softened. 'You always look beautiful. Even when you're splattered with mud, when you have measles, when you have been crying and your nose is all snotty.'

'Thanks.' Louise said, in a sarcastic voice. 'Well, I'd better look surprised. This is my surprised face.' She widened her eyes, opened her mouth, and clasped her hands together.

Dicky did his own improvisation of surprise. Laughing, they raced to the front door.

'Act normal,' Louise hissed.

'Surprise.'

. . .

Kurt was there looking gorgeous. One cheek dimpled when he smiled. By now, Louise should have got used to him, but her love seemed to have multiplied. His presence did strange things to her body, made her knees feel wobbly, her stomach lift, as though on the wooden roller-coaster at Hampstead Heath fairground. He flashed a smile at her and Louise felt as though they were the only two people in the room.

'Chin chin,' Joan shouted, breaking the spell.

'Cheers.' Pa chinked his glass with Joan's.

Elderflower wine for Pa and Joan. Ma, Kurt, Dicky, and Louise were drinking ginger ale with a maraschino cherry. It was new to Louise, making her feel grown-up and sophisticated.

'Who can play the piano?' Joan shrieked. Had her voice always sounded so loud and annoying? Louise felt guilty. Joan was her friend.

'Ma can,' Pa said. Ma pretended not to hear, busying herself at the kitchen counter, preparing tinned peaches and evaporated milk. 'Come on, lass. It's Christmas.'

Ma sat at the piano and opened her music. Then, after nodding herself in, played *Come All Ye Faithful.* Louise stopped singing and closed her eyes. Pa's warm, low voice — comforting, Joan's girlish and exuberant, then Dicky— no longer reaching the high notes; his voice stopped and started, sometimes hoarse. Her friends. Her family. And then there was Kurt, a faint accent, his voice deep, caressing. His intake of breath sent shivers down her spine. Louise opened her eyes and joined in the chorus.

The tinned peaches had been eaten with a pot of brew. Torn Christmas crackers and crumbs littered the oil clothed table.

'I've got something for you,' Dicky said.

'But I bought nothing for you!' Louise had hoped there would be no exchange of presents. Even if she had some spending money, there were no shop— just Braithwaite's grocery.

'It's nothing much.' Dicky handed her a package wrapped in brown paper. 'I made it.'

Inside was a polished wooden egg cup. A swirl of green decorated the rim. Louise stroked the smooth edges. 'It's beautiful. How did you make it so even?'

'A lathe. I checked, it's the right size for an egg.'

'It's lovely. Thank you.'

'I have something for you too.' Kurt stood behind Dicky, dwarfing him. 'I made it in the camp. Maybe my skills are not so good.'

Louise blushed. Kurt had a present for her. She found it hard to breathe.

He handed her a wooden box. She held it as though it were a bird with a damaged wing. 'A jewellery box.'

There were three sets of tiny drawers—for earrings and brooches, Kurt said. Hooks on either side for necklaces, and a lid beneath which was a foam cushion covered in velvet.

'It is the most precious thing,' Louise said, her voice a whisper. 'Thank you, Kurt. It's perfect. The best present ever.'

As soon as the words were out, Louise regretted them. It sounded as though she didn't value Dicky's gift. She threw him an apologetic look, unsure of what she could say to make things right. Dicky glowered, resentment and disappointment radiating off him. Louise was cross with herself for upsetting her friend, but it wouldn't have made any difference what she had said—Dicky resented Kurt.

Why had Kurt given her the jewellery box? He must like her a lot, to have spent so long crafting it. A bird fluttered within her rib cage—Kurt was in love with her. As a prisoner of war, he had to be careful, but his message was clear. After the war, they would find a way to be together. Louise Müller. Mrs Louise Müller. She drifted off to sleep, imagining the day he could no longer keep quiet about his feelings.

28

MONDAY 25TH OCTOBER 1965

'How was dinner at the Simms?' Fitzpatrick asked as they settled in for their morning meeting.

'Fiona Simms is used to getting her own way.' Louise tried to soften the antagonism in her tone. 'A good business woman.'

'So long as you didn't make any false promises.'

Louise sighed. '*I* didn't.'

'Pete?'

'Not exactly, but he might have given the impression you would be open to negotiation. Reverend Cummins is perfectly content...well okay with…a small chapel of rest alongside the cemetery. It needn't be more than a wooden shack, so long as it's a place where loved ones can sit quietly to reflect or pray. And we've told him the Corporation will pay for the transportation and storage of the stained glass windows until they find a permanent home.'

'Yep. That's all doable. Good chap, the vicar.'

'He is. Fiona Simms is not so easy to please. I think she's working up a proposal for your consideration. An investment in the Braithwaite and Simms department store as a result of having to relocate the business.'

Fitzpatrick frowned and scratched his head. 'What's she talking about? There wasn't a department store. Richard Braithwaite signed a contract for the sale of his grocery shop, which took into account any lost income because of the move. Nice try, but it's not going to happen.'

'If we have to offer up anything else, Pete and I thought it would be a nice gesture to fund a project preserving local history. We've relics from the old mill, and other artefacts discovered in the valley. I'll talk to Esther, the librarian, see if there's a local group who might be interested.'

Fitzpatrick nodded. 'Okay. The technical bods are due today. We should know the reservoir boundary in a couple of days. Then, all systems go.' He rubbed his hands together.

'Reverend Cummins is holding a final church service on 31st October. And he'll want to consecrate the site of the new cemetery. Did Dolly Lombard say a week would give enough time to move the graves?' Louise shivered. The significance of the date—Halloween, a time when the veil between the living and dead was fragile—was not lost on her.

'It will have to be. She's got a big team. High House will be full. How are we progressing with clearing all the properties?' He slugged down the last of his coffee.

'All the residential dwellings have been cleared. There's just the big house by the mill, but I'm having trouble getting inside.'

'Take a couple of contractors down there today. They'll need to cut through the lock and provide a skip.'

'What about things of value? A grandfather clock, for example?'

'Get a lorry too. We'll put anything of value in storage. You'll need an auctioneer to do a valuation when we've finished clearing everywhere out. Is that all? I need to prepare for the techies visit.'

'Do you think we should have a party or something to mark the occasion? A "goodbye to the valley," event?'

'That's your department. Happy to go along with whatever you suggest. You know the community, Jane. I trust your judgement.'

He wouldn't if he knew the truth. Thankfully, Pete hadn't cottoned on to Fiona's barbed remark about the reservoir boundary. *Please God, let it remain the same.* There had been a few precious moments at the dinner party when Richard had softened, and it felt as though they were on the same side. He had always been her champion and protector, even when she didn't deserve his unswerving friendship. If Becks Farm was destroyed by the flood, it would break her heart. It was typical of Richard trying to safeguard the farm, even though Ma and Pa were long gone. What had he said? It's part of *our history.* For a heartbeat, she thought he meant *their* history—Louise and Dicky. But Richard didn't know, did he? She thought he had recognised her the day they moved the polyphons, and there were occasions on Saturday night when their connection was strong. He *had* to know. But why pretend? Now, it would be awkward to say, 'It's me, Louise Pearson.' Maybe he really had forgotten her. It had been twenty years. He had obviously meant more to her than she had to him, if he had obliterated her memory.

That afternoon, Louise cycled down to the Mill House to meet the contractors. She was looking forward to visiting it again. That was where she had found her memory box. An old cash tin, but it had meant the world to her. She could still remember every item carefully stored: Dicky's lucky marble, a penny, a broken eggshell, a stub of lipstick, Dicky's home-made Get Well card, and a wooden eggcup. Louise could not recall whether she had left the box behind on purpose, or was rushed away with no time to gather her belongings. Whatever the reason, she regretted losing it. At least she had her diary, and Dicky's gift—Jane Eyre.

A skip had already been delivered to outside the Mill House. There was no sign of the contractors who were to help her break in. Louise propped her bike against a stone wall and went to investigate. Today, the windows had been boarded up. No climbing in through a downstairs one like last time. In twenty years, the trees had grown, pushing against the walls of the house, setting traps of raised roots to trip intruders. The valley resembled the enchanted word of Disney's Sleeping Beauty. But her prince would not kiss her and magic the world back to how it once was.

A Transit pulled up and tooted its horn. The contractors, a middle-aged man and a younger one, climbed out. 'Hardwicks will be down within the hour with a removal van. How much stuff are you expecting to shift?' the older one said.

Louise felt foolish. What if the Mill House was empty? She had assumed it would be as she remembered. 'Shall we get inside and take a look? We can cancel Hardwicks if there's nothing to move.'

Ten minutes later, they had cut through the lock and entered a dim, dank hall. The old grandfather clock stood in the hall as if he had been waiting for her return. Louise felt like throwing her arms around him. The two men stood back, waiting for her instructions.

'I'll do an inventory of the downstairs first. It won't take long.' She wanted to revisit each room alone.

The first room leading off the hall was the one where they had found the cash box in a desk drawer. The desk was still there, much smaller and less imposing than when she had been a girl. Stuffing spilled out of the seat of a high-backed chair where the green leather had been nibbled away. A family of mice had likely made a nest in there. Louise marked each item in the inventory book. She didn't want to investigate the desk drawers, afraid of dead rodents or birds.

There was a fancy glass chandelier that she didn't remember from before, and so this too was noted in her book.

This was the room where they had sealed their friendship. A ribbon and a marble. It was the day she fell in love with Richard, although she didn't know it then.

'What time do you think we'll be finished here?' Voices coming from the hall reminded Louise to get on with the job.

'We'll definitely need Harwicks for the grandfather clock, and there's a desk and chandelier in there. You could take the chair out to the skip. I won't be long finishing downstairs.'

The room behind the study had looked like a library. Louise could remember blowing dust off a couple of books about weaving, but not much else. She had barely opened the door when she sensed an energy that wasn't there before. It was as if the room breathed. It smelt different, too. Wood shavings, and a slight chemical scent. In the seconds it took her to open the door fully, Louise had prepared herself for a surprise, but not this.

She gasped. Fortunately, the men were outside wrestling the chair into the skip. She wasn't yet ready to share her discovery. A workbench stood under the window, although the carpenter would not have any light now it had been boarded up. A saw, lathe, and a chunk of wood covered in sandpaper were lined up on the bench. Curls of wood littered the floor as though the craftsman had been called away unexpectedly. How long since he had last been here?

Louise fell to her knees to admire the craftsman's work. He had recreated Thorncrest valley in miniature. A model village. Each home was a doll's house with attention to detail. There were no trees choking the cottages. A river twisted through the valley. There was the little bridge, the church, the mill. Braithwaite's shop. Tiny packs of sugar, mustard, cornflakes. Bread rolls, and jam buns made from modelling clay.

She looked for Becks farm, but it was missing. Louise traced her fingers a little up the hill from the shop and away to the left. He had made the track leading to the farm, but then it stopped.

A school exercise book peeked out from beneath the bookcase. Louise shook away the dust. Dicky Braithwaite 4GF. He would have been in the fourth year of secondary school. Louise counted on her fingers. Sixteen. Two years after she left Thorncrest. Inside the book were plans for the model village. Why had Richard left his precious tools here? How long since he last visited?

'What do you want us to do with that?' The younger man joined Louise in the library.

'I think I know who it belongs to. If we can find some boxes to pack it away, I'll hang on to it until I can return it.'

The man picked up Ma Widdle's cottage and turned it with care, examining the craftsmanship. 'Amazing attention to detail. My little girl would love to play with this.'

'Hardwicks are here.' The older man joined them. 'Anything else for the skip?'

Louise roused herself from the past. It was no good dwelling on the years since she left, wondering what had happened to Dicky. Had he missed her? Did he think about her as he recreated the valley in which they had played?

'What about these old books?' The men were eager to get on, and she still had a few rooms to check.

'Could you pack them up and load them on the lorry? Some of them might be valuable.'

Louise travelled back in the Hardwicks lorry. She didn't

want to be parted from the model village. It had been transported in six packing boxes. The last of them was being carried up to her room when she stopped for a chat with Fliss at the front desk.

'I just booked three lads in to the men's dorm. One of them from London.'

'Are we expecting any more?' Louise idly flipped through a pile of unopened mail.

'We are, as a matter of fact. One male and two women. Now we have a date for the trial flood. It's all systems go. Bet you're glad you have a private room.'

'I am. Who's Jenny Rutter?'

'Must be one of the women we're expecting. Pass it over and I'll put it with the one for Louise Pearson.'

Louise went cold. She must have misheard. 'What was that name?'

'Louise Pearson. I haven't checked the names of our new arrivals; just guessing this mail is for them. Hold on, I'll take a look.'

Fliss consulted a diary, the letter still in one hand. 'Jenny Rutter, Mary Jones, and Sue Forbes. No Louise Pearson. That's odd.'

'Can I look?' Louise's heart was beating so hard she was afraid it would give her away. The letter had a typed address for Louise Pearson at High House.

'Oh. I know what this is. Leave it with me and I'll pass it on.'

Fliss shrugged. 'Okay. I'll let you know if anything else arrives for her. Will Louise Pearson need a single room? There's not much accommodation left upstairs. You don't want her booting you out of your room.'

Louise gave a half-hearted laugh as she took off up the stairs, the letter grasped in one hand.

The man from Hardwicks passed her on the stairs. 'I pushed them up against the wall of your room. Stacked. Hope that's okay,'

It took a couple of seconds for Louise to register what he was talking about. 'Yes. Thank you.'

In her room, she sank on to the bed. Maybe it was another Louise Pearson. The post mark was local. Not London. Eddie would not have used her maiden name. It was a different Louise. Her fingers trembled as she opened the envelope. Inside was a handwritten message:

Your secret is not safe with me.

Louise's mind raced through the people who could have sent this warning. Susan Jeffreys. It had to be. What was she intending to do with the information? Blackmail? Louise felt sick. She could imagine the headlines: 'Corporation employee returns to the scene of her crime.' 'Teenager Louise Pearson, branded a cold and heartless killer.' And if Susan shared the incriminating evidence, and Louise was convicted—a life sentence? The death penalty?

Louise was tired of running. The Mob. Susan Jeffreys. Richard Braithwaite was the only light in her life. If the reservoir swallowed Becks farm, he would never forgive her. Her light extinguished.

29

WEDNESDAY 27TH OCTOBER 1965

Fitzpatrick rapped a ruler on the table and a hush fell across the room. 'Is everyone here? Public health? Contractors?' He scanned the hostel's bar where all the staff had gathered. 'Peter Murray? Jane Cox?'

'Here,' they both shouted.

'Then I'll waste no more time. Two weeks until the trial flood. Have all the properties been cleared, Jane?'

'They have.'

'Dolly Lombard. Will a week give you sufficient time to clear the churchyard? The last service is on Sunday, so work can start immediately after,' Fitzpatrick said.

Dolly narrowed her eyes as if giving this some thought. She balanced the burnt ash of a half-smoked cigarette and Louise was transfixed, waiting for it to drop onto Dolly's tweed skirt. 'It will need to be cordoned off. Tents erected over each of the graves. In most cases, the coffin would have disintegrated, leaving just the remains of the body—a skeleton. My specialist team will transfer them into marked caskets and store them inside the locked church until we're ready to move them. So long as everyone follows the schedule a week should be fine.'

Louise flinched. Ma and Pa's bodies, Dicky's mam and da, cleared. As if they were debris. She didn't want to witness the relocation exercise. It was too distressing.

'The reservoir boundary,' Fitzpatrick said.

Louise's scalp tightened. Hairs on the back of her arms stood to attention.

'Do we know the actual perimeter now? There were some technicalities to resolve.' He put this question to some techies sitting near the front. Louise shifted her weight to the edge of her seat. *Please God, let it be unchanged.*

'The volume of water in the reservoir is calculated by measuring the contours.' The young man went into a lengthy explanation. Louise hung on to every word, desperately trying to squeeze some meaning from the jargon. 'The trapezoidal formula and prismoidal formula will …' No, he might as well be talking in a different language.

'Excuse me,' Louise raised her hand.

The techie stopped mid-sentence; his eyes big behind myopic lenses. He gave a couple of owl-like blinks.

'I'm sorry to interrupt but please could you explain in plain English? Will the reservoir boundary be the same as in the original plan?' She let out her breath.

The techie cast a glance at Fitzpatrick, who nodded for him to continue.

'Um. No. That's not possible. You see, the volume of water would be inadequate. The reservoir will have to come up higher.'

'How much higher? The farm. Becks Farm. Will it be affected?' Her mouth was so dry, she could barely speak.

The techie frowned. 'I'm sorry I'm not familiar with the dwellings.'

A tall man, one of the contractors, cleared his throat. 'We'll be embedding posts around the perimeter to mark the water level in the trial flood. It will give an indication of the trees and buildings to come out.'

He made it sound as though they were extracting teeth. A surgical procedure. In a way, it was. They were removing vital organs: trees—the lungs, church—the heart, and if Becks Farm was a casualty, then all the memories it contained. But surely the farm was safe? It sat above the valley.

'When? When are you planning to mark out the boundary?' Louise's face burned.

'Tomorrow?' The contractor looked at the techie, who nodded his agreement.

'So, next on the agenda,' Fitzpatrick said.

The next day, Louise could think of nothing else: Susan Jeffreys threatening letter—who else would it be? Eddie. The Mob. If Becks farm was safe. If the perimeter posts were just *a bit* further out, surely that's all it would be—these techies were pedantic, probably making a big deal over a few inches difference—then she would take off. To hell with Susan bloody Jeffreys. Let her do her worst. And if Eddie tried to throw her under the bus by telling Big Jim she'd done a runner with his money, then she would tell him the truth. *Just let Becks farm be safe,* she prayed.

Fitzpatrick wasn't available for their meeting that morning. High House buzzed with activity, people coming and going, carrying tripods, trowels, canvas bags, and mysterious boxes. Louise questioned anyone and everyone. Had the perimeter posts been erected? Did they know whether any buildings needed to be cleared?

Her answer came that afternoon, when Fitzpatrick called her into his office.

'Becks farm. Can you get it cleared out by Wednesday or Thursday next week?'

Louise's knees gave way, and she sank into a chair. 'Why? The reservoir's not coming up that far.'

'No, but it will come dangerously close, making the foundations unstable. We'll demolish it along with the other properties after the trial flood. The original boundary was calculated back in 1911, so not surprising we were a bit out.'

'The landscape's not changed much in that time,' Louise argued. 'Aren't they being a bit overzealous?'

'No, but industry has progressed and with it the demand for hydroelectric power and resilient water supplies.' Fitzpatrick was moving on to his favourite topic—the wonder of engineering, unaware Louise's heart had stopped.

'But the farm,' she cried. 'Can't we do something to strengthen its foundations? We should at least try to save it.'

'Not worth the effort or expense. It belongs to the Corporation, so we don't have to get permission. But I would like it cleared. So, next Thursday at the latest? You'll need to arrange a few skips, Hardwicks, and book some contractors before another team nabs them.'

'Does Richard know?'

'Who?'

'Richard Braithwaite. Does he know?'

Fitzpatrick threw up his hands. He shrugged. 'What's it to him? Okay. Can I leave that with you?'

Louise left his office in a daze. She had to tell Richard. He had said at the dinner party the Corporation had made assumptions about ownership. They *had* to talk. If there was any way to save the farm, they had to try.

She jumped on her bike and headed down into the valley,

searching all the while for perimeter posts. Once they went up, everyone would know the new plan.

Richard's Land Rover was not parked at the side of the maisonette. There was a notice on the shop door saying it had closed for the last time. Louise pressed her face to the glass. It was completely empty. Even the till and advertising boards had been stripped out. Just an empty counter and shelves.

Louise knocked on Richard's door, but there was no reply. She hadn't thought to ask him where he was going to live. Above the new shop? Had he moved in with the Simms? There were enough rooms in the family manor and he had looked very much at home on the night of the dinner party. She couldn't visit him there.

'Good morning, Jane.' Reverend Cummins trilled his bicycle bell. 'Will you be coming to our last service on Sunday?'

Louise turned away from the empty shop front. It was starting. The beginning of the end. The life support machine turned off as they waited.

She sighed. 'I wouldn't miss it, Reverend. Do you know where Richard Braithwaite is living now?'

'Sorry, I don't. Have you asked Fiona Simms? Or Kaye White?'

'No. But if you're free, could I ask you something?'

'That sounds intriguing. I was headed for the church. Why don't you accompany me and we can set the world to rights over a cuppa?'

Louise smiled. 'Thank you.'

She mounted her own bike and followed the Reverend up the hill to Thorncrest Church.

Louise made their tea in the shabby kitchen at the back of the vestry. She knew she was clutching at straws but if there was the remotest chance the reservoir boundary could be challenged, she had to try.

'How long have you lived and worked in the parish, Reverend?' Louise said, after handing him a cup of tea with four sugars.

'I moved here from the Lake District, let me see, 1957. Eight years ago.'

Six years after Ma died, Louise calculated. 'Was anyone living on the farm above the valley—Becks farm?'

'I know the place you mean. No. It's always been empty, to my knowledge. Why do you ask?'

Soon everyone would know. She might as well tell him. 'I heard today the reservoir is going to come up higher than expected. Becks farm is to be demolished as the foundations will become unstable. I understand the Corporation has claimed ownership, but this has been contested. Do you know where I might find the deeds for the farm, maybe a will, anything? If there's a living relative of the Becks, I can make a case for strengthening the foundations. It would be terrible to lose it.' Louise realised with a jolt she had said the wrong thing. 'I mean, it's a tragedy that we are losing this church. The entire valley.' Emotion overcame her—the bursting of her personal dam.

'There now.' The Reverend handed Louise a crisply laundered white handkerchief. 'Sean Fitzpatrick has been working you too hard. Endings are always sad. Beginnings scary. And it is a new beginning for all of us.'

Louise shivered. Goosebumps peppered her arms. 'There's nothing for me after this.'

'Oh, I'm sure you'll find another project, a clever girl like you. And we have a new church. It may not be as beautiful as this one, but Christ was born in a lowly cowshed. An austere environment will focus the mind, no glitz and glamour to distract us from our true purpose. You asked about the deeds for the farm or a will. Kaye White unearthed some interesting documents charting the history of the valley and some of its inhabitants. Letters written to the church about paupers from the workhouse being employed for hard labour in the mill. I can take a look, see if there's anything that might be of interest.' He cast a glance at Louise to see if she had recovered.

Her breathing steadied. 'Thank you. That would be helpful.' Concerned that he would ask questions, Louise moved the conversation on. 'We are interested in funding a project which will preserve the history of the valley for future generations. The papers you mentioned, for example.'

'Indeed. Splendid idea. And don't worry about our dear church. Everything and everyone has a beginning and an end. Part of God's great plan. Come along to the service on Sunday. We will say goodbye together and give thanks for all the valley has given us—including the reservoir. Yes. The reservoir. It is giving us water. Time to wash away the past and start anew.'

As Louise cycled back to High House, she felt calmer. The Reverend was wrong. She had no future, but maybe he would unearth something of the farm's history. Richard knew something or he wouldn't have challenged the Corporation. Maybe it wasn't too late to save the farm. If only she knew how much time she had left. Eddie was coming for her. Big Jim must know her whereabouts. The day they found her she was as good as dead. At least she would die knowing she had done everything in her power to save the farm and protect Richard.

30

SUNDAY 31ST OCTOBER 1965

The perimeter posts had been in place for two days now, and news of Becks farm's demise had become public. If only she could have warned Richard. Explained how it had taken her by surprise—that she honestly believed the plan would remain unchanged. How naïve and self-centred she had been. When she lied to Richard, she had fooled herself it was to set him free, to allow him to live the life of his dreams. When those dreams did not include her, when she discovered she didn't know Richard at all—that he was happy, living with Fiona in the valley, working in retail—reality dawned. He had been far more important to her than she had ever been to him. He didn't even recognise her. The lie had cost them the farm. Louise had let Ma and Pa down—again, and Richard hated her.

She had arrived early to offer moral support to the Reverend, not that he needed it. That man was as solid and consistent as a lighthouse in a storm.

'It is a sad day as we come together to say goodbye. Thorncrest Church has been at the heart of this community for more than a hundred years. Our grandparents, and their grandparents before them, knelt on this stone floor to give thanks, to ask for salvation, and to find peace.'

The candle-lit church was packed. Villagers dressed in their finery filled the aisles and crammed together at the back. It was hard to believe that in eight days' time it would be underwater. Louise imagined a school of fish weaving between the columns. A fat pike resting its weight on the lectern.

'Seeing your loved ones moved to another burial site will be deeply distressing. When we laid them to rest, we asked that they might rest in peace. But they *are* at peace. They are with our Lord in heaven. Moving their mortal remains does not change that. Let us now pray for those we have loved and lost, and for the families who are grieving as they say goodbye once again to loved ones.'

She had not said goodbye to Ma and Pa the first time. Poor Ma would have buried Pa alone, with only her neighbours there to offer comfort. And who was there for Ma? Richard's mam, villagers—everyone loved her, but Louise should have been there. Ma and Pa were family. She imagined a group of callous strangers digging up her beloved's remains, chatting and laughing as if it were of no importance, and she shuddered. The image was too distressing. Pa would have been matter-of-fact about it. From ashes to ashes, he would have said. *Everything in nature has a cycle*. It was the only time he would become philosophical, talking about the land and nature.

Ma would have reminded Louise that she was now with her maker, with no use for her mortal body. Ma had a strong faith. Louise smiled, imagining Ma directing her wandering attention back to the service.

'Taking away our church will not destroy our community; God's love unites us. Community is how we behave. It's not about buildings or even place. So, look after your neighbour and your neighbour's neighbour. Keep our community alive with kindness, not anger.'

Louise's attention wandered to take in the congregation. Kaye White. Esther and Bill. Everyone for miles around had gathered to say goodbye. There were too many people. More standing outside, it was whispered along the aisle.

'Let us sing hymn 368. Rock of Ages.'

The Reverend brought the service to a close with words of love and wisdom. This was the last service ever. A few minutes of silence followed as they each remembered loved ones and cherished moments in Thorncrest Church. A tear trickled down Louise's cheek. So many happy memories, standing between Ma and Pa, feeling protected and loved. The organ played, signalling the end of the silence. It was a cue to leave, but nobody moved. The woman to her right fished in her handbag for a handkerchief and blew her nose. A couple of women in the pew in front hugged one another. People started to move. Slowly. Shuffling along each pew and up the aisle for the last time.

The congregation gathered in the churchyard. It was twilight and would soon be dark. Richard and Fiona had joined other villagers who were paying their respects at each of the graves, remembering all who had passed. Louise felt her presence as an outsider might be unwelcome. Her grieving would have to be done in private. She stood under an old oak tree and drew comfort from the earthy scents of peat and rotting leaves.

'You should have worn a warmer coat,' Kaye White said, joining her.

Louise nodded, cursing herself again for snatching a

bloody anorak off the coat stand when she left home. And then Susan Jeffreys was walking towards them. There was no time for her to prepare. Caught in the depths of her grief, Louise felt vulnerable.

'Hello again,' Susan said.

Kaye greeted Susan, then left to chat with the Reverend.

'Hello Susan.' Louise's voice came out croaky.

'I've been racking my brains trying to place you. I knew we'd met before. You're the evacuee who stayed with the Becks.' She was playing a game. Pretending to be friendly. Hiding her meaning—her threat.

Louise nodded. 'I changed my name.'

'That's what confused me.' Then Susan laughed. 'It's funny I should meet up with you now. I found something of yours in the Becks cowshed.'

Bile gathered in Louise's throat. Let Susan do her worst. She had no fight left.

'Amazing Grace. How sweet the sound.' A lone voice filled the starlit night.

'Did you?' What else could she say?

From the dark expanse around them, a cigarette lighter clicked on. Then another tiny flame. And another. Voices joined in the hymn. *That saved a wretch like me.* Soon, everyone was singing. Lights dancing like fireflies.

Susan was talking, but Louise couldn't hear her. She was smiling. Laughing.

But now I'm free.

There was a hushed silence. Then Susan whispered, 'You and I must have a proper catchup. I've an interesting story to share.' And then she disappeared into the huddled groups of people.

Susan knew who Louise was and what she had done. Soon everyone in the village would too. No matter. She would clear

Becks farm, her final goodbye to Ma and Pa. A bit like preparing a body for burial. Then, when the valley was ready to be laid to rest, she would disappear. Run until the Mob found her.

'Jane!' Reverend Cummins attracted curious glances as he strode across the churchyard towards her. She met him halfway and found herself enveloped in a fold of his flock. Everyone wanted his attention.

'Jane. I almost forgot to tell you. I had a good look through all the archives. Fascinating. We have lots of material for your history project. Alas nothing about the ownership of Becks farm. Some correspondence regarding arrangements for Elizabeth Becks burial. Unfortunately, nothing that might help us save it from being demolished.'

Louise could feel his presence behind her, as if a ghost had wrapped its arms about her shoulders. She turned to see Richard. His eyes, deep pools of torment, reflected her own sorrow. They had lost everything: their loved ones, their church, the valley, their childhood, and their friendship. Now Becks farm was to be demolished. Her soul was being pulled apart, and there was nothing she could do. For a fleeting second, Louise imagined herself in Richard's arms, crying and comforting one another as they had once as teens. Then Fiona appeared at his side and pulled him away. The vicar was waiting for her response.

'Thank you, Reverend Cummins. It was a beautiful service.' She was Jane Cox, attending the service on behalf of the Corporation. *Try to keep focused.* 'Do you think I could ask one more thing of you? I need to get word around that there is to be a goodbye party for the village. Saturday 6th November in the old school. I'll let Esther know so she can hand out fliers from the mobile library. But if you could help spread the word?'

The Reverend agreed. His flock now took his attention and Louise watched as Richard and Fiona walked away, arm in arm. At the church gate, Richard turned to look directly at her.

'Goodbye Richard,' she whispered.

31

MARCH 1945

Louise couldn't concentrate on the algebra equation chalked up on the blackboard. The other girls were scribbling away, but Louise was gazing out of the window. The moors were cloaked in their spring colours: shades of green and gold. A band of sunlight highlighted the crest as if underlining the day.

She had pleaded with Ma that morning to let her skip school. 'You let me off for haymaking and this is more important.'

'If Gertrude's time comes before you get home, there are plenty of hands to help with calving.'

'But I want to be there! I'm the one who milks Gertrude. I should help deliver her calf.'

'Get off to school. It's likely she won't calf until late into the night.'

'If she does, then you must wake me.'

'We'll see. Now get going before you make yourself late.'

As soon as class was dismissed, Louise ran home without waiting for Dicky. She pictured her and Kurt working together, the emotional tension as they struggled to save mother and calf, their relief and jubilation at the miracle of birth. He had promised they would deliver Gertrude's calf.

Ma was in the kitchen when Louise hurtled through the door, throwing her school bag ahead of her. 'Whoa. Slow down. First, you can pick that up and then go and change. No Dicky today?'

'How's Gertrude?'

'Oh, she's fine. A perfect little calf.'

'When? It's not fair! I was meant to deliver her calf with Kurt.'

'Go on out. Forget your bag and getting changed. It can wait. She's not long had it. They should still be with her.'

Joan was sitting on *her* milking stool beside Gertrude. In front of her, Louise glimpsed a black and white calf suckling its mother.

'Close the door,' Kurt said a little sharply.

Louise felt the prickle of tears. Kurt wasn't even looking at her. She edged closer to Gertrude, resisting the temptation to push Joan off her stool. 'When was her calf delivered?'

Neither of them looked at her. They were both gazing at the calf. Eventually, Kurt said, 'About forty-five minutes ago. She's feeding well. Bravo, Joan.'

'I can take over now,' Louise said.

'It's all done,' Kurt replied, turning his head briefly to acknowledge Louise. 'Joan did an amazing job.' His shirt was open at the collar, exposing the Saint Christopher. *Their secret.*

'No. It was all down to your experience, Kurt,' Joan said.

Kurt crouched down next to Joan, their shoulders touching. 'He's a fine calf.'

Louise watched them, waiting for someone to say something to include her, but they were in their own world. Unable to witness this scene where she had imagined herself to be the star, Louise slipped away, carefully closing the barn door behind her.

It was hard to like Joan after that. Louise knew she was being unfair, that Joan had only ever been kind to her, but she couldn't help her feelings of rage whenever she saw them together. And it seemed they were always together now. Kurt spent more time in the fields, assisting Joan and Pa with the winter harvest, and less time around the farmhouse, leaving Louise and Ma to do the milking and tend to the chickens.

Two weeks later, a poster went up in the Braithwaite's shop. The Thorncrest annual tea party was to be revived. There would be a dance and refreshments in the village school. A chance for villagers to let their hair down after enduring five years of war and hardship. The war was not over, but there was a feeling of optimism that things were going the right way. Louise heard about the party from Dicky when she called at the shop one Saturday to buy her weekly ration of sweets.

'Are you going?' she asked, nodding at the poster.

Dicky shrugged. 'Probably not.'

'Why are you always such a grump? You used to love dancing.'

'When?'

'When we used to dance to the polyphons.'

'When we were little kids.' Dicky rolled his eyes. 'Is that all you want? A bag of humbugs?'

'Yes. I was hoping you would hang out with me.'

'Can't. Got to mind the shop.'

'Then I'll see you at school on Monday.'

Louise didn't think she had done anything to offend Dicky. Although she accused him of being a grump, he wasn't really. Dicky was mostly gentle, kind, and funny. He had his moods, everyone did, but in the past, he would have confided in her. Maybe it was just an off day. Louise shrugged away her worries and instead focused on the tea party. What kind of dance would it be? What would she wear? Had she been nice enough to Joan lately to ask if she could borrow a frock?

32

MAY 1945

The tea party was on a Wednesday afternoon. The school was to close for the day, a holiday for everyone.

'Does that mean Kurt can go?' Louise asked, when they were eating their tea, vegetable pie with mash and gravy.

'Doubt it,' Pa said.

'We'll have to let the prisoner of war officer know that he's not to come to work that day.' Ma bustled around the kitchen.

'Come and sit-down, Ma. It's a right good'un this pie. All vegetables from our land?'

'That they are. I thought Joan would join us, but she's off meeting her friends.'

'Will the Land Army girls be invited to the party?'

'Of course they will. I expect they'll enjoy dressing up. I'll see if I have a dress that can be altered for you, Louise.'

She ought to have been excited, but Louise was agitated. 'Won't they need extra hands to set everything up?'

'Aye. There's a lot to organise. The wood burning tea urns. They'll need to be moved from the church up to the school.

Braithwaite would normally transport them but with Frank missing in action, well he's got a lot on his mind.'

'Kurt could help. There will be furniture to move into the school hall as well,' Louise said.

'We could ask if they would let him help out at the tea party instead of the farm for one day,' Pa said.

Louise crossed her fingers under the table. 'Do we have to ask, if he's just helping you?'

'Aye lass. We do.' Pa filled his mouth with pie. The conversation was over.

It was the day of the tea party. Kurt had been given permission to assist with getting the hall ready. He would be escorted back to the camp at his usual time and so there was a chance he might dance. Louise imagined herself in his arms waltzing around the hall whilst villagers stood back to watch. In her daydream, she looked like Rita Hayward and danced like Ginger Rogers.

'Do you want me to style your hair?' Joan asked Louise's mirror reflection.

Louise fluffed up the waves she had created by sleeping with her hair in rags. 'If you could make some pin curls around my face, it would be great. Thank you.'

Joan set to work. 'You have a pretty face, Lou. No wonder that boy of yours can't keep his eyes off you.'

Louise suppressed a smile. Joan had noticed Kurt's interest in her too. 'Do you think he'll admire me in this dress?' It was a red gingham dress that Ma had taken in and edged in rick-rack ribbon.

Joan stood back. 'Honestly?' 'It's not very glamorous. A bit country girl. But maybe he likes that look.'

Joan was right. Her cotton dress looked like a kid's

compared to Joan's V-neck swing dress. But she had to wear it. Ma had sat up late unpicking the ribbon from one of her skirts. It would hurt Ma's feelings to reject the dress.

'I know. You could wear this one.' Joan sprung across the room and pulled a silk shirt waister from her wardrobe. 'It would look amazing on you.'

'It's beautiful. Are you sure?' Louise felt herself wavering.

'Try it on.'

With her hair pinned up in curls, make-up and the gorgeous green dress, Louise felt like a film star. Ma's gingham dress lay on Joan's bed—the bands of rickrack ribbon hand-stitched.

'Louise,' Ma called up the stairs. 'Dicky's here to see you.'

'Can you send him up? I'm dressed, but need a bit more time to get ready.'

Dicky's feet echoed on the wooden stair. Louise stood at the top to greet him, excited to see his reaction to her transformation.

He was wearing an old sweater, wool unravelled around a hole at his elbow. 'I just came over to let you know I won't be going to the party.'

'Oh. Okay.' She clutched the gingham dress to her.

'What's that?'

Louise followed his gaze. 'A dress Ma made me for the dance.' She held it up.

'So, why are you wearing that other one?'

'Do you like it?' Louise held back her arms so that Dicky could admire her.

'I like the gingham better.'

'Oh, you don't know what's fashionable, Dicky. You're a fuddy-duddy country bumpkin.'

'And you are a vain, selfish cow.'

They stared at each other. Louise felt as though Dicky had slapped her hard across the face.

'I'm sorry, Louise. It's just that--'

'--Leave me alone. Go away.'

When Dicky had left, his boots scuffing across the courtyard, Louise sunk onto her bed. He was right. To discard the dress that Ma had lovingly made was unkind.

Ma clapped her hands together when Louise made her entrance into the farmhouse kitchen. 'Oh my goodness. Aren't you the bee's knees? I'm surprised Dicky didn't change his mind when he saw you — a vision of beauty. Poor lad. It would have done him good to get out.'

'Are my two girls ready for their carriage?' Pa came in from outside.

'As ready as I'll ever be. Unless you think I should make up some more sandwiches?' Ma took a step towards the pantry.

'Absolutely not. Everything's set up in the hall. I'll have us there in a few minutes, and when we get there, try to relax and enjoy yourself. No scurrying off to make yourself busy serving drinks. Let someone else volunteer for a change. My, you both look grand.'

Louise daren't ask whether Kurt was waiting for them at the school. It would arouse suspicion and if the answer was no, her disappointment would show.

Kurt was there. Sitting on one of the chairs lined up along the wall. A few of the farming families had also arrived early. Ma joined a group of women hovering around the serving counter, and Pa wandered over to the musicians, a pianist and fiddle player, to check that they had everything they needed. Louise swayed from one foot to the other, unsure whether she should approach Kurt. Maybe he had been told not to socialise. She tried to catch his eye, a smile fixed on her face, but his attention was focused on the entrance door.

The hall was filling up. Men and women Louise recognised from the village shop, or market, farmers who did business with Pa, helping each other out. There was Dicky's friend George, with his younger brother. And then Louise spotted Brenda Button and her entourage, the bitchy girls from school. If Dicky had been with her, Louise would have felt braver, but standing alone, clutching a paper cup of warm orange squash, she felt awkward and self-conscious. Brenda was wearing a swingy dress, with a wide belt and buckle. Her hair was styled like Louise's, but she didn't wear lipstick. Louise wanted to feel superior, but she just felt stupid in her gingham dress.

At last, Joan and her friends burst through the door, a colourful whirlwind of energy with their chatter, laughter, and glamour. Louise made a beeline for them, striding across the hall with a newfound confidence. She was a few paces away from Joan, about to greet her, when Kurt beat her to it. It was as though he had been watching the door waiting for Joan's arrival, and now they were walking together towards the refreshments. They were not holding hands, but might as well be. Their heads were bent together. Joan giggled. Her hand stroked the sleeve of his shirt. He turned to look down at Joan and Louise's heart plummeted. Why didn't he look at her like that?

The fiddler tried a few bars of a reel. Paused. Then the piano picked up the tune. Everyone clapped in time. The party had begun and Louise wanted to be anywhere but in the middle of the school hall with Kurt and Joan making eyes at each other across the room, and bitchy Brenda Button, no doubt sneering at her country-style dress.

Louise headed straight for the door. She didn't want to spoil Ma and Pa's fun, but she couldn't stay.

'Can you tell Ma Beck that Louise remembered something that she had to do back at the farm? I won't be long. But if I don't return, then they're not to worry. I'll be fine.'

'If you're sure?' The woman who sat at the entrance greeting new arrivals looked concerned.

'Really, it's fine. I walk back to the farm from this school every day.' *With Dicky,* Louise thought. Everything would have been better if Dicky had been there.

33

MAY 1945

Ma, Pa, and Joan arrived back at the farm not long after Louise. She was sitting on the bed, writing in her diary, when the kitchen door slammed, startling her. Then raised voices. At first, Louise thought they were angry that she had left early spoiling the party for them, but when she crept to the top of the stairs to listen, she heard Pa shouting.

'What were you thinking of, lass? Now, we've lost our best farmhand.'

'It's a huge over reaction. I'll explain; tell them it wasn't his fault,' Joan pleaded.

'You are damn right you are going to explain. And apologise. Making an exhibition of yourself.'

Joan was sobbing. Loud, gasping cries and sniffles. The door slammed. Pa had left the farmhouse, probably heading to the fields to work off his anger. Whatever had Joan done?

The door at the bottom of the stairs opened, and Louise dived back into her bedroom. Joan's feet pounded on the wooden stairs. Then her bedroom door closed. The house was silent. A whine from Kara.

Louise didn't know whether to knock on Joan's door to see if she was alright or go downstairs to Ma. Kara yelped and that decided her. At least Kara would offer a warm welcome.

Ma Beck was sitting by the fire. Louise could not remember seeing her sitting in the living room during a work day unless it was to entertain a visitor. "Ma? Are you alright?'

Ma looked up at her. 'There you are, pet. We were worried about you. I hope you've not got a bad tummy from eating and drinking too much. I'm afraid I wasn't keeping a proper eye on you. What time did you leave?'

'Not long before you.'

Ma put a hand to her forehead. 'Then you didn't see …'

'See what?'

'Nought for you to worry about, lass.'

'Please tell me Ma. I heard Pa shouting at Joan. I ought to know if it's something that affects our farm.'

Ma smiled. 'You are right. It's our farm. You've become like a granddaughter to us. Pa and I are going to miss you so much when you leave.'

'Hopefully that won't be for a long time and even when I do, I can come back. When I'm a grown-up, I'm going to move back here.'

'You are always welcome here, pet. You know that. How about you make us both a brew? I don't think I have the strength.'

As Louise prepared a pot of tea, she thought through every scenario. Joan had drunk too much elderflower wine and had thrown up in the middle of the hall. That brought a smile to her face. Kurt wouldn't want to smooch with Joan if she smelt of sick. But Pa had said they would lose their best farmhand. They didn't have many—Joan, Kurt and herself. A couple of men on casual labour at harvest time. Maybe Joan and a couple of the farm boys had been having a lark. She was a bit high-spirited. They had left Kurt at the dance. Louise hoped he wouldn't get in trouble for not being at the farm when his officer arrived to escort him back to camp.

Louise set Ma's cup and saucer down on the occasional table. 'It's nearly time for Kurt to be collected. How is he getting back from the school?'

'Did you sugar it?'

Louise nodded.

Ma blew on her tea and took a sip. 'Lovely. Kurt is being collected from the school. I'm afraid we won't be seeing him on the farm for a while, pet.'

'Why?' Louise felt as though her heart had been scooped out, leaving a hollow ache.

'It was the excitement. The farm girls got high-spirited. You can't blame them; the war has brought us all down. They were just letting off steam.'

'Tell me what happened.'

Ma sighed. 'The girls were dancing. The Jitterbug. Jive. Whatever it is they do when they swing each other around. Being lively. There weren't many fellas to partner and so Joan grabbed hold of Kurt. At first, it was okay. He let her twirl under his arm, but you could see he was being careful, not really joining in. If Joan had left it at that, nobody would have minded.'

'What did she do?' A surge of anger kicked Louise's heart into over-drive.

'Kissed him. In front of everyone. The silly girl.'

'What in the middle of the dance floor?'

'No. She was trying to get him to dance. Larking about. Putting her arms around his waist. Teasing him. Of course, when they left the floor, everyone had eyes on them. Not all folks are comfortable with prisoners of war working on the farms, what with husbands and sons fighting them. That's why the Braithwaite's didn't show. Dicky told you about his brother, Frank?'

'Still missing?'

'No, pet. They got a telegram, "Presumed dead."'

Louise gasped. 'He didn't tell me. Poor Dicky. Oh, his mum and dad must be heartbroken. I had no idea.'

'So, when Joan kissed Kurt full on the lips, you can imagine the hoo-ha. A couple of the men wanted to take him outside and give him a beating. If it weren't for Pa calming them down and telling them he was responsible for the boy, I reckon they would have.'

'No. It's not fair!' Louise cried out in anger.

Kara whimpered, roused from her sleep by the fire and skulked out of the room.

'There's a lot that's not fair. But we have to make the most of it. Pa will forgive Joan once he's calmed down. She's young and just got a bit carried away. Maybe they'll let Kurt come back. We'll have to wait and see. But if they don't…I don't like Pa doing heavy work. Perhaps we can get the local lads to do a bit more.' Ma was thinking ahead. Being practical. But Louise's world had been blown apart.

Pa came in from outside and Louise, not wanting to stay and hear them discuss the kiss, or to go upstairs where Joan was crying, went outside. The birds sang as though it was an ordinary day. The cows still needed milking. She hadn't bothered to ask who would do it when they were all at the tea-party. Maybe Pa had arranged help, but everything changed when Joan kissed Kurt.

It wasn't fair. Joan had ruined everything. Kurt would be confined to the camp. Would they punish him? The thought of Kurt suffering made Louise's stomach lurch. And Dicky. No wonder he was angry and upset. His brother had died. Frank, the son his mother, seemed most proud of. Dicky had never been jealous, just accepted that Frank was the clever one, the one that women admired. He was going to run the family business when he returned from the war, expand it to sell household goods, records, anything and everything. A store to compete with Woolworths. All of their dreams – the future which Mrs Braithwaite had described as though it were a certainty. Gone. He must have come around earlier to tell her and they had a row about her stupid dress. *Oh, Dicky. I'm sorry.* She wanted to hug him, to tell him everything would be alright. Dicky was her best friend—she loved him, heart and soul. Without him, nothing felt right. Why did they have to grow up and change?

Louise creaked open the barn door and felt some comfort in the warm scent of hay. Gertrude and her calf were settled happily in their stall. Soon, they would have to wean the calf off her mother's milk because they were collecting less milk for cheese and butter sales. She sat on Kurt's milking stool. Her fingers caressed the wood as she thought of him, how he had taught her to milk. The song he had hummed to the cows. And then, no longer able to keep back the tears, she cried. Big, heaving sobs that raked her body. The Germans may have killed Frank, but Joan had destroyed Louise's world.

34

MAY 1945

When Louise awoke, the morning after the party, a heaviness was pressing down on her. At first, she thought it a bad dream, but then the change in sounds and energy alerted her that something was different. Their lives had been shaken and nothing was going to be the same again. Ma and Pa were talking in hushed voices outside her window. No shrill cries from Joan or the clutter of milk pails being carried from the cowshed.

It was Saturday, so no school, but the cows would need to be milked and the chickens fed. The sound of the army vehicle delivering Kurt had not awoken Louise that morning and she had overslept. It was too quiet. She dressed in breeches and blouse, determined to show Ma and Pa they didn't need a Land Army girl. Joan was more trouble than she was worth—surely Pa would realise that and get rid of her. Then Kurt could come back. Maybe he would arrive later that morning when everything had been sorted out.

Louise creaked down the stairs and opened the kitchen door. There was nothing cooking on the stove—no freshly baked bread or fried bacon waiting for her. Ma came in from outside to greet Louise.

'How did you sleep, pet?'

'Okay. But I was worried. Has Pa spoken to the prison warden? Explained that it wasn't Kurt's fault?'

Ma sighed. 'It's more complicated than that. I don't think Kurt will be leaving the compound for some time. We'll miss the extra pair of hands. He was a good worker. And Pa...' She shook her head and sighed. 'Well, Pa needs someone younger to help him.'

'Like me,' Louise said.

Ma gave her a loving smile. 'You are exactly what we both need. I'll make you an egg for breakfast.'

Louise felt like crying. She might never see Kurt again. Maybe she could visit him at the prisoner of war camp. Or send him a letter.

'That smells good.'

Louise's head whipped up. Joan. Why hadn't *she* been sent packing?

'Move up, squirt.' Joan pulled a chair alongside Louise at the table.

Louise kept her head bowed. Her teeth clenched. Then she caught a glint of silver at Joan's neck. She swallowed hard and looked up.

'I didn't see your boyfriend at the party yesterday,' Joan said.

Tears clouded Louise's vision. Dicky's brother had died, and she wasn't there to comfort him. He hated her.

Ma carried over two plates of scrambled egg and set them in front of Joan and Louise. 'Poor lad. His brother Frank is missing, presumed dead. I don't expect he felt like going to a party. Maybe later you could carry a basket of produce over to the Braithwaite's Louise. Give our condolences.' She squeezed Louise's shoulder.

Louise sat very still, afraid that if she tried to speak or move, she would fall apart.

'I'm sorry about what happened at the party, Mrs Beck.' Then Joan laughed. 'A bit too much wine, I'm afraid.'

Louise's head whipped around to glare at Joan. Hatred filling her veins. Kurt's Saint Christopher was fastened around Joan's neck.

'I'm not hungry,' Louise said. 'May I be excused, Ma?'

'I don't like you wasting food. You need the protein and despite our hens we are rationed the same as other folk.'

'I'll eat it,' Joan said.

Louise wished she had poisoned it. Or that Joan would choke and die. She could barely see through her tears as she stumbled to the door and fled upstairs to her bedroom.

Kurt had thrown his love away on Joan — a worthless floozy who cared nothing for him. Now he would be confined to prison. Away from the farm and animals that he loved. Louise's heart ached as she remembered the lullaby he sang to the cows. Everything was perfect until Joan came along. She had taken everything away from her. Hate burned in her chest, filling her until she felt she would explode.

Joan clipped up the stairs humming, *We'll Meet Again*. Unable to be within hearing distance of Joan, Louise waited until her bedroom door closed and then went downstairs. Ma had disappeared, probably to the dairy, and so Louise went to the chicken coop. Her body went through the motions of feeding the chickens and collecting eggs whilst her soul felt crushed, her heart broken.

She remembered how Kurt had discovered the egg shells. He had always made her feel special. They had a bond. If Joan hadn't taken Louise'sher place delivering the calf, Kurt would never have looked at her. Louise was meant to be in that cow shed alongside Kurt, experiencing the miracle of birth. And he loved her. Louise knew he loved her—he made a jewellery box, said she was pretty. Joan may have turned his head at the party, dressing up like a floozy, but he would have seen through her. Only now, they might never be reunited. Like Romeo and Juliet. It wasn't fair. Joan had ruined everything. She hated Joan.

There were only two eggs that morning, and Louise felt bad for leaving her scrambled egg at breakfast. Maybe she should stop eating until Kurt came back. Someone would send for him, saying, 'You have to come quick. We believe Miss Louise will die if she doesn't see you.' Die of a broken heart.

As she walked across the courtyard, a coin winked in the sunlight. She bent down to pick it up—Kurt's Saint Christopher. One of the chain links had loosened. It must have slipped off Joan's neck. Louise squeezed it in her palm. It was a sign. She smiled to herself.

Jobs done, she returned to her bedroom. Ma always encouraged Louise to relax on a Saturday. As kids, she and Dicky would explore the valley, playing house in the old Mill House. Poor Dicky. She would visit him later with the basket of produce and be the friend to him she should have been yesterday. Dicky had known about his brother, and all she had gone on about was what she would wear to the party. Dressed up in one of Joan's dresses like a tart. How could she have ever thought Joan glamorous? She was hideous. A witch. Rotten to the core.

Louise trailed the silver chain through her fingers, imagining it around Kurt's warm neck. His mother had given it to him for luck. He had to have it back. Louise's heart quickened as she imagined the scene, Kurt behind bars distraught—he would have realised Louise was his true love and be full of regret for his rash behaviour. Then he would see her waiting for him. A couple of years older now. Sixteen. Beautiful. So beautiful he couldn't take his eyes off her. She would return his Saint Christopher and he would clasp her hand—pull it to his lips.

Outside, Louise heard Joan chatting to Pa. He was instructing her on a job, Louise could tell from the tone of his voice. He was probably still angry with her. So many good people die at war, innocent civilians and soldiers like Frank. Why couldn't a bomb drop on Joan? A freak accident? She could get trampled by a bull. Or step on a land mine. There was an unexploded bomb found on the moors. So many lives lost—what was one more?

Louise knew she was playing—creating a story to make herself feel better—when she took a sheet of notepaper and pen and started writing.

Dear Mr. Kurt Müller

No *Dearest Kurt,*

I hope that life has been kind to you—she had read that once in a letter addressed to her aunt and it sounded elegant. *Life on the farm is busy, as always. Gertrude and Henrietta miss you, as do I. We had such good times together. Remember how we filled an egg shell with mustard when I was a little kid?*

I am sorry to be writing with sad news. You may remember our Land Army girl, Joan? There was a tragic accident on the farm and sadly Joan died. Louise stopped writing to enjoy the moment. No more Joan. With Joan out of the way, Kurt would realise that it was her he loved. Louise Pearson. Louise Müller. *I am writing because I believe she had something of yours. The Saint Christopher that your mother gave you. I know how precious this is to you and wanted to return it. I will visit you at the POW camp and hide it in a handkerchief so that the warden doesn't see it and take it away from you.* She couldn't spell confiscate. What else could she write to make herself sound grown up, alluring and mysterious? *Like the Saint Christopher you wear around your neck, I will always hold your friendship close. My heart is yours and always will be.*

Louise paused, filled with thoughts of Dicky. How he had lost his brother and she hadn't been there for him. Writing always made her feel better. But it was time she found her friend to comfort him. Her dearest friend.

She was slipping the Saint Christopher into the envelope with the letter for safe-keeping when Ma knocked on her door.

'Hold on,' she said. But Ma came straight in. Flustered, Louise clutched the letter to her breast, trying to disguise it. If Ma saw it was a letter, she would insist on posting it.

'What's that you're hiding?' Ma said.

'Nothing.' Louise scrunched the envelope into her pocket. 'What did you want?'

'I've made up a basket for Mrs Braithwaite. Would you deliver it for me?'

Louise longed to be with Dicky again. To let him know she would always be there for him. The pain of losing him made her realise with a jolt that what she felt for Dicky was love. It was different to the way she felt about Kurt. With Kurt, it was make-believe, as if she was living a story, instead of just telling it. Her feelings for Dicky ran deep. They had scared her when she was younger and when she was old enough to know, he had turned his back on her. Kurt had come between them before she became infatuated with him. From the day Dicky saw the prisoner of war on their farm, he had changed towards her, and now Frank was dead. Maybe it was a good thing Dicky wouldn't have to see Kurt again. If only she could have her friend back. Return to the days when they trusted one another, and he told her everything.

'I'll go straight away,' she said.

35

MAY 1945

Ma had filled a basket with eggs, butter, preserves, elderflower wine, and a loaf of bread. 'There's a note in there offering our condolences. Poor Elsie. She worshipped Frank. Just leave the basket and come back. They won't want visitors, so don't be a nuisance.'

'Dicky will want to see me.' He had tried to tell her before the party, but she had been too full of herself and the impression she would make on Kurt. It was Joan's fault, making her look like a tart in that green silk dress.

Louise almost ran down the hill in her impatience to see Dicky. There was a handwritten sign on the door of the grocers. *Temporary closure due to family bereavement.* Louise went to the side door where Dicky had sneaked in on the day they had played truant. She rapped the knocker, thinking of her friend, how sadness had clouded his sparkling eyes once so full of mischief. Dicky lost his sparkle the day Frank went missing, but she had been too wrapped up in herself to give him the attention he deserved.

When nobody came to the door, Louise rapped harder.

They must all be out. Maybe it was the funeral today. Or they were staying with a relative. She was knocking repeatedly, not expecting an answer, when the door flew open and Mrs Braithwaite stood there in her working overall. Her hair was loose, and her face pale and ghost-like, with no make-up.

'What do you want?'

Louise held out the basket, which was covered with one of Ma's best linen cloths. 'Ma Beck sent this for you with our sympathies for your loss.'

Mrs Braithwaite sniffed. She took the basket and her fragile looking body swayed with its weight. 'Tell her, thank you.' She started to close the door.

'Mrs Braithwaite. Is Dicky in?'

'No.'

'Where is he? I would like to pay my respects. I didn't know.' Louise choked back tears. It would be poor form to cry in front of a bereaved mother.

'I don't want Richard going to Becks farm or associating with you. I didn't want to be blunt, and I appreciate Ma Becks kindness, but under the circumstances I think it best we keep our distance.'

Louise stared at the closed door. First Kurt, and now Dicky. She was alone. Completely and utterly alone. Mrs Braithwaite had lost her son, but Louise was suffering too. She had lost her two best friends. And it was all Joan's fault. Joan had thrown a grenade into her life and now, while Louise was picking the shards from her heart, bloody Joan was acting like nothing had happened.

She stomped up the lane, anger numbing her pain. If Joan had not arrived with her foolish frippery and vanity, then life would have continued as it was. Dicky might have got over his resentment of Kurt if Louise hadn't tried emulating Joan's glamour. She'd made a complete fool of herself. Dicky had told her as much. He knew her better than anyone. And now, she wasn't to see him. Life without Dicky was unbearable—he had become part of her. The better part.

Louise's coat snagged on a thorny shrub. She tugged it free, and the fabric tore. 'I hate Joan,' she shouted.

Hate. Hate. Hate. With each step, rage built. An all-consuming hatred. Joan was responsible for everything that was wrong in Louise's life. The blood in her neck pulsed. Her palms throbbed. By the time she reached the farm, Louise was shaking with anger.

Joan was crouched on her haunches searching the yard with eyes and hands.

'Lost something?' Louise said, glad Joan could not see her mouth twitch.

'Oh, it's nothing. You didn't happen to see anything lying around out here?'

'No. But if you tell me what you've lost, I'll keep my eyes open.'

'It's okay. I've just misplaced something. It'll turn up. If you're free, do you want to help me service the tractor? I'll show you how to disable it in case of capture by the Jerries. There was an article in the Land Girl this month.'

She was carrying on as if nothing had happened. As if she wasn't responsible for Kurt being grounded, for Dicky being banned from the farm, and for breaking Louise's heart.

'Is Pa Beck still angry with you?' Louise said.

Joan sighed. 'Oh, you know about that? Probably. That's why I'm going to service the tractor and then I'll do some muck spreading on the middle field. Pa was complaining about that job, so I'll surprise him. Coming?'

He wasn't *her* pa. Pa Beck or Mr Beck. Kurt always called him, Mr Beck. Louise seethed as she followed Joan into Pa's work barn. The tractor had already been dismantled; the back wheel removed and pieces of machinery lined up along the workbench.

'I'll talk you through what I've done so far,' Joan said.

She didn't apologise for the chaos she had caused on the farm, or explain why she had behaved like a cow – that was an insult to Gertrude. It was as though she had done nothing wrong. But she took her time explaining to Louise how the engine worked. Treating her like a grown-up. Another Land Army girl. *You won't win me over this time,* Louise thought. How foolish and gullible she had been to put Joan on a pedestal. At one time, she had even wanted to be like Joan. Dicky had seen through her.

'Look at these brake shoes,' Joan exclaimed, when she opened up the casing. 'Rusty. They need a good clean.'

They worked side by side, rubbing down the brake shoes, freeing them of rust.

'Now we just need to reline them.' Joan went to her tool box and returned brandishing two brake liners, as proud of them as she had once been of her nylons and lipstick. 'I got these from one of the other Land Army girls. Got to help one another out. Right, Lou?'

'What would happen if you hadn't cleaned them up and lined them?'

'That depends. I'm surprised Pa didn't hear squeaking or grinding. Although that could be his hearing. I've got most of the rust off and the brake liners will make a difference. I wouldn't want to be on the road, or heading down to the lower field with no brakes. She's a heavy girl, so builds momentum downhill. Just as well we spotted them. Right. That's done. I'm taking a break. You coming in with me? See if Ma's done any baking?'

'What about putting the tractor back together?'

'I'll do it when I've had a cuppa. Then I'll get started on the mucking.'

'I'll follow on. I've a couple of jobs to do first,' Louise said.

As soon as she was alone, Louise set to work, reversing the steps Joan had just demonstrated. First the bolts holding on the cover plate. One. Two. Three.

The hairs on the back of her neck prickled and she froze, feeling like someone was watching her. All was quiet and so Louise opened up the casing. Joan had screwed the bolts in hard. Removing the brake liner was easy. Louise scoured the brake shoe and threw in a handful of gravel from the barn floor for good measure. It was wicked. She knew it was, but Louise was driven by fury. She hated Joan with every fibre of her being. When the cover plate was back on, Louise hid the brake liner beneath an oil drum.

Ma was kneading bread when Louise arrived back at the farmhouse. She had flour on her forehead and nose. Her face flushed. 'Hello, pet. How were Dicky and his folks? Did you give them the basket?'

'I did. Mrs Braithwaite said to say thank you. I didn't see Dicky. I don't think he's allowed to be friends with me anymore — because of what *she* did.'

Ma wiped her hands on her apron and gave Louise her full attention. 'They are going through untold grief, pet. We cannot imagine the pain. Give them time. You and Dicky have a strong friendship. Nothing and nobody can come between you, if you've a mind to treasure that gift. Be kind to Joan, lass. She's not much more than a girl herself. And she's far from home. We have to forgive people when they make mistakes, otherwise people might not forgive us and we all make mistakes.'

Louise felt bad. Ma was so good and kind. Shame swept

over her. 'Where's Joan? She said she was coming in for a break.'

'I haven't seen her. Must have got waylaid.'

Good. There was time to go back to the barn and undo her evil. What had she been thinking? It was stupid to do something so dangerous. She didn't want Joan to die in real life—only in her head. 'I'm just going to Pa's work barn. Joan's teaching me how to service the tractor.'

'That can wait. I need you to deliver a roll of butter and some eggs to Blackmoor Farm. Mabel's daughter has had a baby girl and they're going to visit. I promised I would get the provisions over there before they leave. Besides, Mabel helped me out last week with some extra rashers of bacon to feed the local lads helping Pa. It won't take long. I've made up a parcel in the pantry.'

No. She had to make the tractor safe. 'Please, Ma. I promised Joan. Can't it wait until after?'

'No. Best not. Pa was going to drop off the butter and eggs on his way to the pub, but there was some sort of emergency with a broken fence. Thank you, Louise. One less thing for me to worry about. But please be quick. No dilly dallying.'

'Okay, but please, please, please don't let Joan reassemble the tractor before I get back.'

Ma laughed. 'I'll do my best. Be quick and you'll get back before she makes a start.'

'Just don't let her start without me.'

'Go!' Ma laughed.

Everything was going to be alright. She would tell Joan she'd been having a go, putting into practice what she'd learnt and ask her to check if she'd done it right. So long as she was quick. Joan hadn't even started her break, so there was time.

The sky was bright blue. Not a single cloud in sight. Above her starlings wheeled in a kaleidoscopic pattern--formations fragmenting, then gathering. A perfect dance of nature. Louise watched them in wonder. And the trees. A vibrant green, with the first leaves of spring. Energy surged through her. She wanted to run, to release her pent-up emotions. Louise trotted and skipped; the parcel banging against her leg. Then she laughed, remembering her rage. It was often like that when her period was due—great swings of emotion. Ma was right. She and Dicky would always be friends. Now that Kurt was no longer working on the farm, she would work hard to rebuild their friendship. Her problem was living too much in her imagination. In the future, she would write romantic stories and those of revenge instead of trying to act them out. Louise laughed at herself, anxious to share this revelation with Dicky. He would understand—sometimes he knew her better than she did herself.

At Blackmoor Farm, Mabel insisted Louise drink a glass of ginger beer as a special treat. She couldn't say "no thank you" without seeming rude, and then Ma Mabel kept talking about the birth of her granddaughter. So, it was later than she hoped when Louise ran back to Becks farm.

She headed straight for the work barn, but the tractor had gone. Henrietta clucked around Louise as she stood staring at where it had once been. The hen squawked. Louise ran back out into the lane, hoping to see Joan driving away, but all was quiet. A Magpie cawed. *Please don't let her die. I'm sorry, God. Please let her be safe.*

'Louise, is that you?' Ma called from the back door.

She couldn't face Ma. Her face would give her away. Louise hurried across the yard and hid in the cowshed.

The cows were out grazing. Louise sat on her milking stool and took deep breaths. It would be okay. Maybe the tractor would take longer to stop, or skid around in the mud. Joan was most likely exaggerating about the brake shoes to make herself seem important. As soon as Joan returned the tractor, she would confess and together they would put right the damage she had done.

'Help! Help!' One of the farm boys was shouting. 'Come quickly. Phone an ambulance. There's been an accident.'

The back door slammed. Ma screamed.

It was too late. What had she done? Louise was about to run out to comfort Ma when she remembered the letter in her pocket. It would look as though she knew Joan was going to die. That she had planned the accident. And she had. Louise was shaking. Ma was calling for her.

The loose flagstone. She lifted it and hid the letter with the Saint Christopher still inside the envelope.

'Louise. Louise. Where's Louise?' Ma was crying.

As Louise stepped out into the courtyard, she saw Joan comforting Ma. She let out a huge sigh of relief. Joan was alive. Thank God.

'I'm here, Ma.' Louise rushed to her side. She wanted to hug them both, Joan for being alive, and her beloved Ma, who was sobbing as if her heart was broken.

'Oh Louise.' Ma left Joan's side to hug Louise tight. 'Thank the Lord you're safe.' Her body juddered. 'It's Pa. Oh, Louise.'

'What's happened?' Louise went cold.

'He was out on the tractor.' Ma couldn't finish the sentence. She gasped and cried.

Joan rubbed Ma's back. 'A car's being sent over for us Ma. They've taken Pa to the hospital. I'll follow with you.'

'What about Louise?' Ma said.

'Lou will be okay. She's almost a grown woman.' Joan smiled reassuringly at Louise.

Pa was in hospital because of her. She, Louise Pearson, caused his accident. If her darling Pa died, she would never forgive herself.

. . .

When the black Wolsely pulled away with Ma and Joan in the back seat, Louise felt as though she had died and wished that she had. She couldn't move. And then she did as her body shook in violent tremors. If Kara had not sat on her feet and then nudged her to move, Louise might have stayed planted to that spot all night.

36

WEDNESDAY 3RD NOVEMBER 1965

Louise closed her fingers around keyring twenty-four. The handwritten labels, now faded: cowshed, chicken coop, workroom, backdoor. Louise couldn't remember there being a front door. Maybe once upon a time, opening into the living room. They had always entered through the kitchen where a warm stove and the scent of freshly baked bread, or a casserole, greeted them. Louise closed her eyes to imagine Ma locking up for the last time. Had she been taken into hospital on that day? Who would have looked after Kara, the sheepdog?

A skip would be delivered tomorrow morning; Hardwicks in the afternoon, to transport anything of value. At least Ma and Pa's treasured possessions would be kept in storage until they were auctioned off. Today, Louise was visiting alone. She didn't know what awaited her behind the farmhouse doors. A place that had always represented love and comfort; she was afraid of finding it neglected and abused. The temporary home of squatters or foxes. Tears welled up, clouding her vision. It couldn't be put off any longer.

She had come equipped with a claw hammer. The boarding was chipboard and easier to remove than expected. On closer inspection, it looked as though it had jus been wedged into position. Lazy workmanship. The yard was empty. No chickens clucking, no cow muck, or abandoned tools. She stood a while summoning ghosts from the past. Dicky pushing his glasses up his nose, impatiently kicking the satchel dangling from one hand. Ma calling out to her, 'How was your day, darling?' Pa plodding across the yard ready for a hearty stew. Kara's bark.

Louise shivered and wrapped her arms across her chest. 'I'm home, Ma,' she whispered.

The key was a big iron Chubb, the same one that had hung just inside the pantry door. It turned easily. Louise took three deep breaths to prepare herself. Then she leaned her weight against the heavy door and it swung open. The sweet smell of wood-smoke. How could you imagine a scent so strongly your brain believed it was real?

At first, Louise believed all of it was a mirage. How she wanted to remember the kitchen because everything was exactly as it had been then. A scrubbed pine table in the centre, which had been used to roll pastry, to peel potatoes and to share the many meals Ma lovingly prepared. A big cast iron fireplace, with a side-oven on the left and boiler on the right, dominated one wall. And that was when Louise saw the flicker of flames. Someone had lit the stove. The wood-smoke was real. And then her heart faltered. She wasn't alone. Her instincts had been right all along. Someone had been living in the farmhouse. At least they had preserved it, and for that she was grateful. But who? Dare she believe Ma was alive? No, she had seen her gravestone. Whoever it was, they would have to move out now. Louise's heart hammered in her chest. Fear? Anger? They were trespassing. Had no right to be there.

'Hello?' Louise called out as she entered the living room. The two armchairs sat on either side of the fire. No Kara to steal the warmth. No fire today, but the kitchen stove seemed to warm the entire house. Maybe that was why there was no mildew or damp. If Ma walked in that door now, she would be proud of her home. Louise sank into Ma's chair.

'I'm sorry I wasn't here for you when you needed me. Oh, Ma. I've made a complete mess of my life.' Louise gave in to self-pity and let the tears roll.

Don't sit there feeling sorry for yourself. Finish what you came to do, Ma said in Louise's head. But she couldn't move. This was where she had wished herself almost every day since leaving the farm. All that was missing was Ma and Pa. She closed her eyes and imagined them to be there with her. *I'm so sorry, Ma, Pa, for what I did. I would never in a million years have caused you harm, darling Pa. I loved you both so much. Thank you for everything you did for me. For giving me a loving home.*

If only she had come sooner. Would Ma have forgiven her?

She could feel Ma's presence. Her love and concern. Ma was emotionally strong and pragmatic. Louise sighed and tried to draw strength from Ma's example — her role model.

'Okay. I'll get on with it,' she said, as if Ma was standing behind her.

Every item of furniture, every possession, had to be recorded and then safely stored. The Corporation would auction everything off. If she took anything to remember them by it would be stealing, but she could bid for them. The monopoly board and chequers were in the bottom drawer of the sideboard, where they had always been. Pa's farming magazines in another. Louise prepared herself mentally for going upstairs. It may not be as well preserved as downstairs, and she was afraid a squatter might lurk up there.

She opened the door to the staircase and called up, 'Is

anybody there?' There was no movement and so she creaked up the stairs.

Her own room was as she remembered it, just smaller, as everything was. Without her few belongings, it was sparse. She moved on to Ma and Pa's room. Their bedroom door was closed. As a child, she rarely visited them in their bedroom. It felt private, out of bounds, and even now she hesitated before turning the handle.

The scent of cold cream and lavender greeted her. Sunlight dappled the silky eiderdown. Ma's dressing table looked as though it had been polished. Not a single dust mote was visible in the light streaming through the leaded window. Louise picked up Ma's bristle brush, the decorative back now faded. One hundred strokes had been their night time ritual, Ma's hand stroking Louise's hair after each draw of the brush. She lovingly tugged a few strands of long white hair from the bristles and held them to her cheek. There was little evidence of Pa in this feminine room, but then Ma would have lived there alone for several years after he died. Louise checked a tear before it splashed on to the polished wood.

A photograph of Ma and Pa stood in a little ornate frame. They looked so young. She hadn't seen it before. There was another photograph in a similar frame. A girl with long brunette hair and a shy smile. Twelve-year-old Louise. Ma hadn't thrown it out. Maybe she had forgiven her.

Ma wasn't one for jewellery, but anything of sentimental value was bound to be kept in the dressing table drawers. Whoever had been using the house had at least been respectful of their things. It wasn't how you would expect squatters to leave a place.

When Louise opened the top drawer and saw her memory box, she cried out in delight. 'Oh Ma. You kept it!'

Her hands trembled with excitement as she lifted the lid.

Dicky's card was on top. Warped and stiff as though it had once been damp, and then dried out, his childish handwriting inside, faint from age. *Get well soon and come back to school. I miss you.*

Louise handled it as though it were an ancient manuscript before setting it aside to investigate further. The beautiful wooden egg cup that Dicky had made for her.

'Oh, Dicky.'

There was something else in the box that Louise did not expect. Mail. Unopened letters. She prised them out of the bottom of the box. They were addressed to Louise Pearson and had been returned. *Not known at this address.* But it was where she had been living at that time with her mum and Joe. Ma had tried to keep in contact. Four letters. They had been sent in the years following her return to London. She had moved out of Joe's flat by the time the last one was sent, but her mother knew where she lived. Why hadn't she passed them on? Had her mum been jealous of Ma — the strong bond Louise had made with the Becks? It was cruel of her to send them back unopened.

There was the penny and the stub of lipstick. The egg shell would have turned to dust, but a pressed, dried flower--a rosebud--had survived. And there, rattling in the bottom of the tin, was Dicky's lucky marble. Louise closed her fist around it and held it to her heart.

The stairs creaked. Someone was coming. She was about to dive under the bed when the door opened. It was Richard.

37

WEDNESDAY 3RD NOVEMBER 1965

He stood in the doorway, as if conjured by her longing for him. 'Louise. I saw your bike.'

'Dicky.'

He grinned. 'I've not been called that for a while.'

Louise unfurled her fingers to reveal his marble nestled in her palm.

Richard reached into a back pocket, keeping his eyes locked on hers. He opened his wallet, and, as if in slow motion, plucked a silky ribbon from within. It fluttered like a fragile butterfly unused to daylight.

'You kept it?'

'Of course I did.'

'When did you discover I was me?'

'How could I not know it was you? You've not changed *that* much. Reckless. Passionate. Obstinate. Foolhardy. And very, very annoying.'

'But you didn't say. I didn't know.'

Richard sat beside her on the bed. 'When you helped me

move the polyphons. I hadn't really taken much notice of you and then you played the waltz and I knew.'

Louise let the marble roll off her hand and into the box. She faced him. Richard. Dicky. Her dearest friend, now a man. He was everything—the missing part of her soul. She needed him to feel complete, and yet there was too wide a chasm between them—all that had gone before, increasing the gap until it felt too big a leap—to just reach out and take his hand in hers.

'I'm sorry, Richard. For this. For everything.'

He sighed. 'So, this is the end. Is there nothing we can do to save the farm?'

'I wish there was. When I lied to you about the perimeter, I had no idea the farm was at risk. You have to believe me, Richard. I love this place. Who has been living here? Do you know something I don't? You said an assumption had been made about ownership. What did you mean?'

Richard sighed. 'It doesn't matter anymore. Even if I found the will, it would make no difference.'

'Ma left a will?'

'Towards the end, Ma Beck and my mam became close. That's how I came to have a spare key.'

'So, it was you who lit the stove?'

'Yes. To keep out the damp. I've been popping in and out, maintaining it. I hoped you would return one day and wanted it to be as you remembered it. Fiona told me I was crazy. You'd think this place was my other woman the way she carries on. I told her about you, how we were friends as kids and that you might return one day to claim your inheritance.'

'*My* inheritance?' Louise thought she must have misheard.

Richard nodded. 'I tried to stop the Corporation taking ownership. I did everything in my power, and enlisted the help of solicitors, but without evidence that Ma Beck left it to you, it was impossible.'

Her world was turning too quickly. Nothing made any sense. 'Why on earth did you think Ma would leave the farm to me after what I did? I was a wicked girl.'

'Not wicked. Foolhardy. Passionate.' Richard's mouth twitched in a smile. 'If you stop crying, I'll tell you a story. Something I should have told you twenty years ago. I tried. The day that you left the farm. Do you remember I came running up to the car?'

Louise wiped the tears from her cheeks and nodded. Every word. Every breath. Etched in her memory. She had hung onto their parting words, like a safety rope keeping her tethered to that past life. 'You wanted to tell me something. I wrote to you, Richard, but you didn't reply.'

He gasped. 'I did. I wrote back as soon as I received your letter. Didn't you get them? My letters?'

'Letters? More than one?'

'I wrote every couple of days. Then weekly. When you didn't reply, I thought you had forgotten me. Moved on.'

'Never. Oh Richard. I hate my mother. How could she have done this to me?'

'I don't know. But I have to tell you this now. Are you listening?'

Louise took a deep breath, afraid of what was to come.

'It was after the party. Frank had died. I was in my bedroom when I heard you rapping on our door. I kept you waiting because I was furious with you for throwing yourself at that German. You broke my heart, Louise. You have no idea how much in love I was.'

'I loved you too.' She wanted to say, *I still do. I haven't stopped loving you*. 'We were so young. Children.' And yet nothing in her adult life had come close to the love she felt for him then. And now.

Richard took a deep breath and continued. 'So, when my mam sent you away with a flea in your ear, I made an excuse to go out and followed you back to the farm. I remember rehearsing in my head all the names I would call you. A German soldier had killed my brother, and you were shamelessly flirting with one under my nose.'

'I'm sorry. I was a stupid teenager. I might as well have had a crush on a film star. It meant nothing. Just make-believe. I had gone to your shop to say how sorry I was about Frank. I wasn't the friend I should have been. I'm sorry, Richard. You deserved better.'

'You were fourteen. All kids are selfish and stupid at that age. Including me. Anyway. I followed you back to the farm. Then, I saw that Land Army girl and didn't want to get into a conversation with her. There was a rumour going around that she had disgraced herself at the party. So, I spied on you both around the door of the barn. I was waiting for you to come out alone so we could talk. She was showing you how to clean the brake shoes and fit a liner.'

'That's right,' Louise said, amazed he could remember in detail.

'When she left, I was about to reveal myself, but then I saw that furtive look in your eyes. Honestly, Lou, I don't know how you've got through the past twenty years without me getting you out of trouble.'

'I don't think I have,' Louise sighed. 'So, you saw? I took off the brake liners and made the tractor unsafe.'

'And I put them back on.'

It took a while for this information to process. 'You replaced the brake liners? I hid them--'

'--under an oil drum.'

'And Pa?'

'Died from a heart attack.'

'I didn't kill him?' It took a moment for Louise to process this news. To rewrite the story of her life. 'But you said... When we met in the old Mill House, the day before I was sent away.'

'I was winding you up. Getting my own back. I tried to tell you before you left. Then I wrote to tell you. When you didn't reply, I thought it was because you were angry.'

Louise let out a long breath. The angst of twenty years. 'I didn't kill Pa. That was a horrid thing to do, Richard.'

'I know. I hated myself for hurting you. As soon as I said it, I regretted it. But seeing you cry, holding you, released something in me.'

'I remember you crying too.'

'I hadn't been able to until then. Frank dying. Mam's grief. It was too much. But holding you like that, crying together, felt good. Can you forgive me?'

'I've spent twenty years punishing myself. Living in fear of retribution. How could you have done that to me?'

'I know. I'm sorry.'

They sat in silence.

'I probably deserved it,' Louise said. 'I was unkind to you. If only my mum hadn't interfered, I would have received your letter, and Ma's. Oh Richard, what a waste.'

He went to stroke her hair, but his hand stopped halfway, falling back into his lap. 'I honestly thought you knew. Ma wrote to tell you how Pa Beck died and to say sorry you were sent away. Some official decided the Becks could no longer support a placement with Ma Beck widowed, and they sent you away without telling her. But if you never received that letter...'

It was too much. Emotions gushed through Louise's body

as though a dam had broken. And it had. A wall she had built around her heart, denying herself any joy.

'Oh, Dicky.' Louise's tears were now happy ones. He would always be her Dicky. 'I didn't kill anyone. I'm innocent. Ma did love me.'

He shifted his weight on the bed and Louise thought he was about to embrace her, but he stood up abruptly. 'So, I wasted my time maintaining this place. The Corporation won. When are you clearing everything out?'

It was as though they were strangers again—on opposing sides. 'Richard? You know I didn't want this. I lied about the perimeter being finalised because I thought… I thought you were putting everyone else's needs before your own. And you were. You were thinking of me, trying to protect what you believed to be my inheritance.'

Richard shrugged. 'I'd been looking after the farm for so long, I guess it became a habit. At first, I was certain you'd come back, and then when you didn't, I suppose I didn't want to let go.'

'But I did. I'm here now.' Louise spoke softly, trying to coax him back to the warmth they had shared seconds before.

'That day. When you played the waltz. I could hardly believe it.' He slumped down onto the bed beside her. 'Then, at the meeting…'

'You heard that the reservoir boundary hadn't been confirmed. That I'd lied to you.'

Richard nodded. 'I thought you'd come back to Thorncrest to further your career. That you didn't care about the valley, Ma and Pa Beck, me, anything.'

'Oh Richard! How could you possibly think that? You know how much I loved them. And you. You meant everything to me. I've missed you so much.' Louise dabbed her eyes with an already sodden handkerchief. 'Why are women's handkerchiefs ridiculously small compared to men's?'

'I wanted to believe in you. Seeing you in the Mill House that day, it felt as though the girl I knew and loved had come back. That time had stood still. I really wanted to believe, but I was wrong. Just as I had been wrong back then. First the lie and then on the moors when you told me to keep my distance, so he didn't see us together.' Richard threw up his hands. 'You *knew* Fiona and I were serious. And yet you thought I would fool around with you?'

'No. It wasn't like that. If you hadn't plied me with drink, I might have made more sense.'

'Well, now you know about the missing will, and that you had nothing to do with Pa Becks demise. So, I'd best leave you to decide what to do with this lot. My job's done.'

She deserved that after all she'd put him through as a kid. But what about him? Dicky had caused her untold grief—twenty years believing she had killed Pa.

Richard was backing out of the room, a bewildered look on his face. 'I'll leave the spare key on the kitchen table.'

'Not so fast, Richard Braithwaite. Hard as it might be for you to believe, I was not trying to seduce you on the moors. I had twisted my bloody ankle. I clung on to you because I couldn't walk. I didn't want Eddie, my husband, to see us together. Yes, I'm married. And not because I was hiding my undying love and lust for you, but because I didn't want you to be the next victim of the Mob.' Louise stopped her rant to draw breath.

Richard starred at her, mouth open. Then, pushing his glasses up his nose, he said, 'Oh. Um. Do you want a cup of tea?'

'I don't suppose you've another bottle of medicinal brandy in your car?'

'No. But I discovered an unopened bottle of whiskey in the pantry, when I was searching for the will.'

'Okay. If you can trust me not to take advantage of you whilst under the influence.'

38

WEDNESDAY 3RD NOVEMBER 1965

It felt like old times, sitting at the kitchen table with Richard. He poured them each a glass, more at home now in Ma's kitchen than Louise.

They chinked glasses. 'To Ma and Pa,' Louise said.

'To Ma and Pa Beck. And all our happy memories here,' Richard added.

'Yes. The happy ones. There were more of them than sad.' Louise took a sip, savouring the peaty warmth as if a fire had been lit within. They sat a while in silence. There was so much they needed to share, but after twenty years, it could wait a while longer.

'I'm sorry about what I said upstairs.' Richard was blushing.

Louise hid her grin, taking another sip. 'About me fancying the pants off you and trying to have my evil way on the moors?' She laughed out loud. 'I'm sorry. I did. *I do* fancy you. You're a very sexy man. But you are engaged to Fiona.'

He looked so awkward; Louise couldn't stop laughing. It

was a relief after all the tension. More tears. Happy and sad merging.

Richard took a long slug as he waited for her to become calm. He was incredibly handsome; who would have thought that gawky Dicky had such potential and yet in his face she saw the boy and the man—she loved them both. Every version of him.

'We're not engaged. At least I haven't proposed. Fiona talks as if it's inevitable we'll get married one day. I should have asked her but all of this business,' he shrugged and held out his hands, 'This farm. You. Well, the memory of you. Anyway. Enough about me. You'd better tell me what you've got yourself into this time.'

'You're not engaged?'

He glared at her.

'Sorry. You are a good-looking and wonderful, kind man. But I wasn't trying to seduce you. I was trying to apologise about lying to you and to warn you that the Mob were after me and I didn't want you to be a target as well.'

Richard frowned. 'You'd better explain.'

Louise would, but something else worried her. She finished her whiskey as she contemplated. 'If I didn't kill Pa, why is Susan Jeffreys threatening to blackmail me?'

Richard raked a hand through his hair. 'Susan Jeffreys? Simon's wife? Susan wouldn't do that. She might cheat by getting ahead on the Boxing Day hunt, according to Fiona, but blackmail?'

'I received an anonymous letter. *Your secret's not safe with me.* It was addressed to Louise Pearson and delivered to High House.'

'When?'

'The Monday after we had dinner with you and Fiona. And I saw Susan Jeffreys at the last church service. She said she knew who I was. So, it must have been her.' Even as she said this, Louise doubted its truth. Her brain was computing. They arrived at the same conclusion together.

'Fiona,' they both said.

'I was careful not to give anything away. I knew she would be jealous of you as she was during the time I spent here, maintaining this house it in case you came back.' Richard shook his head. He reached for the bottle and poured them each another generous measure.

'My book. Jane Eyre. It had your inscription in the front. It was handed into the library by mistake and Fiona returned it to me for Esther.'

'You kept that?'

'Of course.'

Richard chinked his glass with hers. 'I'm sorry about Fiona. You can't blame her for being jealous. I think my memory of you has always threatened her. You'd better tell me about Eddie and the Mob.'

'Okay.' Louise took a deep breath, then a slug of whiskey, and began. 'My mum and Joe, her boyfriend, didn't seem thrilled when I was sent back to London. We never spoke about how the accident happened, just that Pa had died and Ma didn't want me around anymore.'

'That wasn't true,' Richard interjected.

'I know now—but then… Anyway, the flat was too small for three of us. Joe was always talking about finding a bigger place, but he got little work after the war. I never really worked out what it was he did. I moved in with my aunt for a few months, just until I found a job that paid enough for me to rent a room. Maynard's sweet factory.'

'A factory? Why didn't you go back to school? You were the clever one.'

'I had to support myself. Anyway, I'm telling you this so you understand how I got myself into the mess that I did.'

'Go on.'

'I lived hand to mouth, just about getting by. It was okay. Factory work. Cleaning. Anything that paid the rent. I was working in a cafe when I met Eddie. She explained how Eddie's charm, his philanthropic ways, and promises of a better life had persuaded her to marry him. 'Until then, I had seen myself remaining single. Can I be absolutely honest with you?' Louise gulped. She was a little drunk.

Richard nodded, holding her gaze.

'I was a bit obsessed with you. The feelings I had for you when I was young were unlike any other. I measured every relationship against that, because for me, that was what love should feel like. And it didn't with Eddie. Or anyone.' She sighed.

Richard nodded. 'I know.'

He wasn't going to say anymore, so Louise continued. She told him about Big Jim. How she discovered too late that she had married into the Mob. And the letter she wrote before leaving for Thorncrest. When she had finished her story, her glass was empty and her mouth dry.

'Shit. That's serious,' he said. 'Bloody hell. How do you get yourself into these things? Do you really think they're coming after you?'

Louise poured them both another glass. 'I do. That's what I was trying to tell you on the moors. The Quality Street Gang—the Bellamy brothers--were staying in High House. Big Jim must have sent them to keep an eye on me, or to send a message. He knows where I am, Richard. If Eddie doesn't come for me, the Mob will.'

'Okay. Here's what we'll do. I'll go with you to the police. Tell them about Big Jim. Everything. You can't go on living like this, always looking over your shoulder, afraid of being found.'

'Why not? I've been doing that for the past twenty years.' His eyes went stormy, and Louise smiled. 'Well, I have.'

'That's not the same. You had nothing to be afraid of then. But that's my point. You wasted your life when you could have been something great.'

'Thanks.'

'You know what I mean. You were—*are*—clever. Look how you stepped into the public relations role with the Corporation. You are amazing, Louise. I remember the stories you made up as a kid. You wanted to be a writer. What happened to your dreams?'

'I could say the same about you, Richard. When did owning a chain of department stores become your dream? The boy I knew hated capitalism. He was going to build a village. Timber houses. I saw the model village you made. It was in the old Mill House. You are an amazing carpenter. The detail.'

'I guess we both grew up.' He finished the bottle into their glasses.

'I wish it were 1944 and nothing had changed. I would do everything differently,' Louise said.

He glanced out of the window. It had become dark outside. 'I can't drive home tonight. Do you mind if I stay here until morning when I'm sober?'

'What are you suggesting, Richard Braithwaite?' Louise giggled, but corrected herself when she saw his disapproval. 'I'm joking. Of course, you can stay over. Why don't we light the fire next door and pretend we've gone back in time?'

. . .

They played Monopoly, sitting on the floor in front of the fire. Sharing memories from their childhood.

'I didn't understand back then how losing your brother Frank had affected you,' Louise said.

Having won the game, Richard was tidying away the money. 'My mam was never the same. She died with him.'

'Do you think, Richard,' Louise spoke softly, afraid of alienating him again, 'Do you think this Braithwaite and Simms enterprise is your way of keeping their dream alive—your mam and Frank's?'

He finished packing the pieces into the box. 'It is. They would have loved it.'

'I know. But is it *your* dream?'

'We can't always have what we want. Fiona and her dad are excited to be going into business with me, and he's been very generous.'

'I'm sure he has. It is, of course, a sound business idea, but he believes you're planning on marrying his daughter. That might have something to do with his generosity. *Are* you going to marry her, Richard?'

He sighed. 'I don't know. It feels as though I ought to propose. We've been together for a couple of years.'

'Do you love her?'

He didn't answer for several heartbeats. Eventually he said, 'Not like I loved you.'

Loved. Not *love.*

'Maybe our feelings were so intense because of our age. Maybe we've both been trying to measure adult love against something that you can only feel as teenagers. First love.' Louise knew that wasn't true. She loved Richard more than ever.

'You could be right. Fiona is okay. She deserves better. What's the time?'

Louise stretched. She was feeling sleepy. 'Two-thirty. Do you want to have a nap upstairs on Ma and Pa's bed? I'll stay down here.'

'I couldn't sleep. But you go ahead.'

'I won't lie down, but maybe I'll just rest my eyes.'

'Here, I made you a cup of tea,' Richard said, waking her.

Louise rubbed her eyes. The fire had almost died. Outside, the cool blue of a new day was seeping from the darkness. 'The contractors are due today.' She took the cup and saucer from Richard. Ma's best china.

'Do you want me to stay?' Richard sat opposite her in Pa's chair.

'No. It's okay. I don't really want you to go. Never, if I'm honest. But as I said last night, I don't want Eddie to be jealous and target you. I have to clear up my own mess this time.'

They drank their tea and Richard took their cups through to the kitchen to wash up. Louise followed him.

'Are you going to marry Fiona?' she said.

'I don't know.' He washed up with his back to her. 'I want to do the right thing.'

'Then do what's right for you, Richard. Stop putting everyone else's needs ahead of your own.'

He gave a half-laugh, reminding her of his twelve-year-old self. 'It was fun pretending we could turn back time, but I think I'd better go now. I'm staying at the Coach and Horses. Here's the number in case you need me. Try to keep safe, Louise. If you're afraid. If Eddie or the Mob come looking for you, call me there. I know you don't want me to get involved, but I will. Honest to God, I'll kill anyone who lays a finger on you.'

Louise wanted to hug him, to kiss him goodbye, but she

knew where that would lead. From the way he kept his distance, she guessed he did too.

'Goodbye, Richard. Dicky. Thank you for looking after the farm for us. It meant a lot to me, finding it like this. Loved and cared for.'

When he drove away, Louise felt as bereft as she had all those years ago when she waved goodbye to him from the back window of the Red Cross lady's car.

39

THURSDAY 4TH NOVEMBER 1965

When Louise was alone in the farmhouse, she retrieved her memory box from the bedroom and settled herself back in Ma's armchair by the dying fire. The blackened logs resembled sleeping alligators; their backs striped with cracks. As a child, mesmerised by the images she saw in the fire, she created stories for herself. Richard was right. She had dreamed of writing books, of being a landowner, a farmer. Richard wasn't the only one who had abandoned the dreams of his youth. Was he right? Did life happen, and you just had to get on with it? After the flood, she would leave Thorncrest, once again a fugitive living hand to mouth, taking any job that paid, trying to keep one step ahead of the Mob. Who was she kidding? Big Jim knew where she was and would come for her when he was ready.

Louise sighed and opened the box. Ma's letters were at the bottom, and so she gently removed each of her treasures, stopping to read Dicky's Get Well card before placing it with the marble, lipstick, and penny on Ma's footstool. Then she wriggled down in the armchair and imagined Ma's arms around her.

May 30th 1945

My darling girl,

I'm so sorry I wasn't there to say goodbye when you left for London. I had no say in the decision to send you back. The authorities took it upon themselves, thinking an evacuee would be too much trouble for me. As if you, our darling Louise, could ever be thought of as trouble. Having you at home would have been such a comfort. Instead, I lost both you and Pa.

It must have all seemed so frightening to you. It was for me, too. One minute, life was normal. You had gone on an errand to deliver eggs and milk. I was kneading dough, and Pa was ploughing the far field. Why don't we appreciate every second of normal? It is more precious than we realise at the time.

We knew Pa had a weak heart. That's why we took on extra help — the Land Army girls and a POW. And you, dear Louise, because I know you would say, 'What about me?' You were a tremendous help to Pa and me, but we thought of you as our own. It was probably wrong of us. You have your dear mother, but we grew so fond of you. Sadly, Pa and I could not conceive a child. This might be too much information for you; sometimes I forget you are a child — I know — ***a teenager.*** *But I want you to understand why you mean so much to us. We will always love you, dear heart. Thank you for the joy you brought into our lives.*

I'm sure your mother is pleased to have you back home and I must be glad for her. Maybe you can come back one day for a visit, or stay for a week in your school holiday.

If you can find time to write, I would love to hear from you.

With all of my love,

Ma xxx

A tear splashed on to the page and Louise dabbed it with her sleeve. 'Oh, Ma. I loved you both, too.' Did Ma think she had been forgotten when Louise didn't reply? Maybe she had talked too much about Ma and Pa to her mum, making her jealous. As an adult, Louise better understood the challenges her mum had experienced, single-handedly trying to raise a child during a war with little income and no home to call their own.

She opened the next letter. News of the farm, how Joan was organising the farmhands to keep things going. There was no news of Kurt. Young Louise would have been disappointed. *Mrs Braithwaite has been very kind, making sure I have eaten and putting aside groceries. Last week there was a delivery of tinned pineapple. There were queues almost down to the bridge, but she kept a tin for me. I treated Joan and the other farmhands. I don't have much of an appetite.*

The sound of an engine, and then a chain clattering, alerted Louise to the skip being delivered. She returned everything to the memory box, except for the letters which she placed on the seat of the armchair to read later, and went outside to say hello.

A man waved as he unloaded a skip from the back of the lorry, but Louise's attention was on another delivery. Someone had left a cardboard box and a brown paper bag on the doorstep. Mystified, she gathered them up and, after shouting her thanks to the men, hurried inside to investigate. They had not been there earlier when she said goodbye to Richard, and the men knew nothing about the items, so someone had dropped them off in the past couple of hours. Louise was cross with herself for not hearing a car or footsteps in the yard, but she had probably fallen asleep.

She peeked inside the paper bag as she carried it through to the kitchen. Groceries. And a note:

I thought you might be hungry. Richard

Louise smiled. That was an understatement. She hadn't

eaten a thing since lunchtime the previous day. He had packed sandwiches—cheese and ham, an iced bun, two apples, and a banana. And, bless him, a pint of milk. Would he have come in and shared the feast if she had heard him outside?

Excited now to open the cardboard box, Louise prepared a cup of tea and took it with her sandwiches, in to the living room. Wanting to make the moment of anticipation last, Louise bit into a sandwich. Thick cut ham from the bone. Delicious. She finished the sandwich and sipped her tea. Then she knelt in front of the box and unfolded the flaps. Whatever was inside had been wrapped in newspaper. But there was a note on top.

I'm sorry we couldn't save Becks farm. Here is something to remember it by. When we arranged to meet, I told you there was something I had to do first. I collected this from the Mill House where you found the rest of the model village. Now you can complete the set.

Your friend, always. Dicky.

Louise hugged his note to her heart. If only they could be forever friends, but she was afraid that may not be possible. Fiona would not welcome her presence in their lives. Richard was far too honourable to do anything behind her back, and then there was Eddie and the Mob.

Impatient now, she reached into the box and cradled the package, lifting it free. A couple of wrapped items dropped from the main bundle. Louise lined them up, ready to open. Richard had made a perfect replica of the farmhouse. The front opened like a doll's house. Inside was a room similar to the one she sat in now, two armchairs on either side of the fire, and a lead sheepdog from a toy farm. Upstairs was the room she had used as a girl. A red gingham dress lay across the bed. And a tiny book. Louise extracted it with pinched fingers to take a closer look. Jane Eyre. She smiled to herself. He had thought of everything.

The two smaller packages contained the cowshed, and a chicken coop inhabited by lead cows and a rooster.

Darling Dicky. He was the sweetest, kindest man she knew. He had spoilt her for any other man because nobody could compare to him. She had known it since the day she left Thorncrest and now, just when she had found him, they had to say goodbye all over again.

There was a rap on the door. Richard! She threw the newspaper onto the armchair and ran to open it.

'Is there much to shift?' It was the man from Hardwicks. 'I bought some packing boxes and newspaper; in case it was needed. Or is it all for the tip?'

Louise stared at him with her mouth open. They were here to empty the farmhouse. To gut ready for the flood. She wanted to shout, *Go away. Leave us alone.*

'It's not ready,' she said. 'Everything needs to be sorted.'

'That's what we're here for.' The man squeezed past her into the kitchen. 'Where do you want me to start?'

The flood was in three days' time. Even if they found the will, it wouldn't make a difference. It was the end of Becks farm, and Louise had to find a way to go on.

'If you start packing down here, I'll do the bedrooms,' she said. 'But not that package. That belongs to me.' She put everything back into the cardboard box, wrapping each item in newspaper, and took it upstairs with the memory box to keep them close.

There wasn't time to mull over every item, to linger on each memory: Pa's favourite pipe which Ma had wrapped in tissue paper, a daisy chain pressed within a bible—Louise remembered presenting it to Ma when she arrived home from school. Dicky had helped her, picking the daisies as they ambled along the lane. Downstairs, the men seemed to be throwing the furniture around, careless about any damage caused. Louise packed the pipe, bible, hairbrush, and other items from Ma's bedside cupboard into a box. She opened the stopper of a perfume bottle and inhaled the scent. Lily of the Valley. The perfume, framed photographs, Pa's pipe, everything would be put into storage or thrown away as if it didn't matter. It was all Louise had left of her Ma and Pa. Could she take them or would it be stealing? If Fitzpatrick knew why they were important to her, she might have been able to plead her case, but that was impossible.

When she had finished packing everything upstairs, Louise made the men a cup of tea. 'We won't be throwing anything on the skip. Everything has to be put into storage.'

With her bike wedged into the back of the removal van, Louise went with them to the storage lock-up, a big barn in a field. It had once been part of a working farm, according to the driver. Inside the barn, possessions had been allocated a numbered space, and they sat as neighbouring dwellings—stripped of their outer shell. Louise wandered down the aisle taking in the worn armchairs, polished dressers, and remnants of past lives: a battered trilby, a washing jug and bowl, a one-eyed teddy bear. An idea started to take root. The last thing she could do for her beloved village.

40

FRIDAY 5TH NOVEMBER 1965

'Happy Redheads' Day.' Pete presented Fliss with a string of shiny conkers.

Louise paused on the turn on the stairs and smiled down at them. 'Did you make that, Pete?'

'I did. If you want a conker fight, I'm a mean player.'

Louise continued down the stairs and joined them in reception. Fliss tied the conker garland around her neck. 'Now I know Redheads' Day is a thing I'll be celebrating every year. There ought to be greeting cards for redheads. Have you been out this morning, Louise? I didn't see you at breakfast.'

Pete winked at Louise. 'It's not polite to ask a lady where she spent the night.'

'Ha. Ha. I overslept. It's true, I stayed out the night before. Nothing like that.' She shook her head at Pete, who was smirking. 'I spent all of last night and yesterday clearing Becks farm. Which is why I am shattered today. And,' Louise checked her watch and pouted, 'why I have missed breakfast?'

'Well, Fitzpatrick is out this morning, so you don't need to worry about your ten o'clock. He's collecting his wife from

Harrogate station. They're both going to the party tomorrow. Dion's band has been practicing a new set. It's going to be fab. What are you wearing, Louise?'

'I don't know.' Louise shook her head, trying to kick-start her brain. 'I need caffeine and a bacon sandwich. And I'd better sort last-minute preparations for the party and the trial flood on Monday. Argh, so much to do. Pete, could you give me a lift to Esther's? I don't think I have the energy to cycle.'

'Yes. But first, let's sort out coffee and breakfast. Peggy is not immune to my boyish charm.'

'Then she's the only one.' Louise exchanged a look with Fliss, who grinned back at her.

Pete and Louise sat by the electric fire in the bar lounge. Peggy had supplied a pot of coffee and a plate piled with bacon sandwiches. Thickly cut bread, slathered in butter, and bacon dripping with fat. It was heaven. Louise took a satisfying bite and felt life return.

'So, this is it. Job done.' Pete said through a mouthful of bread and bacon. 'Who would have thought when I jumped into that car with you we'd achieve so much together?'

Louise took her time chewing and pondering before she replied. 'Were you following me that day?'

'I had my eye on you, if that's what you mean. I thought a pretty girl will hitch a ride quicker than me. And I was right. It meant I had to leg it from under the bridge, but everything worked out okay. Didn't it?'

'Yes. But it seems a bit of a coincidence that you were headed for Thorncrest, too.'

'Destiny. We were meant to be.' He winked.

Louise didn't believe a word of it, but she would not get the truth out of him. 'I visited the lock-up for the first time yesterday. How and when does everything go to auction?'

'I don't think we've got that far yet. At some point, the

Corporation will have to work with an auction house. It's mostly all rubbish. I expect we'll have to pay them to take it away.'

Louise tingled with excitement. It was just an idea, but her mind had taken it and was running like a rugby player with the ball. 'Who owns the barn and land?'

'Don't know. The Corporation. Probably.' He pointed at the plate. 'Do you want that?'

Louise shook her head, and Pete helped himself to the remaining bacon sandwich. 'It feels like the last day of term. A party tomorrow and then the big day on Monday,' he said.

Peggy cleared away their plates, and Pete asked Louise to meet him outside in thirty minutes for her lift to Esther's. She went upstairs to collect her jacket and stared longingly at the cardboard box she had brought back from the farm. Inside was the model farmhouse. Her fingers itched to remove it from the packaging and set up the completed village, but it would have to wait until the weekend. Esther was relying on her help to get things ready for the party. Pete was leaning against his bike when Louise stepped outside.

'For you.' He presented a spare motorbike helmet.

'You're full of surprises this morning. A garland for Fliss, and a helmet for me.' But his kindness touched her.

'Got to make a fuss of my two best girls before we have to say goodbye.' He put on his own helmet and revved the engine before Louise could ask where and when was he planning to leave. She too would have to move on soon. With Richard getting married, the reservoir project nearing completion, and her reason for being there was no longer valid—she had not caused Pa's accident—it was time to start the next chapter of her life.

'Ready?' Pete called over his shoulder.

As I'll ever be, Louise thought.

. . .

A tray of tea things had been set up on a small table in the backroom, overlooking a garden where a red berried, Berberis and bright yellow Choiysa made a valiant attempt to defy winter.

'Dion's band are setting up at six. The flier says seven start, but most people will get there around eight,' Esther said, pouring the tea.

'Peggy and her husband will get there early. I bet a few of the oldies will queue outside from about six-thirty. Are we having someone serve drinks or is it help yourself?' Louise was embarrassed that she knew so little about the arrangements when she had volunteered to assist.

'Everyone will bring food and drink to share. I was thinking of keeping it casual. If we cover a couple of long tables with cloths and provide plates and glasses, that should be enough.'

Louise nodded. 'I've asked the caretaker for plates and glasses. We'll have to go back the next day to help wash dishes and tidy up. Fitzpatrick and his wife will be there.'

'Everyone's going. It's a momentous occasion, Louise. The end of life as we know it. I can't imagine everything being under water. Our little church. Braithwaite's.'

Louise's stomach turned. Ma and Pa's farm demolished. 'No,' she whispered.

There wasn't really anything more to do. Esther had arranged everything with her usual efficiency.

'Have you had any thoughts about the history project?' Louise asked Esther.

'Not really, I've been busy organising the party.'

It wasn't meant as a criticism, but Louise cringed. 'I know. I have had a few thoughts. I visited the lock-up where all the unclaimed property from the vacated dwellings is stored. It's fascinating. The stories they tell of people's lives. It seems a shame to just auction everything off. Okay, some of it, but what if we curated rooms to show what life was like in the forties and fifties? And there's the stuff from the textile mill. Books with names and wages. The old spinning machines and looms. And Reverend Cummins has communication between the parish vicar and the workhouse about the welfare of apprentices.'

'It sounds like an interesting project for someone who has the time,' Esther said, when Louise stopped to draw a breath.

'I wish I could do it myself.' The idea had been going round and round in Louise's head. The collection of possessions telling her stories that she longed to write.

'If the Corporation agreed to fund a local museum, it would be the answer to Fiona and Richard's problem.'

Louise cocked her head and frowned.

'The jukebox things.'

'The polyphons. They're displaying them in the Ripley shop. I know Fiona wasn't keen at first, but she seems okay with it now.' Louise went to take a sip of tea, but her cup was empty, as was the pot.

'I'll make us a fresh brew,' Esther said, standing up. 'I think things might have changed there.'

'Oh?' Louise followed her out to the kitchen.

Whilst Esther boiled the kettle and made a fresh pot of tea, Louise washed up. She was desperate for her friend to finish the story. Eventually, with a tray of tea things, they returned to the backroom.

'You were saying about Fiona and Richard?' she prompted.

'Oh yes. I was out walking Bouncer this morning. Fiona was out with her Labradors. Have you seen them? They're gorgeous. I was surprised because she wouldn't normally take them out on her own. A bit of a handful.'

'You were saying about the polyphons?'

'Oh yes. We walked together. Our dogs get on. It's good for Bouncer having the boys to play with. Seems Fiona had a lot on her mind and was glad of my company to get things off her chest. Apparently, Richard split up with her last night. She's devastated. I told her to give him a couple of days, this trial flood's unsettling everyone, he'll come around. Her father was planning to go into business with Richard Braithwaite. Nothing was finalised but now the Simms have bought the lease on the shop they're stuck with it. They had a huge row about the jukeboxes. So, maybe you could include them in this museum you're planning?'

Louise wanted to be alone, to unwrap this information and feast on the possibility it promised, but the walk home she planned was sabotaged by Bill, Esther's husband, returning from his shift at the hospital and with Esther's prompt, insisting he drive Louise the few miles.

There was a festival atmosphere around the valley. A caravan was parked on a scrap of green close to the road. Smoke from a bonfire drifted across the road, temporarily obscuring their view. Louise turned in her seat noting more caravans and a couple of tents. A man strummed his guitar whilst a couple of women in long skirts danced, waving their arms around and swaying their hips.

'Let's hope they move on once the excitements over. That's all we need, a hippy commune,' Bill said.

'I hope that bonfire wasn't prepared for a Guy Fawkes party this evening,' Louise said.

They passed beaten-up camper vans, and fancy state-of-the-art ones parked bumper to bumper outside the perimeter.

'At work, they were saying some schools are closing for the

day on Monday so the kids can witness the dam opening for the first time,' Bill said.

'It's hard to believe it's actually going to happen,' Louise said with a heavy heart.

She relaxed and let Esther's revelation sink in. Richard had left Becks farm yesterday morning and finished with Fiona the same day. He had not indicated that was his plan. If anything, he had defended Fiona when Louise bad-mouthed her for sending a spiteful letter, and he sounded as though he was committed to the idea of going into business with the Simms. A bad idea. But she had tried to keep her thoughts to herself. What was he planning now? She wanted to phone him, but that would be unfair. Maybe Esther was right. Richard had been unsettled by the pending flood—and spending time with her in Becks farm. Richard and Fiona just needed a little time to sort things out between them. It was going to be torture keeping her mouth zipped, resisting the urge to go running to him with declarations of her love. And she did love him. More than she believed possible. Louise now understood what writers meant when they described an all-consuming love. This love was eating her up—she could think of nothing but Richard. Hoping against hope they had a future together, because she couldn't imagine a life without him.

41

6TH NOVEMBER 1965

Dion's band was playing *It's been a hard day's night,* and the hall was packed with villagers, reservoir workers, and visitors. Earlier that day, Louise and Esther had covered a few tables with white cloths. Villagers had left Tupperware boxes and plates covered in foil: home-made sausage rolls, shortbread, and devilled eggs. Peggy was arranging the offerings, tidying half-filled platters by combining them. Two tables were littered with bottles of beer, spirits, and wine. Booze was flowing faster than the anticipated flood. A couple had dressed up as a mermaid and merman. Another as King Neptune.

Louise took a moment, hugging to her the joy of seeing people she had come to think of as friends and family celebrating what they had achieved together and all that had gone before—the textile mill which had once dominated the valley, the church, and Ma and Pa's farm. Her heart ached with love. She would help create a museum to preserve their memories, including Richard's model village depicting what life was like before the flood.

'Good. I was hoping I would see you again, Louise.' Susan Jeffreys use of her name, startled Louise. But now she had nothing to fear, and she was pleased to see her.

'I wanted to tell you that you are responsible for my friend Joan getting married. I don't suppose you remember Joan? She was a Land Army girl back in the day. We both worked on Becks farm where you were evacuated. Anyway, when I was clearing out the cowshed, I found an envelope addressed to a German prisoner of war and posted it. Kurt, that's Joan's husband, received it and went looking for her. I believe you thought she'd had an accident, anyway she was fine. Once they got together again, with the war being over, they fell in love. And now they've been married for fifteen years. So, they have a lot to thank you for.'

Fliss interrupted them, slipping an arm around Louise's waist. 'I love you in that gingham dress.'

Susan went off in search of another drink and Louise took a deep breath. So, that's what Susan had wanted to tell her. Young Louise would have been mortified to learn she had brought Kurt and Joan together.

'The Locomotion. I love this one. Come and dance.' Fliss propelled Louise on to the dance floor. Esther joined them. Both friends grinned madly.

She had two wonderful girlfriends. *They* were worth celebrating. And Peggy, who acted as though she were her mum, and was now waltzing around the floor in the arms of her husband. Louise tried to relax and look as though she was having fun, but all she could think about was Richard. The song came to an end and Louise used it as an excuse to leave the dance floor. She wandered out of the hall into the corridor, welcoming the cooler air. Somewhere fireworks exploded. A confetti of diamonds reflected in the window. Kurt and Joan were together. It made sense. She was happy for them, recognising now the obvious attraction between them years ago. And Kurt's Saint Christopher had been returned. At least that story had a happy ending.

The outside door opened and then Richard was before her. Alone. He brought with him the scent of fresh air and bonfire. Everything else faded. He took a step towards her. Close enough to touch. Louise resisted throwing herself into his arms. She focused on his lips. Full and sensuous.

'I wasn't going to come,' he said.

'I'm glad you did.'

A firework rocket squealed and banged.

'I heard you and Fiona had split up,' Louise said, unable to hold back any longer. 'I hope it wasn't anything I did or said.'

Richard gave a half laugh. 'You don't mean that.'

'I do! If she's right for you, then my opinion shouldn't matter. Why did you finish with her?'

'It felt wrong letting Fiona think I would marry her one day when I was in love with someone else. Fiona's known for some time that my first love was my greatest, but neither of us expected that love to be rekindled. From the day you turned up in Thorncrest, Fiona's been on high alert. I think she would have guessed who you were, even without my inscription in your book. So…' He sighed. 'I did the honourable thing and let her go. Fiona deserves to have someone love her as if she is the brightest star in the sky.'

'I love you, Richard. I've always loved you.' Louise spoke softly. 'It's bigger than anything I felt as a teen.' She traced her finger along his cheek bone until it came to rest lightly on his lips.

He grasped her wrist. His eyes were like a torrent of waves sweeping her in. 'I can't …Don't…' As if tossing words and caution to the wind, his mouth pressed against hers. She abandoned herself to his taste, his touch, wanting to be one with him. He pulled away and looked deep into her eyes. 'I can't lose you again, Louise.'

'You won't. I promise.'

The door from the hall opened, music and laughter spilling out. A couple of girls giggled as they stumbled past on their way to the Ladies.

'Can we go back to your place, Richard? I don't think I can go back in there and pretend there's nothing between us.'

'Do you need to collect your jacket?'

'Yes, but then everyone will try to persuade me to stay.'

'Wait here. I'll get it for you.' But he stood as if unable to leave her side.

'Be quick and we'll get out of here.' Louise grinned.

She gazed into space, the feel and scent of Richard hung like a cloak around her. Nothing mattered anymore. Where they lived. How they lived. So long as they were together.

A pack of Scooter boys ambled in clutching cans of beer. Louise stirred from her reverie, but not enough to prepare her for the vision when they parted.

'Pete said I would find you here. It's time to come home, Princess.' Eddie stood before her, polished and unflustered, as though nipping out to bring her home was an everyday occurrence.

'No, Eddie. I meant what I said. I'm not going back.'

He gave an exaggerated sigh. 'Big Jim would be unhappy to hear that. I promised him I'd return you safely when you'd finished having your bit of fun. I've been a patient man. Given you time to cool off. But time's up. Come on.' He grasped her upper arm and pushed her ahead of him out of the building.

'I can't just leave, Eddie. People will look for me. You kept the money Big Jim gave you to fix the fight, and blamed me, didn't you?'

'Sorry, Princess. It had to be done. Got me out of a

scrape. Big Jim was keeping an eye on you. Giving you the money was a test, so he sent one of his boys after you. We've always known your whereabouts. So...' he sighed as if dealing with a petulant child, 'now you've had your fun, it's time to come home. I'll clear things with Big Jim. I've made a bob or two so I'll see him right. He'll come round. And I'll keep your secret about the accident. Can't be fairer than that.'

Louise had barely been aware of her movement, but now she was being led towards his car. She twisted in his grasp to look behind her. Richard. Where was Richard?

'That's right, Princess. Just get in the car.'

'Where are we going? I can't just leave. My role here's important. Mr Fitzpatrick will be looking for me.'

As if on cue, Pete skulked towards them across the car park. 'Ah, you found her. Sorry, Louise.'

'How could you, Pete? I trusted you.'

'I know. I'm sorry. Eddie, mate, what's the hurry? It's going to arouse suspicion if Louise disappears with no explanation. Why don't you join the party and then tomorrow Louise can tell Fitzpatrick that she has to go back to London? He'll want her to stay for the opening of the dam on Monday. We don't want to create a huge drama.'

'I've got business to attend to in Harrogate. A game to fix. So, she'll have to come with me now.'

'If you go to Harrogate alone, I'll keep an eye on Louise. She won't be going anywhere, will you?' Pete looked at Louise and she shook her head.

'Hey, what's going on?' Richard ran over. He took a few deep gasps, waiting for his breath to return.

'It's okay, Richard,' Louise said. 'This is Eddie Boyd, my husband.'

Richard's face darkened and Louise was afraid he might

throw a punch. Fortunately, Pete stepped between them. 'Everything's fine. Mr Boyd was just leaving.'

'I'll be back for you on Monday.' Eddie spat the words at Louise, each one a slap. He'd never raised a hand to her, but his expression was murderous.

'Okay.' Louise's voice was barely a whisper.

The three of them watched Eddie drive away. Then Louise said, 'Can you give us some time alone, Pete? I'm not going anywhere.'

'Sure. And I really am sorry, Louise.'

Louise shook her head. She was disappointed in him, but not surprised. Deep down she had known all along Pete Murray was with the Mob.

'So that's the infamous Eddie Boyd,' Richard said when Pete had gone back in. 'Why didn't I just knock him out? Smug bastard. I should have pummelled him.'

'I'm glad you didn't try. Beneath his fancy suit, Eddie's a thug. A well-connected thug who can bring in the heavies. He could have us both murdered and it would look like an accident. I know how they operate, Richard. I thought we were safe. I honestly thought we might have a life together, but it's impossible. I'm married to the Mob until death us do part. I'm sorry.'

'You can't. I won't let you. We'll go to the police.'

She wanted to pretend everything would be okay, but couldn't. It would put Richard at risk. 'I wish it was as easy as that. I love you more than life itself and would do anything for you--'

'--then leave him. You don't have to do as he says.'

'He would come after both of us. The Mob always wins.'

'No,' Richard shouted. His fists were clenched, his eyes flashing. 'I'll kill the bastard.'

People were stopping to stare. Louise tried to take his arm. 'Let's go inside.'

Richard pulled away. 'Tell me you're not going back to him.'

She hesitated, trying to find the right words.

'Tell me!'

'I can't.'

'So that's it?' He threw up his hands. 'You're leaving me again?'

'Richard.'

He looked bewildered. 'No. I can't do this.' He bit his lip.

Louise touched his arm, but he stepped back. 'I can't watch you throwing your life away. Do what you have to do, but don't involve me. It's best we don't see each other. It's just too painful.' He turned and walked away from her.

'Richard,' she pleaded.

He raised his hand but did not look back. 'Don't try to contact me.'

42

SUNDAY 7TH NOVEMBER 1965

By sunrise, Louise had constructed the model village complete with Becks farm and made a decision. She wasn't going anywhere with Eddie. Richard was right. It was time to stop running. It was one of the hardest decisions she'd ever had to make because, in refusing Eddie, she risked endangering Richard's life. But a life without Richard was meaningless. He had to know how much he meant to her, that she wouldn't hurt him for the world. Last night he looked broken. She had to see him, to make things right between them.

As Fitzpatrick and his wife Carole had stayed in High House overnight, Peggy arrived for work on Sunday morning with her husband, Bert, to prepare breakfast for them all. They sat around a long table, passing toast and marmalade and exchanging stories from the night before.

'Who was the fellow I saw you with outside?' Peggy asked Louise.

'Has Jane got an admirer I should know about?' Fitzpatrick said, feigning a father role.

Pete shot Louise a look. He might have covered for her, but Louise decided it was time to tell the truth. Well, some of it.

'I think the gentleman you're referring to was…well *is* my husband. Eddie.'

Fitzpatrick's mouth fell open. 'You're married?'

Louise sighed. 'Yes. And my name's Louise. I called myself Jane Cox because I was trying to be someone different. It was wrong of me. But now you know.'

Carole broke the stunned silence. 'Whatever Louise's reason for using an alias it doesn't concern us. Plenty of people work under a different name. Authors have pen names, and actors change their names. Jane or Louise, we think you're amazing. Don't we, darling?'

Fitzpatrick nodded.

'And you gave a terrific speech last night,' Carole concluded, raising her cup of tea as if in a toast.

'Hear hear,' Pete added, raising his cup too.

'Okay.' Fitzpatrick let out a long breath. 'Anything else I need to know?'

'Nothing that can't wait until Monday.' Louise kept her tone light.

After breakfast, Louise was anxious to get going. Every minute away from Richard was torture. She had to find him. She was preparing to leave when Peggy knocked on her door. 'Can I come in, lass

Louise opened the door. 'You know it's Sunday and you ought to be at home with your family?'

'It's okay. Bert's having a chat with young Pete. I wanted to check that you were alright.' She didn't ask what Louise knew she was thinking, was she running away from a violent husband?

'Everything's good, Peggy. Now the project's coming to an

end, I would have had to move on anyway. Eddie coming to find me just speeded things up.'

'So, you *are* planning on leaving us?'

'Not immediately. Eddie and I have some things to sort out first. Don't worry, he's not a bad'un.' Louise smiled at her use of the local vernacular. 'But I don't think we belong together.'

'So long as you're alright, pet. What's all this?' Peggy peered at the model village spread out in all its glory across the bedroom floor. 'I've never seen anything like it. The whole of the valley in miniature. Oh, my lord.' Peggy gasped and fell to her knees. She picked up one treasure after another, exclaiming over the attention to detail.

'I'm sorry about the mess.' Louise nodded at the scrunched newspaper littering the floor. She had discarded the wrapping as a child might when opening presents on Christmas morning.

'Don't you worry about that. I'll clear it in no time. Who made this?'

'Richard Braithwaite.' Louise grinned as she said his name.

'He's a master craftsman. What are you planning to do with it?'

'I'm going to ask Fitzpatrick if we can create a museum for the valley. This model would be displayed in the centre so future generations can see how the valley once looked. It could hold Mr Beacon's polyphon collection. Artefacts from the church. Historical papers. Old spinning mills.' Louise gabbled excitedly, words chasing ideas as the dam in her imagination broke. 'I need to find Richard to tell him. It's not been finalised, but Fitzpatrick seemed keen and indicated the Corporation would be supportive.'

'It's a marvellous idea.' Peggy's eyes shone.

'Isn't it?' Louise leapt to her feet and planted a kiss on Peggy's cheek. 'I'll see you later!'

Pete was at reception. 'Where are you going?'

'I have to see Richard. I can't leave him like this. I'm not going to make a run for it. Where would I hide? I'm not stupid. Big Jim would find me. I just need to talk to him.'

'I'll give you a lift.'

Louise accepted reluctantly. Why did a young man like Pete Murray—or whatever his real name was—ruin his life by joining the Mob? 'Are you even an engineer?' she asked as she took the spare helmet from him.

'Engineer in training. I am now. In fact, I've been looking into the qualifications I would need to do the full course. Big Jim's my uncle. My mum told him I've got to get a professional qualification. Doesn't want me going down the same road as him. So, Coach and Horses? You can buy me a pint.'

'No, I bloody won't,' Louise said.

The Coach and Horses had just opened up for Sunday lunch time when they arrived. Pete waited outside while Louise went inside to find Richard.

'He's not here,' the landlord said, testing the beer tap.

'No. He's in a room upstairs,' Louise said impatiently.

'Was. He left an hour ago.'

'Where? Out for a walk?'

A couple of punters strolled in and the landlord greeted them. She tried to get his attention, but it felt as though he was ignoring her on purpose. A young woman who Louise recognised from the night Dion's band played looked up from polishing a table. 'Are you looking for Richard Braithwaite?'

'Yes.' Louise could have hugged her. 'Where is he?'

'I saw him leaving in his Land Rover this morning. Last night in the bar, he said he was going away for a few days. Got a bit drunk and depressed.'

'Where? Did he say where he was planning to stay?'

The girl shook her head. 'Sorry.'

He could be anywhere by now. On the ride over, she had imagined a life with Richard. Somehow, they would free her from the Mob. Explain to Big Jim what had really happened. Go to the police. The strength of their love for one another made anything feel possible, but now reality sank in. Tomorrow, Eddie would come for her. It was useless trying to resist. She would never see Richard again.

As Louise left the pub, thunder rolled. The sky turned black and heavy drops of rain fell.

'Maybe we should wait inside until this clears,' Pete yelled as they were pelted with what felt like ball bearings.

'No. Let's go.' Louise didn't care if they soaked. She didn't want to spend any more time than was absolutely necessary in his company.

Water sprayed as they took off, soaking her thighs. It was a downpour, like something out of the bible. Noah would be building his Arc. Pete was right, they should have waited it out. It felt as though he was driving too fast. The bike lent to one side as they rounded a corner and Louise had to hang on tight or risk falling. A clap of thunder. The sky flashed with lightning.

Louise was relieved when they arrived back at High House in one piece. Her anorak and jeans were saturated. She took off her helmet and handed it to Pete, then went inside, her feet squelching inside her shoes.

Reception was unmanned with it being Sunday. Pete came in behind her, exclaiming about the weather, but Louise couldn't make small talk with him. He had deceived her. She went straight to the bathroom, where she ran a bath before peeling off her sodden clothes. If Richard had been in his room at the Coach and Horses, she would have told him how much she loved him. That she would do anything to be with him, but she had to protect him from the Mob.

Laying in the bath, Louise considered her options. She could tell Pete the truth, that Eddie had stolen the money, but that would be as good as executing Eddie because Big Jim would show no mercy. Eddie had promised to protect her by paying off 'her debt' and squaring things with Big Jim. She knew he would so long as she stayed with him or he tired of her. A life sentence married to Eddie.

Warm and dry, Louise took her memory box to the bed and snuggled into a nest of pillows and blanket. She held Dicky's lucky marble in the palm of her hand, as if holding his love. The egg cup he had crafted, wanting only to please her. And his Get Well card. The vision of Dicky as a schoolboy pulling it from beneath his pullover—earnest, embarrassed, brought a lump to her throat.

Ma's letters. Where were Ma's letters?

Louise leapt up, spilling the contents from her box across the bed. She had been reading them in Becks farm when interrupted by the arrival of the skip. Her skin prickled with anxiety. She couldn't lose Ma's letters. They were all she had left. The newspapers that Peggy took away.

Please let the letters be safe, hidden within them.

There was nothing more she could do until Monday, when Peggy returned to work.

43

MONDAY 8TH NOVEMBER 1965

Today the dam would open. The reservoir flooding would begin and she, Mrs Louise Boyd, would return to London with her husband, Eddie.

'I'll be sorry to see you go,' Fitzpatrick said in his office that morning. 'Pete Murray is leaving, too. You arrived together like a couple of angels and now you are both deserting me. At least the project is almost complete. I couldn't have done it without you, Jane. Sorry, Louise.'

Louise stood at the window, looking out. 'Bad luck about the rain. It hasn't let up since yesterday afternoon. It would have chased away the visitors I saw camping on the roadside. I doubt we will have much press coverage, either.'

'You know, I don't mind about that in the slightest. The valley is flooding itself before the dam has even opened. I don't think it's worth doing an official opening with the press. Nobody will want to stand around in this.'

Louise sighed. He was right. They would be lucky to get any press coverage. She had already taken a few calls from newspaper offices telling her that photographers and reporters could not reach Thorncrest because of fallen trees or flooding. 'I'll arrange a press briefing here in High House. You can do something when the trial flood is complete. It will be a better photographic opportunity. But that's the best we can do.'

'It's fine. I'm going down there at ten this morning to open the dam. Will you be joining me?'

'Is Pete going with you?'

'Absolutely. He won't want to miss that.' Louise wondered at Pete's acting skills; he'd convinced Fitzpatrick that he was as excited about opening the dam as his boss.

'If you don't mind, I'll stay here to take calls and set up the press briefing.'

'Good idea. What time are you planning to leave for London? I wish you'd let us give you a proper goodbye.'

'I don't know what time Eddie's arriving. He's travelling from Harrogate and with problems on the road, created by the storm it's anyone's guess. Another reason to stay here where he can find me.'

Her clothes were packed. The model village had been boxed up with instructions for it to be displayed in a local museum, with Richard's permission. That morning, she had asked Peggy about the missing letters.

'Can't remember seeing anything, but I'll have a good look through Bert's stack of newspapers when I pop back home. I didn't throw them out. Waste not want not.'

Pete came out of his office as Louise passed by. 'Thought we were going to sail home last night. Did you feel the bike slip under us?' It was the first time they had spoken since she climbed on the back of his bike yesterday.

'Do you mind if I stay here to communicate with the press and manage operations whilst you are with Fitzpatrick opening the dam?' She spoke in monotone, communicating the minimum necessary.

'If that's what Fitzpatrick wants you to do. You'd be crazy if you tried to go anywhere…in this.' The pause was sufficient to convey his meaning.

'I'm not going anywhere,' she said.

'Good.' He winked. 'Then let the show begin.'

By mid-afternoon, Louise had arranged a press briefing for the following morning. Pete and Fitzpatrick had not returned to High House, but contractors popped in and out, updating her with news. The dam opened as planned, with no ceremony. The valley was filling far quicker than expected, helped by the torrential downpour. Police and council workers were working flat out trying to keep the area safe. Flooding, a threatened mudslide, and an influx of excited visitors undeterred by the rain were creating a challenge.

'You're wise staying here. It's Armageddon out there,' a contractor said, wet hair plastered to his face.

'It's certainly drier. Why don't you dry off a bit and I'll make you a hot drink,' Louise said.

'A cup of tea would be grand. But no point drying off. I've got to head back out once I've picked up summat here.'

Louise went through to the kitchen, where Peggy was busy chopping onions. 'I should have started this earlier, but it was a nightmare getting here. A lovely hot pot to warm them up. Will you still be here at tea?'

Louise had no idea. Eddie hadn't given a time, but she expected him soon. He would have been up most of the night in a club working the tables. 'I doubt it, Peggy. Eddie will want to start our journey back to London.'

'Oh. I nearly forgot.' Peggy wiped her hands on her apron.

'I found those letters you were looking for. Hold on, I'll get them for you.'

Louise's spirit lifted. The thought of losing Ma's letters on top of all her other losses had broken her heart.

'Here you are, pet. I'll finish making that cup of tea. You look as though you need a few minutes.'

Louise wiped the tears from her eyes. 'Thank you, Peggy. For these. And yes, if you don't mind making the tea. It's for the contractor who just came in.'

'Fred. Maggie's boy. I'll warm him a scone too.'

Louise took Ma's letters to a corner of the empty lounge and settled in a high-back armchair, hiding herself from view of anyone glancing in. There was one unread letter; Louise kissed it in gratitude. She had almost lost it. Prolonging the joy of anticipation, she reread the other letters first. Then, with a smile lighting her face and heart, she snuggled further into the chair to hear what Ma had to say.

2nd October 1951

Darling Louise,

I hope you are well and enjoying life. I think about you every day, wondering how your studies are going, what work you are planning to do when you leave school. Maybe you are already working. You always worked hard. Whatever you do or plan to do, I know you will be a great success. Aim high, precious one. You can be anything that you set your mind to. Life goes by far too quickly. One day you are a young woman with the world at your feet, the next, counting your days left on this earth, which brings me on to why I am writing now.

I managed to keep the farm going as long as I could after Pa died. It was a miracle that I did. But folks around here are kind and Pa was popular, so I got lots of support. In the past few months, I have had to slow down and today closed the business. No more cows or chickens. Just me and this big old farmhouse and land.

The Corporation has been hounding me ever since Pa died, trying to get me to sell them the farm. Over my dead body! I may not have much say in it, as I am sorry to tell you, I am dying.

Louise put a hand over her mouth. 'Oh Ma. I wish I had been there to care for you.'

Ma Braithwaite has been a great help. She lost her husband the year after Pa. Poor woman. First her boy and then her husband. I suppose we have been looking after one another.

It's cancer. I'm afraid it had spread to several organs by the time it was discovered in my liver. So, I'm looking forward to being reunited with Pa.

I've left you the farm in my will. The farmhouse, the land, everything. My letters to you have all been returned, but I'm hoping that this one will reach you. In any event, I have hidden my will under the loose floorboard in the cupboard under the stairs. Ma Braithwaite knows of my wishes. She has a spare key and will let you in when you visit. I wish I was still alive to see you, darling. I'll ask her to post this letter as I'm going into hospital today and don't know if I'll return. I am praying that you get this letter and will take good care of the farm. You always wanted to be a farmer! Do anything that you want with the house and the land, darling.

Pa and I have and always will love you.

Your Ma

xxx

The will! It was under the floorboards. She had to find it before it was too late. Everything she had removed from the farmhouse was now hers: Pa's favourite pipe, their marriage photo, Ma's bristle brush. The Corporation would compensate her for the value of the house and land, but it was the precious items within that Louise longed to claim as her own. Then it occurred to her that compensation would be more than enough to pay off Eddie's debt to Big Jim and set her free.

She ran to the kitchen where Peggy was chatting with

Fred. 'I've got to go out, Peggy. Fred, can you give me a lift to Becks farm?'

'Do you have to go out, pet? The rain looks as though it might be easing, but Bert says another storm's on its way.'

'I'm afraid I do. Can you put these somewhere very safe, Peggy? If Fitzpatrick or Pete ask where I am, tell them I won't be long. Can we go now, Fred? It's kind of urgent.'

The sky was dark– storm clouds or dusk? Louise wasn't certain. Becks farm looked forlorn, as if it knew it had been abandoned and was awaiting its fate. Water whooshed and gurgled in the valley below. Ma Widdle and Beaky's cottages would be flooded by now.

The cupboard under the stairs. Louise didn't remember there being one. The kitchen had a flagstone floor. There was a door leading to the stairs and then a closed narrow staircase. She opened the door and looked up into darkness. Ma said *under the stairs*. Could she have been muddled in her last days?

Louise checked the pantry. The meat safe. She and Richard had already taken a good look when they spent the night. There wasn't time to play hide the thimble. Where else could it be? The living room was also paved with flagstones. There weren't any floorboards anywhere.

'Louise. What are you doing in there? It's not safe. We've got to get out.' Richard stood at the back door, yelling to be heard above the storm.

Richard. 'I thought you had gone. That I'd never see you again.'

'Peggy told me I'd find you here.'

Louise threw herself into his arms. 'I love you, Richard. I was crazy thinking I could live without you. I tried to tell you but...'

The house creaked—it sounded like a low scream. A tree was sliding down the hill, and Louise was reminded of a scene in a book, *The Railway Children*.

'Come on. We've got to leave now.' Richard turned with her in his arms, steering her away from the house, but Louise broke free.

'*No.* The will. It's in there somewhere. Under the floorboards. We've got to find it.'

Richard held up his hands as if fighting against his better judgement. 'Okay. But we have to be quick.'

Louise returned to the kitchen, relieved to have Richard's help. Her brain felt scrambled in the panic. 'Cupboard under the stairs. Where?'

'In the living room. The stairs are behind that wall.'

'Of course!' Louise tugged open the cupboard door and, crawling on all fours, felt each of the floorboards. Her finger slid into a groove and she grasped the broken edge of a board. It lifted easily. Soft padding, paper—Louise retrieved what was hidden inside. A thick envelope. Thank God.

'I've got it!'

She checked there was nothing else hidden before crawling out backwards, the envelope tucked into the front of her jeans.

Richard grinned at her. 'You're amazing. Can we go now?'

They left the farmhouse and struggled up the hill. Trees advanced as though on skis. Louise fell onto all fours, clawing at the ground to find purchase. Ahead, on the road above the valley, a car was parked. In its headlights stood a familiar figure. Eddie. It felt as though her hopes and dreams were sliding into the reservoir, along with the trees. She'd been fighting for so long. And for what? Eddie had come to claim her. She belonged to the Mob. Louise froze. She was slipping. Away from Richard. Away from Eddie.

'Louise,' Richard shouted. 'Don't give up, now.'

His voice triggered her resolve, and she lunged forward, taking his outstretched hand. He dragged her until they reached solid ground--where Eddie was waiting.

Louise squared up to him. 'I'm not going with you.'

'Just get in the car. I'll deal with your boyfriend later. You know, he's going to pay for your stupidity, princess? But he served a purpose leading me to you.'

'No. It's over, Eddie.'

Eddie grasped hold of her hair and yanked her closer. 'I said, get in the car.'

Whack. Richard punched Eddie on the side of his jaw. Louise knew Eddie would make mincemeat of him.

'Eddie, stop! I'll give you five hundred to pay back your debt. Just let go of him.'

The men continued wrestling, oblivious to her plea. Louise launched herself at Eddie and lost her footing.

Slick mud carried her like a waterfall down into the valley. Her right shoulder hit a boulder. The pain was excruciating. Then her head. She was turning over and over, her body flying, then thumping a rock. A street sign. Water. It was dark now. She couldn't see Richard or Eddie.

'Help,' she cried, desperately trying to keep herself above water.

The current was strong, pushing her in a torrent away from what would now be the bank. It was like being in a washing machine, the water sweeping her where it willed, her attempts to swim pathetic, as she could not compete with nature.

Freezing cold, disorientated, and scared, she lost sense of time as she struggled to keep above water. A loud splash--something or someone falling into the reservoir.

Please don't let it be Richard.

He wasn't a strong swimmer, and his asthma would be

triggered. She opened her mouth to shout but swallowed water.

Just stay alive, Louise. Keep going.

The church steeple protruded from the dark water. She sent up a silent prayer. *Thank you, God.* The reservoir had swept her to safety. If she could summon the strength to clamber onto the spire, she would be safe.

44

TUESDAY 9TH NOVEMBER 1965

Louise lay in a hospital bed, one leg in plaster, suspended in a pulley. Her ribs were broken and her shoulder badly bruised.

'Fitzpatrick sent these.' Pete's voice came from behind an enormous bouquet of roses.

Louise sighed. He was the last person she wanted to see. 'Thank you. Just leave them on the table.'

Pete put the flowers down and made himself comfortable in the chair alongside her bed. Louise turned away from him, hoping he would take the hint and leave.

'I'm sorry for your loss, Louise.'

She said nothing. There was nothing she could say.

'I'm sorry for everything you've been through. Honest I am. I didn't want to get involved in my uncle's business. My mum warned me against it. She lost my dad, Big Jim's brother, when he was doing a job for the Mob. I should have listened to her.'

Still, she said nothing, hoping he would leave.

'I didn't know where you were going when I followed you

from London, but when our driver told us about the reservoir, it was perfect. I've been wanting to train as an engineer since leaving school and this job gave me work experience.'

'I'm happy for you,' Louise said, monotone. 'Shut the door on your way out.'

Pete laughed. 'I know I deserved that. Seriously, Louise. Tell me what I can do to make it up to you.'

She sighed and turned to face him. 'Tell Big Jim the truth about his money and the bet.'

'Already done. My uncle sends you his sincere apologies for any grief you've experienced because of this misunderstanding. And of course, his condolences on your loss.'

'So, I'm free to live as I please when I get out of here?'

'Yes. I thought I'd made that clear. We can put all of this behind us.'

A nurse opened the door. 'Mrs Boyd has another visitor waiting. We don't want to tire her. What lovely flowers. I'll put them in some water for you.'

'Okay. Goodbye then,' Pete said, standing up.

He was at the door when Louise called him back. 'Pete? I don't think you're a bad person deep down. Eddie wasn't either. But your uncle is bad news. Don't let him ruin your life like he did Eddie's.'

'I won't.' He blew her a kiss. 'Take good care of yourself, Louise. You're one in a million.'

Louise shut her eyes and let the knowledge seep in. She was free of Big Jim and the Mob.

'Are you awake?' Richard's voice stirred her heart.

She opened her eyes to see her beloved, looking a bit battered, with a swollen eye, a purple jaw, and his arm in a sling. 'Come here,' she whispered.

He bent over her and they kissed gently, aware of one another's injuries. 'I bought you summat,' he said.

She smiled. As an adult he rarely used the local vernacular. 'Not flowers, I hope.'

'No. You've got enough of them. This.' He reached inside his jacket pocket and pulled out a notebook. 'It's time for you to write the next chapter of your life.'

Louise hugged it to her. 'Thank you. I'm going to fill it with happy memories.'

'I'm sorry about Eddie. He was okay when I left him to get help.'

'Was he trying to rescue me?' Louise said.

'I don't know. Maybe. I'm sorry, Louise.

'They tried to resuscitate him. I can't believe he's dead, Richard. I'd never have wished that upon him.'

'There'll be an inquest,' he said, and she was reminded of the last time he had said this--when Pa died. 'I told the police we had been fighting.'

'Eddie drowned. It was an accident. He wasn't concussed or anything when you last saw him?' Louise went cold.

'I don't know. It all happened so quickly. I whacked him on the jaw, but to be honest he was getting the better of me. There's no way I knocked him out.'

'No. I'm sure you're right. When I was swept away, I hit my head on a rock. Everything came flying, road signs, bricks. We're lucky to be alive.' Louise sighed as she took in what might have been. 'I won't waste another moment of my life, and I'm never going to let you go. Sorry. You're stuck with me, Richard Braithwaite.'

'For better or worse. Until death do us part,' he said.

And as they sealed this declaration with a kiss, Louise knew she had found the missing part of her soul. She was complete.

Before You Leave

If you enjoyed The Evacuee's Secret, please leave a review on Amazon to help other readers discover this book.

Sign up to my newsletter for giveaways, information about future publications, and behind-the-scenes information. http://eepurl.com/g5URFD

www.deborahklee.com

AUTHOR'S NOTE

The photograph of a church roof and steeple emerging from a reservoir in North Yorkshire haunted me. Like many people, I am fascinated by lost villages and one that existed underwater had me hooked. It was a story I yearned to write. But first, I had to find the whereabouts of this reservoir and discover its history. It was, I discovered, Thruscross reservoir and the lost village – West End.

I visited Thruscross reservoir, staying with a wonderful local woman, Sheila, who generously arranged for me to meet with people whose families had lived in and around Thruscross before the floodgates opened in 1966. As I heard about the compulsory purchase orders that destroyed the village, the disastrous relocation of the church and graveyard, and listened to the post office owner—the last business to close—reminisce about life before the reservoir, a story began to emerge. Before visiting the area and talking to local people, I had started to plan a story, but it was based on assumptions. I left with a very different one, inspired by the words of the people I met.

'The village was never abandoned; it was killed.'

'We knew the day would come, but that didn't make it any easier. It's like a loved one living with cancer.'

'They planted trees everywhere, so there were no roads.'

Whilst West End village and Thruscross reservoir were the inspiration for this story, the people and events are fictitious and bear no resemblance to persons living or dead.

The hamlet of West End was once a thriving community with four mills originally producing cotton yarn, but from 1814, this changed to flax. The collapse of the textile industry and the inaccessibility of West End by rail and road led to a decline in the population from 1840s onwards. Its death sentence came in 1897 with the Leeds Corporation Act, which gave Leeds Corporation the authority for compulsory purchase of property in the valley to create a reservoir.

However, the reservoir wasn't created until the autumn of 1966 with Thruscross dam's official opening on 7th September. The last service at Thruscross Church was held by candlelight on Monday 11th October 1965.

This beautiful little church was replaced by an austere-looking chapel, and the graves moved to a cemetery on the other side of the reservoir to the church.

A family farm and shop were the last inhabited buildings in the 1960s. Locals remember an older woman in the village who had an impressive collection of clocks. This story inspired Horatio Beacon's polyphon collection.

In The Evacuee's Secret, Ma and Pa are discussing a man who was acquitted of murdering his wife but died five years later when he was knocked off his bike. This is a reference to Jesse Peel, who was tried and acquitted for murdering Margaret Peel in 1938. Margaret was bludgeoned to death in the shop where she worked with a wheel brace, which was later found in a nearby reservoir.

The death penalty for murder was suspended in the UK for five years by the 1965 Murder Act and was abolished in 1969 to be replaced with a mandatory sentence for life. In my story, Louise is aware that Parliament is discussing the death penalty.

I carried out extensive research for this book. I even joined a Facebook Group for vintage Fordson tractors and was advised by Josephine Roberts, an enthusiast, on the mechanics of making a Fordson model N tractor unsafe to drive.

Alongside my interviews with people who experienced life before and after the reservoir, my greatest resource was a book by Alastair Laurence, *West End: A Sunken Village* (available from Amazon). The photograph that inspired me to seek this reservoir and its history is on the back cover. Inside the front cover is a fold out illustration and map of West End village when it was a thriving community. My mind wandered those streets: the post office, Mill House, a bridge, the ruins of Patrick's old mill, and of course, Thruscross Church.

I was sorry to leave Louise and Richard behind, as the fictitious Thorncrest had become dear to me. So, I wrote a sequel. *The Canary Girl's Secret* tells Ma Beck's story. Actual events again inspired this story as one or two graves were empty when the graveyard was relocated from the real Thruscross church. In my story, Louise cannot inherit the farm as there is no evidence that Ma died and so her will is called into question. And if that is not trouble enough, a murder enquiry is opened on the cause of Eddie Boyd's death. Did he fall into the reservoir or was he pushed? As their trust is challenged, can Louise and Richard hold on to their dreams or will they risk losing one another?

ACKNOWLEDGMENTS

This book's journey has been aided by many people and would not have been possible without their valued input. I'll start at the beginning, when the story was just an idea that took me to North Yorkshire for research. Sheila Smith, whose kindness and generosity in providing me with accommodation, acting as tour guide and driver, and putting me in touch with local historians, astounded me. Sheila, you sowed the seeds of this story.

Margaret Verity, Keith Murgatroyd, and Paul Myers for generously sharing their memories, photographs, and historical information.

The Facebook group Harrogate Past, Present, and Future. Who would have thought a simple question: Where could I buy a Biba style dress in 1965 could generate so much discussion? Over 200 replies!

The Facebook group Ford/Fordson tractor enthusiasts, and Josephine Roberts (Jo) in particular, who helped me understand the technicalities of tractor mechanics.

Beta readers: Janet Bridger, Anita Belli, Ellie Holmes, Elizabeth Holland, and Sally Freytag. Gerald Hornsby for technical help with publication.

Charlotte Ledger, editor at One More Chapter, who provided editorial feedback on several drafts of this novel. Thank you for your encouragement, support, and expertise.

Chris Towndrow, for his meticulous line and copy edits.

Asya Blue, my wonderful cover designer.
And, as always, my patient and supportive husband.

Printed in Dunstable, United Kingdom

79899428R00214